THE BOURNE SERIES

ROBERT LUDLUM'S THE BOURNE VENDETTA (by Brian Freeman)
ROBERT LUDLUM'S THE BOURNE SHADOW (by Brian Freeman)
ROBERT LUDLUM'S THE BOURNE DEFIANCE (by Brian Freeman)
ROBERT LUDLUM'S THE BOURNE SACRIFICE (by Brian Freeman)
ROBERT LUDLUM'S THE BOURNE TREACHERY (by Brian Freeman)
ROBERT LUDLUM'S THE BOURNE EVOLUTION (by Brian Freeman)
ROBERT LUDLUM'S THE BOURNE INITIATIVE (by Eric Van Lustbader)
ROBERT LUDLUM'S THE BOURNE ENIGMA (by Eric Van Lustbader)
ROBERT LUDLUM'S THE BOURNE ASCENDANCY (by Eric Van Lustbader)
ROBERT LUDLUM'S THE BOURNE RETRIBUTION (by Eric Van Lustbader)
ROBERT LUDLUM'S THE BOURNE IMPERATIVE (by Eric Van Lustbader)
ROBERT LUDLUM'S THE BOURNE DOMINION (by Eric Van Lustbader)
ROBERT LUDLUM'S THE BOURNE OBJECTIVE (by Eric Van Lustbader)
ROBERT LUDLUM'S THE BOURNE DECEPTION (by Eric Van Lustbader)
ROBERT LUDLUM'S THE BOURNE SANCTION (by Eric Van Lustbader)
ROBERT LUDLUM'S THE BOURNE BETRAYAL (by Eric Van Lustbader)
ROBERT LUDLUM'S THE BOURNE LEGACY (by Eric Van Lustbader)
THE BOURNE ULTIMATUM
THE BOURNE SUPREMACY
THE BOURNE IDENTITY

THE TREADSTONE SERIES

ROBERT LUDLUM'S THE TREADSTONE RENDITION (by Joshua Hood)
ROBERT LUDLUM'S THE TREADSTONE TRANSGRESSION (by Joshua Hood)
ROBERT LUDLUM'S THE TREADSTONE EXILE (by Joshua Hood)
ROBERT LUDLUM'S THE TREADSTONE RESURRECTION (by Joshua Hood)

THE BLACKBRIAR SERIES

ROBERT LUDLUM'S THE BLACKBRIAR GENESIS (by Simon Gervais)

ROBERT LUDLUM'S
THE BOURNE VENDETTA

THE COVERT-ONE SERIES

ROBERT LUDLUM'S THE PATRIOT ATTACK (by Kyle Mills)

ROBERT LUDLUM'S THE GENEVA STRATEGY (by Jamie Freveletti)

ROBERT LUDLUM'S THE UTOPIA EXPERIMENT (by Kyle Mills)

ROBERT LUDLUM'S THE JANUS REPRISAL (by Jamie Freveletti)

ROBERT LUDLUM'S THE ARES DECISION (by Kyle Mills)

ROBERT LUDLUM'S THE ARCTIC EVENT (by James H. Cobb)

ROBERT LUDLUM'S THE MOSCOW VECTOR (with Patrick Larkin)

ROBERT LUDLUM'S THE LAZARUS VENDETTA (with Patrick Larkin)

ROBERT LUDLUM'S THE ALTMAN CODE (with Gayle Lynds)

ROBERT LUDLUM'S THE PARIS OPTION (with Gayle Lynds)

ROBERT LUDLUM'S THE CASSANDRA COMPACT (with Philip Shelby)

ROBERT LUDLUM'S THE HADES FACTOR (with Gayle Lynds)

THE JANSON SERIES

ROBERT LUDLUM'S THE JANSON EQUATION (by Douglas Corleone)

ROBERT LUDLUM'S THE JANSON OPTION (by Paul Garrison)

ROBERT LUDLUM'S THE JANSON COMMAND (by Paul Garrison)

THE JANSON DIRECTIVE

ALSO BY ROBERT LUDLUM

THE BANCROFT STRATEGY

THE AMBLER WARNING

THE TRISTAN BETRAYAL

THE SIGMA PROTOCOL

THE PROMETHEUS DECEPTION

THE MATARESE COUNTDOWN

THE APOCALYPSE WATCH

THE SCORPIO ILLUSION

THE ROAD TO OMAHA

THE ICARUS AGENDA

THE AQUITAINE PROGRESSION

THE PARSIFAL MOSAIC

THE MATARESE CIRCLE

THE HOLCROFT COVENANT

THE CHANCELLOR MANUSCRIPT

THE GEMINI CONTENDERS

THE ROAD TO GANDOLFO

THE RHINEMANN EXCHANGE

THE CRY OF THE HALIDON

TREVAYNE

THE MATLOCK PAPER

THE OSTERMAN WEEKEND

THE SCARLATTI INHERITANCE

ROBERT LUDLUM'S

THE

BOURNE
VENDETTA

BRIAN FREEMAN

G. P. PUTNAM'S SONS
NEW YORK

PUTNAM
— EST. 1838 —
G. P. Putnam's Sons
Publishers Since 1838
An imprint of Penguin Random House LLC
penguinrandomhouse.com

Library of Congress Cataloging-in-Publication Data

Names: Freeman, Brian, 1963– author.
Title: Robert Ludlum's the Bourne vendetta / Brian Freeman.
Other titles: Bourne vendetta
Description: New York : G. P. Putnam's Sons, 2025. | Series: The Bourne series
Identifiers: LCCN 2024033337 | ISBN 9780593716489 (hardcover) |
ISBN 9780593716496 (ebook)
Subjects: LCGFT: Thrillers (Fiction) | Spy fiction. | Novels.
Classification: LCC PS3606.R4454 R68 2025 | DDC 813/.6—dc23/eng/20240719
LC record available at https://lccn.loc.gov/2024033337

Printed in the United States of America
1st Printing

ROBERT LUDLUM'S
THE BOURNE VENDETTA

YOU'RE BEING WATCHED!

Johanna glanced across the street from the top of the Las Vegas parking garage and knew why that strange prickling sensation on her neck was warning her about surveillance. The Sphere arena, barely one hundred yards away, had taken on the look of an enormous green eyeball across its metal skin. The feminine eye, with long delicate lashes, stared right at her, winking a couple of times, as if it knew she was there.

She shivered despite herself.

Jesus, that thing gave her the creeps.

It was three in the morning, and for now, Johanna was alone. The nearby office buildings were empty, and so was the parking garage. She'd used a Banish 22 suppressor on her Ruger Mark IV Tactical pistol to silently dispatch the lights over her head, leaving her mostly in darkness. But the whites of the eye on that goddamn Sphere still made her feel like the spotlight of a prison watchtower was zeroing in on her.

A December breeze—cold for Las Vegas—blew desert dust in her face. Johanna's spaghetti-straight blond hair hung down to the middle of her chest, and a wool Golden Knights cap was pulled low on her forehead. She wore black jeans, tight on her skinny legs, plus a white tank top and a gray zipped jacket with extra-deep pockets to accommodate her gun and suppressor. Her aquamarine eyes, as pale blue as Caribbean water, surveyed the quiet corporate campus below her.

Nothing stirred. No one moved in the shadows, and no headlights lit up the street.

Two minutes passed. Then five minutes. Then ten.

Callie Faith was late.

Or was this meeting a trap? Johanna took precautions wherever she went, but these days cameras and scanners were everywhere, and facial recognition technology could peel away most of her disguises. She knew Treadstone was still looking for her. *Shadow* was still looking for her, and she wouldn't stop until Johanna was dead.

Come on, Callie, where are you?

Finally, on the street below her, she spotted the twin high beams of an SUV turning off Howard Hughes Parkway. The vehicle stopped short of the garage, using one of the handful of outside parking places. Moments later, the driver's door opened. With a Zeiss monocular, Johanna watched Callie Faith climb out from behind the wheel. No driver for her tonight. No congressional town car. Callie was using a Hyundai Santa Fe that Johanna had left on Clark Avenue two blocks from her downtown office. If anyone happened to run the license plate, the DMV records would show the owner as Martin Reynolds, who was currently away on a fourteen-day cruise through the Panama Canal. There would be no way to connect the SUV to Callie Faith.

Neither Callie nor Johanna wanted a record of this meeting.

The congresswoman's high heels clicked on the asphalt as she walked into the lower level of the parking garage. A couple of minutes later, Callie appeared at the garage's stairwell door and scanned the empty parking places. When she spotted Johanna in the shadows, she headed toward her.

Johanna's hand tightened on the Ruger. Her finger curled around the trigger. She waited until Callie was ten yards away, and then she removed the pistol from her pocket and pointed it at the woman's head.

"Stop."

The congresswoman did. She raised her hands in the air. Her face was expressionless, and she said nothing.

Johanna closed the distance between them until they were face-to-face. Callie wore a black trench coat down to her knees, and Johanna searched it, finding nothing. Then she undid the belt, which was tied loosely at the woman's waist. With her gun at Callie's temple, Johanna reached inside the coat and did a thorough, intimate pat-down of the woman's body, making sure that the congresswoman carried no weapons or listening devices.

Callie finally spoke.

"I didn't realize this was going to be a Tinder date."

Johanna backed away without smiling and replaced the Ruger in her pocket. "I don't trust anybody, Congresswoman."

"Call me Callie. And you're right. God knows I wouldn't trust anyone in Congress, either. So what do I call you? In Treadstone, your code name was Storm, but obviously, you're not in Treadstone anymore."

"Obviously. The most recent identity I used was Johanna. Let's stick with that."

"All right. Johanna."

Callie removed oversized amber sunglasses from her face and slid them into the pocket of her trench coat. Her steely eyes were dark, her smile wolfish and icy. She was small, barely five feet tall, and in her early forties, although she was trying like hell to look younger. As the wind mussed the thick strands of her shoulder-length hair, which was the color of milk chocolate, she brushed the loose strands away with manicured fingernails. Her makeup was perfect despite the lateness of the hour.

They'd had months of electronic communication back and forth between them. Even so, Johanna took an immediate dislike to Callie Faith in person. She sized her up as the kind of ambitious, manipulative narcissist that women wanted to slap and men wanted to fuck. But it didn't matter whether she liked her. The enemy of her enemy was her friend.

"It's your meeting," Johanna said. "Let's not waste time."

"Of course. Thank you for agreeing to see me face-to-face. You've been very useful, Johanna. Until recently, the House Intelligence Committee has been mostly toothless. Your tips on clandestine operations have been a big help in finally putting the DNI on the defensive. Everyone on the committee is jealous of my sources. I'm grateful. Someday I hope I can find a way to pay you back."

"Destroy Treadstone. Let Shadow rot in jail. That's all the payback I need."

"That's my plan," Callie agreed. "I want to yank out the deep state by its roots, and that starts with its spy ring. Without Treadstone to back them up, they're deaf, dumb, and blind. But we're also talking about smart, resourceful opponents. They won't go down without a fight, and they have no hesitation about using dirty tactics to win. That's why I wanted to see you."

"What do you want?" Johanna asked impatiently. "You said in your message that you needed my help, but you couldn't risk any record of what we talk about. I assume you're looking for more than information this time."

"That's true. I need your skills. Your *Treadstone* skills. Because everything we've been trying to accomplish is suddenly at risk."

"Why?"

"Why do you think?" Callie replied. "Shadow."

Johanna's whole body heated up like a fire. She glanced at the Sphere again. For a moment, the huge woman's eye on the metal ball became Shadow's piercing eye, studying her like a psychiatrist, examining her and tormenting her. Shadow. She was the woman who had turned Johanna's life upside down. The woman who had given her a mission that haunted her dreams whenever she closed her eyes. An innocent man died. Children died.

Shadow.

The new head of Treadstone.

"What has she done?" Johanna asked, her voice frozen.

"It's what she's trying to do," Callie said.

"Go on."

Callie shoved her hands in her coat pockets. "My position has always been very clear. The intelligence community is hopelessly corrupt, from the FBI through the entire alphabet of secret agencies. I want to defund them and start over. Salt the ground and build something new. For Shadow, that's an existential threat. I want to destroy her, so she wants to destroy me. I'm also sure she suspects that you're the one who's been feeding me operational details. That means you're on her list, too."

"Shadow may be many things, but she's no fool," Johanna agreed. "I've been on her list for a long time. If she finds me, I'm dead."

"In other words, we both have a vested interest in stopping her plans. This is a race. We need to win."

"A race to do what?"

The congresswoman glanced at the Sphere. The huge green eye seemed to be watching them closely. "Have you heard about something called the Files?"

"No."

"There's a kind of database on the market in Washington. Hacked information. Secrets. Corruption. Shadow is after it. Needless to say, if she got her hands on something like that, no one would dare move against the deep state again. They'd have too much power."

"What's the source of this information?" Johanna asked. "Where did it come from?"

"I don't know."

"Who has it?"

Callie hesitated, and her lips squeezed into a frown. "I don't know that, either."

"Does Shadow?"

"I don't think so. Not yet anyway. That's what makes it a race. You need to get to the Files before she does."

Johanna gave a hollow laugh. "In other words, you want this mystery database for yourself. Right?"

"Well, I wouldn't complain if it came my way," Callie admitted. "Politics is war. The ends justify the means. I expect a lot of different people, including other governments, are chasing this information.

If they get the power, they'll use it. So will I. I'm not going to apologize for that."

Johanna was silent for a while.

She was sure Callie wasn't sharing the whole truth, but no one ever did. That was the intelligence world. In Treadstone, she'd been fed nothing but lies, and those lies had nearly destroyed her.

"Will you help me?" Callie asked, watching Johanna's face. "I know I'm sending you back into the lion's den."

"If it means fucking over Shadow, of course I'm in," Johanna replied. "If she kills me, she kills me. Those have always been the stakes. But I have an advantage over her that no one else does."

"Which is?"

Johanna pictured him in her head.

She could still see his features so clearly, that imperfect face that always seemed perfect when she stared at him. His dark brown hair messy and swept back. A small scar near the line of his forehead, an indentation in his jaw. Pale lips, a mouth that rarely showed any expression. And those blue-gray eyes, hot and cold at the same time. When he stared at you, you felt it deep into your blood.

Months had passed since she last saw him, but the memory of their bodies wrapped together still brought a flush to her pale skin. She hadn't met him in order to fall in love with him. She'd met him only to deceive him.

In the end, she'd done both.

"I know the agent Shadow will use," Johanna told Callie. "His name is Jason Bourne."

PART ONE

1

A COLD MIDNIGHT RAIN FELL ON GROSVENOR SQUARE. THE DAMPNESS made the fifty-degree temperature feel as if London were freezing. Jason Bourne took what shelter he could under the gnarled branches of one of the park's plane trees. He sat astride an X-PRO street bike, a full-face blackout helmet covering his head, a black rain jacket and waterproof black pants over his clothes. The rain and the darkness made him almost invisible.

The bike sat in the wet grass near the statue of FDR, which gave Bourne a vantage on the entrance to Gordon Ramsay's Lucky Cat restaurant across the street. Flipping up the visor of the helmet, Bourne retrieved his phone from a zippered pocket in his jacket. He opened an app that synched with the spy camera he'd hidden inside the restaurant earlier in the day. Immediately, the screen gave him a 4K view of the late-night activity. It was Friday, and the Mayfair hot spot was alive with people feasting on monkfish tempura and duck leg bao. Every table was full to the max.

No, not *every* table.

The two booths closest to the kitchen, which would normally seat eight to ten people squeezed together, included just two men, one at either booth. Bourne zoomed in the camera. He assessed the men: both Middle Eastern with short black hair and trimmed beards, both dressed in white sport coats over royal-blue silk turtlenecks, both armed with machine pistols positioned discreetly in their laps.

Faisal al-Najjar always traveled with protection.

Focusing the camera beyond the guards, Bourne took a close-up look at al-Najjar himself. The Saudi banker sat at the square chef's table, enjoying Asian dishes fresh from the clattering kitchen woks and washing them down with expensive white wine. Al-Najjar wore a dark pin-striped suit that looked as if it came directly from Savile Row, but his head was covered by a red-and-white-checkered kaffiyeh. He wasn't alone at the chef's table. Two girls sat with him, both Russian, both blond, both barely more than teenagers. Their cleavage spilled out of glittering thigh-high cocktail dresses.

With a buzz of vibration, a text message crossed Bourne's screen. It was from Shadow.

Is he there?

Jason texted a quick reply. *Yes.*

Shadow wrote back moments later. *Let me know when you have him.*

Bourne didn't bother answering. This was a kidnapping, and kidnappings were always a delicate business.

On the video feed, he took note of the empty plates and the three empty bottles of wine. It was almost time. Al-Najjar would be leaving soon. According to the assistant concierge at the London Hilton, the banker had a set routine whenever he was in London. Two or three fresh-faced young escorts, always Russian and blond.

Live rock music at a Soho club. Dinner at one of the city's trendy restaurants. And then a limousine back to his top-floor suite after midnight with the girls in tow. By morning, the concierge reported with a sniff, the maids needed hazard pay to clean up the room.

Outside the restaurant, gauzy headlights cut through the rain. Bourne watched a limo glide down the street from the direction of Park Lane and come to a stop near the steps of the building. He checked the camera and saw al-Najjar getting up from the chef's table, one stunning girl on each arm. The Saudi thanked the men in the kitchen in a booming accented voice, thanked the tuxedo-clad maître d', who was there to bow in gratitude, and then took up position between his two guards. The men made no effort to hide their weapons as they led the banker through the maze of tables.

Moments later, Jason watched the Lucky Cat door open across from the park. One of the guards came through first, machine pistol level and ready to fire. The banker followed with his companions. The driver of the limo greeted al-Najjar with a huge umbrella, and the Saudi and the girls descended the steps, safe from the rain, and climbed into the back of the town car. One guard took the passenger seat to the left of the driver. The other climbed into a black Mercedes parked behind the limo at the curb. The engines of both vehicles purred to life.

Bourne flipped down the visor on his helmet. Time to go.

But as he got ready to fire up the street bike, he stopped. Through the dank London rain, cigarette smoke drifted his way. Someone was hiding in the darkness. Not far away, a voice whispered, low and urgent, in an Arabic language. Bourne followed the sound of the voice and spotted a small man crouched near the hedge that bordered the street. The man had a phone pressed to his mouth. As the two vehicles pulled away from the curb, the man watched them go, still murmuring into the phone.

He was the lookout. The hunters followed immediately.

The growl of street bikes rose above the pounding downpour. Bourne watched two compact motorcycles, much like his own, wheel around the corner of Audley Street and pursue the Saudi banker's limousine and the trailing Mercedes. Two drivers hunched over the handlebars, both shrouded in black like he was. As they passed under the glow of a streetlight, he knew what they were.

Assassins.

Bourne swore under his breath. He shoved his foot down to kick-start the X-PRO. The noise of his engine drew the attention of the lookout near the street, and the man spun around and shouted in surprise. Bourne watched the man thrust one hand inside his jacket, then saw the silver glint of a pistol reflected in the light. He accelerated, kicking up spray and mud. Bullets thudded into the tree trunk beside him and pinged off the stone of the Roosevelt Memorial. He leaned left on the bike as another round ricocheted off the metal frame, and then he drew his Sig Sauer and awkwardly returned fire. His body was off balance; his shots missed. He wheeled the X-PRO in a circle and gunned it at the man in front of him, using a tight serpentine motion. Arms extended like a V, the man fired back. One round cracked the shell of Bourne's helmet; another shattered his mirror.

But the game of chicken finally forced the man to jump aside to avoid the stampeding bike. Following the man's rolling body with the barrel of his Sig, Bourne squeezed the trigger twice, putting two rounds in the middle of his back. Then he braked hard, jerking the bike sideways. He splashed the X-PRO through the sodden grass and onto the path that led out of the park.

On the street, the other vehicles had already disappeared. Al-Najjar was staying at the Hilton, so Bourne assumed the limousine would be heading for Park Lane. He followed the road around Grosvenor Square and sped up toward the glow of the brightly lit thoroughfare a few blocks away. His engine whined like a cloud of angry hornets. As he reached Park Lane, he whipped around the corner, dodging cars and taxis. Even at midnight, London traffic was heavy. He weaved in and out of the four southbound lanes, with expensive hotels flashing by on his left. It didn't take him long to spot the limousine and the trailing Mercedes, with the two street bikes practically hugging the rear bumper.

Motorcycles were a dime a dozen on the London streets. The vehicles hadn't taken evasive maneuvers yet; they didn't know they were being targeted. Bourne shot forward using the taxi lane, then cut across the street in front of a Range Rover that slammed on its brakes with a squeal and a blare of its horn. Keeping one hand on the handlebars, Bourne drew his Sig with the other. Only a short stretch of empty pavement separated him from the two killers on street bikes. He aimed low, the gun barrel impossible to keep steady at high speed, and he fired at the rear tire on the bike immediately in front of him.

The bullet bounced off the street and missed. One of the cyclists glanced back and saw him. The man shouted to his companion on the other bike, and that motorcycle broke to the right and bumped onto the curb that ran along the tree-lined median. With a burst of speed, the bike drew alongside the driver's window of the Mercedes. In an instant, the man drew a gun and unleashed a barrage of fire.

The Mercedes driver had no chance, but neither did the cyclist. The sedan lurched out of control, veered right, and crushed the bike and its rider against the low iron fence that bordered the median. The cyclist toppled off the machine, his lower body now pulp. The car bounced off the fence and swerved across multiple lanes, and Bourne heard the tortured metal thuds of a chain reaction crash behind him as other drivers braked wildly. He swerved far left to avoid the spinning Mercedes and lost his Sig in the process; the other bike in front of him swerved right.

The limo driver realized what was happening. The long, sleek town car had slowed as the vehicle neared the Hilton, but now its tires screeched as it accelerated past the hotel. It made a hard left, wheels coming off the ground, then righted itself and sped down Piccadilly. The second street bike stayed on its tail. Bourne closed the gap, coming up directly beside the other cyclist, but he had to break off as the man thrust out an arm to knock him off the X-PRO. He snaked back, striking a glancing blow on the rear of the other machine that made both of them wobble and nearly go over.

Bourne reached for his ankle, detaching his backup Ruger from its holster. The cyclist drew his own gun. They targeted each other, but before either one of them could take a shot, the rear window of the limousine ahead of them shattered outward. Machine-pistol fire erupted from the security guard inside. One round seared across the top of Bourne's left shoulder, ripping through his jacket and drawing blood. The next exploded the front tire on his X-PRO. His bike careened to the pavement, and he rolled hard on the street as he lost his grip, elbow pads and knee pads taking the punishing blows.

The other cyclist took a burst of bullets squarely in the chest. Bourne watched the man lose control and fly backward, somersaulting and slamming headfirst into the street. The bike roared forward, riderless, then crashed sideways as if in slow motion and spun to a stop, wheels still turning. The man on the street didn't move. Blood stained the pavement. He was gone. Behind them, traffic came to a dead halt, backing up as far as the Hard Rock Cafe and leaving a long stretch of Piccadilly deserted.

Bourne got to his feet slowly, bones and muscles all protesting. He tasted blood in his mouth. Dizziness made him stagger, but he shook it off, limping toward the sidewalk. He heard the shrill up-and-down wail of sirens drawing closer. Fifty yards away, the limo carrying al-Najjar stopped, blocked by vehicles ahead of it. Its rear window was a jagged line of glass fragments. The passenger door swung open, and the guard with the machine pistol climbed out and surveyed the street.

His eyes immediately went to Bourne.

The man marched his way, his face hard and dark, his gun level in his arms. Bourne realized he'd lost his backup Ruger, too; it was sitting in the middle of the street near the X-PRO. He took a couple of steps backward, gauging the distance between himself and the guard. The sheer volume of bullets the machine pistol could unleash didn't leave him anywhere to run. If he moved, the man would cut him down.

Then a siren screamed, nearly on top of him.

From behind, another motorcycle rocketed down the middle of the lane between the stopped traffic and careened around him. Bourne caught a glimpse of the reflective yellow jacket and white helmet of a London police officer. The cop closed in on the security guard, who squatted and put his machine pistol on the pavement and held his hands out from his sides, fingers spread wide.

The bike jerked to a stop next to the guard. The cop flipped up his visor.

That was when Bourne noticed that the police officer wasn't riding a police street bike. It was black and unmarked, like the vehicles the other men had been riding. Bourne began to shout a warning, but he was too late. The police officer's hand dove into the pocket of his yellow jacket and came out with a semiautomatic. He fired three bullets into the face of the guard, who collapsed immediately to the street.

Bourne ran, but his legs gave way beneath him, and he stumbled and slipped to his knees. It didn't matter. The killer posing as a cop had already revved his bike again. As he sped past the limo, the man paused long enough to grab something from his pocket, separate a metal pin, and lob a grenade gracefully into the vehicle's broken back window. Then in the next instant, the bike roared away down Piccadilly.

It took five seconds.

Bourne—knowing what was about to happen—threw himself to the pavement and covered his head. A muffled explosion erupted inside the limo, making the ground shake. The remaining windows of the vehicle blasted outward in a shower of shrapnel and glass, along with the tissue, organs, bones, and blood of the limo driver, the two Russian prostitutes, and the Saudi banker named al-Najjar.

2

BOURNE SHOWERED IN HIS ROOM AT THE LONDON HILTON, WASHING OFF dirt and tending to the cuts and scrapes all over his skin. The scalding-hot water eased the soreness in his body, but as soon as he dried himself off, the pain returned, making him move stiffly. The long hotel mirror showed a rainbow of bruises across his naked body. He was just over six feet tall, toned and muscled from his intense daily workouts, but in his late thirties, he didn't bounce back from punishment as quickly as he once had.

His body bore many scars from his past, some from bullets, some from knives, wounds that all came with stories. But they were stories he largely didn't remember. A few years ago, a bullet had left him floating half-dead in the Mediterranean Sea. He'd been rescued and taken to a lonely French village called Port Noir. Only the quick action of a drunk expat English doctor, who'd gone off the booze long enough to steady his hands for surgery, had saved his life. But he'd awakened as a nowhere man. He didn't remember his past. He didn't remember his identity. Even the name he carried—Jason

Bourne—turned out to be one more fiction in a life created by an organization called Treadstone.

His real name was David Webb, but David Webb didn't exist anymore. All that was left of him was a ghost.

Bourne got dressed again, this time in a gray British business suit. He returned to the Hilton lobby, which was a hive of activity even in the middle of the night, thanks to the murder of Faisal al-Najjar. Police, agents from MI5, and at least a dozen Middle Eastern men, some he recognized as Saudi embassy officials, clustered in small groups on the marble floor. Pretending to check his phone, Bourne eavesdropped on the conversations for several minutes, but when one of the MI5 men began to study him with more than casual interest, he continued through the revolving doors and left the hotel.

The rain had stopped. He crossed through a gaggle of tabloid reporters to Park Lane, where he had no trouble flagging a black cab even at the late hour. With no traffic, the taxi's transit through the city was quick. He gave the driver an address on the south bank of the Thames, but when they reached the far end of Westminster Bridge, beyond the Houses of Parliament, he told the man to let him out. He took the steps down to the Queen's Walk and noted a twentysomething woman sitting on the stone wall over the river. She had blue hair and wore a black dress over fishnet stockings and calf-high combat boots, with a white lace shawl draped over her lap. He assumed her gun was there. She didn't look at him, which was a dead giveaway that she was the first of the watchers.

Treadstone took no chances when its new boss was in town.

He passed three more agents as he neared the London Eye, which loomed bright and motionless over his head. Beyond the wheel, not far from the railway bridge into Waterloo Station, he spotted a woman standing alone by the river. She was in profile, but he recognized her, as distinctive as a diamond on black velvet. Her dress outshined the surroundings, a navy-blue strapless bodycon gown that emphasized her wide, curving hips and came together tightly below her knees, with a slit to the middle of her thigh. She wore matching high heels. She should have been cold, but she seemed unaffected by the December chill. As he approached her, she turned to face him. Her wavy blond hair fell to her shoulders, and her face was beautiful but distant, with cool blue eyes and burgundy lips that showed no emotion or expression. She was in her midforties, but she had an ageless look that never seemed to change.

"Shadow," Bourne said.

"Hello, David."

He found himself irritated that she called him that. Not Jason. Not the man he was now. It was no accident that she used his old identity. Everything Shadow did was intentional, part of a psychological strategy. They had history together that made him vulnerable to her, and Jason didn't like feeling vulnerable to anyone. More than a decade ago, when he was still a young man called David Webb, they'd been lovers. They'd been *in* love—or so he thought. He hadn't realized that everything she'd told him was a lie, that she'd been grooming him and measuring his skills as an agent in the field.

For Treadstone.

It had been four months since he'd last seen her. Since he *remembered* her from the empty mists of his past. They'd been together on a small island off the British coast, which was when he finally found out who and what she really was—a spy climbing the ladder, about to take the reins of the entire agency. Shadow had appointed herself his handler. He'd report to her, directly, alone, like a new game of control between them.

Then she dropped off the radar. Four months of silence followed with no contact or assignments, until one week ago, when she'd left a message for him at their prearranged drop in Paris. *I need you in London.*

"You're a little underdressed, aren't you?" he commented.

"I was at the theater. I didn't have time to change. Do you like it?"

He didn't answer.

Her gown was part of the sexual game she played, like the double entendre of the message she'd sent in Paris. She wanted him distracted by her legs, by the swell of her breasts, by the aura of her perfume. She was like a museum sculpture he could admire but not possess. What bothered him was that her strategy worked as intended. Being near her again after so many months apart left him off balance.

"Al-Najjar is dead," Bourne said.

"So I heard. What happened?"

He explained about the ambush on Piccadilly. The failure of the mission didn't seem to faze her. Her blue eyes drifted away to the river and her deep red lips furrowed into a frown, as if her mind were calculating the next series of moves in a chess game.

Always turn a setback to your advantage.

Treadstone.

"Do you know why I wanted him?" she asked a few moments later.

"I assume because of the media reports last year linking him to the president's son. With an impeachment scandal looming, Congress was after him to testify about foreign bribes going into the president's pocket. Al-Najjar was the Saudi moneyman."

"Very good, David."

"Let's stick to Jason," he reminded her coldly. "Or Cain."

"I thought you might want a little of your past back. At least when it's just the two of us."

"I don't."

"As you wish. *Jason*." Her face remained inscrutable. "Anyway, the Saudis didn't want al-Najjar talking to Congress. They had too much to lose if the financial arrangements became public."

"You think they sent the assassins?"

"I'm sure of it. Mostly because they told me that was their plan. I was hoping we'd get there ahead of them, but he's dead, that's the main thing."

Bourne stared at her. "You were going to kill him, too."

"After I'd interrogated him? Yes."

"Why?"

"The country doesn't need another political scandal to bring down an administration," Shadow replied. "Were there bribes? My God, of course there were bribes. The president has been lining the family pockets for years. Show me a politician that doesn't do the same thing. But the extremists in Congress don't stop when they chop off one head. They always want more. These fools are hell-bent on eviscerating the entire intelligence community, even if it means creating a national security risk. My job is to stop them by any means necessary, and that's what I plan to do."

"Why put me in the middle of it?" Bourne asked. "If you knew the Saudis were going to take him out anyway, why risk getting caught?"

"Because I wanted to know *how* al-Najjar was exposed," Shadow explained. "Do you think I wasn't looking into the president's son myself? Do you think I wasn't turning over every rock to get that kind of leverage? But I never got a whiff of his connection to al-Najjar, and as far as I can tell, nobody else in the intel agencies did, either. And yet the whole thing got splashed over the front page of the *Washington Post*. Details, dates, emails, bank records. Nobody should have been able to put their hands on that kind of information. But somehow, they did."

"You wanted al-Najjar to help you find the leak?"

Shadow nodded. "Yes, but it goes deeper than that."

"How?"

She didn't reply. Not immediately. Bourne saw two older Brits walking side by side on the walkway toward Westminster Bridge. They were close, not even twenty feet away, talking loudly to each other. The men weren't threats, but he was sure that at least two Treadstone guns were tracking them, and if Shadow gave the signal, they'd both be dead in a matter of seconds. Instead, she took Jason's hand and pulled him next to her. She leaned into him with her arms around his waist. Her body was soft, her skin cool to the touch. Their faces were obscured. If the old men looked their way, they'd see nothing but two lovers silhouetted by the river.

When the coast was clear, she separated herself as if nothing had happened between them, but her presence lingered in all of his senses.

"There's a database out there," Shadow told him, smoothing her dress. "People are calling it the Files. We haven't seen anything like this since Hoover's death, when someone stole his FBI archives and began using them for blackmail. The exposure of al-Najjar is just the tip of the iceberg. Secret leverage is being used to influence policy and personnel decisions all over the government. Outside contractors, too. A few months ago, the CEO of a rocket component start-up in Florida suddenly pulled out of a Space Force RFP they were about to win. No explanation given. Wilson Scott, the senior congressman from Arizona, resigned last year in the middle of his term. Rumor is, he was ducking some kind of sex scandal. A member of the Joint Chiefs did a public one-eighty on Ukraine, then shot himself. Those are just the high-profile examples. The influence racket goes way down the chain. Everybody's scared, but no one wants to talk about it."

"Where's the dirt coming from?" Bourne asked.

"That's what I was hoping al-Najjar could tell me. How did anyone tie him to the president's son? Where was the information stored? Who had access to it? There has to be a common thread linking this activity together. If a private or public database got hacked, I want to know what it was and who else is in it. That will give us an idea of the depth of our exposure."

"Is there any chatter about who's behind it? Foreign or domestic?"

Shadow shook her head. "Rumors are all over the board, but I don't trust any of it. Nobody knows."

"You mentioned the general who flipped on Ukraine," Bourne said. "Wilson Scott was also one of the loudest anti-Russian voices on the House committee before Callie Faith took over. And it may be nothing, but al-Najjar had a taste for Russian girls, according to the concierge at the Hilton. That's three Russian connections."

Shadow's lips pursed. "It's worth checking out."

"I got pictures of the girls who were with al-Najjar tonight. Can you find out where they came from?"

"I can," Shadow said.

"I'll talk to Wilson Scott," Bourne told her. "If he resigned to avoid a scandal, somebody must have threatened him. Maybe that will tell us where the Files originated. And who has them."

Shadow nodded. "Given what happened to al-Najjar, you should hurry. Scott may already be on somebody's target list. He's an obvious link in the chain, and there are other people after the Files. They may want to keep him from talking to us."

"And when I find whoever has the database?" Bourne asked.

"Eliminate them."

He stared into Shadow's blue eyes. "What about the Files?"

"Get them for me."

"To destroy the data? Or to use it yourself?"

"That's not your concern, David," Shadow told him.

Her voice had a hard chill. This time he didn't bother correcting her about his name.

Bourne turned to go, but Shadow reached out and curled her cool fingers around his wrist.

"One more thing."

He stopped and waited.

"When did you last see Storm?"

Bourne hesitated. He heard the code name Storm, but in his mind, he saw Johanna's face. She would always be Johanna to him. Johanna was a rogue Treadstone agent who'd been declared unfit for operations. She'd manipulated Bourne the previous summer in order to locate Shadow and try to kill her.

Johanna.

There was a strong attraction between them. He'd fallen for her in ways he hadn't felt since the love of his life, a Canadian journalist named Abbey Laurent, had walked away from him and his Tread-stone world. But just like David Webb's relationship with Shadow, Jason's relationship with Johanna had been a lie from the beginning.

A betrayal.

He'd had a chance to kill Johanna when he discovered the truth. He'd had a gun pointed at her head. Instead, he let her go.

"I saw her in Paris a few months ago," Bourne said.

Shadow didn't look surprised. "You can't trust her."

"I know." He didn't add: *I don't trust you, either.*

"Give Storm half a chance, and she'll betray you again."

"Maybe so," Bourne agreed.

"I never asked when we were together. Did you sleep with her?"

"Why do you care about that?"

"I don't," Shadow snapped, but he wondered if he saw a flash of jealousy in her eyes. Then she went on. "Did Storm tell you about her plans? Do you know what she's going to do next?"

This time Bourne was the one to lie.

"She didn't tell me anything."

In fact, Johanna had told him exactly what she was planning to do.

She was on a mission to destroy Treadstone. And Shadow.

3

"WOULD YOU MIND TAKING OUR PICTURE, SIR?" THE ELDERLY CHINESE man asked Bourne. He smiled, extending a Konica camera that looked as if it dated back to the 1980s.

Bourne took the camera and focused on the couple through the viewfinder. The man appeared to be in his seventies and leaned on a heavy wooden cane. He wore a wool sweater and dress slacks, both too heavy for the warm Arizona day. His wife was of similar vintage and wore a handmade yellow dress, with flat shoes and white lace socks. She stood stiffly next to her husband, not touching him. Behind them, a prickly, wizened saguaro cactus rose out of the desert terrain, even older than the Chinese couple.

"Smile," Jason said, but neither of them did.

He handed the camera back to the old man, who slung the strap around his neck and then inclined his head in thanks.

With a few long steps on the dusty path, Bourne left the husband and wife behind. He climbed the low slope past more tall, multi-armed saguaro, interspersed with squat barrel cacti, organ pipes, and tufts of pink and purple flowers that grew between the rocks. In the distance, the stony peaks of the Tucson Mountains made a jagged line on the horizon. It was late afternoon. Sunset shadows stretched out over the up-and-down trails of the outdoor garden.

Somewhere among the cacti and high brush was Wilson Scott.

Bourne had arrived in Phoenix that morning on an overnight flight out of Heathrow. He'd allowed himself a one-hour nap in the terminal to combat jet lag, and then he'd located the former congressman's estate home among the luxury golf courses of Scottsdale. But Wilson Scott, according to the maid who answered the door, was away on a weekend trip to paint watercolors at the Arizona-Sonora Desert Museum. So Bourne had driven south out of the city toward Tucson.

Now, hours later, Bourne and the elderly Chinese couple on the trail behind him were among the few people still on the museum grounds in the last minutes before the area closed for the day. But Scott's blue Corvette was still in the parking lot, so Bourne assumed the man was somewhere up ahead applying Winsor Orange to his canvas to match the clouds around the waning sun.

He walked quickly on the trail. A near-deserted desert landscape made a good place to talk about blackmail, but it was also a good place for a hit, if anyone wanted Wilson Scott dead. The vegetation rose high enough that he couldn't see far ahead of him, and the landscape provided plenty of hiding places for an assassin. Every now and then, he pushed off the path into the brush, listening for threats, but he heard only the whistle of the desert wind and the occasional maraca music of a rattlesnake warning him away from the rocks.

Over the summit of the next slope, he found Scott.

The former congressman sat on a small wooden stool, a square canvas on a tripod in front of him, along with a palette of paints and brushes on a metal table. His vantage looked out over the tops of the cacti toward the mountains. His painting, which was almost done, was actually quite good, and Bourne stood behind the man, admiring it for a moment. Then he took a couple of steps past Scott and turned around.

"Congressman."

The man wore half-glasses on a long, bumpy nose, and his squint didn't deviate from his canvas at Bourne's greeting. "Not anymore. That part of my life is over."

"I see you're a painter now," Bourne said. "And a good one, too."

Scott still didn't look away from his work. "I don't live in Washington anymore. Ass-kissing is no longer necessary or effective with me. You're not a tourist, and you're not an art lover, so who are you and why are you getting in the way of my light?"

Bourne smiled. He liked the man.

Scott was in his sixties, tall, and slightly cramped as he fit his gangly limbs around the wooden stool. He wore baggy cargo shorts, tan sandals, and a loose white T-shirt smeared with paint stains of various colors. His salt-and-pepper hair jutted up in spikes like the quills of a porcupine. He had the leathery dark skin of someone who'd spent most of his life baking under the Arizona sun.

"My name is Paul West," Bourne told him, using the cover identity he'd presented on a passport at Heathrow the previous day.

"West, huh?" Scott said, sounding unconvinced. "Who are you, Mr. West? FBI? CIA? No offense, but after twenty-four years in Congress, I know the look."

"It's something like that," Bourne admitted.

Scott wiped his brush on his shirt, dipped it in a milky slurry of water on the metal table, and dabbed at the bluish-gray paint on his board. He made a couple of tentative strokes across the canvas. "Something like that. Well, Mr. West, one of the few perks of being an *ex*-congressman is that I don't have to talk to people like you anymore. I'm an old man, my wife is dead, I've got a fat pension and a seven handicap. I don't want much else. So how about you leave me alone with my mountains, okay?"

"Actually, I'm worried about your safety."

The man stripped off his half-glasses and finally focused his dark eyes on Bourne. "What do you mean by that?"

"I mean, I know about the Files. I think you know about the Files, too. Whatever you know may be enough to get you killed."

Scott frowned. "What exactly do you want?"

"I'd like to know why you resigned your seat and what information they had about you."

The congressman's thick eyebrows wrinkled with anger. "Get away from me, Mr. West. Or whoever you are."

"Anything you tell me stops right here."

"Anything I *don't* tell you stops right here. That's the way secrets work."

"I'm serious about the danger," Bourne told him. "Did you read about the Saudi banker who was murdered in London a couple of nights ago? We think he was part of the Files, too. Somebody didn't want him talking."

Scott patted a bulge in the pocket of his cargo shorts. "I'm a Second Amendment Republican, my friend. Don't worry about me."

"Faisal al-Najjar had armed security. They got to him anyway."

The congressman sighed. "Look, Mr. West. They've already done the worst they can do to me. I'm out. I quit. I don't see why they'd come after me now. Once the horse is dead, you don't keep shooting it."

Bourne assessed the man's stubborn independence and concluded that he wasn't going to get any further on his first attempt. He jotted down a cell phone number on a blank white card and put it on the metal table next to Scott's paints.

"If you see anything that concerns you, call me," Bourne said. "I'll be hanging out in the area for a while. Just to be sure no one comes after you."

"I know, spooks don't give up easy. Then again, neither do I, Mr. West. If I find you leaning against my Corvette when I get out of here, the answer's going to be the same. Just don't scratch the car or I'll have to kill you."

Bourne smiled again.

He retreated across the top of the trail and nearly bumped into the elderly Chinese couple coming the other way. The old man leaned into his cane and nodded at him; his wife's face was stolid and unmoving, her eyes studying him with naked suspicion. Bourne shot a quick look across the couple from top to bottom in a routine way, then continued past them as they disappeared down the other side of the slope.

He took a few more steps before his brain caught up with what he'd seen.

Always look at the hands.

Treadstone.

People wearing disguises paid special attention to their faces, but they often forgot about their hands. Bourne had noticed the Chinese man's wrinkled face, but the hand clutching tightly to the cane wasn't the hand of an old man. It was smooth, with strength in its grip. And the woman! She had her hands folded behind her back, but a narrow patch of skin showed between the hem of her dress and the lace tops of her white stockings, and the skin there was unblemished and young.

Bourne bolted back up the trail. As he cleared the top of the slope again, he spotted the two Chinese killers, still in character, only steps away from Wilson Scott. The congressman paid no attention; his focus was on his painting. Bourne heard the heavy, singsong tap of the Chinese man's cane on the dirt as he neared the congressman and spotted Scott's bare feet in his sandals, jutting far enough out on the trail that it would be easy to prick him with an accidental jab of the cane.

Poison.

"*Stop!*" Bourne shouted, drawing his new Glock G47 into his hand.

All three people below him turned in surprise. Scott began to get to his feet, then stumbled backward, tipping over his palette of paints and splashing color on the ground. The accident saved him. The Chinese man took a look at Bourne and knew the game was up, and he picked up the cane and jabbed it toward Scott, only to have the man fall out of reach. Before the man could rear back for another assault, Bourne fired his Glock, needing only one shot. The bullet drilled through the man's neck, dropping him where he stood. The cane toppled, too, a glint of metal at its tip.

The Chinese woman yanked up her yellow dress to reveal black panties and a holster on her thigh, like a garter, that held an enormous Desert Eagle semiautomatic. Bourne fired, but missed wide as she danced sideways with all the speed and grace of a ballerina. In the same instant, she drew the pistol, and he found himself staring down its silver barrel. The huge gun looked ridiculous in her tiny hand, but she wielded it like a pro, and Bourne had to throw himself to the ground as bullets sang around him. If she'd kept firing, she would probably have killed him with a headshot in the next couple of seconds, but instead, she sensed movement on the ground and swung back to her primary target.

Second Amendment Scott, propped on one elbow on the ground, had his Smith & Wesson revolver in his hand, the hammer already cocked. His bullet blasted an arm off a saguaro cactus but missed the Chinese woman entirely. She drew a dead aim on the congressman, but Bourne fired first. The round from his Glock hit the meat of her shoulder, jigging her arm and sending her next two shots into the air. He didn't let her fire again. He squeezed the trigger three more times in succession, landing two shots in her neck and one in the side of her skull above her ear.

The Desert Eagle hit the ground. So did she.

Bourne scrambled to his feet. He ran to Scott, who was staring wide-eyed at the two bodies sprawled in the rocks, his revolver loose in his hand. The tripod with his watercolor painting lay face down in the dust.

"Come on," Bourne said, extending a hand. "We need to go. There may be others. They may have backup."

"The police," Scott murmured.

"You can call the police when we're clear."

He helped the congressman to his feet. He kept his Glock aimed and ready as he dragged the man along the Desert Loop Trail. In the waning light, he saw no one else; the two killers had apparently been working alone. As they neared the museum entrance, a man in a brown zoo uniform sprinted toward them, but the man skidded to a stop and threw his hands in the air when he saw Bourne's gun.

"FBI," Bourne told him, holding up an ID folder at a distance.

"There's been an attempt on the congressman's life. Call 911. I've got to get Mr. Scott to safety. Tell the police he'll make a statement once I'm sure the threat is past. *Go.*"

"Yes! Yes, right away!"

The museum employee disappeared in the opposite direction.

Scott, breathing heavily, steadied himself on the trail. He glanced at Bourne with appreciation on his face. "I guess you were right. Thank you. Sorry to be a stubborn fool, but it comes with the territory after a couple of decades in Washington."

"It was my mistake to let them get close to you," Bourne said. "I passed them once before. I should have spotted them immediately."

"Who were they?"

"I don't know, but obviously they were trying to make sure you never had a chance to tell your story." Bourne dragged the man forward again, but Scott had the strength now to walk on his own. "I need the truth, Congressman. Somebody had enough leverage on you to get you to give up your seat. I'm trying to figure out who it is and *how* they got the information they did. I can't do that without knowing what you're hiding. Tell me what happened. Believe me, a sex scandal isn't worth getting killed over."

"It was never about sex," Scott replied with a rumbling sigh. "I think I would have weathered the storm if it were just that. But this was much worse."

"What was it?" Bourne asked.

Scott drew himself up to his full height and closed his eyes. The paint smears on his shirt made it look as if he'd been shot multiple times. "They had evidence that I'd hired a hit man to kill my wife."

4

AS THEY LEFT THE ZOO, SCOTT STOPPED AT HIS CORVETTE AND RETRIEVED
a small leather-bound box from the glove compartment. Bourne
then drove the two of them deeper into the desert in his rented Land
Rover. When he was sure they weren't being followed, he pulled
onto the shoulder of a highway called Mile Wide Road, with nothing
but empty desert around them. Thousands of saguaros jutted up like
totem poles from the flat, rocky landscape, and mountains ringed the
horizon. The falling sun flirted with the peaks.

Bourne dropped the tailgate. They sat next to each other amid
the rush of the desert wind, surrounded by gray shadows. A few
hawks circled far above them in the blue sky. Scott opened the small
box, which contained a bottle of twenty-five-year-old Dalmore
single malt whisky, plus two Waterford crystal tumblers. The congressman poured shots for each of them, spilling a little with his
trembling hands.

"I always keep this bottle with me," Scott said. "Virginia and I
first tasted the Dalmore on our honeymoon in Scotland in 1988.

Helluva trip, helluva drink. After that, we always had some on hand for anniversaries. Since she died, I've nursed this last bottle, only dipping into it now and then. But you can only hold on to the past for so long."

They clinked the tumblers. Both drank the shots down in a bracing swallow.

Bourne saw the congressman wipe a tear from his eye and inhale with a large sniffle. Carefully, the man cleaned the glasses with a small white cloth, then shut away the bottle and glasses in the leather box again.

"Virginia had a slow-moving form of ALS," Scott told him after a long silence. "It started with numbness in her leg. She progressed to a cane, then a wheelchair. It began to get worse from there. This was over the course of three years. A nightmare."

"I'm very sorry," Jason said.

"Thank you. Don't feel bad if you don't know what to say. Nobody does. Virginia bore up well under the torture, but it killed me seeing her that way, seeing the disease steal away her body."

"A lot of people would consider extreme measures in those circumstances," Bourne commented.

"Like murder?" Scott replied.

"Assisted suicide is legal in some places."

"True, but not here in Arizona. And not for Catholics, I can tell you. Suicide wasn't an option Virginia would ever have considered. For her, it would have been like giving up her soul. I went so far as to tiptoe around the subject once, and she shut me down. She was determined to tough it out to the end, no matter how bad it got."

"What about you?" Bourne asked. "You must have thought about finding an easier way out for her."

"Of course I did. But I did *not* kill my wife."

"She died," Bourne pointed out.

"Yes, she did. Of the disease. Of natural causes, if you can call what happened to her *natural.* I sat by her bedside and held her hand while she died in an excruciating way. Believe me, I wish I could obliterate the memory."

Bourne, who'd had most of his own memories obliterated, said nothing.

"But all that makes me sound like some kind of hero," Scott went on, "and I'm not. In fact, I humiliated myself and dishonored Virginia. I couldn't bear for her to find out what I'd done. I didn't want her to die knowing the kind of man I was."

Scott studied the leather box of Dalmore, which was cradled in his lap, with a strange disdain, as if he wanted to throw it away into the desert. Instead, he lifted it up and pushed the box into Bourne's hands. "Here, you take it. I don't deserve it anymore. I'm just fooling myself."

Bourne took the box from the congressman without a word and shoved it into the back of the Land Rover.

"What happened?" he asked.

"Well, this should be no surprise, but Virginia didn't have much interest in sex after the diagnosis. Her body was betraying her, so it was difficult for her to celebrate her body, if that makes any sense. I didn't push her. But me, I still had needs. Jesus, I feel dirty saying it like that. I was disgusted with myself, and I still am. I mean, my wife is dying, and I'm worried about sex. I figured I should be able to shut off those feelings, but I couldn't. I needed some kind of physical release. And not just that, I needed someone to have a kind of *intimacy* with. That was what I really missed. Someone to talk to."

"You had an affair?" Bourne asked.

Scott shook his head. "Not that way. Not like you're thinking. No. I've slept with one woman my whole life, and while Virginia was still alive, I was determined to keep it that way. But what I did felt even more pathetic. I signed up for one of those interactive adult apps. Something called mygirlnextdoor. I saw it advertised on a porn site. It was supposed to be an upscale girlfriend experience, but let's face it, it was a place for lonely men to jerk off to pretty girls taking their clothes off in private chat rooms. I signed up. I visited the site all the time, sometimes at home after Virginia was asleep, some-times even in my congressional office. I was lucky an aide never walked in while I was . . . busy. Every night it was a different girl. All young, all gorgeous. They were mostly Russian."

"Russian," Bourne said sharply. "Are you sure?"

"Oh, I know a Russian accent. Plus, they'd tell me about their lives, and they were all from cities like Moscow and St. Petersburg. I'm sure most of the shit they told me was made up, but even if they were fairy tales, they were definitely Russian fairy tales."

Bourne frowned. "Go on."

A faraway look crossed the congressman's face. "Then every-thing changed for me. One night I met Irina. I'd seen her face in the private rooms, but she'd never been available before. Men were al-ways with her, paying her, tipping her. But that night I was able to have her for myself. Jesus! She wasn't like the others. Her body was perfect. Just perfect, oh my God. She couldn't have been more than twenty years old to look like that. At my age, it takes a lot to get me excited, but when she took off her clothes—"

He stopped, another scowl of self-disgust on his mouth.

"There's no fool like an old fool, right? I gave her a lot of money.

I stopped seeing the other girls on the site. I only wanted Irina. We arranged dates, times when I could log on and be with her. It wasn't just sex. I mean, I won't lie, sex was a big part of it. But I found myself talking to her, too. Irina was a good listener. She was smart, funny, well-educated on so many different topics. You couldn't design a more perfect girl if you built her yourself. I know what it sounds like, but the fact is, I fell in love with her. It wasn't the kind of love I had for Virginia, but I developed a crush on Irina that was like a tidal wave. She just washed me away. And I kept going back for more."

Scott laughed bitterly at himself.

"I began to tell her things," he went on.

"Personal things?" Bourne asked.

"Oh, yeah. Things I had never admitted to anyone else."

"Do you think you were targeted because of your position in Congress? Do you think this was all arranged as a trap?"

"Looking back, sure, I wonder about that, but I don't see how they could have done it. It was all anonymous. I never revealed my identity online. I never even showed any of the girls my face! Not even Irina! I was always in the dark, always in shadow. Fuck, I was so careful. I set up a PayPal account with a generic Gmail address for email. I literally never used that address or that account for anything except mygirlnextdoor."

"But someone found out," Bourne concluded.

"Yes. Someone found out." Scott squeezed his eyes shut and gripped the tailgate with his fists. "I began to talk to Irina about Virginia. Not by name, of course. But I told her about my situation, about the ALS, about what it was doing to our relationship. Like I said, I craved sex, but what I really craved was intimacy. Irina gave me that. I poured out my heart to her. Stupid, sure, I know now it was stupid. Hell, I even knew it was stupid while I was doing it. But it felt so good to talk about how fucking awful it was and to have this beautiful girl listen to me. Like she really understood."

Bourne let silence drag out between them for a while. "What else did you tell her?"

"I talked about how much I hated what the disease was doing to Virginia," Scott said. "How she was suffering. How I wanted her suffering to be over. I felt incredibly guilty about that, but I said if God was going to take her, I wished that He would just do it and not drag it out. I said I wanted my life back. I said I would—I said I would do just about anything to give her peace."

"And then?"

"The next time I saw Irina online, she was different. Colder. More distant. Uncomfortable. She gave me a phone number to call. She said it was contact information to reach out to someone who could make my problem go away. There was a man who could end Virginia's suffering and make it look like an accident or natural causes. She said it would be painless, and I would be free. She gave me a code to use to prove to the person on the other end that I was . . . approved."

"What did you do?" Bourne asked.

"I ended the call with her. I canceled my account on the website. I terminated the credit card I'd used. I never spoke to Irina again. I was terrified. You have to believe me, I never meant for something like that to happen. All I was doing was sharing my feelings with her. I never would have considered—"

Scott stopped.

"What about the phone number?" Bourne asked. "Did you call it?"

The congressman pressed a fist hard against his forehead. "Once. I left Washington, and I drove out in the country. I used one of those pay-as-you-go phones. I called the number. I don't even know why. I guess I was curious."

"Did someone answer?"

"A man."

"You gave him the code?"

Scott hesitated. "Yes."

"What did he say?"

"He asked for the target name, the fulfillment date, and any special requirements. It was sickening. I could have been calling a department store with a phone order."

"Then what?"

"I hung up. I threw the phone into a lake, and I got the hell out of there. For weeks, I was scared it would somehow all bounce back on me. But it didn't. Months passed, and I didn't hear a thing. I thought I was in the clear." He shook his head. "I wasn't. About eighteen months ago, I received an anonymous call on my congressional phone. A woman. She said she was sending greetings from Irina. Wondering how that special project worked out for me. I arranged to call her back that evening, and I got another pay-as-you-go phone. I called, and the woman laid it out for me. She knew everything, about mygirlnextdoor, about Irina, about Virginia, about the contact with the hit man. If I didn't resign immediately, it would all come out, and I'd have to resign anyway."

"Did you recognize the woman's voice?" Bourne asked. "Could she have been another girl on that same website?"

"I didn't recognize the voice," Scott replied, "but I don't think so. The thing is, she knew that I'd called the assassin. She knew where I went to call him. I don't even understand how that's possible. So it definitely went far beyond the website."

"You resigned," Bourne said.

Scott nodded. "Yes. One way or another, I knew I'd be out. If I was exposed, I might even have faced criminal charges for attempted murder. Even though I didn't actually do anything—well, not really. But most of all, I didn't want Virginia finding out about any of this. She was still alive, but she was failing. I didn't want her knowing about my sins before she passed away. The things I did on the website. And the hit man. She didn't deserve to die with those kinds of doubts about my love for her in her head."

Bourne pushed himself off the tailgate. He stared out at the dark mountains, then turned around and faced the congressman. "You have no idea who approached you? Or how they found out what you'd done?"

"No idea at all."

"Did you tell anyone about the hit man?"

"Sort of. I thought someone in authority should know about it. I mean, this man was a contract killer, and he was linked to Irina and the website. So I sent an anonymous tip to the FBI with as much information as I felt comfortable sharing. But I don't believe there's any way the agency could have traced it back to me."

Bourne frowned, trying to assemble the puzzle pieces in his mind. An online porn star and a U.S. killer-for-hire. Somewhere in that unholy alliance was a link to the Files and whoever had them.

The Russians? They were behind the website.

The Chinese? They'd been hacking U.S. government data for years, and the assassins in the desert museum were both Chinese.

He wandered away from the congressman among the rocks and cacti adjoining the highway. It was nearly dark, and the air cooled quickly. He slid a phone from his pocket and tapped out a text to Shadow.

Have you had any luck tracing the two girls who were with al-Najjar?

The head of Treadstone replied a few seconds later. *I just got a report on that. They were flown to London from Estonia specifically to meet him.*

Let me guess, Bourne texted back. *He met them on an escort website called mygirlnextdoor.*

How did you know that?

Bourne put away his phone without answering. His next step was clear. He needed to find a girl named Irina.

5

AFTER DROPPING WILSON SCOTT BACK AT HIS CORVETTE IN THE MUSEUM
parking lot, Bourne headed out of the city, leaving the lights of Tucson behind him. It only took him a few minutes in the darkness on I-10 to realize that he was being followed.

The driver hung back, keeping a couple of vehicles between them, but when Bourne slowed enough that cars began to pass him, one set of headlights in his rearview mirror slowed, too, staying nearly half a mile behind the Land Rover. Then he took the SUV up to ninety miles an hour, and the headlights kept pace, decelerating as soon as he slowed back to his cruising speed. He wondered when the car had picked him up and whether the driver had spied on his meeting with the congressman in the empty desert.

Not long after he passed the town of Marana, Bourne saw an exit sign for Pinal Airpark. He took the lonely cloverleaf from I-10 and headed west through flat scrubland toward the airport. The GPS screen on his dashboard guided him. With an arrow-straight road ahead, he switched off his headlights, making the Land Rover mostly invisible. Half a mile in his wake, the glow of the other car kept following him. No doubt the driver was wondering where Bourne had gone, and he or she certainly knew that Bourne had spotted the tail.

Even so, the car kept coming.

He drove until the road ended with the lights of the airfield just ahead of him. Beyond the barbed-wire fence, he saw the white bodies of dozens of jets lined up like ghosts across the tarmac of the maintenance facility. His tires scraping, he pulled the Land Rover off the road and shut down the engine. He got out and jogged to the other side of the highway, his Glock in his hand. Less than a minute later, the trailing headlights got larger.

A dark Mercedes slid to a stop on the road as the driver spotted the Land Rover parked near the airfield. It stayed where it was, not moving at all, its engine purring. Bourne waited, his gun trained on the door of the car. He couldn't see through the windows.

How many were inside?

Were they in league with the Chinese assassins at the museum?

Then the driver's window rolled down.

"It's me, Jason," a voice called.

Bourne's heart quickened. He knew that voice. Even so, he didn't reveal himself from the darkness or loosen his grip on the Glock. The driver's door opened and a woman got out, nothing but the palest shadow in the distant lights from the airport. He recognized that tall, lean outline, with its waterfall of wheat-colored hair. He knew her body from head to toe. He remembered the taste of her mouth and the scent of her skin.

He also remembered her pointing a gun at his head and threatening to kill him.

"Johanna," Bourne said.

Hearing his voice, she raised her arms in the air. He was sure she had a gun, but she hadn't drawn it from her holster. She walked into the middle of the dusty, deserted road, and he listened to the click of her heels.

Bourne drew a penlight and bathed her in a circle of light, making her squint. He crossed the road, his Glock still aimed at her heart. She didn't move. Her pale blue eyes took note of the gun in his hand, and her mouth bent into a small smile. She was dressed much as she'd been when he first met her, in jeans and a tie-dyed tank top, untucked, with a swirling design that looked like the radar map of a hurricane. He wondered if that was an inside joke for his benefit. Johanna had previously been the Treadstone agent known as Storm.

"What do you want?" Bourne asked.

"No foreplay?" Johanna replied. "That's disappointing. As I recall, you were really good at foreplay."

"What do you want?" he repeated.

She shrugged. "Same as you. The Files."

He appreciated that she didn't lie. Not that he would have believed a lie. He'd already heard too many lies from her in the past.

"My gun's in the car, Jason," Johanna went on. She turned around slowly and lifted the tank top high on her torso so he could see that she wore no holster in the small of her back. "You can put the Glock down."

He did. He knew Johanna well enough to know that if she'd wanted to kill him, he'd already be dead. She was every bit as good an agent as Bourne, and she was almost ten years younger. She was also—according to Shadow's psychological profile—emotionally unstable and prone to fits of violence and revenge. He'd become involved with her not knowing who she was, but even after he learned the truth, he'd been unable to give her up. They were drawn to each other. When they had sex, it was with the frenzied passion of two wounded souls. But being with her was risky and potentially deadly, like two scorpions trying to mate.

"How did you find me?" Jason asked.

Johanna, who was a techie and a hacker, gave him a look that said it was no big deal. "I broke into the London street cams to take a look at al-Najjar's murder. I saw you there. So I knew you were after the Files. After that, it was only a matter of time before you came looking for Wilson Scott."

"Two assassins tried to kill him in the park," Bourne said. "Did you send them?"

"No. I spotted them, though. I'm surprised they got by you the first time, Jason. Did you forget to look at the hands? But I assumed you'd be able to take them out. I was watching in case you needed help."

"And what about Scott? Did you eavesdrop on my meeting with him?"

"No."

"You don't want to know what he said?"

"Tell me or don't tell me. I don't care. I'm not interested in him. I'm interested in you, Jason. But you already know that."

Bourne ignored the innuendo. "Again, what do you want?"

"I told you what I'm after the last time we talked in Paris. You know what I'm trying to do. I want you with me, not against me. I know Shadow is sending you after the Files, just like me. I don't intend to get in your way. It's a race, and I intend to win, but who knows? You may outsmart me and get there first."

"Then what?"

"Then I think you should fuck Shadow and give them to me," Johanna said.

"Why would I do that?"

"Lots of reasons. First of all, you can't trust her. She lied to you and tricked you once before. She'll do it again."

"I could say the same about you."

"Yes, you could," Johanna agreed, "but I haven't lied to you since you found out who I am. It's cards on the table for the two of us now, Jason. Shadow is an evil, conniving bitch who would slit your throat if it got her what she wanted. She'll play you, she'll seduce you, and then she'll throw you away when she doesn't need you anymore. You're expendable to her."

"Whereas you?"

"Whereas you and me make a fucking good team. In every sense of the word. Give the Files to me. They're gold. With them, we can bring down Treadstone and the rest of Alphabet City."

"It's tempting," he admitted.

Because it was. There were days when he wanted to destroy Treadstone as much as Johanna did. Every time he tried to get away from them, the agency slithered its way back into his life. And now, with Shadow on top, he felt himself more bound to this life—and to her—than ever before.

Maybe Johanna represented a way out.

Or maybe she was lying to him again.

"Who are you working for?" Bourne asked. "You're not doing this on your own."

Johanna hesitated, as if she were weighing what to say. "You're right. Are you familiar with Callie Faith? The Nevada congresswoman?"

"The new head of the House Intelligence Committee?"

"That's her. I've been feeding her information about Treadstone. I know a lot of dirt, believe me. I hacked Shadow's files last year, remember? Callie wants to see Treadstone obliterated as much as I do."

"You can't trust Callie Faith any more than I can trust Shadow."

"Oh, I know that," Johanna agreed, "but we share a common goal. For now, that's enough."

"Is it? You're being used, Johanna. Callie Faith is where she is because Wilson Scott resigned and set up a domino effect that elevated her on the House committee. She got exactly what she wanted. So maybe Callie already has the Files."

"If she did, she wouldn't need me. She reached out to me because she's scared that Shadow will get them first and be able to destroy her. Those two hate each other. But I'm not saying Callie didn't find a way to use the Files. She obviously did. If she paid whoever has them to get rid of Wilson Scott, then I'm sure that whetted her appetite to get the whole database for herself."

"Do you think she knows who has them?"

Johanna frowned. "She knows more than she's saying, but she had no leads to give me about how to find them. All she could tell me was that Shadow is looking for them, too. When I heard that, I knew our paths would cross again, Jason. I admit, I liked that idea. I've missed you."

He didn't reply, but he couldn't deny to himself that he'd missed her, too.

"Where are you going next? Want to give me a clue? Come on, do you really want Shadow to get the Files? You know her, Jason. You know what she's capable of."

"Do you really want Callie Faith to get them? She's no better."

"Maybe I have no intention of giving them to her," Johanna replied with a wink. "But first we have to find them before anybody else does. Why not work together?"

"I work alone," Bourne said.

"So do I, but it doesn't have to stay that way. I know your weakness, Jason. You're *not* a loner, not by choice. You need someone in your life."

"As I recall, you used that weakness against me."

Her face darkened. "Yes, I did. I'm sorry. But my own weakness is even worse. I *hate* the idea of having someone in my life. I don't want to rely on anyone but myself. And yet here I am with you. No gun. No hidden agenda. This is me, Jason. I want you back. I can't say it any plainer than that. I want you in my bed. I want you in my life. You and me side by side. Isn't that better than Treadstone?"

She took a step toward him, raising her arms as if to wrap her body against his. He wanted that. He wanted to feel her softness on his skin again, but instead, he raised the Glock, which made her freeze where she was. A flash of anger crossed her face, and Johanna's anger had a life of its own.

"Seriously? You think I'm playing you?"

"No. I don't."

"Then what is it? I know you want me, too. We're good that way."

"You and me? That's not happening, Johanna. Not again."

"Because of Shadow?" Her blue eyes narrowed, squinting at him. "No, it's not because of her. It's still Abbey Laurent, isn't it? She's the problem."

Bourne didn't like hearing Abbey's name on her lips. He'd never seen Johanna jealous, and he didn't think he'd enjoy the experience. But she was right. He'd made the mistake of telling Johanna all about his relationship with Abbey, how they'd loved each other without being able to stay together. She didn't fit in his world. She didn't belong with killers.

Like Shadow. Like Johanna. Like himself.

"I haven't spoken to Abbey in more than a year," Bourne said.

"Does that matter? You can't let go of her."

He saw no point in lying. "Maybe I can't."

"So you don't know," she murmured. "Interesting."

Concern flitted across Bourne's face. "Know what?"

"About Abbey."

"How do you know anything about Abbey?"

"I keep an eye on my rivals, Jason," Johanna replied with a sharpness in her voice that gave him a chill.

"What about Abbey?" he asked, emphasizing each word.

Johanna leaned forward until their lips were almost touching, and then she whispered to him in the quiet desert. "She got married last month."

6

THE SMELL OF SMOKE FOLLOWED ABBEY LAURENT INTO HER OCEAN-
front home off Highway 1 west of Malibu.

For six months, as she did research for her next novel, the smell
had stayed with her and never really gone away. It lingered in her
clothes, in her car, in her closet, on her skin, and in her hair. Every
breath she took brought a faint, charred aroma through her nose. But
Abbey didn't mind. She couldn't write about things without living
them herself, and for months she'd been living the aftermath of the
La Sienta Ranch fire.

Forty-five thousand acres blackened in the tinder-dry Santa
Monica Mountains. Fifteen hundred homes destroyed. One hundred
and three people dead. And no explanation of how it had started.

It was almost one in the morning. Abbey didn't turn on any
lights as she got home, and she tried to move quietly in the darkness,
not wanting to awaken Garrett. He was used to her strange hours,
but he wasn't a night creature like her. She lit the way through the
house with her phone. Despite the months she'd spent here, she still

made wrong turns sometimes and bumped into furniture in the five-thousand-square-foot hillside mansion. Abbey didn't own the house. She'd rented it from a Hollywood producer who was away on a year-long film project in New Zealand. He was a fan of her books, so he'd let her have it for a price so ridiculously cheap for Malibu that she couldn't turn it down. The house was only half an hour across the mountains on Highway 23 from the worst of the fire's devastation.

Abbey slipped inside the den she used as her office and writing space. It was a front-facing room with an enormous balcony that overlooked the crashing waves of the Pacific. The double doors to the adjacent bedroom where she and Garrett slept were open, and she could hear the quiet rumble of his breathing from the king-sized bed. Keeping the lights off as she went into the bedroom, she opened her walk-in closet, which was almost as large as the entire studio apartment where she'd lived in Quebec City a few years ago. Another pent-up wave of fire smoke wafted from her clothes inside. She stripped naked, then padded across the plush carpet to the master bathroom.

With the door closed behind her, she finally turned on a light. She started the water in the walk-in shower, and when it was scalding hot, she let the water cascade over her body. She soaped herself up from head to toe and shampooed her shoulder-length burgundy hair, but even when she was clean and dry, the ashy smell lingered on her pale pink skin. Still naked, she turned off the lights and went back into the bedroom.

She was too riled up to sleep. That was typical. This book was the most emotional project she'd ever pursued. She'd spent the day interviewing a lawyer who'd lost his house, his wife, and his four-year-old son in the fire. The numb look on his face had stayed with her, that empty desolation of someone who had seen his entire life stripped away. He hadn't been back to the scene since it happened; he said he couldn't bear to see the remnants of what had once been his home. All he wanted was answers.

How had the fire started?

And *who* did it?

Those were the answers Abbey wanted, too.

Her huge success over the past couple of years had been as a novelist. She'd followed in the heels of the late Peter Chancellor by writing ripped-from-the-headlines conspiracy thrillers, the kind of books where readers wondered if that was how it had really happened. So she was writing the La Sienta Ranch book as a novel, but she wanted it grounded in reality. The more she dug into the fire, the more the real mysteries got inside her head. Even if this was fiction, she was still a journalist, and she wanted to figure out the truth.

In the midst of her research, she'd also done something she never expected.

She fell in love.

Abbey stared down at the dark shape of the man in the bed. She could make out his bare chest above the thin sheet, his head turned sideways on the pillow. She loved how he looked: his long dark hair, almost as long as hers; the smooth, neatly trimmed line of his beard; his bony frame, athletic but a little gangly. The sheet bulged from the mound between his long legs. He always slept naked, like she did. She felt a strong desire to slip the sheet aside and reach down and arouse him with her fingers, and then climb on top of him and make love to him in quick, sweaty silence.

Garrett Parker.

He was twenty-nine; she was thirty-six. He was still a kid, really, but she liked the novelty of being with a younger man. Most of the men she'd loved in the past were older. They'd met by accident five months ago at a bar in the O'Hare airport, when she was on her way back to LAX and Garrett was on a layover flying from Washington, DC, to Seattle. Abbey didn't think she'd ever met anyone quite so charming. He was funny, brilliant, and movie-star handsome, like a nerdy version of Harry Styles. They'd talked for hours, losing all track of time between martinis. When they both realized they'd missed their flights, they rented a room together at the airport Hilton, and Abbey did something she'd never done before in her life. She fucked a man only hours after meeting him.

And it was good. Very, very good.

After that, things moved crazy fast. Too fast. She found that she wanted to spend every waking minute with Garrett, but she had a book to research, and he had a senior IT job in Seattle. They stole weekends together when they could. They Zoomed all night. They had real sex when they were together and video sex when they weren't. Only six weeks later, Garrett sublet his Bellevue condo and moved in with Abbey in her rented Malibu mansion. Another three months after that, they took a weekend trip to Reno, won big at craps, and got very drunk to celebrate. She didn't really remember whether he'd asked her or she asked him, but when they got on the Southwest jet back to Los Angeles, they had rings on their fingers.

That had been two weeks ago.

She'd lived two whole weeks as a married woman.

Abbey was still floating. She'd found the man of her dreams, something she'd never expected at this stage of her life. Standing in the bedroom, naked, she wanted to make love to him. She wanted to feel him inside her at the end of a long, difficult day. Her body was damp and ready. But she didn't reach for him. She went back to her walk-in closet and found a silk robe, and then she took her laptop to the balcony outside her office. She sat on one of the patio chairs, with the low hills all around her and the hypnotic noise of the waves rising from the Pacific, which glittered like millions of stars under the California moonlight.

This was paradise. How could anyone not be happy with this life? And yet she wasn't.

Yes, she loved Garrett, but as Abbey sat on the balcony, it wasn't Garrett's face she saw in her head. It wasn't Garrett's arms that she wanted around her. The gravelly voice that aroused her didn't belong to her husband. Her heart told her what she didn't want to hear, that she'd fallen in love and gotten married for all the wrong reasons. She was trying to fill a hole at the bottom of her soul, and that void had a name.

Jason Bourne.

Jason.

Where was he now?

She'd said goodbye to him more than a year ago. Her choice. She'd walked away. She'd had no contact with him since then, nothing, zero. He'd given her a way to reach him if she ever needed to find him again, but she'd deliberately chosen not to do that, even on those lonely nights when she would have loved to hear his voice and be reminded of their time together.

He hadn't reached out to her, either. Not that she'd expected him to. They were doing what they'd promised each other when they split up on the boardwalk in Quebec City. They were living their own lives, apart from each other, in different worlds. She couldn't share the life of a killer. She couldn't accept who he was and the things he had to do. She'd tried, and she'd fooled herself for a while, but it was too hard.

But every time she thought she'd put Jason behind her, he crept into her mind again.

"Fuck!" Abbey said out loud, exasperated with herself.

She opened her laptop, hoping work would push all the other thoughts out of her mind. Her focus now was on the La Sienta Ranch fire and the novel that would come out of it. She had an idea in her head of how the book would start, with a desperate man anxious to cover up a crime. A murder.

Chapter One.

Her fingers tapped on the keys:

Death always carried a scythe, and so did the midnight man.

Sweating, panicking, he hacked at withered thistles and tall brown weeds filling the scrubland, which had seen no rain in months. He dragged armfuls back to the hilltop house, stacking it against walls and under windows, making kindling for the blaze. This was the burn season. The season of fire. Warning signs alerted the people who lived here to be ready to run with just the shirts on their backs.

From a single spark, infernos came. One little flame would hatch the egg that became a dragon. And the body left behind in the house would simply be one more victim.

Abbey read the words and then reread them. She liked the idea of the midnight man starting the fire. But who was he? Why was he willing to go so far? Did he start the fire knowing it would spiral out of control, or was he horrified at the monster to which he gave birth?

The body. Whose body? Who was it?

She shook her head. The concept wasn't there yet, and she couldn't rush it. She needed to know more about the real mystery in order to craft the fictional mystery. In a few days, she was supposed to meet a conspiracy blogger with whom she'd crossed paths once before. He'd reached out to her online when he read in *People* magazine that her next book was to be inspired by the La Sienta Ranch fire.

There are things about the fire you don't know!

Most of what he published was QAnon-level nonsense, but he'd been right once before. He'd pointed Abbey toward a Washington conspiracy that had nearly killed her. She was only alive now because Jason had been there to save her.

Jason!

Everything always came back to Jason.

Abbey slapped the laptop shut. She tugged her robe tighter against the nighttime chill. The bitter smell of smoke stayed in her nose, never going away.

Except . . .

This was not the smoke of a fire. This was a cigarette.

Her brow furrowed with puzzlement. Abbey got out of the chair and went to the balcony railing. Rolling hills stretched in both directions in the darkness. Below her, beyond the highway, the ocean reflected the moonlight. She inhaled, and what she smelled was definitely a cigarette, rising with the wind that blew up the slope. Someone was down there, in the shadows not far from the house.

Watching her.

"Hello?" Abbey called. "Who's there?"

She found herself adding, "I have a gun."

Which was a lie. If whoever was down there had night vision binoculars—*Jesus, why would she think that?*—then he could see that she was unarmed. She was also keenly aware of being naked under the thin robe. But she had a CZ P-01 9mm in the bedroom steps away, and she knew how to use it.

Thanks to Jason.

To live in his world, he'd told her, she needed to know how to use a gun. *If they come after me, they'll come after you, too.*

"If you're looking for money or drugs, you won't find any here," she added in a conversational tone to whoever was hiding down there. "But if you get close to me, I swear, I'll blow your fucking head off."

She heard nothing. Even the cigarette smell seemed to vanish, as if it had been snuffed out underfoot.

Was she talking to herself?

No. She wasn't. On the slope leading toward Highway 1, she heard a faint crackling of brush. Her eyes narrowed, and just for a moment, she was sure she saw the silhouette of someone walking away.

7

THE FLIGHT OUT OF PHOENIX BROUGHT BOURNE TO DC IN THE EARLY EVE-
ning. He used an app on his phone to hail a car, and ten minutes later,
a black SUV pulled up curbside outside Terminal 1. The driver, who
was built like Jack Reacher, wore a turtleneck and black jeans and said
nothing as he came around and opened the rear door. Bourne took
note of at least three weapons concealed on the man's Godzilla body.

He climbed inside the vehicle, then nodded at the man who was
waiting for him in the back seat. "Special Agent Fox."

"Cain."

The SUV shuddered with weight as the driver got back inside,
and the FBI vehicle shot off into Washington traffic. A glass shield
separated the front seat from the back seat, and Bourne was sure it
was soundproof. But even if the driver couldn't hear them, he expected
that Fox had the back seat bugged to record their entire conversation.

"It's the Christmas season, Billy," Bourne said, noting Fox's
standard-issue gray suit. "Shouldn't you be wearing a light-up tie or
something?"

"Ho ho ho," Fox replied. The FBI man checked his watch. "Speaking of Christmas, my wife has reservations at a tapas bar in Arlington. It's kind of a holiday tradition for us. If I miss it, she says she'll kill me. And you know, she's a Ranger, so I take that sort of threat seriously."

"Tell Farah it's my fault if you're late," Bourne said.

"She won't care. She'll kill you, too."

Bourne smiled.

Farah wasn't actually an Army Ranger anymore—something Billy Fox didn't realize. She was actually a Treadstone assassin code-named Magician. She was Indian-born, thin and dark, and utterly lethal. Bourne had seen her in action once on a mission outside Almaty, when they'd had to shoot their way past a team of terrorists who'd taken over an oil refinery. She'd gunned down seven men with cool accuracy using her H&K, then nearly beheaded two more after a Kazakh militant shot the pistol out of her hand.

Later that night, after the violence was over, he'd bumped into her by accident at the Barakholka market, where she was sharing a plate of horsemeat sausage with her FBI husband. A quick look from Farah told Bourne that her husband knew nothing about the day's lethal activities. He'd kept her cover, and he'd also developed an unexpected friendship with Billy Fox, who had a shorter stick up his butt than most FBI agents. Since then, they'd met up for an occasional Nationals game when Bourne was in Washington.

They also had a quid pro quo relationship when it came to trading interagency secrets.

"I hear you've been spending time in Tucson," Billy commented. "Looking for a winter place? Maybe a condo with a mountain view?"

"I don't like the desert," Bourne replied. "I prefer cities."

"You mean like London? Word is, you spent time there recently, too. You need to be more careful, Cain. An MI5 man spotted you at the Hilton. He put two and two together with the death of al-Najjar, and he passed the tip up the chain to Tony Audley. Tony called me to see if I knew what you were up to."

"What did you tell him?"

"I said you liked Christmas tea at the Ritz," Billy said with a chuckle. "Tony didn't appreciate the joke. He started burbling on about Treadstone body counts and the special relationship and the Saudis owning most of London. You didn't actually kill al-Najjar, though, did you?"

"No."

"Do you know who did?"

"Shadow thinks it was a Saudi hit team trying to shut him up."

"Yes, we thought the same."

A muffled ping sounded in the vehicle. Billy removed his phone from inside his suit coat, then checked the text message without replying and put the device back in his pocket. He ran his hand back through his wiry red hair, which, when combined with his long thin nose and pencil mustache, made him look vaguely like his namesake animal. He was as small and cunning as a fox, too.

"That's Farah. She's already pissed that I'm not there. We should make this quick, okay? I can connect the dots. London and al-Najjar. Arizona and Wilson Scott. You're hunting for the Files."

"I am," Bourne admitted. "Are you?"

"Oh, sure, everybody wants them. FBI, CIA, NSA, DOJ. Plus most of our enemies overseas. Some of our friends, too."

"Are you willing to trade intel?" Bourne asked.

"You've got something?"

"A possible connection. It's worth exploring, but I don't know where to start. You may know more about it than I do."

"If you tell me anything, I'll be forced to pass it along," Billy announced, enunciating his words as if his superiors were listening. And maybe they were.

"Fair enough. All I ask is some room to run."

Billy pursed his lips. He leaned forward, digging his hand into one of the seat pockets and coming out with a small recording device. With a fingernail, he popped open the back and removed the batteries. "Okay. I'll give you a twenty-four-hour head start. I can't do any better than that. What's the connection?"

"First, what do you know about the Files? Where does the data come from?"

Billy shook his head. "We assume some kind of hack, but we haven't found any common ground to determine the source. Believe me, we've looked. Plus, some of the knowledge seems to go beyond what you'd find in a database. There are instances of blackmail that involve information that's not likely to be written down anywhere."

"Like someone hiring a hit man to kill his wife?" Bourne asked.

Billy's eyes narrowed, and the fox resemblance got even stronger. "Yeah. Like that."

"My sources say a rumor along those lines made its way to someone in the Bureau," Bourne said. "Did you hear about it?"

"I did. That was last year. We never found out who fed us the tip. There was also no reason at the time to suspect it had anything to do with the Files. The caller didn't mention blackmail. But I can put two and two together as well as the Brits. Was it Wilson Scott who told you about this? I know his wife died, and there was a lot of talk behind the scenes about whether it was a mercy killing. Not that anyone around our shop was going to look into it. Everybody knows what ALS does. Fucking awful disease."

"Scott says he didn't help her along," Bourne replied. "He insists she died without any help. But he said someone put him in touch with a man who could speed it up. He made a call, but he claims that's as far as it went."

"Do you believe him?"

"I'm not sure, but it doesn't really matter either way. The point is, someone knew all about it, and whoever it was leveraged the secret to get Scott to resign. He claims he was very careful, that there's no way anyone should have been able to connect him to this. But they did. That means it's probably part of the Files."

Billy frowned. "As I recall, the tip mentioned a website. Sort of an OnlyFans kind of thing for online sex."

"Mygirlnextdoor," Bourne told him.

"Yeah. Right. We checked it out as best we could. You use a site like that, you know you run the risk of being exposed. It doesn't mean there's a link to the Files."

"Except al-Najjar used the same site to hook up with Russian girls. Escorts. They got blown up with him in London. That's two connections to the same website, which makes it feel less like a coincidence."

"Yeah, agreed," Billy said.

"You said you checked it out. What did you find?"

"I said we checked it out as best we could. The site's not operated in the U.S. We couldn't get to any of the programmers or the people running the hands-on parts of the scheme. Our IT guys hacked open a lot of the code, but according to them, it didn't raise any red flags. There wasn't any obvious spyware other than the usual cookies and trashy ads. So we figured the leak was probably the girls themselves, using info their clients provided to operate lucrative side businesses. Killers-for-hire, real estate scams, in-person prostitution, human trafficking, take your pick. Lonely men with hard-ons try to impress naked girls, and they wind up saying things they shouldn't. They may think it's anonymous, but it ain't for long. It's not a new story. But remember, we were looking for a hit man operating in the U.S. That's all we knew. We weren't looking for a blackmail ring."

"Did you find him?" Bourne asked.

Billy shook his head. "No."

"What about the site itself? What can you tell me about it?"

"Not as much as I'd like," Billy said. "As far as we can tell, the app appears to be based out of a town called Narva in Estonia. It's on the Russian border, so there's heavy Russian influence throughout the town. That ties our hands. Like you said, the girls on the site seem to be primarily Russian, too."

"Did you try getting any HUMINT off the site?"

"Yeah, we created fake accounts and dangled some bait. They smoked us every time. One of my boys thought he was getting close. He was playing hot and heavy with a girl on the site and complaining about troubles with his boss, like he'd love to see his boss have an accident or something. The girl said she knew someone who might be able to help him with his problem. Gave him a phone number and a contact code."

Bourne rolled his eyes. "And?"

"And the number belonged to a burner phone used by the labor secretary."

"Cute."

"Yeah. Real cute. Apparently, the secretary was a fan of the girls on the site. He wasn't too happy when we ran a sting and surrounded him with half a dozen agents in a DC parking lot because we thought he was a hit man. Even worse, someone tipped off the press, so video of the whole thing ran on Politico. The secretary's divorced now."

"Maybe he can find a nice Russian girl," Bourne said.

"Ha."

"What about the website server in Estonia? Did you put anyone on the ground in Narva?"

"Sure we did. After they fucked with us, we wanted to fuck them right back. So we sent in a Latvian agent who passes info to us from time to time. Two weeks later, a ten-year-old Estonian girl found his body washed up on the beach of Lake Peipus. These guys do not mess around."

"So who are they?" Bourne asked.

"Russians, but we don't believe there's any official connection to Moscow or Putin. The only name we've got is somebody called Cody. Nothing more than that, no photos, no real identity. We don't know much about his background, but we think he's an ex-Wagner guy who was tight with Prigozhin. Needless to say, we assume he's been laying low and finding other sources of income ever since his boss went down in that plane."

"Income like hookers and hit men," Bourne said.

"Yeah. Plus God knows what else."

"So could Cody be behind the Files?"

Billy looked dubious. "Maybe, but a site like mygirlnextdoor is a pretty narrow niche. The Files seem to be casting a much wider net. I think it's more likely that whoever is running the Files has been able to tap into the website's info, and somehow it's being combined with dirt from a lot of other sources."

"Still, the website seems like the place to start," Bourne said. "That means a trip to Estonia."

"Well, if you go, steer clear of Cody. Our friend in Latvia died very unpleasantly before they threw him in the lake. I'd rather you not go the same way. Not that I give a shit about Treadstone, but you always seem to get first-base seats for the Nationals."

Bourne smiled. "What about the Commanders?"

"Nobody gives a shit about the Commanders," Billy replied. "Are we done here, Cain?"

"One more thing. Wilson Scott mentioned a relationship with a particular girl on the site. She was the one who made the connection to the hit man. According to him, the name she used in the chat room was Irina. Did you look into her? She may be a pawn, but she must know something. She's the one I'd really like to find."

Billy gave a sour laugh. "Good luck with that."

"What do you mean?"

"I mean, yeah, we found Irina. She's still on the site. Still posting pics. And I can see why Scott was obsessed with her. That body, shit, it would make just about any guy weak in the knees."

"So what's the problem?"

"The problem is she doesn't exist," Billy told him. "That's why we didn't get anywhere with her."

Bourne's brow furrowed in confusion. "What are you talking about?"

"She's an AI model. The pics, the videos, they're all computer-generated. There's no such girl as Irina."

8

THE BORDER BETWEEN ESTONIA AND RUSSIA WAS CLOSED, THE GATES chained and locked, the river bridge empty of traffic. No one came or went through the checkpoint where thousands usually crossed every day. Putin had flooded the neighboring country with too many migrants, and the Estonians had finally had enough.

Bourne sat in a park near the border's barbed-wire fence and stared across the water at a stone fortress located in the Russian town of Ivangorod. When he put a pair of binoculars to his eyes, he focused on a Russian soldier marching by the river's edge with a Kalashnikov slung around his shoulder. The soldier, feeling watched, spotted Bourne and lifted the barrel of the rifle in his direction. Bourne didn't think the man would risk an international incident by shooting across the river, but with Russians, you could never really be sure. He put down the binoculars and wandered away from the deserted bridge.

Despite the closed border between them, Russia cast a long, dark shadow over every aspect of the Estonian town. Everything about Narva had a Russian flavor. A third of the people had Russian passports. Nearly everyone spoke Russian. Many of the city's buildings still looked like stone giants from the Soviet era. Even the old yellow paint on the walls had a drab Soviet feel. It may as well have been 1980, with the Cold War still hot.

There were also Russian spies everywhere.

Bourne stopped along the water and held up his phone, reversing his camera as if to take a selfie. He spotted the young man with the short, greasy brown hair and the heavy green combat jacket about fifty yards behind him. The man had picked him up at the hotel when he arrived by rented car from Tallinn earlier in the day. Bourne wasn't sure if the man actually knew who he was, or whether the spies in town had standing orders to observe any American who came to Narva. The man made no effort to hide his surveillance, staring openly at Bourne and smoking a cigarette by the river. He may as well have been holding a sign that said: *We know you're here.*

Was he one of Putin's men?

Or was he connected to the Russian called Cody?

Regardless, he was an obstacle.

Bourne headed away from the river toward the heart of the town. A light snow fell, dusting the overgrown green grass with white. He neared the ruins of a building that had once been a hotel, its rows of square windows now open to the elements, its crumbling stonework covered over with graffiti. When he reached the far corner of the building, he turned right, temporarily out of view of the man following him. He approached one of the boarded-up doors and shoved it open with a sharp slam of his shoulder. The interior had a musty smell of dampness and mold. He hid in the shadows on the other side of the door and waited for the man to come inside.

A smart spy would stay outside and wait. Bourne didn't think this man was smart.

A few seconds later, he heard footsteps, and he caught cigarette smoke in the cold breeze. The cracked-open door groaned on its hinges. The young man took a step into the hotel's gloomy shadows, and Bourne whipped his Glock through the air into the back of his skull. The spy collapsed into Bourne's arms, and Jason lay him on the wet floor and returned to the streets of Narva. He walked four more blocks, confirming that the man had been working alone, and then he hailed a cab.

The cab dropped him near a McDonald's in the Westernized section of Narva, close to a large, modern shopping mall called the Astri Center. Walking inside was like entering one of a thousand covered U.S. suburban malls back in the 1990s. People crowded down corridors on multiple levels, bags in hand, as they did their Christmas shopping. Bourne knew where he was going. He took the escalators to the mall's top floor, which was dominated by a gray planetarium dome that showed the surface of the moon.

He took his burner phone and opened the most recent photo he'd downloaded from mygirlnextdoor. It had been posted only two days ago. The photo showed a girl with long chestnut hair and a sweetly innocent face that belied the other pictures he'd found of her online, which were mostly nudes. She wore a tight-fitting white dress with tiny red polka dots, barely held up by thin spaghetti straps on her tanned bare shoulders. The dress hugged her curves almost like a bodysuit and sank low enough on her chest to tease the pink areolas on her large breasts.

This was Irina.

According to Billy Fox, Irina didn't really exist. She was an AI

creation. But in her latest picture, this imaginary girl was standing right here in the Astri Center, with the craters of the moon on the planetarium framed behind her. Bourne could also see the cropped fringe of an electronics store in the photo's background, and he saw a clerk standing at the store window, ogling the girl in the dress.

The clerk was real. In fact, the same clerk stood twenty yards away from Bourne in the electronics store, ringing up a customer.

Bourne went inside. He browsed the shelves of phones and fitness trackers while studying the clerk, who was probably still a teenager. He had jet-black hair, a pale pimply face, and a bright smile. He didn't look like a spy, and he didn't look like he'd been anything other than an accidental bystander in the photo of Irina. If he'd been eyeing a pretty girl, it also meant that there really had been a girl in the picture.

When the customer was gone, Bourne went up to the counter. "*Da zdravstvuyet tovarishch Putin,*" he said in Russian.

Long live Comrade Putin.

The young clerk's eyes narrowed as he decided how to respond. Even if you despised Putin, you had to be cautious about saying so in Narva. But Bourne could tell from his strained expression that the kid was no friend of the Russians.

"*V Sibiri,*" Bourne added with a wink.

In Siberia.

This won a broad smile, and the clerk nodded vigorously.

"I need your help," Bourne went on, sticking with Russian.

"If I can. What do you need?"

Jason removed the burner phone from his pocket and called up the photo of Irina outside the planetarium. He tapped the screen, pointing at the image of the clerk in the background of the picture.

"This was a couple of days ago. You were here, you saw the photo shoot. You remember it?"

The clerk's smile vanished. "Who are you?"

"I'm not the police, and I'm not with the intelligence services, either Estonian or Russian. But I want to know more about this girl."

"She's one of Cody's girls," the clerk replied. "I don't want trouble with Cody."

"I don't know your name, and I don't know who you are. We never talked."

"Yeah, but if you found me, so can he. Particularly if anyone starts messing with Irina."

"I'm not going to mess with her. I just want to talk to her."

The clerk shrugged. "I can't help you. I don't know where she is or who she is. Her real name isn't Irina. And she doesn't—"

He stopped talking and bit his lip.

"Doesn't what?" Bourne asked.

The kid shook his head. "I've said too much. You need to go."

Bourne slipped a hand in his pocket and then put a two-hundred-euro note on the counter. "Doesn't what?" he asked again.

The clerk looked around the store to confirm they were alone, and then he palmed the bill. "She doesn't look like that," he said.

"What do you mean?"

"That's not her face. That's not her body. I mean, don't get me wrong, she's a beauty, and I don't know why anybody bothers making her look different online. I've been there when she does nude photo shoots, and she's plenty hot. But when the pics come out, they make her breasts bigger, her hips wider, no blemishes on the skin, whatever. Plus, they give her a younger face, make her look like she's sixteen or something. I guess that appeals to the online perverts."

"What does she really look like?" Bourne asked.

"The real Irina—whoever she is—is older. Probably thirty or close to it. Really pretty, though. I'd take her over the fake-ass girl they create for the website. Her hair is dyed sort of lilac purple. She's skinny, bony, small breasts, but in great shape. She wears black glasses, too, makes her look like a professor or something. She takes them off when the camera's shooting, but she's blind without them."

Bourne listened to the description, and something pinged in his memory, as if he'd met a girl like that before. But he couldn't place her. Then he tapped the photo again. "This other woman, the real one, she was here in the mall this week?"

The clerk nodded.

"And she's one of Cody's girls?"

"Yeah, but you didn't hear that from me."

"How do I find her?"

"I told you, man, I don't know."

Bourne placed another euro note on the counter, but when the kid reached for it, Jason held it in place with his fingers. "You said you've seen Irina shooting naked. I don't imagine they allow spectators around the girls, not unless you've got a connection with the model or the photographer. So if you don't know her, I bet you know him."

The kid sighed. "You didn't get his name from me. Okay? If he knew I ratted him out, he'd beat the shit out of me."

"I told you. We never talked."

"Yeah, all right," the clerk said, and Bourne let him grab the euro note and stuff it in his pocket. "His name's Kepler. He's my cousin. He finds most of the girls for Cody. He lets me help out at the nude shoots sometimes. Believe me, I'd be with him right now if

I didn't have to work. He's got a new girl, a gorgeous redhead named Ariel. You'll find them both in his studio. He shoots out of an old garage near the railroad tracks on Puuvilla. But if you go, you better be careful."

"Why is that?" Bourne asked.

"Sometimes Cody shows up to bang the girls himself."

BOURNE FOUND THE GARAGE ON THE SOUTH END OF NARVA. RAILROAD tracks ran beside it, but the tracks were overgrown with weeds and hadn't been used in years. It was almost night, and waves of heavy snow fell from the slate-gray sky. The shells of abandoned cars, mostly Russian models, filled the gravel parking lot, but he saw one gleaming black Porsche near the building's stone wall. He also spotted the red light of a security camera mounted near the roof.

It made him wonder if Cody was watching.

The rusted door to the garage was half-open. Inside, the lights were off. He shined his phone onto a concrete floor littered with tools and empty oilcans. The air was cold; there was no heat in the building. Bourne stopped to listen, and he heard a low murmur of voices somewhere in the darkness ahead of him.

He kept walking. The building was long and narrow, and although there were a few wrecked cars inside, it wasn't a functioning garage anymore. He reached a wall with open double doors in the middle, and he went through to the other side. Ahead of him, a glow of lights illuminated a huge white sheet hung from the ceiling. The voices got louder, one male, one female. He also heard a whirring noise, the quick metallic click of a camera shutter firing.

Bourne slipped his Glock into his hand. If Cody was here, he wanted to be ready. But when he came around the corner of the white sheet, he saw only two people caught in the klieg lights of a photo shoot. One was the photographer, who wore a leather jacket and jeans. He was pale and bald, in his thirties, barking instructions at his model as he bent over a Hasselblad camera mounted on a tripod. The other was a girl with orange-auburn hair who was every bit as attractive as the mall clerk had said. She stood in front of the garage's crumbling stone wall, caught by light from two sides. Her chin was tilted upward, her green eyes focused on the ceiling. She wore a white-and-silver fur coat, open wide enough to reveal one pink-tipped breast and the long bare expanse of her right leg.

The girl noticed Bourne first. And the gun. But she showed no fear. She broke pose, letting the fur coat hang fully open against her body, and reached for a bottle of vodka on a stool and took a swig. The photographer straightened up with an irritated curse, but then he sensed motion behind him and turned around and saw Bourne. Unlike the girl, he reacted to the gun with a nervous shudder.

"Who are you?" the photographer demanded, covering his fear with false bravado. "What are you doing here? What do you want? I'm busy!"

"You're Kepler?" Bourne asked.

"Yeah, that's me. I said, what do you want?"

Bourne holstered his Glock. "I'm looking for one of your models."

"Why? Are you from the website? Shit, are you one of the fools who thinks the girls are really in love with you? My advice is, get the hell out of Narva. Men have shown up here before, and bad things happen to them, okay?"

"This girl is called Irina," Bourne went on, ignoring him. He added, "I don't mean the AI version who shows up online. I'm look-ing for the real girl who poses for you."

Kepler's sallow skin got even paler. "What do you want with Irina? Fuck, it doesn't matter. I can't help you, man. Go away."

Bourne said nothing, but his dark eyes drilled into Kepler's face, making the photographer wilt.

"Look, I already told Cody, and now I'm telling you. I don't know where Irina went! For all I know, she skipped town. She's not in her apartment. She's not answering her phone. If I knew where she was, don't you think I would have told him? Jesus!"

"What does Cody want with Irina?"

"How should I know? You think he tells me? If Cody didn't send you, then you need to get out of here before he shows up and kills us both."

"Do you know any of Irina's friends? Does she have family in town? Somewhere she might go?"

"I don't know anything about her. Cody sent her to me last year, okay? She needed money, she had no problem with nude pics. That's all I needed to hear. She said she was from St. Petersburg, but she didn't tell me anything else. She takes off her clothes, I take her pic-ture, end of story. Cody and his men do the rest. She and I aren't friends, and we're not lovers. One time I hit on her, and she slapped me so hard I almost puked."

"What's her real name?" Bourne asked.

"Are you not listening? I don't know! Trust me, you're wasting your time. Cody has a dragnet for her all over town. If she's within fifty miles, he'll find her, and she'll end up at the bottom of the lake."

"Then help me find her first," Bourne said. "You saw her a couple of days ago. What happened? She must have said something to you."

"She said nothing," Kepler snapped.

Which was a lie. It was all over his face.

Bourne reached for his Glock again to encourage Kepler to talk, but as he did, he glanced over the photographer's shoulder at the redheaded model. She caught his eye, put a finger to her lips, and inclined her head toward the far end of the garage.

Bourne hesitated, then left his gun in the holster.

"If you tell Cody I was asking about Irina, I'll come back here for another visit," he told Kepler. "You really do *not* want me to come back. Understand?"

"Yeah, I get it, I get it. Fuck!"

Bourne turned away from the photographer, then headed around the high white sheet into the cold darkness of the garage building. He walked all the way to the entrance, where the outside light was mostly gone, and he waited.

Five minutes passed. Then ten.

Finally, he heard the click of high heels.

The girl named Ariel appeared through a cloud of cigarette smoke. Her sunset-colored bangs hung down to her eyebrows, and her hair seemed to glow despite the low light. She made no effort to close the fur coat over her body, and snow blew through the doorway, melting on her bare skin from the full swell of her breasts to the V between her legs. Her green eyes narrowed as she stared at him.

"You're looking for Irina?" she asked. Her voice was Irish, not Estonian.

"Yes."

"And Cody didn't send you?" Her lips bent into a smirk. "No, he didn't, I can see that. His men are all stupid gorillas. Not like you.

Well, if you want to find Irina, you better move fast. Kepler wasn't fucking with you. If Cody gets to her first, Irina is dead."

"Why?"

The girl said nothing for a while. She sucked on her cigarette, and the smoke enveloped Bourne. "If I tell you where she is, will you help her? She needs to get out of Narva. She needs to get far away from here. When you go, you take her with you, okay? Otherwise, you get nothing from me."

Bourne didn't make promises lightly, because when he did, he kept them. That was the opposite of all his Treadstone training, which had taught him how to lie to get what he wanted. He studied the beautiful girl in front of him, assessing whether this was part of a trap. But he didn't think so.

"Okay," Jason agreed. "Irina comes with me."

"Good."

"Where is she?"

"She's staying in an apartment above an Irish pub on Paul Kerese Street," the girl said. "She's safe for now, but not for long. Cody has spies everywhere."

"Do you know her real name?" Bourne asked.

"No, I don't. She never tells anyone. To me and the other models, she's just Irina."

"Why does Cody want her? What happened?"

Ariel glanced back into the garage to confirm that Kepler hadn't followed her. "He thinks she sold him out. He thinks she leaked the identity of one of his assets in the U.S. A hired killer. Now he wants to know who she told."

9

BRIGHT LIGHTS SHINED IN THE WINDOWS IN THE FOUR-STORY APARTMENT
building on Paul Kerese Street. Bourne waited in the trees at the
center of a traffic circle across from the ground-floor Irish pub. Snow
whipped in mini-tornadoes down the wide street, gathering in drifts
against the building wall. Only a handful of cars cut trenches through
the slippery street, and no footsteps disturbed the virgin snow on
the sidewalk in front of the restaurant. He could hear a faint din of
music from inside.

He checked his watch. He'd waited in the darkness, invisible, for
half an hour. No one else was watching the street. With his hands in
the pockets of his leather jacket, fingers curled around his Glock, he
headed for the bar. His boots kicked through a couple of inches of
snow. When he opened the door, warmth spilled from inside, along
with the singsong twang of violins playing an Irish jig.

The pub was wide but not deep. He faced the bar, which glowed
with neon, and every stool was taken. A few wooden tables stretched
along the windows on his left and right. A wooden stage had been

built against the east wall, and a small band played there, led by a redheaded singer who bore a resemblance to the model Ariel. The similarity was striking enough that Bourne wondered if they were sisters and whether Irina was hiding out in their apartment above the bar.

He approached the counter and flagged down the bartender, who was a thin, dour man in his forties, wearing a black Guinness T-shirt. The man sized him up as a foreigner and spoke in English.

"Want something?"

Bourne pointed at the man's shirt. "Guinness."

The bartender wiped his hands on a towel at his waist and slowly pulled a dark, chocolaty pint from the tap until foam overran the glass. Bourne took a sip, then put enough money on the counter to triple the price of the ale. He leaned closer to the man, speaking just loud enough to be heard over the music, and he took a chance that he was right about the redheaded sisters.

"Ariel sent me. I'm here to help Irina."

The bartender studied Bourne with hooded, suspicious eyes. "I don't know who you mean."

"I think you do, and I think you know I'm not from Cody. Irina needs to get out of town. I can do that."

Not blinking, the man drummed his fingers on the bar. His lips puckered into a frown, and he gestured at the singer on the small stage. "Talk to Sara. They've got a break coming up after this song."

Bourne added another bill to the counter. Then he took his Guinness and found an empty window table close to the stage. He watched a meaningful look pass between the girl at the microphone and the man behind the bar, and the girl focused on Bourne and sized him up with her blue eyes as she sang. She was a few years older than her sister—if Ariel was her sister—but just as pretty, with fiery red hair to the middle of her back, a deeply freckled face, and a glow of sweat on her white skin. She wore a low-cut flowered blouse and a tattered jean skirt with multiple pockets. Her voice rose, warbling the high note at the end of the song, and a ripple of applause made its way through the bar. As it died down, the girl hopped off the stage and took a seat at the table, opposite Bourne. Without a word, she reached for his glass and drank a long slug of Guinness. A little bit of foam clung to her lip and she licked it off.

"Who the fuck are you?" she inquired in a thick Irish accent that matched her sister's.

"Ariel told me about this place."

"Oh, Ariel did, did she?" One of the girl's hands disappeared under the table, and Bourne stiffened as the blade of a knife pressed against his femoral artery inches from his groin. He was impressed at her quickness.

"I'm not lying," he told her. "Ariel asked me to get Irina out of the city."

"And you thought you'd just come in here where everyone could see you? Did you not think Cody would have a spy in here who would spot a stranger? Particularly someone who fucking screams American?"

"Then let's not waste time," Bourne said. "Take me to Irina."

The knife disappeared from his thigh.

"Give me two hundred euro," the girl said. "Make it obvious. Everyone's watching us."

"What's the money for?"

"First, because I want it. And second, because you don't think my voice pays the rent, do you? My sister earns her money taking off her clothes for pigs like Kepler and his camera. Me, I earn it on my knees. Or at least that's what the men around here think. They don't need to know I'm Interpol, *Cain.*"

Bourne wasn't often surprised in his life, but his jaw dropped. "Well, damn."

He took two hundred-euro bills from his wallet and slapped them on the table. The girl grinned at his startled expression and shoved the money into her low-cut blouse between her breasts. "I'm Sara, by the way," she said. "Now come on, I figure we've got ten minutes before Cody's men storm this place."

Sara took him by the hand. He felt the rest of the men in the bar watching them, and Sara gave them a wink. She led him to a rear door beside the counter, and the two of them went through to the other side. They were inside the apartment building here, with a corridor running the length of the building and stairs leading to the upper floors.

The Interpol agent led him up the stairs.

"We've been trying to penetrate Cody's operation in Narva for almost a year," she told him as they climbed. "Every time we get close or find someone who will talk to us, the witness disappears. You know about the Latvian agent who wound up in the lake?"

"I do."

"Well, he's not the only one. We lost one of our agents, too. That's why my sister and I have been undercover here since the summer. Cody has a stranglehold on Narva, and the crime ring he's operating ripples through Eastern Europe. He's into everything. Drugs. Prostitution. Smuggling. Murder."

"You know about the website?" Bourne asked.

"Mygirlnextdoor? Sure. But that's just one piece in the puzzle. Cody's ambitions go way beyond that."

"What about Irina? How does she fit in?"

"As far as we can tell, she's just a pawn for the app. She seduces customers, gets information out of them, and then Cody figures out how to make it work for him."

"So is that what the Files are all about?"

Sara shook her head. "Don't think so, no. The Files are bigger than this one app. But there's a connection somewhere. Cody thinks Irina sold out one of his hit men in the U.S., but Irina swears she didn't. So maybe someone is watching the watchers. Whoever has the Files may be spying on Cody and his girls."

"Can we trust Irina?"

"Judge for yourself," Sara said.

They reached the top level of the building, and the Interpol agent rapped her knuckles on the first door on the left side of the hallway. Then she added a code phrase in Russian to assure the person inside that everything was clear. A few seconds later, the door opened. A woman in her early thirties, with a rough bob of blond hair streaked in purple and thick black glasses that slipped down her nose, stood in the doorway. She was tall and skinny to the point of malnourishment, wearing tight blue jeans and an untucked red flannel shirt with the sleeves rolled to her elbows. A gold pendant dangled from her neck, with a Russian cameo hanging from the chain. She had a very pretty face, but with the solemn, distracted expression of a woman who didn't pay much notice to her own looks.

She stared at Sara. Then her gaze went over Sara's shoulder, and she spotted Bourne.

Seeing him, her eyes suddenly widened with surprise and joy. Her serious mouth broke into a huge, excited smile. In a voice loud enough to be heard down the hallway, she shouted in thick accented English, "Jason! Oh my God, Jason, it's you! You've come to save me!"

Her long arms reached out and grabbed him by the neck. She threw herself against him, and her full lips pressed into his mouth. The kiss went on long enough that Bourne found it hard to breathe, and when he finally peeled away the woman's arms, he looked into her gray eyes again and finally remembered who she was.

"*Tati.*"

THREE YEARS EARLIER, BOURNE HAD FOUND A RUSSIAN CLIMATE SCIENtist named Tatiana Reznikova in the little town of Whitby in northeast England. She was escaping with her husband—who turned out to be an environmental terrorist—from a gang of Russian assassins. Bourne had saved her life, but when he'd given her the opportunity to take American asylum, Tati had chosen instead to go back home to her scientific work at a university in St. Petersburg. The last time he'd seen her had been on a California beach as she took a Zodiac out to a Russian submarine off shore.

Tati was Irina, and Irina was Tati.

"I take it you two know each other," the Interpol agent said sarcastically.

Tati continued to kiss Jason all over his face, leaving lipstick smears on his cheeks and forehead. "Oh my God, I love this man, he save me, he give me my life back! Jason, I can't believe you are here! How did you know I needed you?"

"I had no idea you were here," Bourne admitted. "I'm as surprised as you are."

She pawed him as if she had to convince herself he was real. "I think about you every day, I pray you come! I want to reach out to you, but I do not know how to find you!"

"Well, I'm here," Bourne said, trying and failing to keep Tati's roaming hands off his body.

"This is real sweet and everything," Sara interrupted, "but we need to get the fuck out of here right now. Irina—Tati—whoever the hell you are—grab your go bag and let's move before Cody's men get here."

Tati's pretty faced paled at Cody's name. "Yes! Yes, right away!"

She disappeared inside the apartment and returned seconds later wearing a worn, unzipped down jacket, with a small canvas backpack slung over her shoulder. Sara unholstered a Ruger from her inner thigh, and Bourne drew his Glock. Tati clung to his left hand, and the three of them took the stairs down to the ground floor of the apartment building.

"Not through the pub," Sara said. "We'll use the side exit. I've got a car across the street."

She led them down the hallway, her Ruger cocked at her waist. At the end of the building, a door opened onto the tree-lined street, and they pushed outside into the cold. Snow poured over them, hitting their faces like the prick of needles. The whistling wind drowned out other sounds. Bourne saw no vehicles, and the tire ruts on the street had softened as more snow began to cover them up.

Sara gestured toward a grassy park near a gas station. It looked like a white meadow. "My car's there."

The three of them single-file tramped through the drifts. Tati stayed in the middle, and Bourne brought up the rear, circling every few steps to check behind them. In the trees lining the sidewalk, a few Christmas lights blinked in dots of red and green. The sheeting snow began to gather on their clothes, and Bourne had to keep wiping his eyes to see. He squinted at the roads leading in and out of the traffic circle, but they were empty. No one lurked in the doorways of the buildings around them.

Still, he didn't like it.

The most dangerous threat is the one you can't see.

Treadstone.

They were in the middle of the street when a voice shrieked above the wind. *"Sara!"*

Bourne and Sara both swung their pistols toward a tan brick building bordering the roundabout. A woman bolted around the corner, screaming and waving her arms at them. Her red hair glistened through the downpour of snow, and she was underdressed for the cold in a tank top and shorts. Frozen blood made streaks down her arms and legs.

It was Ariel, the model from the auto garage.

"Sara! Run!"

Sara froze as she recognized her sister making a desperate attempt to warn them away. In the next instant, automatic-weapons fire erupted behind Ariel from the same corner. The bullets riddled her and made her body twitch like a puppet on strings. She staggered, then collapsed, red hair and red blood shining in the midst of six inches of snow.

The bullets kept coming.

Bourne threw himself against Tati and Sara, spreading his arms and taking both women down into the cold drifts covering the street. Two men stood near the building, aiming machine pistols their way and filling the winter air with a burnt smell. With his Glock, Bourne fired back, and Sara did, too, her shots accompanied by a guttural, angry wail for her dead sister on the ground. But they were outgunned. The men began to advance, rounds zeroing in on their position and blowing up silver spray with each ricochet. One bullet ripped through the shoulder of Tati's coat in a mixture of down, snow, and blood. Tati screamed.

They were sitting ducks on the street. In a few seconds, they'd all be dead.

Sara reached into one of her skirt pockets and pushed a cold piece of metal into Bourne's hand. Car keys.

"It's the Citroën in the last space. Get Irina out of here. I'll cover you."

"Sara, *don't*—"

He knew what she was going to do. He reached out to grab her, but the Interpol agent was already on her feet, running an awkward zigzag pattern through the snow directly at the two men. Her shots momentarily forced them back. Jason grabbed Tati off the ground and dragged her toward the park on the opposite side of the street. Sara's revenge fire bought them time to reach the sidewalk and jump over the low railing. Ahead of them was a lineup of snow-covered cars.

On the street, he heard a cry of pain.

He glanced sideways and saw Sara frozen in place over Ariel's body, not even twenty feet from Cody's men. The shooters fired nonstop, eviscerating her with deadly aim from their machine pistols, but somehow she stayed standing and kept firing her Ruger. She was close enough to take one of the men down with a bullet in the middle of his face, but the man's partner kept firing. Sara was done, her whole body a mass of blood. The gun slipped from her hand, and her knees bent, and she crumpled to the snow on top of her sister.

Bourne and Tati kept running. The other shooter retrained his gun, and bullets chased them across the snow, getting closer with each round. In another second, they cleared the side of the building, and the wall temporarily blocked them from the machine-pistol fire as they charged down the alley beside parked cars. The shooter followed, and the gunfire began again when they were near the end of the alley. Bourne threw Tati sideways between two vehicles, and they crouched as they hurried to the Citroën a few yards away.

The lock was frozen. The key wouldn't go in. Bourne had no time to waste. He simply lifted his Glock and shot out the driver's-side window and opened the door from inside. He lofted Tati across the seat to the passenger's side and got behind the wheel. When he turned the key, the engine chugged without catching. He tried again, and again, listening to the starter whine, and finally the motor rattled to life.

"Stay down!" he barked at Tati.

Bourne shoved the Citroën into gear and stamped on the accelerator. The car fishtailed in the snow as he swung into the alley and then shot forward, kicking up waves of snow as he headed for the street. With slick ice under the snow, he had almost no control, and the car swerved, bouncing between the parked cars and the curb beside the building.

The shooter was directly in front of him, his weapon aimed at the car. Bourne ducked down just as the entire windshield exploded and showered them with glass. His foot stayed on the gas, his hand on the wheel. An instant later, he felt a heavy thud as the front bumper hit the man and somersaulted him over the roof of the Citroën. The gunfire stopped. The car crashed through the metal barrier near the sidewalk and spun in circles into the middle of the lanes of the E20.

Bourne threw open the driver's door. He ran to the bodies of the two Interpol agents, who lay prone in the street. When he checked their pulses, he felt nothing.

Sara and Ariel were both dead.

Slowly now, his steps heavy, he returned to the Citroën. The snow kept falling, and the wind roared, blowing away the acrid stench of the gun battle. He got inside the frigid car, and Tati stared at him, her gray eyes wide and sad, but neither one of them said a word. He pushed the accelerator, listening to the tires grind for traction on the slippery pavement. Finally, the car lurched forward, and he sped down the highway that led out of town.

10

BOURNE STAYED ON THE FLAT, EMPTY E20 HIGHWAY THROUGH THE DARK-
ness and snow. Dormant farm fields lined the two-lane road. He
hoped to make it all the way to Tallinn, but half an hour outside
Narva, Tati moaned as the numbness of the cold gave way to pain.
Her shoulder began bleeding profusely. He checked the side
mirrors—the front mirror had been shot away—and saw that they
still had the road to themselves. No one was pursuing them. Not yet.
Hopefully, the snow had erased their tracks and Cody and his men
didn't know which direction they had gone.

Two miles later, he spotted a lonely farmhouse tucked into a
band of trees, and he turned off the highway. As they neared the
house, he saw that it was in disrepair, the wooden siding peeling
away and many of the windows broken. He parked the Citroën out
of view of the road, and he helped Tati out of the car. The door to
the house was boarded over, but he kicked it open easily. He led
them inside and found that the owners had left most of the furniture
behind when they abandoned the house. Other residents had moved

in. Spiderwebs dangled from the ceiling, and droppings littered the floor. A large rat scampered through the glow of his flashlight. He draped Tati across an old blue sofa, and then he checked the go bag that Sara had prepared for her escape.

Sara had done well. He found a Mylar thermal blanket and spread the silver foil over Tati to keep her warm. Using the medical supplies in the bag, Bourne sterilized and bandaged her wound. The bullet had grazed her shoulder but not penetrated muscle or bone. She'd be fine in a couple of days. When he was done, he gave her a small bottle of Powerade to drink, and she began to improve quickly, the color coming back to her face.

He checked his watch and wanted to get back on the road immediately, but Tati wasn't ready to go. She wrapped part of the thermal blanket around his shoulders as he sat on the floor next to the sofa.

"Let's stay here for a while, yes? I like the quiet."

"A few minutes," Bourne agreed. "Then we need to leave."

"Is there vodka in that bag? God, I could use a drink."

Jason checked and found a bottle of Estonian Viru Valge. Sara had thought of everything. He opened the bottle and gave it to Tati, who took a Russian-sized swallow from the neck. When she handed it back, Bourne shrugged and did the same.

"Better," she said.

Bourne smiled. It *was* better.

The blanket kept their body heat from escaping, but the house was still as cold as the outside air. Wind screeched through broken windows. After a while, Tati sat up and patted the sofa for Bourne to join her. He sat down next to her, and she clung to his body. She put her arms around him and leaned her head into his neck. The chain of the Russian cameo she wore was cold on his skin. They drank more vodka.

"How did you get here, Tati?" Bourne asked finally. "The last I knew, you were doing research at a climate university in St. Petersburg."

She shivered a little against him.

"The war," she said. "The war changed everything."

"But you were protected. You were close to Putin and the *siloviki*."

"Not close enough. I made a mistake by speaking out. I said what Putin was doing in Ukraine was wrong. Barbaric. One day at the university, I heard they were coming for me, to make an example for others to stay silent. My choice was to be tossed in prison or to run. So I ran. All I had was the clothes on my back. No money. No identity. I made my way to the border at Narva, but I had no way to cross. And yet I needed to get out of Russia. That was when I heard about Cody."

Bourne heard sourness and shame take over Tati's voice.

"Cody controls this region on both sides of the river," she went on. "He can make anything happen. I didn't tell him who I was, but that didn't matter. He already knew. He could have destroyed me with a phone call. But he told me there was another way. I could earn my way across the border."

"The website," Bourne said.

Tati's head moved gently, and her cheek was soft against his neck. "Yes. He said I was perfect. I spoke English. I'm pretty. Plus, I have no inhibitions. I don't care if people see my body. Sex means nothing to me. You remember my husband, Vadik? I learned not to care about sex because of him. All men are like Vadik. Well, maybe except for you."

Bourne said nothing. After he'd rescued her in Whitby, he remembered her coming to his bed at a safe house in London. She'd offered to sleep with him, not because she was in love with him, not because she had any desires herself, but because she wanted to thank him for saving her life. To Tati, sex was simply a way to give men what they wanted, and she was surprised when he turned her down.

"What happened?" he asked her.

"Cody got me over the river to Narva. He set me up in an apartment in town. But I still had no money. No identification. He said if he was happy with my work, then the day would come when he would set me free. At first I believed him, but the more I talked to other girls, the more I realized we were really slaves."

"How long have you been here?"

"A year and a half."

"What did he have you do?"

Tati took a while to reply. "Kepler took pictures. Every day a different outfit. Beautiful, expensive clothes, swimsuits, lingerie. Something to tease the men, you know? Showing off my breasts, my legs, my ass, my smile. They made me an Instagram star. I have like a million followers. But that was just—what is it called?"

"Bait," Bourne said.

"Yes. Bait. Men who loved my free pics could sign up to see more at mygirlnextdoor. There, Cody posted the nude shots. Very explicit ones. Me touching myself. Me with toys. You know the kind. The price was very, very high. He wanted to screen out ordinary men. He only wanted those who had the money to pay for anything they wanted. Those were the men he wanted to influence."

"But the girl wasn't *you*. It wasn't your face."

Tati shook her head. "That was Cody protecting me. Or so he

said. He said Putin was still looking for me, and if he found me, he'd send men to kill me or drag me back to Russia. So I took the pictures and the videos, but then Cody had tech boys who used artificial intelligence to create a new, younger woman out of the images. Irina. She is me, but she is not me, you see? I move, I pose, but the computer modifies me and makes me into her."

"The men you met on the website," Bourne said. "Did you know who they were?"

"Some of them. There were powerful men. Wealthy men. Some of these men I had even met. I'd met their wives, too. That was strange. I wondered if they would recognize me, but of course, it wasn't really me they were seeing. It was Irina. But I enjoyed the power she had over them. I admit that."

He felt her head turn, and her lips kissed his neck. Her hands began to explore, reaching inside his clothes, caressing and squeezing between his legs. But there was a strangely robotic quality to her movements, as if she really were nothing but a computer simulation. He took her wrists firmly and moved them away from him.

"I don't understand you," Tati said, her brow furrowing. "Why don't you want me? In London, it was the same thing. I came to you, and you sent me away. Multiple times now, you save my life. I owe you. This is how I repay."

"You don't owe me anything," Bourne said.

Tati shrugged, still not understanding.

"But I do have more questions for you," he went on. "Among the men you met online was a U.S. congressman. Wilson Scott."

She looked puzzled. "I don't know him."

"He says he talked to you almost every day."

"Well, maybe, but I don't know this man."

"His wife was sick. He says you gave him contact information for an assassin based in the U.S. who would kill her."

Tati's eyes widened. "Oh, Phil! That must be Phil. He was nice. I felt bad for him, what was happening with his wife. But he was cautious, too. I never saw his face. I didn't know who he was. I'm not surprised he was powerful. He needed to have a lot of money to be with me. But I didn't know his real name."

"Cody never told you?" Bourne asked.

"As far as I know, Cody didn't know this, either."

"But Wilson Scott was being blackmailed over the hit man in the U.S."

"Not by me. I don't think by Cody, either. I never heard about that, anyway. The only thing I knew about was passing along contact information. That was the money Cody wanted to make. One hundred thousand dollars for a kill. I hoped Phil would do it. Better for him, better for his poor wife. But I never heard. After I told him about the hit man, he shut down his account. I never talked to him again."

"Who was the hit man?" Bourne asked.

"I have no idea," Tati replied. "I passed along contact details to Phil, but that was all anonymous. The person could be anyone."

"So what happened between you and Cody? Why is he looking for you?"

"Apparently he thinks I gave info about the hit man to someone. The killer contacted Cody, furious. He said somebody knew all about him. This person was threatening to turn him in to the FBI if he didn't do a job. He told Cody there was a leak in his organization, and Cody assumed it must be me. But it wasn't. I never told anybody. That doesn't matter, though. Cody sent men to get me, and I went to

Ariel for help. That was when I found out she and her sister were really part of Interpol. They've been trying to get me out."

Bourne put his head on the tattered back cushion of the sofa. Something scuttled on the floor near them, but he didn't bother using his flashlight to see what it was. He thought about what Tati had told him and concluded that Billy Fox had been right. Cody didn't have the Files. Someone else did. Whoever it was had hacked mygirlnextdoor and been able to find the real identity of Wilson Scott.

And the real identity of a hit man.

"We need to go," Bourne said. "The sooner we get to Tallinn and get you out of Estonia, the better."

"Yes, okay."

They got off the sofa and made their way through the wreckage of the house to the front door. Bourne listened, hearing only the wild screams of the wind. The snow continued to fall, slapping their faces. He led her to the Citroën and situated her inside, and then he went around to the driver's side and started the engine.

Before he could put the car in gear, bright lights dazzled him, forcing his eyes shut.

When he could see again, he made out the silhouettes of at least ten men surrounding the car, rifles pointed at them. There was nowhere to go and nothing to do. Then he heard a guttural voice booming through the storm.

"Please keep your hands on the wheel. Don't make my men cut you to ribbons . . . *Cain.*"

"YOU REALLY DON'T NEED TO COME WITH ME," ABBEY LAURENT TOLD HER husband. "I've met Jerry before. He's harmless."

Garrett shook his head. "A conspiracy nut? Somebody who wants to meet you in the middle of nowhere? No, Abbey. I want to be there."

He swung the wheel, guiding his Lexus convertible along the tight switchbacks of Decker Edison Road as it climbed into the Malibu hills. An emerald-green down coated the landscape, thanks to a rainy December. Creeks raced across the one-lane road, and the sedan's tires splashed through muddy water. Garrett had the top down, and the higher they climbed, the colder the air seemed, whipping Abbey's red hair into a bird's nest.

The ocean crept into view behind the hills like a blurred blue glow on the horizon.

"We should be close," she said.

Garrett slowed on the curves. "Abs, I don't know about this. You're writing a novel, aren't you? It's *fiction*. Isn't that where you make shit up?"

"Yes, but I want the books to feel real. Peter Chancellor's novels always felt real. That's because they were grounded in things that actually happened. My last book? The one about the media disinformation conspiracy? I had people in Washington calling me up to say the novel should be required reading. That it was so close to the truth about media manipulation, they were wondering about my sources."

"Washington," Garrett replied with a cynical smile. His long dark hair was tied up in a man bun, and sunglasses covered his eyes. His beard made a neat line around his jutting jaw. "They're the ultimate conspiracy nuts. I had to testify in front of a House committee, remember? Callie Faith kept trying to get me to expose all the data mining behind Jumpp. Like the Chinese were desperate to get contact info for millions of fourteen-year-olds dancing around to Taylor Swift songs. I told her I'd been through the code myself and didn't see anything. And she still didn't believe me."

"Except you're not so sure anymore, are you?" Abbey asked.

Garrett shrugged. "I said I spotted anomalies."

"Well, I see anomalies in the fire," Abbey retorted. "We're not being told the whole story about what happened. The feds are covering something up. I want to know what it is."

Her husband reached over and squeezed her thigh. "Just be careful, okay? The other day, you said someone was watching the house. I don't like that."

"It was probably nothing," she replied, trying to convince herself. "Some stoner looking for an easy target to break in and grab cash or jewelry. I scared him away. I haven't seen anybody around since then."

"Uh-huh."

Abbey didn't want to argue, mostly because that meant admitting Garrett was right. The incident in the night, with the stranger watching her on the balcony, had made her nervous. She'd had plenty of close encounters with danger in recent years, but Jason had always been with her to protect her. And now he wasn't.

She pointed at a bluff at the end of a grassy trail leading from the road. A tall young man stood near the end of a high promontory, buffeted by the ocean wind. "There. That's him. Pull over."

Garrett steered the Lexus onto a narrow shoulder off the road, behind a red Toyota Corolla that had seen better days. Jagged boulders made a kind of guardrail where the land sank sharply into the seam of the valley below them. They parked, and Abbey picked her way past the rocks to the trail that led through the tall grass. Garrett stayed at her side. Ahead of them, about fifty yards away, she saw Jerry, whom she'd only met once before, outside a post office in Maryland. He was in his twenties, Asian, with wavy dark hair and feminine features, pacing nervously with his hands shoved in the pockets of his jeans. A pair of high-powered binoculars swung on his chest.

"This is your source?" Garrett asked dubiously.

"You're a techie. You know what nerds are like."

"Fair point."

They closed on Jerry, who saw them coming and began rubbing his hands as if wiping away sweat. When they were within earshot, he pointed a finger at Garrett. "Who's he? I said I would only see you alone."

"He's my husband," Abbey replied.

"Garrett Parker," Garrett told him.

Jerry's knee twitched nervously. His eyes narrowed, and he made a careful analysis of Garrett as if he were running him through a scanner. "I know you. I know all the tech bros. You're a senior programmer with Jumpp, right?"

"I was. I'm a private consultant now."

"Jumpp is fucking spyware," Jerry snapped.

"Isn't everything these days?" Garrett asked, as if he'd heard that comment thousands of times before, which Abbey assumed he had. "Social media, search engines, AI, we're all dancing with the devil, spying on everybody else. That's how the game is played. Abbey says you're part of a hacker group. You try to get information that the government is hiding. Doesn't that mean you're a spy, too?"

"I do it to *expose* evil," Jerry replied.

"Maybe so. Maybe you're a good guy wearing a white hat. But I don't know you. So you want to talk to my wife, you put up with me being here. Got it?"

Jerry scowled at Abbey. "I drove across the country to see you, and you don't trust me?"

"You *drove?*" Abbey asked.

"You think I'd give my ID to the government by getting on a plane? If they knew I was on it, they'd fucking take the thing down. They can do that, you know. Crash it by remote control and make it look like an accident."

Garrett rubbed his beard to cover his mouth and murmured in her ear in a singsong voice, "Fruitcake."

Abbey put a hand on Jerry's shoulder. "Look. I trust you. You know I do. You gave me a tip that led to my first novel. It was legit. But that's why I need to be cautious and why Garrett worries about me. I'm the one in the public eye. My name's on the books. If they want to get to you, believe me, they want to get to me even more."

"Yeah. Yeah, I'm sure you're on the hit list, too. But you got guts. You keep doing what you do. We respect that. Plus, you listen." Jerry shot a resentful glance at Garrett. "A lot of people just think we're nuts."

"I know you're not," Abbey said. "That's why I reached out to you. I've heard rumors about the fire. The feds aren't telling us everything they know. I figured if anyone had heard what was really going on, it was you and your group."

Jerry glanced around at the nearby hills. He put the binoculars to his eyes to check out the nearest ridgeline and then let them dangle on the strap. "Oh yeah. The government is trying to bury this. No question."

"Bury what?"

"How the fire started," Jerry said.

"It was intentional?"

"Definitely."

Garrett shrugged. "Everybody knows it didn't start naturally. That was in the papers. The first responders on the scene said it appeared to be a reckless fire that got out of control. It was probably kids doing something stupid."

Abbey shot her husband a look to silence him. She was a journalist, and she knew how to interview sources. You didn't interrupt them or throw cold water on their stories. You let them talk to see where they would lead you.

"Go on, Jerry. Tell me. What have you heard?"

"This wasn't just a *reckless* fire," he retorted, eyeing Garrett again. "The fire investigators lied. They were *told* to lie. This was arson. Somebody wanted that fire to start, and they wanted it to be big."

"Why?"

"To cover up a crime. A murder."

Abbey blinked in disbelief. She remembered the lines she'd written, the draft of the prologue to her novel. Fiction made up from inside her head. *From a single spark, infernos came. One little flame would hatch the egg that became a dragon. And the body left behind in the house would simply be one more victim.*

"A body," she murmured. "He wanted to hide a body."

Jerry's face flushed with excitement. "Yes! You know about that, too?"

Abbey felt her head swim, lost in one of those moments when her imagination blurred with reality. Her novel, the stories she invented, had begun to bleed into things that were actually happening. "Keep going, Jerry. Please."

"There was a house being used as an Airbnb," Jerry went on. "The owners had rented the whole place out. They found a body inside."

"I remember. A woman. Her name was—it was Debbie, wasn't it? Debbie Robertson."

"Yeah, that was the name she used to rent the place," Jerry said. "Thing is, it turns out her ID was fake. Fake name, fake address, fake credit card. Nobody knows who the hell this woman really was or what she looked like or why she was there. But the feds are sure *she* was the real target."

"Why?" Abbey asked.

"Because that house is where the fire started."

11

THE WHITE PANEL VAN BUMPED OVER A RUTTED DIRT ROAD. HALF AN hour had passed. Bourne tried to keep track of the turns in his head, and he calculated that the vehicle had taken them somewhere into the rural lands southwest of Narva. He and Tati lay in the empty back, wrists and ankles tied, mouths gagged. With each lurch of the chassis, they rolled in the darkness, smashing against the walls and against each other.

Finally, he felt the van jerk to a stop. A few seconds later, the rear doors swung open, letting in a burst of cold and snow. Two flashlights lit up the interior. He blinked, then focused on half a dozen men with automatic rifles waiting for them on the snow-covered ground outside. They'd already searched Bourne and removed all of his weapons, but Cody was taking no chances.

One man yanked Tati out by her ankles and let her fall into the snow. Then he did the same with Bourne. He let them squirm in the cold for a while before he grabbed their feet and dragged them behind him across a dirt driveway that had recently been plowed.

Sharp rocks cut their arms, shoulders, and faces, and left both of them bloody. Bourne couldn't see where they were being taken, but soon after, their bodies thumped painfully over wooden steps and then over a threshold into a house. The hard, frigid ground turned to deep, soft carpet.

It was warm inside. The man left them face down, but Bourne was able to turn his head sideways and see that they were in the middle of a large ranch-style room with flagstone walls. Somewhere close by, wood popped and crackled in a fireplace, and the radiating heat felt good after so much time in the cold.

He heard heavy footsteps.

"The fuckers are bleeding on my carpet," a voice growled. "Untie them."

Someone kicked Bourne heavily in the kidney, causing a jolt of pain. A knife cut through the bonds on his wrists and ankles, and a large redheaded man yanked the tape off his face, then removed the dirty cotton towel that filled his mouth. He did the same for Tati, whose beautiful features were bruised and bloody. Bourne caught her eye and tried to give her a look of encouragement that he didn't feel.

He stretched his limbs, then sat up on the floor. Next to him, Tati did the same.

"Welcome to Estonia, Cain," a man said from a leather armchair near the fireplace. He had an open bottle of Stoli Elit in his huge left hand. His other hand held an MP-443 Grach pointed at the floor. "I'm Cody."

Cody wore green fatigues, with a belt around his waist that boasted a nine-inch knife. His black calf boots were unlaced. He was tall and large, at least six foot five and built with the bulging physique of a wrestler. He had dirty, curly dark hair, long enough to hang below his shoulders, and a thick, unkempt beard. His eyebrows slanted in a wicked arch, and his eyes were blue and bright. Despite the sunless winter, his skin bore a chocolate-brown tan.

Bourne sized up his chances of fighting back and concluded he had none. His limbs were stiff, and by the time he leaped at Cody, the man would have delivered several rounds from the Grach into his face and chest. Plus, there were still four men with AK-12s forming a circle around the two of them. Cody had won.

And yet Bourne and Tati weren't already dead. The man wanted something.

"I know a lot about you, Cain," Cody went on. His accent betrayed his Russian roots, but he spoke English flawlessly. "I know you're the man with no memory. What an interesting thing that must be, to have your past wiped out like a blank slate. I know all about Treadstone, including many of your missions for them—a big one in Tallinn, as I recall. But most of all, I know that you're the one who murdered Lennon last year. Putin's personal assassin. You realize what that means, don't you? With you in my possession, I have quite the currency in my hands. The Moth would give me just about anything to take hold of you. I could deliver you across the border and name my price. Or I could throw you in a cell and keep you alive as—what do you Americans call it? My get-out-of-jail-free card. I'm sure Prigozhin wished he'd had something like that."

Cody hoisted his muscled bulk out of the armchair. His footsteps thudded heavily on the carpet as he made his way to Tati. He traced the line of her jaw with his Grach, making her twitch and cry. Then he held out the bottle of Stoli.

"Want some, darling?"

"Cody, it wasn't me," she pleaded. "I didn't do it. I told no one!"

The man shrugged. "Open your mouth and drink. Open!"

Tati's mouth fell open, and he tilted up her chin and shoved the bottle between her lips. He poured vodka down her throat until she gagged and choked, spitting it down her chin. Then he took a giant drink himself. When he was done, he suddenly twisted around and threw the bottle into the fireplace, where the glass shattered against stone and sprayed glistening fragments onto the gray carpet.

He placed the barrel of the Grach between her eyes.

"Shall I make it quick, my love?"

"Oh, Cody, God, please, don't, don't. I did nothing!"

He racked the slide on the pistol. "Trust me, pretty one, you won't feel a thing."

"*Cody!*" Bourne hissed at him from six feet away as Tati whimpered. "Enough. What do you want?"

The big man smiled. "What makes you think I want anything other than to see this little bitch die and send you on a train to Lefortovo?"

"Because you're a smart man, and smart men don't waste their time on petty revenge. Only fools do that. Plus, I think you know that Tati isn't the one who betrayed you. She's telling you the truth."

Cody yanked away the gun. He sat back down in the leather armchair and snapped his fingers, and a new bottle of vodka appeared from one of his men. He satisfied himself with another drink, then wiped his wet beard. His eyes glittered, and his white teeth shined in his smile.

"You're right, Cain. I do know that. But only because I've been listening to Tati and tracking her for days. That pretty little cameo I gave you, my love? It told me everything. It was very sweet of you to wear it just like I said."

Tati's eyes turned angry. "Then why hunt me down if you know I didn't do anything? Why make me think you wanted me dead?"

"Because I wanted to see what would happen next," Cody snapped. "I wanted to know who you would talk to and what you would tell them. And don't play innocent with me. You were ready to sell me out to Interpol to get out of Narva. But Cain is right. I know the leak didn't come from you. I was actually planning to come see you myself and tell you that all was forgiven—but then something unexpected happened. Cain showed up. That changed everything."

"What do you want?" Bourne repeated.

Cody jabbed a thick finger at him. "You tell me. I think you can guess."

Bourne didn't have to guess. He knew. "The Files."

The big man laughed. "*Yes.* Yes, of course, the Files. I've heard about them for more than a year, like everyone else. For a while, I thought it was nothing more than rumor—but then strange things began to happen. Wilson Scott resigned, and the stories on the dark web pointed at *me.* At my website. But how? *I* didn't even know the congressman was one of the men playing with Tati. And yet someone did. Someone knew enough to get him to resign—and that had to be about more than his sexual appetites. Someone had unearthed his interest in my assassin. So naturally, I began to suspect that the information on my own site had somehow become part of the Files. But not just my site. There had to be much more. Other databases. Other information. My little enterprise had become one piece in a bigger puzzle. To be truthful with you, Cain, I've become somewhat obsessed with the Files. My funny little tech people have combed the code on my site, trying to figure out how anyone could be stripping our data. But they've come up empty. I was beginning to give up. And then, very recently, I got a phone call."

"From your hit man in the U.S.," Bourne concluded.

"Very good, Cain. That's exactly right. He called me. He said he was being blackmailed. Someone knew who he was, his name, his cover job, his history of kills. Needless to say, he was furious and wanted to know how this had happened. How had the information leaked? But I was as shocked as he was. You can imagine that I guard his identity quite religiously. There is absolutely nothing about him on our website. Literally the only person with whom I've shared even his anonymous contact information is the lovely Tati here. That's why I suspected her initially. However, I soon realized that I was wrong. Whoever reached out to my assassin knew much more than Tati could ever have given them. This person knew everything about my man. There's only one way that's possible."

"The Files," Bourne said.

Cody swigged more vodka. "Yes indeed, my friend. It had to be someone with access to the Files. Most likely the person behind the whole scheme. Whoever has the Files wants someone dead. So they needed a hit man. *Voilà*, they comb through a million databases and do whatever voodoo they do, and it delivered the name of my assassin. That's the opportunity, you see. That's the way to get the Files. Through my killer."

"I don't see how the assassin helps you," Bourne said. "The approach he received had to be anonymous, right? Maybe you could figure out which databases led to your man, but that's a needle in a haystack. It would take months of coding, if not years, to trace it back. Plus, it still wouldn't narrow down who's behind it."

"Cain, Cain, Cain, keep up with me," Cody bellowed cheerfully. "It's not my assassin. He's not the lead."

Bourne thought about it, and then he understood. "It's the target."

"Exactly! Now we're on the same page. Whoever has the Files wants the target dead so badly that he's willing to risk using an assassin to do it. Maybe it's personal. Maybe it's professional. But there are only so many motives for murder. Somewhere in there is a guided trail that leads back to the Files."

"Who's the target?" Bourne asked.

Cody shrugged. "I have no clue. My man refused to tell me. He no longer trusts me, you see. And the person who hired him made it very clear that the anonymity of the deal was the only thing that would keep my man alive and out of prison. However, I can give you the name of the assassin. I have absolute faith that you have the skills to take it from there."

Bourne frowned. "Why would you do that?"

"Because when you find the Files, you're going to bring them to me," Cody said.

"I don't work for you. Take me to Putin if you want. I'm not going to do your dirty work."

"Oh, I think you will, my friend. You see, if you don't, Tati dies."

Bourne's mouth went dry. "Tati's not a part of this. She had nothing to do with exposing your hit man. Let her go."

Cody holstered his Grach. Then he drew out the long, wide knife from the scabbard on his belt. He pushed himself out of the armchair again, and he approached Tati and dragged the dull side of the blade along her throat. Bourne watched her whole body tremble like leaves in the wind. She stared at him, gray eyes wide.

"*Jason!*"

"Maybe Tati means nothing to you, yes?" Cody mused, turning the knife sideways and putting its point against her windpipe. "No matter how beautiful she is. Is that true? If so, tell me, and I'll kill her now, and we'll come to some other arrangement. But I told you, Cain. I know a lot about you. That means I know you have a weakness for women in trouble. That is your Achilles' heel. I'm told that, in the past, you saved Tati's life more than once. Are you really willing to let her die right now?"

Bourne held up his hands. "Stop! Okay, you win. Let her go. I'll get you the Files."

"Let her go?" Cody chuckled. "Oh, no, no, no. Tati stays with me. You see, Cain, now you *do* work for me. You're my own private spy. Go get me the Files, and bring them back here. If you do, I'll set Tati free. If you don't, she dies. And she won't die easy, my friend. Believe me. I will make a video of her death, a long, long video, and I will put it in your hands so you can see the results of your failure."

Cody snapped his fingers. The men with the rifles jerked to attention. He nodded at the redheaded killer who'd dragged them from the van. "Take her away. Lock her in the wine cellar. Strip her naked in case she gets any ideas about trying to run."

"Jason!" Tati screamed, bolting off her knees and throwing her arms around Bourne's neck. He held her hard as the man began to drag her away, and she clung to him desperately, her nails scraping on his skin.

"I'll get you out," he whispered. "I promise."

"Jason!" she screamed again, limbs flailing, her whole body fighting back. The redheaded man pulled her off, and she collapsed to the carpet, and he began wrestling her out of the room.

"*Wait!*" Cody said suddenly, holding up a hand.

His voice had changed. It had a frozen hardness to it. The glitter in his eyes vanished and became cruel. His mouth pushed into a thin, mean line above his beard. Everyone in the room sensed the change in atmosphere. Especially Tati. She knew this man. She knew his capacity for evil, and her face bled white.

"Do you believe me, Cain?" Cody asked calmly.

"What do you mean?"

"Answer the question, please. Do you understand that Tati will die in a terrible way if you fail?"

Bourne didn't like the darkness in what he was hearing. His body went cold with sweat. "I understand."

"I'm not sure you do. I must impress upon you my absolute seriousness."

"*I understand,*" Bourne repeated. He noticed several of Cody's men drawing closer, preparing to restrain him.

"Alas, I am not convinced. I think you need a demonstration."

Alarm bells went off in Bourne's brain.

"*No!* I understand. I'll do what you want. You don't need to do anything."

Cody held up the sharp blade of the knife. He strolled over to Tati, who struggled in the redheaded man's arms, and he squeezed his hand around her thin wrist, locking it in his grasp. He nodded at Bourne. "Pick a finger."

Tati began to shriek with wild terror.

"Cody, *don't do this*!" Bourne shouted at him. "I will get what you want!"

"Pick a finger," Cody repeated.

"You fucking monster! Don't do this!"

The big man sighed, as if bored by the delay. "I'm a man of my word, Cain. I always do exactly what I say. It's very important that you understand that. Now pick a finger. You have five seconds. If you don't, I take her whole hand."

12

CALLIE FAITH DID A CATLIKE STRETCH, THEN WALKED TO THE WET BAR
and retrieved a bottle of Riesling. She poured herself a large glass
and returned to the floor-to-ceiling window behind her desk. Her
top-floor congressional office in the Lewis Avenue building looked
southwest toward the dazzling lights of the Strip. Seeing the casino
towers made her want to play. Craps was her game, but it had been
ten years since she'd tossed the dice and felt that surge of adrenaline
in her veins and the wetness between her legs. Gambling was in her
blood, but she'd had to choose between her ambition and her addiction.

Ninety-six thousand dollars.

That was how much she'd owed when the senior vice president
of a casino conglomerate had invited her to his suite for a midnight
meeting. She'd overrun her line of credit that night. At the time,
Callie had been a two-term Clark County commissioner, a rising
star in Nevada politics who was easy on the eyes and had a knack for
self-promotion. But rumors had begun to bubble to the surface about

her gambling problem. The *Ralston Reports*, which was the go-to blog for Las Vegas political gossip, mentioned a certain Republican brunette who'd been spotted losing big at the tables in the middle of the night.

So the casino exec gave her a choice. Give up gambling. Let the casino wipe away her debt, and get the full support of the industry in a run for the open congressional seat in the next election. In return for favors on legislation in the future.

Or declare bankruptcy, see her addiction hit the headlines, and watch her career implode like the Sands.

Callie chose wisely. Since then, she'd won five elections, each one by larger margins than the time before. Now she had her eyes set on taking down the incumbent Democrat in the next Senate election. After that, anything was possible.

But damn, there were days when she missed the thrill of the tables.

Callie sipped her sweet wine. She yawned; it was three in the morning. Her staff was gone. She'd sent them home. The aides didn't like to leave before the boss, but Callie was used to gambling all night, and she'd shifted her late-night obsession to work. Most nights when she was home in the district, she caught a couple of hours of sleep on the office sofa before getting up at seven and juicing her system with coffee. Somehow she never slowed down.

Behind her, she heard a muffled text tone from her bottom desk drawer.

Callie was surprised that anyone would be reaching out to her at this hour. She also grew nervous when she recognized the ringtone. This wasn't her congressional phone. It wasn't even her personal phone. This was the *other* one. The burner phone. Untraceable.

The one she'd used to destroy Wilson Scott and pave her way up the congressional ladder. The one she'd used to expose Faisal al-Najjar and the president's dirty laundry. The one she'd used right up until the moment of catastrophe.

No one had that number.

Well, one person did. Just one. But that person was dead.

Callie didn't even know why she'd kept the phone. No good could come of having it in her possession. And yet she found she couldn't throw it away, on the off chance that the day would come when it would ring again.

Like now.

Who was sending her a message?

Callie knelt behind her desk and punched in the combination code that unlocked the bottom drawer. She dug out the phone at the back, still powered on, still fully charged because she always kept it that way. Just in case.

Could it be?

Was her contact alive?

But if so, why had there been months of silence? Her messages had gone undelivered. Unread. It seemed impossible.

Callie opened the phone. The app showed one new message, but she didn't recognize the number that had sent it. It wasn't her contact. It was someone else. She wondered if maybe the message was a mistake, a slip of the finger by someone typing a number. But when she opened the app, she realized she was wrong. The message was just two words.

Hello, Callie.

The phone felt hot in her hands, as if she wanted to drop it. Sink it in water. Set it on fire. Throw it in the waters of Lake Mead. But she didn't. Fingers trembling, she tapped out a reply. *Who is this?*

Callie waited. A bubble appeared, telling her that the person on the other end was typing a response. Seconds later, she saw the next message.

I have something you want.

Callie put the phone on her desk. She finished her wine in a single swallow and paced in her office. She thought about her days on the casino floors, where everything came down to a decision. Do you take your money and run? Or do you let it ride? She'd always been one to let it ride, to play out the game.

And too often, she'd lost.

Callie grabbed the phone. *Don't contact me again.*

She should have powered down the phone at that moment and destroyed it, but she didn't. She waited. She had to see what the person would say next. She had to push her finger closer and closer to the fire, even when she knew she would get burned.

Do you want the Files, Callie? Because I have them.

Shit! Fuck!

Callie thumped her fist against her pretty chin and tried not to panic. This was a trap. A setup. She knew who was using this phone. Shadow. Treadstone. They were luring her into a game, trying to get her to admit what she'd done. What she knew. They were trying to destroy her before she destroyed them.

But what if she was wrong?

She couldn't stop herself. She had to play the cards she had.

If you have the Files, describe them.

The person wrote back immediately. *Everything you need is on a laptop, Callie. But you know that. You tried to buy it once before. Don't you remember?*

Oh my God.

He knew! How could he know?

Callie breathed hard and loud. Her heart hammered in her chest. She told herself to stay calm. Be in control. Every threat is really a deal to be made. She grabbed the wine bottle, filled her glass to the rim, and sat back down at her desk. She made sure the office door was closed. No one was outside; no one could hear her.

How do I know you have the laptop?

A couple of minutes passed. There was no reply. Was this really just a Treadstone game? Then a message appeared, and she had to clap a hand over her mouth to stop herself from screaming.

Ninety-six thousand dollars.

She felt as if she'd rolled a seven before the point and watched her bet get swept from the table. This was impossible. No one could know about that. Her debt had been wiped out years ago, the records erased.

If this came out . . . If people knew the truth . . .

Callie breathed into her hands until the tightness in her chest finally loosened. Then she typed: *How much do you want for the laptop?*

In her head, she could see a grin taking shape on the person's face. Whoever it was knew they'd won. They'd beaten her.

Fifty million dollars.

Callie let out an audible gasp. *You are fucking kidding me!*

You're in Congress, Callie. Just open up one of those black boxes where all the money gets hidden.

She shook her head. *That's not how it works.*

You were prepared to pay twenty million last time. Inflation comes for us all.

Fuck, how could he possibly know that? Jesus!

Things have changed. Budgets are being watched.

Find a way.

It's impossible! she began to write.

Because it was. There was no way to hide that kind of payoff or bury it in the intelligence slush funds. If she went after a pot of gold like that, Shadow would spot it instantly. Even the transfer of twenty million dollars had been a lie, a ruse to draw the Files into the open. She'd never had any intention of paying the money once she got the laptop.

But maybe what had worked before would work again.

Callie deleted what she'd written and typed a new message.

All right. I'll get it. Give me some time.

Another long pause followed.

You have one week, Callie. After that, I talk to other buyers. And when they ask for a free sample of what secrets the Files can give them, I'll start with yours.

13

BOURNE SAT BELOW THE COLUMNS OF THE LINCOLN MEMORIAL. IT WAS A gray afternoon in Washington, the mood somber despite the holiday decorations everywhere.

He heard Shadow's footsteps approaching from the steps above him with that distinctive, confident click of her high heels. She stood beside him, breath clouding in front of her, hands buried in her pockets as she admired the view. She wore a long winter coat with a fur collar that framed the sharp line of her chin. Her makeup, as always, was perfect, her lips deep red. Her wavy blond hair spilled onto her shoulders. When she finally sat down next to him, smoothing her coat beneath her, she was close enough that their legs touched.

They were silent for a while. The Reflecting Pool in front of them stretched toward the pinnacle of the Washington Monument. Christmas tourists shivered in the cold, but the hard ground in the park was brown and snowless.

"So you're back," she said finally.

Jason didn't reply. He surveyed the people around them by habit—assessing threats, identifying the half dozen Treadstone agents assigned to protect Shadow—but his soul felt dead. He'd been virtually silent since he'd left Cody's ranch house outside Narva. Silent on the road back to Tallinn. Silent on the Treadstone jet back to Washington. The only thing he could hear in his head were Tati's screams.

Idly, he stroked the little finger on his right hand. Part of him wanted to bend it back until he heard the crack of the bone breaking. His whole soul tightened into a ball of fury aimed at the Russian called Cody.

He was a *monster*!

"Is everything all right?" Shadow asked, her lips pursing into a frown.

"Fine."

He felt the intensity of her eyes as she watched him, that damn psychiatrist's stare that was both icy and intimate. He had to suppress the wave of anger he felt toward her. Or was it desire? With Shadow, the two became tangled up in his mind until he had no idea whether he wanted to kill her or sleep with her. Or both. He knew she wanted a report. She'd rerouted his Treadstone flight out of Tallinn from Los Angeles to Washington because she wanted an update on his hunt for the Files. But he found it nearly impossible to drag the words out of his chest.

Instead, he couldn't stop thinking about Tati. He saw her face. The pleading in her eyes.

"You're distracted," Shadow said. "That's not like you. What's going on? What happened in Estonia?"

Bourne dragged a cloak over his emotions. "It was a long flight. I haven't slept."

Her blue eyes hardened. A wrinkle of annoyance came and went on her forehead. It was obvious she didn't believe him, and Shadow didn't like agents lying to her. But he didn't care. There was no way he was going to tell her the truth. The secrets of Narva belonged to him and him alone.

"This is a race, Jason. There's no silver medal for the loser. I need you at your best."

"Then get out of the way and let me do my job," Bourne snapped, trying to turn the conversation against her. "You're the one who insisted the jet stop in DC. We could have done this over the phone. Or we could have done this when the mission was over. I'm losing time being here with you instead of in L.A."

"What's in Los Angeles?" she asked.

"A county parks worker named Rod Holtzman."

Shadow waited again, saying nothing. The standoff between them drew out, until her impatience won over her stubbornness. "All right. Who is Rod Holtzman? Why is he important?"

"His parks job is a cover. It's fake. Rod Holtzman is a contract killer. His assignments come via a Russian strongman in Estonia named Cody. Cody's the one who masterminds the escort website. He finds rich clients for Holtzman via the website—people like Wilson Scott—and then Holtzman splits the fee with him. It's a lucrative business, five- or six-figure payouts on every job."

"What's the connection to the Files?"

"Someone on the outside figured out who Holtzman is and what he does. They went directly to him to get him to do a hit. If he refused, he'd be exposed. Turned over to the FBI, along with evidence of his jobs."

"Someone?"

"I think it's the person we're looking for," Bourne said. "Whoever has the Files found Holtzman's secret occupation, and they blackmailed him. Just like they did with Scott, al-Najjar, and the others."

"So you want to follow Holtzman to his target," she concluded. "Is that the idea? There can only be so many people who might want the target dead. Presumably, one of them has the Files."

"Exactly."

"And *why* did the Russian give you Holtzman's name?" she asked.

Bourne had been anticipating that question. He'd prepared a cover story to throw her off the scent. Shadow was smart, which was what made her dangerous. He could see suspicion on her face, because she could play every chess game several moves ahead.

The only reason for Cody to give up his hit man was to help Bourne get the Files.

"He didn't give me anything. Irina did. She's the girl on the website."

"Except my understanding is Irina doesn't exist," Shadow pointed out.

"The girl in the pictures doesn't, but there's a real girl behind her. She builds the relationships on the website. She's the go-between in the whole operation. Cody treats her like his girlfriend and keeps her around. So she hears a lot of names. She's in the room for most of his phone calls."

"How did you get her to talk?"

"She wanted to get away from Cody," Bourne said. "I said I'd help."

"And did you?"

"I tried to get her out, but Cody ambushed us on the road to Tallinn. He killed her. I was lucky to get away."

Always build a lie on a foundation of truth.

Treadstone.

But Shadow was the head of Treadstone. She knew the rules backward and forward and knew how they could be manipulated. Her cool eyes drilled into him, trying to peel back layers of deceit, looking for holes in his story.

"I got a report that Interpol lost a couple of agents in Narva," Shadow said. "Was that part of your operation?"

"Yes. They were working with me to evacuate Irina. Cody killed them, too."

"Unfortunate."

"I'm not giving you excuses. I'm telling you what happened. I take the blame. It's my fault."

"But the bottom line is, you got the information we needed," Shadow said.

"Yes."

"Then nothing else matters." She nodded at one of her protection agents nearby and then got to her feet. "I won't keep you any longer, Jason. Stay the night in DC. Meet me at the airfield in the morning. We'll take the Treadstone jet to Los Angeles together."

"Together? Why?"

"If we need to move on the Files quickly, I want to be prepared. I have assets on the coast that can help us."

"I don't need you looking over my shoulder. And I don't need any help."

"Is there some reason you don't want me with you?"

"Not at all," Bourne replied, because there was nothing else he could say. She wasn't lying that backup might be necessary when they went after the Files, but he also knew that she didn't trust him.

She sensed his deception. She was going to babysit him until the mission was done.

Shadow stood over him, one hand on her hip. "I hope you're not concerned about our history together."

"Our history is dead and buried," he replied.

But Bourne didn't believe that. Not for a minute.

JASON GOT A ROOM AT THE HYATT REGENCY NEAR THE CAPITOL. HE SHOW-ered, changed, and reserved a late table for dinner at Charlie Palmer's, where he ordered New York strip steak done rare. He drank red wine with it. Too much. He stayed until the restaurant was almost empty, finishing the bottle on his own and following it up with two shots of Macallan. When he finally took the short walk back through the darkness to the hotel, he had a stabbing headache behind his eyes.

But none of it drove Tati from his mind.

Jason, oh God, make it stop!

His eyes closed. His fists clenched. But all he could do for Tati was get the Files.

At his room, he noticed that the sliver of a toothpick he'd shoved into the crack of the door when he left was now on the carpet of the hotel hallway. Someone had entered his room while he was gone.

He wasn't surprised. He'd been expecting her to show up and wondered when she would make an appearance. Bourne had his Glock in his hand as he opened the door. Just in case. Inside, the room was dark, but the glow of city lights from the window was enough to show him the naked woman lying on his bed. He could see her bare skin in the shadows, her long straight blond hair draped in loose strands across her full breasts, her legs parted with one knee bent.

"I wanted you to see I'm unarmed," Johanna said.

He didn't say anything. He returned his gun to his holster, then took off his sport coat and draped it over a chair. He put the holster on top of the coat and walked over to the bed, where he sat down next to her.

She rolled over on her side, and her fingers grazed his thigh.

"I saw you with Shadow today," she said.

"You were watching me?"

"I was watching her. God, I hate that bitch. I could have taken her down, you know. I was close enough to get off a shot. Six agents and none of them spotted me. Pretty pathetic for Treadstone."

"I spotted you," Bourne said.

"Did you?"

"Taking selfies by the Reflecting Pool. Blue down coat, jeans, orange scarf, white wool cap, sunglasses."

"Of course. I was wondering if you made me. At one point, I thought I saw your eyes look my way. But you didn't say anything to Shadow?"

"No."

"Why not?"

Bourne decided to be honest. "Because it turns out I may need your help after all."

"Well, I like to hear that." She pushed herself up on the bed, and her arms snaked around him, her lips kissing his neck. "Tell me something. If I'd gone after Shadow today, would you have protected her? Or would you have let me kill her?"

"I protected her the last time you tried to kill her," Bourne said. "Nothing's changed."

"You also let me go last time. You could have shot me, and you didn't."

"True."

"One of these days, I'm going to try again. It'll be her or me. You'll have to choose."

Bourne frowned. He was tired of being in the middle of their game. Shadow and Johanna were both playing him, both pulling him into their vendetta. But Johanna was right. A final confrontation was inevitable. He didn't know, when the moment came to choose between them, what he would do.

"Why are you here, Johanna? I thought we covered everything outside Tucson."

She reached between his legs. "Right now I just want to fuck. Everything else can wait until we're done."

"I already told you. You and me? That's not happening again."

"Yeah, you told me that, and I don't believe you."

She grabbed his face, turned his head, and kissed him hard on the mouth. Her tongue pushed between his teeth, daring him to kiss her back, and he did. She was right again; she was always right. He wanted her. Tonight, at that moment, he needed her in his arms. He needed to push everything else out of his mind. The Files. Tati. Shadow. Even the memory of Abbey Laurent. He took Johanna's soft bare shoulders and pushed her down onto the bed and crushed her with his weight. Her hands ripped at his clothes, popping buttons on his shirt, fumbling with his zipper. She couldn't go fast enough for their desire, so he stood up and stripped completely naked in front of her. She rolled onto her hands and knees; she took him in her mouth. His back arched, his breath expelling in a silent groan of pleasure.

Johanna let go, sinking back and spreading her legs. "Now," she whispered urgently. "Now, quick, fast."

The next moment, he was inside her, her legs wrapped around his back, her heels thumping him like a drum. They struggled with each other, gladiators both hungry for control, rolling and switching places, him on top, her on top. He won the first round, drawing a shattering climax out of her as her whole body clenched. Then, in the slow aftermath, she began to move again, her hips undulating like waves as she took him back up the mountain to his own release.

Eventually, they fell back next to each other, sated and sweaty.

"Jesus, I told you, didn't I?" Johanna murmured. "We're good together."

Bourne, still breathing hard, didn't answer. He stared at the ceiling in the darkness, and he knew she was right. There was something between them, whatever it was. But for all of the passion between them, he felt empty.

"What's going on?" she asked.

"What do you mean?"

"That wasn't just sex. You think I don't know the difference with you? That was escape. What are you escaping from, Jason?"

He said nothing, and Johanna sighed at his silence.

"Fine. I get it. We can fuck, but it's nothing personal."

"I thought that's what you wanted."

"You're right. Absolutely. It doesn't have to mean a thing. You tell me the lie you want to hear, and I'll make you believe it."

"Johanna—"

"Forget it. Do you still want Abbey? Is that it?"

Abbey.

Was Johanna right? Was Abbey still his magnet, pulling him back?

"It's not that simple," he said.

"Fine. Then let's get down to business. It's safer that way. You said you need my help, right? And you were in town briefing Shadow. That means you've got something. You've got information. Well, guess what, so do I. If we pool our resources, we'll get there faster. That's important. The race isn't just you and me, Jason. There are a lot of others who want the Files."

"I know," Bourne said.

"So give me something to work with. I've been hunting for leads in Washington, but I've hit a dead end."

"You first," he told her.

"Okay. What I know came from Callie Faith. I'm willing to give it to you for nothing if that's what you want. No quid pro quo. But I'd rather you trust me. I'm taking a leap of faith in you, Jason. Why not do the same with me?"

Bourne frowned. His instinct was always to say nothing. To trust no one except himself. Especially not a woman who'd already betrayed him once. But he knew that Johanna could be useful in the days ahead.

"I'm going to Los Angeles," he told her.

"Do you think the Files are in L.A.?"

"I don't know, but whoever has the Files has business out there."

"What kind of business?"

Bourne turned his head sideways and studied Johanna's face. "A hit."

"Interesting. Who's the target?"

"That's what I need to find out. Hopefully the identity of the target will point us to whoever has the Files."

"Us?"

"Shadow's coming with me. She'll be on the ground, too. So you need to be careful. If you give her a chance, she'll take you out."

"Understood. But why does Shadow want to be there in person? Since when do you need a babysitter?" Johanna put a hand on his cheek, and her face darkened with concern. "What the hell are you hiding, Jason? You're keeping secrets about something. I can tell. She must think so, too."

He shook his head. "I've shown you mine. You show me yours."

Johanna took away her hand, but her eyes stayed on his. "Okay, here's what I know. We're running out of time. We need to move fast. According to Callie, the seller has surfaced with a price. Fifty million dollars. The Files are in play."

PART TWO

14

WITH THE WINDOWS ROLLED DOWN ON HIS RENTED TOYOTA HIGHLANDER, Bourne could smell salt air blowing in from the Pacific Ocean a block away. Hundreds of mop-top palm trees dotted the streets of Long Beach. He took a slug of coffee, then focused his Canon binoculars on the circular tower of the condominium building on Ocean Boulevard. Rod Holtzman owned a tenth-floor unit with a beachside view, the kind of high-end apartment that should have been well beyond the reach of a twenty-eight-year-old worker in the Los Angeles County Parks & Recreation Department. But Bourne doubted that anyone in the parks department would have known who Rod Holtzman was.

He isolated the man's unit in his field of view. He'd been checking the condo since before sunrise an hour ago, and he finally saw movement on the balcony. The curtains swept aside. The glass patio door slid open. Holtzman emerged, drinking coffee like Bourne was, wearing only a pair of plaid boxer shorts. He was tall, with a lean physique, his face square, his brown hair short and unruly. He had the California tan of someone who spent a lot of time on the beach. Anyone who passed him would consider him normal and forgettable, which was an asset for a man whose line of work was as a contract killer.

Who contacted you?

Who are you planning to kill?

Time to find out.

Bourne had Holtzman's private cell phone number. Cody had given it to him. He tapped a single word into his own phone and sent the killer a text message.

Fahrenheit.

Seconds later, through the binoculars, he watched the man pick up his phone from a glass table on the balcony. Holtzman checked it, then closed and locked the patio door in his condominium, and disappeared.

According to Cody, Holtzman received a monthly retainer to reserve the hit man's exclusive services. Ten thousand dollars in cash. On a random day every month, Cody sent a courier to Alamitos Beach. Holtzman provided the courier with the designated code word and received an envelope with the money.

Fahrenheit was the December code. The text told Holtzman it was time for the delivery on the beach.

Bourne and Cody had arranged the timing in Estonia. He hated having the Russian sadist as a partner, but for now, he had no choice.

Tati! If he didn't get the Files, she died.

Jason got out of the Highlander, crossed the parking lot, and jogged up the steps that led to Shoreline Drive. He continued around the corner to the wide expanse of Ocean Boulevard, and he waited for Holtzman to emerge from the condo tower. Ten minutes later, the killer appeared, dressed in a tank top and shorts, a baseball cap over his brown hair. Holtzman set off on foot for the beach, which Bourne estimated gave him at least half an hour before the man would complete the drop and return.

He checked his surroundings before going inside. The morning Long Beach traffic was heavy. Four blond teenagers, two boys, two girls, passed him in beachwear on their way to the ocean. Across the street was a coffee shop, and he could see a handful of people at the tables inside. An older woman in a business suit swirling a tea bag in a mug. A twentysomething Chinese man with red glasses and spiky black hair, using two thumbs to play a game on his phone. Two IT geeks typing on dueling laptops.

No surveillance.

Bourne entered the tower and slipped a magnetic key card out of his wallet. Shadow had given it to him on the Treadstone jet—the latest in universal access technology. A tap of the card got him into the tower's private residence elevator, and he selected the tenth floor. When he was there, he took the empty hallway to the door for unit 1027, where Holtzman lived. Using the same card, he heard the lock click open, and he went inside, drawing his Glock as he did. He wasn't sure if Holtzman would have an alarm or internal cameras, but apparently the man was confident enough in his cover that he didn't opt for additional security.

Or, more likely, he didn't have faith in technology that could be hacked. Where there was a Wi-Fi camera, some stranger could be watching.

He holstered his gun and slipped plastic gloves over his hands. He checked his watch again, giving himself twenty minutes inside the apartment. The condo wasn't large, two bedrooms and two baths, and it was sparsely but expensively furnished. There was almost nothing personally identifiable inside, no photographs, nothing but generic artwork on the walls. He crossed through the living room to the balcony, which looked out toward the water and toward another condo tower across the street. Quickly, he surveyed the rooms in the other building with a pair of pocket binoculars, checking whether anyone had a telescope or camera pointed this way. He saw nothing. The person who had the Files didn't appear to be surveilling Holtzman to make sure the job got done.

Bourne stopped.

Was that a noise?

He waited, listening for the sound to repeat itself, but he heard nothing. Even so, he moved faster. The nearest doorway out of the living room led to a spare bedroom that Holtzman used as an office. Bourne saw a desk and computer at the window, and he booted it up with a Treadstone thumb drive in the USB-C port. Shadow had told him the beta device would be able to unlock most password-protected hard drives, but it might take several minutes to do so. He didn't think he had the time. Even so, he let the computer spin while he checked the rest of the room.

One wall was completely paneled in oak. Bourne thought that was a strange design choice in a condo that was otherwise painted with nothing but white walls. He approached the wall and tapped lightly on the wooden panels, and the hollow sound told him that there was a gap behind the facade. It took him a couple of minutes to find a panel near the floor that unlocked a floor-to-ceiling seam with a quiet click. Both sides of the paneling folded like accordions, and when he opened up the wall, he found a pegboard and shelves that contained the hit man's arsenal.

It was impressive. A dozen semiautomatic pistols, mostly Glocks, but also a couple of H&K and Ruger models. A Daniel Defense V7 rifle. An MK 22 sniper rifle. Boxes of ammunition. Two dozen blades of varying lengths. A bone saw. Chemicals for anesthesia, chemicals for cleaning scenes, chemicals for dissolving bodies. Fast- and slow-acting poisons. Thallium. Cyanide. Tetrodotoxin.

Depending on the job, Holtzman had plenty of options to kill.

"Holy shit, what's all that?"

A woman's voice screeched behind him.

Bourne spun, his Glock already back in his hand. On the other side of the bedroom, a woman of about thirty stood in the doorway, the whites of her dark eyes huge with fear. She had messy black hair and wore a sports bra and shorts, and she had Celtic tattoos across most of her chest. When she saw his gun, her mouth fell open as she inhaled to scream. Bourne crossed the room at a run and clapped a hand over her face. He cut off her cry just as it left her throat.

"Who are you?" he hissed. He shoved the barrel of the Glock into her temple and added, "Don't scream. If you scream, I'll be forced to do something I don't want to do."

He lowered his hand, but left the gun at her head.

"Mindy," she stuttered. "I'm Mindy. Oh my God, don't hurt me!"

"Are you Holtzman's wife? His girlfriend?"

"Who?"

"Rod Holtzman. The man who lives here."

She shook her head over and over. Tears poured down her cheeks. "His profile name was Paul. That's all I know about him. I met him last night, and we came back here. Please! Please, let me go, I don't know anything!"

"How did you meet him?"

"An app. A dating app for L.A. singles."

"Does he know who you are?"

"Well, Mindy's my real name, but I made up a fake last name. Everybody does!"

"Did you give him any details about your life?"

"I said I was a nurse. I am. But that's all. What's going on? Who *is* he? Who are *you*?"

Bourne closed his eyes. He checked his watch and saw that he was running out of time.

Shit! If he left Mindy here, she'd never stay quiet about what she saw. Holtzman would kill her as soon as he returned and realized she knew his secrets.

"Did you talk to him this morning?"

"Yes, he said he was going to get us breakfast. I went back to sleep."

"So he expects you to be here when he gets back?"

"Sure. I mean, I figured we would—you know—again—"

Bourne holstered his Glock. He took the woman by the hands. "Mindy, you need to listen to me. If you see this man again, ever, anywhere, it means he's going to kill you. Do you understand me? The only reason he will track you down is to murder you."

"Oh, fuck! Oh my God!"

"If you see him, don't let him get close to you. Scream, run, get away. You can see from what's on the wall the kind of man he is. *Do you understand me?*"

"Yes! Yes!"

"Get your things, and get out of here. Delete your profile on that dating app. Delete the app from your devices. Never open it again. Don't tell anyone what you saw here, not family, not friends, not the police. My advice is that you quit your job and move. Get out of California. Nurses can find work anywhere. You may be safe staying where you are, he may not be able to find you, but I wouldn't count on it."

"Jesus!"

"Now go."

Mindy turned away, but before she could run from the bedroom, Bourne grabbed her hand again. He decided to gamble.

Don't fight the unexpected. Turn it to your advantage.

Treadstone.

"Wait a minute. I need you to do something for me," he said.

"What is it? What?"

Bourne spotted a pad of paper and pen on Holtzman's desk. He grabbed them and gave them to Mindy. "Write a note. Write it down exactly like I tell you. Okay? The note may help keep you safe. He'll think you're not who you said you were, that you're working for someone else. If he believes that, then he won't bother trying to find you."

He recited what he wanted her to say, and she didn't ask any questions. She simply wrote it down word for word, but she had to labor to keep her hand steady. When the note was done, he told her again to get her things and go. The woman disappeared in a frantic run to the other side of the bedroom, and barely a minute later, he heard the slam of the door as Mindy escaped from Holtzman's apartment.

Silence returned. Bourne was alone again.

The paneled wall hiding the killer's arsenal was still open, revealing its trove of weapons. He left it that way. The Treadstone device hadn't been able to unlock Holtzman's computer, so he yanked it out of the USB drive and shoved it back in his pocket. But he left the computer on. Better to let the man wonder if his data had been hacked.

Bourne crossed to the master bedroom on the other side of the condo. It smelled of sex and alcohol. He confirmed that Mindy hadn't left anything behind, and then he left the handwritten note on a pillow above the tangled sheets.

He read it again:

Hi Rod,

Thanks for last night. Our mutual friend says hi.

You have twenty-four hours to do the job. If not, everyone will know who you are.

15

HOURS LATER, AT SUNSET, BOURNE WATCHED ROD HOLTZMAN DRIVE A
black Chevy pickup out of the condo tower's parking garage. He followed the killer in his Highlander. The pickup stayed on the city
streets out of Long Beach, and Holtzman used several techniques in
the first few miles of his journey to make sure that no one was on his
trail. He accelerated abruptly at red lights, cut across lanes to make
right turns, and pulled over to park for several minutes to let traffic
pass him by.

Bourne watched it all from the computer screen on a laptop in
his Toyota. He'd scoured the parking garage earlier and identified
the vehicle registered to Holtzman, and he'd placed a magnetic GPS
tag on the bumper. So he kept a safe distance from the Chevy and
stayed out of sight as the killer did his elaborate dance to throw off
pursuers.

But Holtzman was no fool.

West of Long Beach, in Lomita, the killer veered off Highway 1
and parked his pickup on a quiet residential street. Bourne waited a

few blocks away, watching the blip of the GPS tracker, but ten minutes passed, and the truck didn't move again. After another twenty minutes, he took the risk of driving close enough that he could spot the pickup at the curb half a block away. From that distance, he could see that the truck was empty, and there was no sign of Holtzman.

The pickup was parked in front of a modest Spanish-style home on 250th Street, with a white picket fence around the front lawn. Bourne did a quick search on the ownership records of the house, and he found that the property was listed in the name of a generic LLC. If Holtzman's target was inside, there wasn't any indication of who it was. But Bourne didn't think the hit man would park his truck outside the house where he was planning to kill someone.

No. This was Holtzman's house.

A staging area where he could leave one identity behind and become someone entirely new. New look. New clothes. New car.

Bourne took the risk of driving past the house. He saw external cameras covering the front and sides in both directions. If anyone approached the house, Holtzman would get an alert, and the killer could also watch the traffic coming and going on the street. At least Bourne was confident that the man hadn't already escaped. The detached garage next to the house was open, with a beat-up Ford Taurus parked inside.

He drove to the end of the block, did a U-turn, and waited.

Night fell soon after. Wherever he was going, Holtzman planned to use the cover of darkness. It would also make him harder to follow. An hour passed, and finally Bourne spotted the red lights of the Taurus backing down the driveway into the street. Holtzman was on the move. Bourne gave him space, then eased the Highlander onto the street and took off after the other car.

The killer made his way back to the crowded city traffic on Highway 1. Every stoplight put Bourne at risk of losing him, so he stayed closer than he otherwise would, hoping the darkness would show Holtzman nothing but headlights when he studied the vehicles behind him. For the next half hour, Bourne got lucky, keeping the Taurus in view, but when they reached Hermosa Beach, his luck ran out. He didn't know whether the man had spotted him or whether Holtzman was just being cautious, but at the next light, the Taurus suddenly accelerated through a red light and then immediately turned right.

Thirty seconds later, when Bourne's Highlander finally turned onto the same street, the Taurus was already gone.

Bourne pounded the steering wheel in frustration.

If Holtzman made it to his destination, if he completed the hit, there was a strong likelihood that they would never know who the target was.

Where are you?

He tried to put himself inside the killer's head and anticipate his next move. For all the diversions Holtzman had made along the way, he'd always returned to Highway 1 eventually. He hadn't headed for the 405 or gone inland. So maybe his destination was closer to the coast, and he'd return to the north-south highway again when he felt secure that he'd lost whoever might be following him.

Bourne swung the Highlander around and returned to his original route. He drove hard and fast now—as fast as L.A. traffic would allow—skipping lights and wheeling around other vehicles, hoping he wouldn't draw police attention. When the traffic on 1 backed up, he switched to side streets and drove through stop signs and parking lots to get ahead of the cars around him. But he kept coming back to the main road. He had only one goal—to get ahead of Holtzman, wherever the man was.

A few blocks south of LAX, in El Segundo, he spotted a parking lot for a Chick-fil-A on Highway 1, and he pulled off the road and waited.

Five minutes passed. Then fifteen.

When twenty minutes passed, he worried that his long shot hadn't paid off. The killer had gone elsewhere.

Then he saw the Taurus.

Holtzman passed the Chick-fil-A, driving slowly and cautiously, attracting no attention. Bourne pulled out of the parking lot and took up position a few cars behind him. At this point, the killer had obviously concluded that he'd ditched anyone who might have been pursuing him. Holtzman stayed on Highway 1 for miles, past the airport, past Marina del Rey and Santa Monica, and finally onto the foggy stretch where the road clung to the coast and followed the ocean northward.

Bourne gave him more space. Holtzman kept driving through darkness and fog, nothing but a gauzy pair of red lights half a mile ahead. Houses thinned, and the headlands crept up to the east shoulder of the road. They passed Topanga Beach, Las Tunas Beach, and then the eastern outskirts of Malibu and the central heart of the rich enclave. Still the killer drove, hugging the ocean. Traffic thinned, until it felt as if only the two of them were driving north on the lonely road. There was nothing around them but the Pacific waves, the highway pavement, and the rocky slopes of the coastal hills. More than an hour and a half had passed since they'd left Lomita.

The fog got thicker. A cloud rolled in from the ocean and billowed onto the land. Bourne drew closer, closing the distance between the two vehicles as visibility shrank. He saw no other lights, no houses, just the looming night hills lost in a milky haze.

Then the red lights of the car ahead of him vanished. One moment they were there, and then they were gone.

Was it the fog?

No. The Taurus had left the road. It couldn't be far away; if he kept going, he'd drive right past it. Bourne slowed the Highlander to a crawl, then pulled well off the highway shoulder and stopped. He got out, his Glock in his hand. The cold air felt damp and thick. He narrowed his eyes, trying to see something, anything, but the fog left him blind. Instead, he reached back into the Highlander and found his gear pack. He unzipped a side pocket and found his TNV10 thermal monocular.

When he put it to his eye, two heat signatures immediately cut through the fog. He spotted the Taurus maybe a hundred yards ahead of him, parked on the sloping land. Beyond the car, moving away as he climbed the hill, was Rod Holtzman.

Bourne set off in slow pursuit. He took a treacherous path up the pitted, uneven slope. The ocean breeze covered the noise of his footsteps, but high brambles scraped at his skin, and the dense brush threatened to lasso his ankles and spill him off his feet. The monocular kept Holtzman in sight. For a while, Bourne had no idea where the man was going. Then, near the crest of the hill, a new heat signature bloomed, showing the outline of an isolated mansion that faced the sprawling hills and the ocean.

It was a rich Malibu house, far from any neighbors. Whoever was inside, Bourne guessed, was Holtzman's target.

As the house loomed closer, the hit man stopped to surveil the property, and Bourne did the same. It was three stories, terraced against the hill, with a large elevated balcony stretching across the entire front of the house. The paver-stone driveway led around to the garage in back. Above the house, power lines followed the ridgeline. The large estate was dark, no sign that anyone was home, no moving heat echoes through any of the high windows that gave views of the Pacific.

The glowing image of Holtzman set off again. As Bourne followed, he watched the hit man approach the side of the mansion. Moments later, Holtzman disappeared entirely.

He was inside.

Waiting.

Bourne reached the house a couple of minutes later. He circled it entirely, confirming that the place was deserted. Using an app on his phone, he identified the house address and unearthed the name of the owner. A Google search told him that the man was a Hollywood producer, but the name meant nothing to him, and nothing about his work history suggested a natural connection to the Files.

Why would someone want him dead?

He took up position in the trees behind the house, crouched on the slope below the power lines. When he checked the estate through his monocular, he saw no movement inside. Holtzman had staked out his own hiding place. He didn't doubt that the man would wait all night if necessary, and into the day, if it meant finishing the job. The alternative was exposure and life behind bars.

Bourne wondered what weapon the killer planned to use and whether the hit carried any special instructions. Make it hard, or make it painless and quick, or make it look like an accident or suicide.

Who ordered the kill?

Another hour passed. Then two. It was past midnight. The dampness got inside his bones, making his limbs stiff. He kept his Glock in his hand, but he had to flex his fingers to keep them loose. The fog stayed dense, nearly impenetrable, and began to play tricks on his eyes. He saw things that weren't there, the shadows so vivid that he kept pointing his gun into the darkness.

When the car came, he heard it before he saw it. An engine growled, getting closer. Twin headlights glowed in the fog, already halfway up the entrance road from Highway 1. Bourne unfolded his legs and got to his feet, his body protesting. He stayed on the fringe of the trees, expecting one of the rear garage doors to open, expecting a flood of spotlights to illuminate the rear of the house.

Instead, everything stayed dark.

The car stopped. The headlights went off. He heard the clicks of two car doors opening, but the vehicle wasn't close to him. It had stopped near the house's front door, and at least two people were getting out. Bourne hurried that way, picking his way down the invisible road. They were going in the front, not the back, and Holtzman might be right inside the door, ready to strike.

Then he heard a voice from the far side of the house, along with the footsteps. Five little words carried by the breeze.

"I think the power's out."

Bourne froze.

The shock left him paralyzed, motionless in the fog. *He knew that voice!*

He'd heard that voice in Quebec City. In Paris. He'd heard that voice in his bed dozens of times, her words twisted up with laughter, joy, and passion. He knew that voice and the woman it belonged to better than anyone else in his life.

It was Abbey Laurent.

Impossible!

It *couldn't* be Abbey! How could she be here? Why?

Then the shell around his mind shattered. The how and why of it didn't matter. Not now. The footsteps kept on toward the house, toward a professional assassin waiting inside. Jason broke into a desperate run. He charged down the driveway and rounded the corner at the front of the house. Ahead of him, the front door was open. He didn't see her, but he heard the sharp stab of that voice he knew well.

Abbey screamed.

He covered the last few steps as if he were flying and cleared the threshold into the darkness. The house was black. The noise of a struggle showed him the way forward, and he dove for the sound. He heard another scream—Abbey—then the guttural gasp of a wounded man.

Was it Holtzman?

Or someone else?

Bourne needed the threat directed at *him*. Holtzman needed to know the game had changed. He aimed his Glock at the ceiling and squeezed off a round, the shot booming like an explosion in the small space. The halo of light as the gun went off showed him three people, Abbey against the wall, a bleeding stranger in front of her, Holtzman plunging at the stranger with a knife. Jason fired high again. Plaster and dust fell, choking them. By instinct, he ducked, expecting an assault, and he got one. Holtzman ran at him, swinging the blade with a deadly rush of air. He missed, barely, and Bourne delivered a roundhouse punch where he thought the man's midsection was. But Jason missed, too.

A boot connected with his wrist. His Glock fell. The knife

swung again, slicing close enough to slash open the sleeve of his jacket. Bourne clutched for Holtzman in the darkness, found the killer's forearm, and bent it sharply back. Holtzman winced. The knife spilled from his fingers, but he twisted free and swung an elbow that connected hard with Bourne's cheekbone and dizzied him. Jason came off his knees, his head and shoulders like a battering ram into Holtzman's stomach, driving him backward into the wall.

The killer expelled a spray of vomit, but then he recovered and drove his elbows down into Bourne's collarbone. A knee snapped upward into Jason's chin. Bourne heard someone running for the front door—was it Abbey?—but Holtzman leaped past him and took whoever it was down to the house's marble floor. Abbey cried in pain as her body landed, but she lashed back, because Bourne heard Holtzman grunt as a blow hit his face. Abbey slithered forward and tried to stand as the man chased her down the hallway.

Bourne threw himself at Holtzman's back, landing on top of him. The two men rolled out the open door into the clammy fog. Holtzman kicked hard, separating himself, and Jason heard the deadly snicker of a wire being extended. A garrote. He had a split second to throw up his forearm as the killer looped the wire over his head and pulled it tight. He felt it cutting his skin, and his own arm squeezed into his throat, cutting off most of his air. Jason struggled wildly. His boot cracked against Holtzman's foot; his hands reached back and clawed at the killer's face. One nail found the liquid goo of the man's eye and he dug it in, eliciting a scream.

The garrote loosened. Bourne ripped it away.

He reached into his jacket pocket, where his Thompson dagger waited. In a single blind move, he spun. The knife hit flesh and opened up Holtzman's throat, nearly severing his head as a fountain of blood cascaded over Bourne's face.

Jason staggered backward. He couldn't see. His eyes saw nothing but blood, darkness, and fog. But he heard the sickening, choking gag as bile replaced the air in Holtzman's lungs and the thud as his body collapsed to the walkway outside the house. Bourne gasped for breath himself. He swayed, reaching out for something, anything to hold on to and lean against. When there was nothing, he began to fall, but then arms held him up. Arms held him tightly, and the scent of a familiar perfume enveloped him.

He knew it was Abbey.

And Abbey knew it was him.

Bourne heard her murmur in his ear. "*Jason.*"

16

THE POWER CAME BACK ON. BEHIND THEM, LIGHTS FROM INSIDE THE house glowed like square beacons through the fog.

Bourne knew what he must look like, covered in Holtzman's blood. He sat in the open back seat of Abbey's red Audi RS 7 as she tended to his face with a cool damp cloth. She stayed very close to him, only a couple of inches away. She used alcohol where the wire had cut his neck, and he flinched as it stung him. Then she covered the wound with a gauze pad. All of her motions were quick, tender, automatic, but she said almost nothing, and she avoided looking into his eyes until she was done.

When she eased away from him, they simply stared at each other. It had been more than a year since he'd seen her. Or talked to her. Or exchanged any kind of message with her. Physically, she hadn't changed, her hair colored to a deep mahogany red, her skin and lips pale, her smart dark eyes always curious, always probing. But she *had* changed. This was Abbey Laurent, successful novelist, not the lost, struggling reporter he'd first met years earlier. In their time apart, she'd grown older, more sure of herself, more comfortable with what she wanted and didn't want. He could feel distance radiating from her, and he sensed the wall between them. Her expression had a reluctance bordering on anger. He'd come back into her life because of a killer—he'd *saved* her life, which he'd done several times in the past—but that kind of violence was also why she'd sent him away.

She broke the silence first.

"You still have this way of showing up when I need you. Thank you for that."

"I didn't know you were here, Abbey. Truly. I didn't."

"Uh-huh." She gestured up the driveway toward the house, where the dead body still lay near the front door. "So who is he?"

"His name is Rod Holtzman. He's a contract killer."

"A *hit man*? Coming after me? Somebody wants me dead?"

"It looks that way," Jason told her. "Do you have any idea why?"

"Well, in the past, it was usually because of you," Abbey replied, and he could hear a little bit of acid in her tone. "But now, I have no idea. It could be anything. My books get a lot of attention. They're drawn from things that really happened, and even though it's fiction, I get a fair amount of threats."

"Anything recent?"

"Nothing worse than the usual nuts."

"What are you working on?" Bourne asked. "What's the new book about?"

"The La Sienta Ranch fire. That's why I'm in this house. Some Hollywood guy offered to let me stay here. It's close to the scene."

Bourne let another long stretch of silence draw out between them. He noticed that neither one of them had mentioned the elephant in the room. The man Abbey was with. The man who was living in the house with her. The man who had kissed and embraced her while Jason was watching them.

Her husband.

As if reading his mind, she twisted the gold ring on her finger, but she didn't say anything about it.

"What now?" she asked. "Do we call the police?"

"No. I'll call my handler. She'll send a team to take care of it."

"'She'? What happened to Nash Rollins? Wasn't he the guy who used to clean up all of your messes, Jason?"

There was more acid in her voice. She looked away and bit her lip, as if unhappy with herself for how she was treating him.

"Nash got shot. He was nearly killed."

"Shit. I'm sorry."

"He's recovering. In the meantime, I'm working with someone else."

"A woman? How are you dealing with that? Are you sleeping with her?"

"Do you really want to go down that road, Abbey?"

She frowned. "No, I don't. Sorry."

"Anyway, she'll send cleaners. They'll remove the body and all the evidence. But you'll need to talk to—you know—you'll need to explain it to him—"

Abbey gave Bourne a cynical smirk. "Really? You think?"

"Will that be a problem?"

"I have no idea. Strangely, using secret intelligence agencies to remove dead bodies hasn't come up in our relationship before now."

He took the comment like a slap, which was how it was intended. "Have you told him about me?"

"Not really. Not in any detail. I told him I used to be in love with a man named Jason. We broke up. That's all."

He didn't miss her choice of words. *Used to be.*

"But he knows you're you," she added. "That you're the one who saved us. I told him I needed a few minutes so we could talk. He's discreet. He said he'd give us time. But I'm going to have to tell him something more about who you are. He deserves to know why we were almost killed tonight."

"Look, Abbey, I'm sorry about all of this," Bourne told her. "I don't know how or why you're involved in this mission, but if I'd known you *were* involved, I would have stayed out of it. I would have asked Treadstone to assign a different agent. I'm not trying to complicate your life. Not any more than I already have."

She sighed and briefly closed her eyes. "No, Jason. Don't apologize. I don't mean to be a bitch. This whole night has taken me by surprise. Coming home, getting attacked, *you* showing up. It's like a blast from the past, you know? I thought I was done with things like that when I left you. The truth is, I *wanted* to be done with it, okay? But I'm grateful to you. Really."

Bourne said nothing.

"So are you going to tell me what's going on?" she asked finally. "I mean, apparently I've pissed off someone pretty badly if they sent a hit man after me. What am I in the middle of? And how are *you* involved?"

"Have you heard about something called the Files?" Bourne asked. "I know you've got a lot of Washington contacts."

Her face clouded over. "I've heard rumors, yeah. The Files are a hacked database with a lot of ugly shit for blackmail. Some of Peter

Chancellor's old sources reached out to tell me about it. They said it reminded them of the Hoover days. They wondered if I was putting it in my next book."

"Are you?"

"No. Like I said, I'm writing about the fire. I don't see any connection."

"Well, I think whoever is running the Files is the one who sent Holtzman after you," Bourne said.

She shook her head. "That makes no sense. I don't know anything about the Files. I don't see how I could be a threat to anyone."

Bourne nodded. He didn't understand it, either. He knew Abbey, and he knew she wasn't hiding things from him. And yet, somewhere, there had to be a connection between the Files and her book. Otherwise, he saw no reason for Abbey to be a target. She had to be getting close to some secret that the person with the Files wanted to keep hidden, even if she didn't know it.

"Listen, I should have asked you before," Abbey said suddenly, touching his hand and then pulling back. "How are you? Are you okay? I don't want you to think I don't care, Jason. I do. Of course I do. I always will."

He hesitated. The safe thing was to say he was fine. But the truthful thing was to say that Abbey leaving him had ripped his heart open and left behind a scar that didn't want to heal.

"I'm fine," he said.

Her eyes narrowed. "Are you really?"

"Really."

"Are you seeing anyone?"

"There's a woman," he admitted, not naming names.

"Your handler?"

"No. My handler was part of my Treadstone past. We were in-volved years ago, long before you, long before I lost my memory. Now she's back in my life. I don't think she wants a relationship. She just likes keeping me off balance. But this other woman . . ."

"You like her," Abbey concluded.

"I'm drawn to her, but it's difficult."

"Difficult how?"

"Difficult in that we're a lot alike."

Abbey blinked. "Oh. Well, at least you didn't say difficult be-cause of me."

"No, it's difficult because of you, too."

"Look, Jason, I hope you're not—" She stopped and didn't finish her thought.

"Still in love with you?" he asked.

Abbey stared at him with a terrible sadness, as if she had no idea what he would say.

"No," Bourne told her. "I'm not. Don't worry. I'm not sure I'll ever be *out* of love with you, Abbey, but I'm not *in* love with you any-more. As for this other woman, she knows about you. She knows what you mean to me."

"Is that a problem?"

"Well, you make her jealous. She doesn't do jealous well. Actu-ally, she's the one who told me you got married."

Abbey frowned. "Almost nobody knows about that. Garrett and I wanted to keep it low-profile. How did she—"

"She keeps an eye on you. She's a wizard online."

"Jesus, Jason. Should I be scared? I mean, it wasn't her, was it? The one who hired the hit man?"

"She will never harm you. I promise."

He wondered if that was a promise he could keep. But he knew he'd already told her too much, and he decided to change the subject. "Anyway, here you are," he went on. "Married. Why didn't you tell me?"

Her eyes looked away down the hill toward the ocean. "I wanted to. I thought about it, but—"

"It's okay. I get it. Who is he? How did it happen?"

"His name's Garrett Parker. He's an IT consultant. He used to be one of the senior guys at Jumpp."

"The social media software?"

She nodded. "We met at a bar in O'Hare. I was coming back here, he was going home to Seattle. We hit it off. Neither one of us was looking for someone, but I guess it happens when you least expect it. He moved in here with me a few weeks later. Earlier this month, we got married in Reno."

"Congratulations. I'm happy for you."

Her brow knitted. "Do you mean that?"

"I do."

"Well, good. I hope you like him. I mean, he's not you, Jason. I needed someone totally different after us. Can you understand that?"

"Of course."

Abbey looked at her watch. "I should check on him. Make sure he's okay. And then you need to tell him what's going on."

"I'll come inside in a few minutes," Bourne said. "I've got to reach out to Treadstone and get the cleaners en route. That will take a while. Once they arrive, they'll be working here most of the night."

"Okay."

Bourne got up stiffly from the Audi. He felt the burn on his arm and neck from the garrote and knew he'd been lucky to survive. He hiked up the steep driveway toward the house with Abbey next to him, and then he made his way to the dead body on the sidewalk near the door. Kneeling next to Holtzman, he began rifling through the man's pockets.

"What are you doing?" Abbey asked.

"I want to see if he's carrying any clue about who hired him. It's not likely, but you never know."

He worked quickly. He found a Samsung phone in the man's rear pocket, but it was locked, with a password requirement and no facial recognition. He'd have to turn it over to Treadstone and hope they could crack it. Holtzman had a wallet, and Jason found several hundred dollars in cash inside, plus a Visa credit card and a driver's license with the Lomita address, rather than the condo in Long Beach. The IDs both used a different name, not Rod Holtzman.

When Bourne checked the killer's other front pocket, he extracted several pieces of printer paper folded together. He separated them and found a series of articles taken from online magazines, blogs, and newspapers.

When he saw what the articles contained, his face darkened.

"*Abbey*," he called to her sharply.

She was on her way inside the house, but she stopped and turned back. "What is it? Did you find something?"

Not saying a word, Bourne handed her the articles Holtzman had been carrying. A shadow immediately crossed her face, like his. The articles were all profiles—including photographs—of Garrett Parker, the programming whiz kid who jumped to Jumpp and then went out on his own. On one of the pages, the killer had written down an address in Malibu.

This address.

The address where Garrett was living with Abbey Laurent.

"I was wrong," Bourne told her. "You weren't the target. Your husband was."

17

"SOMEONE'S TRYING TO KILL *ME*?"

Garrett Parker got out of the Adirondack chair on the balcony. He left a computer behind on the seat of the chair. He paced back and forth, then went to the railing that looked down on the woods. He stared through fog and darkness toward Highway 1 and the Pacific. His long dark hair was oily and loose, and he wore a feminine silk kimono that barely reached his knees. Bourne had already collected their clothes for the cleaners.

"That's insane," Garrett went on, turning back to Jason and Abbey. "I'm a fucking nerd. Who would send a hit man after me?"

"That's what we need to find out," Bourne told him. He added, "By the way, until we do, I'd suggest you not stand at the railing in the open like that. You're an easy target for anyone with a long gun."

"You're kidding."

"I'm not."

Garrett shook his head. "It's pitch-black out here."

"Night vision," Bourne said. "Thermal scopes. A sniper would have no problem taking you out."

"Jesus." Garrett came and sat down at a glass table next to Abbey, and he gestured at Bourne. "Who is this guy? You were really in love with him?"

"Let's not talk about that now," Abbey said. "Okay? Jason's here to help."

Bourne saw the man shoot him a hostile stare with his dark eyes flashing. He couldn't really blame him. Here was his wife's former lover showing up in the middle of the night and rescuing them from an assassin, then breaking the news that his life was still in danger for reasons unknown. No one was going to react well to that.

He couldn't help but wonder what had drawn Abbey to this man. To Jason, Garrett at twenty-nine years old looked even younger than he really was. He still seemed to be a teenage boy, playing with video games, sneaking weed, and erasing porn sites from his browser history. The long hair. The beard. The tall, gangly frame. Not to mention the ridiculous kimono. He was like Gen Z come to life.

All of which was unfair.

God, I've gotten old, Bourne thought to himself.

In fact, he recognized that there was chemistry between Garrett and Abbey. Emotionally, intellectually, sexually, they fit together. Garrett was young, but also extremely good-looking. Physically, he didn't have Bourne's strength or skills, but he would have made girls swoon in a boy band. He probably made Abbey feel young again, in and out of bed. If he was a nerd, he was also wicked smart. The red wine he was drinking was a high-end Russian River pinot noir, and the screen saver on his computer scrolled through images of Qing dynasty artwork. Garrett Parker was no naive kid.

"The first thing to do is determine what makes you a target," Bourne told him. "Abbey says you used to work for Jumpp."

"For eighteen months. I went out on my own six months ago."

"Where were you before that?"

"An AI start-up. The founder screwed me when he sold the business. I didn't read the fine print on my contract. Dumb. I should have walked away with millions, but instead, I had to start over. I went to a conference on AI tech ethics in Washington two years ago, and Jumpp was there looking for someone to replace their head of AI integration. I signed on."

"Jumpp is a social media software, right?" Bourne asked. "Girls posting dance videos and cat memes? What's the AI connection?"

"Everything these days has an AI connection," Garrett replied with a roll of his eyes. "You remember the Prescix software? Social media that could predict what you were going to do next?"

Bourne and Abbey exchanged a meaningful look.

"Yes, I remember," Jason said.

"Well, AI is like Prescix on steroids. That's what I do, and it's what I did for Jumpp. I develop software that intelligently predicts buying behavior based on social media history and creates individualized marketing pitches based on psycho profiles. Advertisers pay a lot of money for that kind of technology."

"Other people do, too," Bourne said.

"What do you mean?"

"Jumpp is a Chinese company."

"Yeah. So? I worked for their American operation. Do you think I'm some kind of spy? I'm a programmer."

"I realize that." Jason nodded at the laptop screen on the Adirondack chair, which showed a landscape painting by a seventeenth-century Chinese artist named Wang Shimin. "But based on your taste in art, I'm assuming you've spent time in China."

Garrett shrugged. "Yes. I took courses in Asian studies at the University of Puget Sound, and I spent a year in China after college. That's one of the things that made me attractive to Jumpp. I also like Chinese art. I'm not sure what the problem is."

"The problem is, a lot of people think software like Jumpp and TikTok are platforms for Chinese spyware. I think whoever wants you dead is in possession of information that might have been gathered from programs like that."

Garrett reached over and slapped his computer shut. "Come on! I don't have any information on anybody. I write code."

"Which would put you in a position to find—and expose—spyware that the Chinese might want to conceal. Have you seen anything like that?"

"Believe me, you're not the first person to ask. A few months into my new job, I got a subpoena to testify at a congressional hearing. They couldn't talk to my predecessor, so they came after me. I'll tell you what I told them. I'd been over the Jumpp code in minute detail, and I saw no evidence that they were gathering any data other than what was outlined in their privacy policy. Just like every app you use on your phone."

Bourne heard Garrett's voice go up, but the louder and faster he talked, the more Bourne realized that Abbey's husband was lying. He was hiding something. More than that, he was *scared* of something.

"Are you familiar with an app called mygirlnextdoor?" Bourne asked.

Garrett hesitated. "Sure. It's basically an exclusive online escort site. Sort of a high-end OnlyFans thing, right? Rich guys talk to beautiful naked girls? What about it? I don't have an account, if that's what you're asking. Not that I could afford it anyway, but I don't need to go online for sex."

He stroked Abbey's leg as he said this, and she gave Jason an uncomfortable stare.

"My point is, there seems to be a connection between the app and the hacked database I'm looking for," Bourne said. "I just wondered if Jumpp was part of the puzzle somehow."

"I don't know anything about mygirlnextdoor," Garrett insisted.

Bourne didn't say anything for a while. He let Garrett stew, and he watched the man grow increasingly agitated by the silence. Finally, he went on in a calm voice. "Do you understand the situation, Garrett? If I hadn't been here tonight, you and Abbey would both be dead. Is that not clear to you? People don't go through the risk and effort of finding someone like Rod Holtzman unless they are very serious. Somebody has a motive to kill you, and I think you know what it is."

Garrett sprang up from the table. So did Abbey, following him. The two of them went to the balcony railing together, and Bourne didn't bother giving them another warning about snipers. Abbey kissed her husband, the kind of sensual kisses she'd shared with Jason many times. Her hands caressed his face, and then her arms slid around his waist. Bourne hated that it bothered him to think of her with another man—with her *husband*—but it did.

Abbey whispered something in Garrett's ear. Bourne couldn't

hear what she said, but Garrett took a long, slow breath and then returned to where Jason was sitting on the balcony. He put his hands on his hips, which didn't make the kimono look less foolish.

"It's not the first time," Garrett said.

"What?"

"It's not the first time someone has tried to kill me."

Bourne leaned forward. "When did it happen before?"

"Last winter. Long before I met Abbey. A homeless guy came at me with a knife in Seattle near Pioneer Square. I figured he was just whacked-out on drugs, except . . ."

"Except what?"

"Well, afterward the police couldn't find him. I gave them a good description, they did a sketch that was dead-on, and then they canvassed the streets around there. No one recognized him. That's weird. Homeless people know each other, and they all know who's violent, because those are the ones you avoid. This guy wasn't on anyone's radar."

"So you think you were targeted," Bourne said.

"Yeah, I'm pretty sure somebody was sending me a message."

"Who?"

Garrett rubbed a hand nervously across his beard. He sat down again without looking at Bourne. "The thing is, I told my boss at Jumpp what happened. How I was assaulted. He said all the right things, how terrible it was, how scary, maybe I should take a couple days off. But then right after that—right after, the very next thing he said—he told me he'd looked into questions I'd raised about the software. I mean, I talked to him about this months ago, but suddenly that's when he tells me he looked into it? Right after a guy came at me with a knife? He said there was nothing to be concerned about and I shouldn't waste any more of my time. The way he said it, the way he looked at me, I knew it was all connected. I better stop asking questions, because if I didn't, they'd find me in an alley somewhere."

"What questions did you raise?" Bourne asked.

Garrett exhaled loudly. "I told you I testified that there's no spyware in Jumpp. Right? There isn't. I know the code backward and forward. But then something weird happened. I downloaded one of those word puzzle games on my phone. DicTrace. The dictionary race app. Remember, everyone was posting on Jumpp and X about their longest words? It was the hot thing. I'd been using it for a few days, and then for the first time, I posted about it on Jumpp. Right after that, I got a security alert on my computer. You see, I wrote my own security software to make sure I don't get hacked, and the alert warned me that it was blocking a large transfer of data to the cloud. I looked. Sure enough, the firewall had blocked a download of most of my personal and financial data, passwords, credit card records, everything. Without my custom security software, I never even would have known it had happened. So of course I dived in to figure out what caused it."

"Where did the breach come from?"

Abbey's husband shook his head. "I don't know. I couldn't find anything. Not to be arrogant, but if I can't find it, it's got to be AI. Okay? The only thing smarter than me when it comes to coding is a machine that can think faster than me. Somehow I did something that triggered an AI program to come looking for my data, and the only thing I could find that lined up from a timing standpoint was posting on Jumpp about my fucking word puzzle game. There's nothing in the Jumpp code. There's nothing in the puzzle code. But when the apps interacted, they began to behave differently."

"Is it just Jumpp and the puzzle app?" Bourne asked.

Garrett frowned. "That was my question. And no. It always seems to be Jumpp on one side, but dozens of other apps seem to have the same trigger."

"Including mygirlnextdoor," Bourne guessed.

"I don't know for sure, but it wouldn't surprise me."

"And this is what you talked to your boss about?"

Garrett nodded. "I told him what I'd found. I said it looked like somebody was piggybacking on our code for nefarious ends. He said he'd investigate. A couple of months later, homeless guy comes at me with a knife, and that same day, my boss says to stop asking questions. I got the message."

"Did you stop?"

"You bet. I dropped it right then and there. And not long after, I quit and went out on my own."

"Were there any more attempts on your life after that?"

"Not until tonight. That's what I don't understand. I haven't pursued this in months. Why would someone come after me now?"

"They think you can identify them," Bourne concluded.

"But I can't."

"Maybe you can, and you don't realize it."

"So what do I do?" Garrett asked. He looked at Abbey, then back at Bourne. "What do *we* do? I don't like that Abbey is in the middle of this now because of me."

"For now, lay low," Jason told him. "I'll see what I can find out from my end. Is there an alarm system for the house?"

"There is," Abbey replied, "although typically we don't turn it on."

"Turn it on," Bourne told her.

He stood up, and Abbey came over and briefly took his hand. "Thank you, Jason. I mean that."

He nodded at both of them, then headed for the door that led inside the house. But he stopped when Garrett called after him.

"There's one other thing. It may be nothing . . ."

"What is it?" Jason asked.

"When I met the people from Jumpp at that conference in DC," Garrett went on, "they were looking for someone to replace their director of AI integration. Mr. Yuan. He was from China, and he brought a bunch of Chinese programmers over here with him. Most of the foundation of the code came from him and his team, so if there really is an AI time bomb in there, it probably started with Mr. Yuan."

"Okay. How do I find him?"

Garrett shook his head. "That's the thing. You can't. That's why Jumpp was looking for someone new. Mr. Yuan quit the company. In his resignation letter, he said he missed his family, his wife, his two daughters. They were still back in Shanghai. Most people thought the government was essentially holding them hostage to make sure Mr. Yuan did what he was told. Anyway, he left Jumpp and went back to China. His whole team quit right after that. No notice, just up and left. A few weeks later, Mr. Yuan took his family to Huang-shan. The Yellow Mountains. He and his wife went hiking, but they never came back. Later that day, one of his daughters found them in a canyon. Dead."

THE WOMAN MOVED LIKE A CAT THROUGH THE UNDERBRUSH, MAKING NO
sound. She crept to the very fringe of the trees, where a sloping
green lawn surrounded the house. The dense fog had finally lifted,
and her keen eyes could see silhouettes on the balcony, framed by
the bright lights inside. She couldn't see their faces, but she'd been
here in this same place on many nights, observing, analyzing, and
planning.

Two of the people she knew from the outlines of their bodies,
which she'd memorized long ago. Garrett Parker. His wife, Abbey
Laurent.

Now there was also a stranger with them. Who was the stranger?

Their voices murmured above the wind, but she couldn't hear
what they were saying. It didn't matter. All she knew was that Garrett was still alive. Holtzman had failed. All that effort to find him,
and the hit man had been a disappointment.

The stranger. The third man. He had killed Holtzman.

Who was he? How had he even known about the assassin?

But she knew. He was hunting for *her.* Hunting for the Files.

The third man came to the balcony railing above her. She couldn't
see his face, but she could sense in the way he held himself that he
was a formidable threat. There was something in the way he looked
into the darkness that made her think he knew she was there. He
sensed her presence.

Like a cat, she left, melting back into the woods.

When she was finally back in her car a few minutes later, heading south on Highway 1 toward the city, she rolled down the window

and lit a cigarette. She'd made a mistake once, lighting up when she was close to the house. The woman, Abbey Laurent, had smelled it and spotted her. It was ironic, really.

Smoke.

Fire.

Her heart burned as it had all those months ago, but she remained calm and focused. If Holtzman had failed, that was a sign. She'd tried to take the easy way out, but she couldn't be a coward. This was more than a mission. It was a commitment. An obligation. She would fulfill it herself.

Garrett Parker would die at her own hands.

18

BOURNE TURNED OFF HIGHWAY 1 AT THE ROAD LEADING TO EL MATADOR State Beach not far from Abbey's house. He hiked a short trail to the cliffside, where steps led down to a narrow strip of Pacific sand. Shadow waited there, standing just outside the reach of the incoming waves. Her flowing blond hair was tied into a ponytail, and she wore a forest-green Lycra top and jeans, which made her look like an athletic Californian. Her Treadstone security was nowhere to be seen. She was alone.

"Holtzman's dead?" Shadow murmured. "That's very unfortunate. Now we can't interrogate him."

"It couldn't be helped."

Her eyes sharpened like twin knife points. "Yes it could, Jason. Of course it could."

"I wasn't going to let him kill two people."

"You mean, you weren't going to let him kill Abbey Laurent," she snapped.

Jason didn't deny it. "You're right. There's no way I would let that happen. But I would have intervened regardless of who it was. My job was to identify the target, not sit there and watch a hit man take him out. Having Garrett Parker alive makes it easier to figure out why someone wanted him out of the way."

"Maybe so, but with Holtzman dead, whoever has the Files will also know that *we* know about Parker. That may prompt a change in strategy. They'll be more cautious, or they'll move faster to unload the data. That makes our job harder."

"You're right," Bourne agreed.

Shadow turned to face him. Ocean mist made her face glow in the starlight. "I'm concerned that Ms. Laurent is in the middle of this, Jason. You have an emotional attachment to her that's likely to get in the way of the mission."

"If you want me out, fine. Tell me to go."

"But you won't, will you? Not while Abbey is in danger."

Bourne shrugged. They both knew that was true.

"Well, it doesn't matter, because we're too far down the road for me to change horses," Shadow continued. "I don't have the luxury of starting over with a new agent. But keep this interaction professional, Jason. Stay out of Abbey Laurent's life, and needless to say, stay out of her bed, too."

"Abbey and I *were* involved. We're not anymore."

"Just tread carefully," Shadow said. Her eyes softened, which was a rarity. "That's personal advice, too, Jason, not just as your handler. You're vulnerable when it comes to women. Especially her."

"Like I was with you ten years ago?" Bourne said. "When you manipulated me and put me under your microscope for Treadstone?"

Shadow's face showed no expression. She didn't apologize; she never apologized. "Yes, I did manipulate you. So what? That doesn't make me wrong. It means I know you better than just about anyone else. Including Abbey."

"Fuck you," he retorted, annoyed with himself that he let her get to him so readily.

Shadow brushed off his anger. "Are the cleaners almost done?"

"Yes, except three of them weren't cleaners at all. They were Treadstone agents. Did you think I wouldn't notice? What were they doing inside Abbey's house?"

"Searching," Shadow replied. "Garrett Parker was Holtzman's intended victim, so that gives him a connection to the Files. I wasn't going to waste the opportunity to see what we could find out about him."

"And Abbey, too?"

"Of course Abbey, too. She doesn't get a free pass because you had a relationship with her. Abbey was a journalist before she followed in Peter Chancellor's footsteps. For all I know, she's after the Files, just like us. Hasn't it occurred to you that Abbey may have discovered Garrett's involvement on her own? And that she sought out a relationship with him in order to pursue the story?"

"You're out of your mind," Bourne replied.

"I'm not. And you know it."

"You don't want me to trust her. That's the bottom line."

"You're right. You're Treadstone, Cain. Do I need to remind you of the rule? *Trust no one.* Including Abbey."

Bourne took a step backward as the rising tide licked at his boots. "Search all you want. You won't find anything about her. And I assume you weren't able to get your hands on Garrett's computer. He keeps it attached to him like a robotic arm."

"You're wrong. We hacked the local Wi-Fi, and we were able to clone his hard drive. If there's anything there, we'll find it. Meanwhile, what else did you learn from him? What did he tell you?"

Bourne related the information that Garrett had shared, including his history with Jumpp and the possibility that he'd been targeted by killers once before.

"Everything he said makes me think this started out as a Chinese espionage operation," Bourne told her. "Their programmers embedded something inside the Jumpp software that's activated by other apps. When the apps come in contact with each other—like mygirlnextdoor or this word puzzle game—they trigger a secret data dump. It's smart and subtle. And we know the Chinese have been gathering sensitive personal data for years, at least as far back as the OPM hack."

Shadow knelt on the beach, letting the waves pour cold water over her hands. She looked up at Jason with a frown. "That makes sense, but you see the problem, don't you?"

He frowned. "The Chinese aren't acting like they have the Files. Why try to kill Wilson Scott? Or Garrett Parker? If they already have what they want, there's no risk to them. They'd only be worried about shutting them up if the Files were in the open and they were afraid we might get to them first."

"Exactly. It seems like they're part of the race, too. But why? If they built the software, something must have happened. Something went wrong with their scheme. They lost control of the program."

"Maybe somebody hacked the hackers."

"Maybe so."

He thought about what Johanna had told him. *Fifty million dollars. The Files are in play.*

"One person," Bourne suggested. "Not necessarily part of a group or connected to a government. Just someone who's after a lot of money."

"Could one person pull this off?" Shadow asked dubiously.

"Someone with the right expertise could. Maybe we're looking for a programmer at one of the companies who figured out what the Chinese were doing and saw the financial potential of using this data for blackmail. Now this person is concerned that Garrett can expose him. Or her."

"That's a reasonable theory," Shadow agreed. She pushed herself to her feet and stepped away from the water. "The question is *who*."

"Garrett's specialty is AI. That's why Jumpp brought him in. His Chinese predecessor, Mr. Yuan, was an AI pioneer, too. Garrett thinks whatever's going on must have an AI component."

"In other words, we're looking for an AI hacker," Shadow said.

"Right."

"Did Garrett have suggestions? This can't be a large community."

"Not that he told me, but he must know something, whether he's aware of it or not."

"Well, perhaps his hard drive will give us a clue," Shadow said.

Bourne nodded. "In the meantime, I know someone who's part of the AI world and knows it better than we do."

He watched Shadow's face darken.

"You want to bring in Storm."

"It doesn't matter what I *want*," Bourne told her. "Storm—Johanna—is already in. She's looking for the Files, just like we are. Callie Faith wants to get to them first, and she's using Johanna to help her. The fact is, Johanna has a deep background in AI. That's why you recruited her to Treadstone in the first place. She was a lone hacker in Salzburg, years ahead of what was going on in Silicon Valley. She'll have names, contacts, people who may know enough to lead us to the Files."

"If Storm is working for Callie Faith, why would she help us?" Shadow asked.

"Not us. Johanna will help *me*. To double-cross you."

"Naturally." Shadow trained her blue eyes on him again. "And how long have you been keeping this information from me?"

"Until you needed to know," Bourne said.

"That's not how it works. I need to know everything, Jason. Is there anything else you're not telling me?"

He saw Tati's face in his mind as he lied. "No."

"I hope you don't trust Storm. She'll turn on you as soon as the Files are within reach."

"That's a possibility," he admitted.

"I'd say it's a certainty. But for the moment, you're right. We can use her. So do what you have to do."

"Good."

Shadow moved in very close to him on the beach, as if she were daring him to kiss her. Her voice was barely louder than the waves, and it came out with the seductive hiss of a snake. "But remember this, Jason. I'm always watching you. I know Storm is out to get me. I know you saw her in Washington. I know you fucked her at the Hyatt. Don't keep any more secrets from me. No one is indispensable, not even you. If you betray me, I'll have you killed."

Bourne stared back at her, his face unmoving. He knew Shadow didn't make hollow threats. She meant every word.

It made him wonder what would happen when he did betray her.

Because once he got his hands on the Files, he had no intention of delivering them to her.

THE RAT STUDIED TATI WITH MALIGNANT CURIOSITY.

It was big, gray, and hungry. Several times a day, it emerged from somewhere inside the walls and snickered close to her on its little rat feet. If she was awake, it stayed out of reach, practically laughing at her when she kicked out with her leg to drive it away. If she was asleep, she would wake up to find its hungry mouth ready to gnaw on her toes.

"Go," she hissed. "Go, get away!"

She stamped her foot on the cold concrete floor of the wine cellar, but the rat didn't move. Its nose twitched, sniffing the stale air. Maybe it smelled the blood from her bandaged hand. Maybe it was just waiting for her to die. Each day, when the rat came back, she could feel herself weaker and thinner.

My God, Tati thought. *How has my life come to this?*

She'd grown up in luxury among the Moscow oligarchs. Putin had always treated her like a daughter. Some people whispered that she *was* his daughter. But for Putin, blood and history meant nothing compared to loyalty. If she'd kept her mouth shut about the war in Ukraine, she would still be doing her climate research at the university, still taking weekends at the dachas of the rich men who wanted to marry her. But keeping her mouth shut had never been an option for Tati. She always spoke her mind.

"Go!" she whispered to the rat again. "Go, or I swear, when Jason comes for me, I will have him cut off your head!"

But the rat just stared at her, its eyes beady and black. The only thing that scared him off were the footsteps, but that was what scared Tati, too. The footsteps were worse than being naked and cold, worse than starving.

Tati drew up her bare knees and wrapped her arms tightly around them. She had a blanket on her shoulders, but the blanket was thin and small and had holes in it. Its scratchy wool gave her a rash. Her blond hair was dirty, and so was her skin. She knew she smelled almost as bad as the chamber pot on the other side of the cellar. Every day the guards brought her a bucket of freezing water to clean herself, but she could barely stand to do more than pour a little over her privates. And the guards all watched as she did.

How much time had passed? How many days?

She didn't know anymore. There were no windows down here, no light except for a single bulb dangling on a string high above her head. Day could be night, and night could be day. Sometimes she sang to herself to quash her fear; sometimes she counted and re-counted the hundreds of dusty bottles of wine. She'd begun to break them open and drink. The crowns of a dozen bottles lay next to her in the corner, their jagged glass teeth grinning at her like jack-o'-lanterns. Her mind swam in a kind of hazy fog, but being drunk made her numb, and numbness was the only way to survive the footsteps.

"Jason," she murmured aloud, her voice cracking, her soul praying. "Where are you?"

She knew he would come for her. She knew he would save her. She never lost faith. But, oh God, *when*?

What would be left of her when he finally returned?

Thump thump thump came the footsteps outside the cellar door.

By instinct, her skin crawled. She could feel the hands of the guards on her before anyone was even there.

On the other side of the cellar, a key rattled in the lock. She heard the squeal of hinges as the heavy wooden door opened. The rat finally scampered away to hide in the walls. It was no fool; it ran away when the guards came. She wondered who it would be today. Would it be Kirill? Or would it be Mikhail or Lev? They were all bad, but she didn't fear for her life with Mikhail and Lev. They put down the tray of watery potatoes and dry stew and replaced the chamber pot. When they forced her to do things, they came quickly and left quickly.

But Kirill.

Jesus.

Jason! Come back to me!

She looked up in the dim light, and her heart sank to her feet.

It was Kirill.

Six feet tall, bald, huge, his stomach jutting out as if he were pregnant with triplets. His eyes were narrow slits, his beard and mustache dirty with crumbs from his last meal. He wore loose fatigues, and she could see that he was ready for her. He always was. She could already taste him, and it sickened her.

He said nothing. He jerked with his fat thumb to tell her to stand up. When her stiff limbs were slow to obey, he grabbed her by the hair and yanked her to her feet. Her knees struggled to unlock; her legs could barely hold her up. Instinctively, she covered her chest, but he slapped away her arm. His eyes pawed over her, hungering after her puffy nipples, which were like bullets in the cold.

His hand squeezed between her legs, his fingers prodding and invading.

Tears leaked from her eyes, but her tears became diamonds, making her hard as ice. She was done with this. Done with him. She was drunk, and she didn't care what happened to her anymore.

"Kitty, kitty, pretty kitty," Kirill grunted, his breath wafting over her like a sour breeze. "What should we do with kitty today?"

Tati inhaled sharply and spat in his face. He scowled with anger, then hit her across the mouth, drawing blood from her lip. But she barely flinched. The punishment was worth it. She would take no more abuse from this pig. If he wanted her on her knees today, he would have to fight.

"You only make it harder on yourself, you little whore," Kirill growled.

"Don't call me that. I'm a scientist. Whereas you—you have a walnut for a brain. And for a dick, too."

The guard's face screwed up with fury. His body swelled, somehow becoming even larger than it was as he loomed over her. "You want to play with me today, huh? You know Cody says I can do what I want to you. As long as I keep you alive, you're mine. What do you want, bitch? Maybe I cut up that pretty face. No more sexy pictures. Maybe you lose a couple more fingers. Hell, I'd cut out your foul tongue, but I like what you do with it."

Tati shoved against his chest, but she had almost no strength in one hand, and Kirill was like a concrete wall.

"Do what you want to me if you have the balls," she snapped. "But whatever you do, I do twice back to you this time. I swear it."

Kirill laughed.

He laughed so hard he closed his feral eyes and tilted his head toward the ceiling. That was a mistake.

Tati didn't think. She acted without any clue about what she was doing. Her knees bent. She leaned down and swept one of the broken bottlenecks off the floor with her uninjured hand. In one lightning-fast motion, she swung it at Kirill's face. All she wanted to do was scare him. He'd jump back; he'd know not to mess with her after that. But the obese guard never moved. He was too busy laughing; he never saw it coming.

The sharpest points of the glass, like the cones of mountaintops, cut through his throat as if it were made of soft butter.

He staggered back, his eyes wide with disbelief. When he inhaled to swell that huge chest of his, no air came with it. He tried to scream and made no sound. Blood poured out of him, more blood than Tati had ever seen in her life. She couldn't believe what she'd done, the terrible mistake she'd made.

Kirill came for her. He was a wounded bear full of rage and bent on revenge. He staggered toward her, arms outstretched. His insanely strong fingers clamped around her neck and pressed deep into her windpipe. He bled; she choked. The cartilage in her throat weakened. She couldn't breathe, couldn't get away. All she could feel was the world spinning and turning black.

But the bottle was still in her hands. Still razor-sharp.

She swung it at him again and cut off his nose.

And again and he lost an eye.

Kirill finally let go. He stumbled away, his face eviscerated, his one remaining eye wild, practically spinning around with terror. He crashed into one of the racks of wine and toppled like a tree onto his back. His fat chest went up and down, clutching for breath and find-ing nothing, until his body twitched with an enormous spasm and went still.

Tati stared down at the corpse on the floor.

Oh, Jason! Oh my God! Oh fuck, what did I do?

She dropped the bottle, and she ran.

19

I'M ALWAYS WATCHING YOU.

Bourne guessed that Shadow had told him more than she intended. If she'd been watching him in DC, if she'd seen him with Johanna at the Hyatt, then she was still watching him in Los Angeles.

He slept in his hotel room at the Delphi until early afternoon, and after he was awake and showered, he searched the room and quickly located two Treadstone 4K cameras. One was in the hanging light over the desk—the obvious one, intended to make him believe there was no need to search further. The other was carefully hidden in the seam of the curtain. As he took it down, Bourne wondered how far Shadow's obsession with him went and whether she was watching him right now as he got rid of her play toys.

In the hotel lobby, he saw that she also had human intelligence tracking him. A twentysomething Hollywood type—lavender suit, matching glasses—lounged underneath the hanging ferns. He noticed Bourne without seeming to notice him, and Jason saw his lips move as he whispered a radio report.

He's heading out.

Bourne skipped his Highlander that was in a nearby garage. He assumed the SUV was bugged with more GPS devices than he was likely to find. Instead, he walked several blocks to Venice Boulevard, picking up two more tails along the way, then lost them as he crossed the street and hailed a cab in the opposite direction. He switched cabs twice more, and when he was convinced that no one from Treadstone was behind him, he finally took a cab to his true destination, which was MacArthur Park.

Johanna met him there.

They walked side by side next to the lake on Wilshire, in and out of the shadows of the palm trees. The sunshine sparkled, and the day was warm. Johanna took his hand, making them look like lovers. She wore a halter top and shorts over neon-yellow sneakers, and her blond hair was long and loose. Ray-Bans covered her eyes. He assumed she had her gun in the satchel purse slung over her shoulder, and the pouch was unzipped for easy access.

"How's Abbey?" she asked.

"You know about her?"

"I still have sources inside Treadstone. I heard what happened."

"Did you know her husband was the target?"

"I didn't know, but I'm not surprised. Callie Faith turned me on to Garrett as a source about data hacking. She called him in to testify before Congress about spyware after he took the job at Jumpp. So I did research on him. Imagine my surprise to find out he was shacking up with Abbey."

"In other words, you were messing with me when you said you were spying on her. You were actually spying on *him*."

Johanna shrugged. "I like messing with you. Seriously, is Abbey okay? Holtzman didn't hurt her?"

"She's fine."

"White knight to the rescue."

"Something like that."

"Did she leave her husband and swoon in your arms?" Johanna asked.

"Not funny."

"It's a little funny."

"Well, as it happens, she asked if there was anyone in my life. I told her about you."

"Really?" Johanna stopped on the sidewalk and whipped off her Ray-Bans. She was still holding his hand. "Really, you told Abbey about me?"

"I did. Obviously, I didn't give her a name."

"Huh."

"Why are you so surprised?"

"I don't know. I just am."

They kept walking. As he examined the tourists around them and confirmed they weren't under surveillance, Jason heard the song "MacArthur Park" in his head, and he had a strange vision of green icing melting along the curb.

"Shadow knows about us," he said.

"She does? How?"

"She bugged my room at the Hyatt."

Johanna shook her head. "So she got to hear the sex, huh? I'll bet that turned her on. What did you say?"

"I said that I wanted your help. She's okay with it. For now."

"No kidding? Well, look at me, back on the Treadstone team. So what did you learn from Garrett Parker?"

"He thinks the data source for the Files involves some kind of interaction between Jumpp and third-party apps," Bourne said. "Individually, the apps are harmless, but when someone uses both of them, the code goes rogue and starts feeding data to the cloud."

"Interesting approach," Johanna said. "If it's Jumpp, then it must have originated with the Chinese."

"Agreed."

"As hacks go, they can do a lot of damage that way."

"But?" Jason asked, hearing hesitation in her voice.

"But it doesn't really get them what they want," she continued.

"What do you mean?"

"Well, hacking huge amounts of data is like building yourself a haystack when what you really want is the needle. I mean, you might be able to troll a few obvious secrets, but it's not like people put the really juicy stuff where you can readily find it. Do you think Rod Holtzman ever talked about being a hit man on any of his devices?"

"And yet whoever has the Files figured it out."

"Exactly. That's the problem. *How?*"

Johanna leaned on the concrete wall and stared at the lake. She didn't say anything for a long time, and he could see her IT mind putting the pieces together and trying to assemble the puzzle. Then she said out of nowhere, "Somebody leaves a cake out in the rain. Really? What the fuck is that about?"

"I was wondering that, too," Bourne replied with a smile.

He was amused that the song was in her head, as it was in his, and something about her offhanded comment drew him in. The more time he spent with Johanna, the more he realized that he liked her. He didn't trust her, but he liked her. A lot. The attraction between them was complicated, but very real.

She turned back to him. Her eyes were now bright with understanding, as if she'd cracked the code. "I think I know what we're dealing with. It's not the data that matters. The hack is secondary. That's just the source material."

"What do you mean?"

"It's the software we really want. The Files are an AI engine. That's what we're looking for. You can grab all the data you want, but for it to mean anything, you need an engine to analyze it. The data is the car, but we want the motor that drives it."

"Garrett figured there was an AI component. But how does that work?"

"Think about it. A data hack gives you an almost limitless supply of personal information for your haystack. But then you need the sophistication of AI to find the needles. Like Holtzman. Nothing in his data is going to point to him being an assassin, right? But aggregate enough info, and an AI engine can see patterns. People who were killed. Where they were killed. Who was nearby. Where they went, where they ate, who they talked to, where they filled up their cars, where their phones pinged, on and on and on. You or I wouldn't spot those patterns in a thousand years. But AI can analyze all of it, and say, 'Hey, you know what? I think this guy Rod Holtzman kills people for a living.'"

"And that's what we're looking for?" Bourne asked.

"Right. Throw the software on a high-end laptop and you're good to go. The data stays in the cloud, while the engine does the heavy lifting. You can say, 'Give me a hit man in Southern California,' and oingo boingo, it finds Rod Holtzman. Or you can say, 'What secret is Jason Bourne hiding that he doesn't want me to find out?' Let it crank, and a few minutes later, I know what you're not telling me."

Johanna winked, as if she wasn't being serious. But Bourne knew she was.

He realized he had to be very careful with her. She was more than smart enough to ferret out his ulterior motive. He and Tati had both left tracks along the way, and with enough time and enough data, it wouldn't take an AI engine to put them together at a Russian strongman's ranch in Estonia. Johanna could do it on her own if she looked hard enough.

So could Shadow.

"So who do you think has the Files?" Bourne asked, ignoring her unspoken question.

"I have no idea."

"Where do we look?"

Johanna tapped a finger on her pale pink lips. "Did Garrett mention Mr. Yuan?"

"He did. He said Mr. Yuan and his wife died in China."

"Yes, everybody assumes the CCP eliminated them. But if the Files originated with a Chinese scheme, and it's integrated with the coding on Jumpp, then it must have started with Mr. Yuan and his team. They were AI pioneers. They masterminded the hack and developed the AI engine to go along with it."

"And then someone stole it?" Bourne asked.

"Could be."

"But Mr. Yuan is dead. It wasn't him."

"Sure, but I'm betting someone on his team saw what happened to Mr. Yuan and figured they needed an insurance policy in case the Chinese came after them. When they had the Files in their hands, they also realized what kind of a moneymaker it could be."

"Do you know who was on his team?" Bourne asked.

"I know who they are," Johanna said. "Everybody in the AI world does. But they all went into hiding after Mr. Yuan disappeared. I communicated with one of them online when I was in Salzburg. His name's Feng. I only knew him by his online avatar, but I was curious enough to go digging. I thought it might come in handy someday to know where he was."

"Did you find him?"

Johanna looked offended. "Of course I found him. Feng's in San Francisco. But we better move fast. If he's kept an ear to the ground, he knows the Files are out there. Whether he took them or somebody else did, he knows people are going to come looking for him. He'll have a target on his chest."

THEIR FLIGHT LANDED AT SFO IN THE EARLY EVENING.

They took an Uber that dropped them at the intersection of Sacramento and Stockton in the heart of Chinatown. The pointed tower of the Transamerica Pyramid jutted out of the Financial District behind them. Johanna led him along a dark street that smelled of sesame and ginger, and she browsed the windows of jade boutiques and antique stores with a strange familiarity, as if she'd been here before. When she pulled him into a tiny, dimly lit Cantonese restaurant, the owner greeted her with a bow and a hug. She returned the favor with a kiss on his cheek.

They got a table at the far back. Johanna sat down with a kind of reverence, stroking the black lacquer with her palms, as if it were filled with memories. A photo on the wall showed a painting of Chinese mountains buried in mist, and she traced the outline of the frame. The owner brought black tea, and Johanna sipped it slowly, her eyes on Jason.

He waited for an explanation.

"I actually knew Feng pretty well," she admitted finally. "This was our table. We came here a lot."

"Tell me about him."

Johanna studied the Chinese mountains again. Her voice was soft. "He was Mr. Yuan's number two on the AI team. He and I clicked when we talked online, so I came here for a visit a couple of years ago. I ended up staying for four months."

"You lived with him?"

"Does that bother you?"

"I'm just surprised."

"Our brains were wired the same," she said. "He was almost as smart as me. Almost. This was the early days of AI, you know? We spent hours talking about how it would all work, what the applications were, where we saw it going, what the dangers were. Feng was cool. We'd sit in his place coding for days with almost no breaks, just coming down here for tofu once in a while, sometimes hopping in the shower together. It was as close to a real relationship as I'd ever had in my life. At least until you. But Feng started keeping some of his breakthroughs from me. I realized I was doing the same thing, keeping new ideas from him. So we broke up. I went back to Salzburg."

"Did Feng talk about Mr. Yuan and Jumpp? Did he ever give you any hints about the programming behind the Files?"

"Not a word. Once, I asked him about Mr. Yuan—I mean, the guy was a legend—but Feng shut it down. He was scared. He didn't want the Chinese finding him or anyone else on the team."

"Do you think Feng stole the AI engine?" Bourne asked.

"I doubt it. That's not his style."

"I'm surprised he wasn't your first call when you tried to find the Files."

"He was," Johanna admitted. "I used my old contact data, but he went off the grid about six months ago. I haven't been able to reach him. Or maybe he's just ghosting me. The breakup wasn't fun. Anyway, at that point, I had no particular reason to think the Files were connected to Jumpp. There are eighteen million hackers out there who could have been behind this. But with Holtzman going after Garrett Parker, that narrows it down. Mr. Yuan's team is definitely high on the list."

"So let's talk to him," Bourne said.

Johanna looked up as the restaurant owner brought them plates of mapo tofu, eggplant with garlic sauce, and sautéed bok choy. They hadn't ordered anything, but apparently the man remembered Johanna's tastes. She thanked him with an irresistible smile and stood up to give him another kiss on the cheek. When she sat down again, she grabbed a piece of tofu with her chopsticks and leaned over to put it in Jason's mouth.

"First we eat," she said. "Then we find Feng."

They had dinner, and the Chinese food was authentic and delicious. Johanna looked relaxed, almost reverent, as if this place and this neighborhood were sacred to her. She opened up to him about her life, and the details bore no relationship to the story she'd invented when he first met her in Switzerland earlier in the year. She'd grown up outside Dallas, she said, which was where her parents still lived, although she hadn't seen them in years. She'd been introverted. Shy. A prodigy at math and computers, but with no friends. Then, at age fourteen, her math teacher had sexually assaulted her, and after that, she ran away from Texas and never went back. But first, she admitted casually between bites of eggplant, she broke into the teacher's house, tied him face down on his bed, and returned the favor with a toilet plunger.

Bourne remembered the warnings Shadow had given him about Storm. Her capacity for extreme violence and revenge. Her inability to shut down her emotions. Her unpredictable behavior and willingness to defy the mission because she thought she was smarter than everyone else. All of that was true. But Bourne saw many of the same traits in himself. That was part of the attraction between them.

He wondered whether Johanna was being honest about her past this time, or whether this latest story was another lie, another attempt to manipulate him. His stare locked onto this woman, who was so different from Abbey. And so attractive.

Who are you?

After dinner, they climbed the sharp slope of Sacramento Street under the wires of the electric trolley cars. Dozens of homeless people slept under blankets in the doorways, and ragged tents and oversized box shelters dotted the alleys. Half the parked cars on the street had their windows open so thieves wouldn't smash them in the night. Some had handwritten signs taped to their windshields. *Nothing to steal.*

Feng lived three blocks away in a five-story Victorian apartment building on Powell. Cable car tracks lined the street, and the lights of the city made a line of fire down the hill that ended at the black water of the bay. Johanna still had a key to the building's gated front door, and she let them inside. They took the stairs upward, guns in hand. Between the second and third floors, they had to squeeze sideways to allow a twentysomething Chinese kid to pass them on his way down the stairs. He had spiky black hair and red glasses, and he wore a baggy white T-shirt over khakis. The kid didn't look at them; he was too busy playing a game on his phone.

They'd climbed to the next floor when Bourne stopped Johanna with a hand on her arm.

"What is it?" she asked.

Bourne frowned. "That kid on the stairs. I know him."

"How?"

"I'm not sure."

"All Asian people look alike to you?" Johanna asked with a smirk.

Jason winced at the joke. Then he closed his eyes. *Think!*

He did know that kid from somewhere. He'd seen him recently, just a passing glance. But it was him.

Or was Johanna right and his brain was blending Asian faces together?

He pictured the kid in his mind—the hair, the red glasses—and he had an impression of that same young man sitting down. Across a street. Behind a window. Jason remembered his eyes sweeping over him, registering who he was, but ignoring him because he didn't seem to be a threat.

Where? Where was it?

Then, with a rush, his brain put the pieces together.

Jesus!

That same twentysomething kid had been sitting in a coffee shop across the street from Rod Holtzman's condo in Long Beach. And now he was coming down the stairs *from Feng's apartment*!

Bourne spun, his Glock still in his hand. Without a word to Johanna, he charged down the building stairs and out to the sidewalk on Powell Street. He looked both ways, seeing no one. The kid was already gone. But an instant later, gunfire erupted, shattering the windows on the ground-floor apartment and forcing Jason to throw himself to the ground. He isolated the source of the fire, between two parked cars halfway down the block. He waited until a passing taxi gave him cover, and then he scrambled to his feet and dashed across Powell.

Footsteps pounded. Ahead of him, the Chinese kid sprinted toward the base of the hill, his pace like the wind. Bourne fired and missed, and the kid fired backward over his shoulder, the bullet going high and wild. Jason followed, running downhill, watching the man dash diagonally across the street at Clay and disappear from view. He reached the intersection a few seconds later, but the kid had already vanished. Bourne listened, hearing nothing. The street was quiet, and he saw only the bright skyscrapers ahead of him, their towers capped by fog. He crossed carefully, staying low, but when he followed Clay all the way to the next street, he saw no more evidence of where the kid had gone.

He'd lost him.

Bourne retraced his steps to the apartment building and climbed to the top floor. The door to Feng's apartment was open, the lights on. The one-bedroom unit smelled of sandalwood incense mixed with the acrid bite of gunpowder. Johanna sat in a lotus position on the worn yellow rug, her lips pushed together in a sad, tight frown, tears running down her face from her wide blue eyes.

Next to her was the body of a Chinese man in his thirties, sprawled on his back with a bullet hole in the middle of his forehead.

20

"I'M SORRY ABOUT FENG," JASON SAID.

Johanna shrugged, pretending not to care. "I don't even know why I'm so upset. I hadn't talked to him in ages, and we weren't really together that long. But I have good memories of him. And this place."

Bourne said nothing. He knew the power of memories better than anyone.

"I lost the kid," he told her. "But I saw him outside Holtzman's building. He's an assassin."

"So the Chinese are closing in on the Files, too," Johanna murmured. She held up her hand, and Jason helped her to her feet. She rubbed the tears away from her face. "They must have guessed that someone from Mr. Yuan's team stole the Files. I'm sure they're hunting for all of them. But why would they be surveilling Holtzman? How would they even know about him?"

Those were good questions, but Jason had already guessed the truth. The Chinese had infiltrated the mygirlnextdoor app as part of their data hack, which meant they were either working with Cody or spying on his operation. One way or another, they'd learned about the hit man and the blackmail. So they'd been planning to track Holtzman to his target, just like Bourne.

But Bourne couldn't mention any of this without telling her the rest of the story.

"Holtzman was in the Files," Bourne said. "I'm sure the Chinese have had him on their radar for a while. They may be watching some key needles in the haystack to see if anyone goes after them for extortion."

"Maybe." Johanna frowned. "Or maybe you're still hiding something from me."

Jason hesitated. He almost told her about Tati. He *wanted* to tell her about Tati. Johanna was skilled in the field, and he might need an ally when it came to the final confrontation with Cody. But he also remembered Shadow's warning.

She'll turn on you as soon as the Files are within reach.

"I'm not hiding anything," Jason lied.

The look on her face made it clear she didn't believe him. Her voice turned dark as she stared at the body on the floor.

"Well, Feng can't tell us who grabbed the software. The kid made sure of that." She looked around the small apartment, which had been thoroughly searched. Cushions and pillows knifed open, stuffing pulled out, cabinets emptied, boxes strewn across the floor, drawers overturned. "But it looks like Feng didn't tell the Chinese anything, either."

"Do you think Feng had the Files?" Bourne asked.

Johanna shook her head. "No. He really was off the grid. Look around. No computers, no devices, no charging cables, no nothing.

You're probably right that the Chinese have been watching multiple targets. My bet is they've known where Feng was for a while and wanted to see if he made a move or reached out to the others. But if the kid saw you at Holtzman's place, then they must know we've identified Garrett. He ties the Files to Mr. Yuan and Jumpp. So the Chinese can't be patient anymore. They're going after the whole AI team."

"Would Feng have been in contact with the others?"

"Probably. I got the feeling they were all close. They might have had back doors or some other low-tech way to exchange messages. But we're not likely to crack that. Meanwhile, if we can't find them, the Chinese will start picking them off one by one."

"So who are they?" Bourne asked.

Johanna kept looking around the apartment, as if she'd missed something. "There were five of them, plus Mr. Yuan. Feng was second in command, and then four others, three men, one woman. Lee, Bai, Haoyu, and Caiji. All single, no family in the U.S."

"And they quit at the same time?"

"Yes, they walked out together. They must have been planning it for a while. They left the company and disappeared. As far as I can tell, they never even went home. They must have known the Chinese would be after them."

"Were there any rumors about why they left?"

"Plenty, but it was mostly people blowing smoke. Nobody knew anything. My guess is they saw what the government planned to do with the AI engine they'd built, and they didn't like it. But Mr. Yuan was the only one who went public about leaving. He sent his resignation letter to the *Wall Street Journal*, talked about spending too much time away from his wife and daughters, wanting to go home.

He said the usual shit about being proud of his work, proud of his people, proud of Jumpp. I don't know, maybe he figured that would keep him and his team safe. He was wrong."

"How did you find Feng?" Bourne asked.

Johanna looked around the apartment again, her brow furrowing.

"Actually, he found me. I was doing some pretty cool AI shit on the dark web. I wasn't too particular about who I sold it to, and some bad people got their hands on it. That's why Shadow found me and brought me to Treadstone, remember? Anyway, I got an email one day in Salzburg from some anonymous avatar. He'd tracked me down, which I didn't like to begin with. Then he pointed out some errors in my code, which I didn't like even more. He said I should be careful because the errors might give Interpol a way to find me. It pissed me off, but it told me the guy was sharp. I followed a long trail of generic accounts and finally connected his IP address to this building in San Francisco. From there, it was pretty easy to figure out I was talking to Feng. That was pretty cool. In my world, the whole Jumpp team was legendary. I didn't tell Feng I was coming. I just showed up."

Her eyes shifted to the body at her feet again.

"Fucking CCP."

She shoved her hands in her pockets and examined all of the apartment's walls, which were mostly empty and painted in a drab shade of beige. She shifted to the small bedroom and did the same thing. Bourne followed, noting the disarray everywhere. The search had been thorough.

Johanna went to an empty hook on the wall and pinched it between her fingers.

"What are you looking for?" he asked.

"Feng kept a framed photo of the whole team in the bedroom. It was from the cover of *Wired*. That was the only thing he seemed to keep from his past. But now I don't see it. No way he would have gotten rid of it. Those people meant too much to him."

Jason checked the floor. He noticed a sprinkling of glass shards near the side of the twin bed, and when he crouched down, he found a large wooden picture frame with a few glass fragments clinging to the edges. The matte had been torn from the back, revealing half of a pencil sketch of Chinese mountains.

"Was this the frame?" he asked.

Johanna nodded. "That was it."

"No magazine cover."

"No. That's Huangshan, where Mr. Yuan and his wife were killed."

"So what happened to the *Wired* cover?" Bourne asked. "Did the kid find it? Was it hidden behind the sketch?"

"No, Feng wouldn't have made it that obvious. Hiding the photo like that, that's amateur shit. He replaced the cover with something else, something that would have meaning to anyone on the team. Or to me, I guess. I wonder if my messages really made it to him, and he knew I'd be coming to see him eventually. He wanted me to remember what used to be in that frame in case something like this happened."

Jason frowned. "Why?"

"To make sure I went looking for it," Johanna said.

Then her eyes widened. "Oh, shit, shit, shit."

She bolted from the apartment. Jason ran to catch up with her, slamming the door shut behind them. They went down the stairs and out to the street, and Johanna fast-walked down the Sacramento hill. It was dark and quiet. They made it back to Stockton, where most of the shops and restaurants were closed now. Johanna hurried halfway down the block to the Cantonese restaurant where they'd had dinner, and she peered through the window. The door was locked, but they could still see the owner inside.

Johanna banged on the glass. He looked up with surprise, but he came and let them in, asking no questions. Jason followed Johanna to the back of the restaurant and the table they'd been sitting at an hour earlier. She reached to the wall with both hands and removed the painting that was hung there. It was a watercolor of the same mountains, made by a different artist.

"Huangshan," she said.

She turned the painting over, undid the clips that held the cardboard matte in place, and removed the backing. Inside, tucked behind the artwork, was a folded piece of glossy paper. When Johanna unfolded it and spread it on the table, Bourne saw a cover of *Wired* magazine from several years earlier. The photo had been taken in what was obviously Mr. Yuan's office at Jumpp. He could see coding books on the shelves, Chinese artwork adorning the man's walls, and a large family photo on his desk of Yuan's pretty wife and daughters. Mr. Yuan himself sat behind his desk, with five people on either side of his leather office chair.

His team.

"Oh, fuck," Johanna murmured.

Bourne knew what she was looking at. Every face in the magazine photograph had a large X drawn across it in black marker. Every face except Feng's. Mr. Yuan. Lee. Bai. Haoyu. Caiji.

All gone. All dead.

"Feng wasn't the first," Bourne said. "He was the last. The Chinese already found the others."

Johanna neatly folded the glossy paper again. She took out her wallet and carefully hid it inside. Her hands came together in front of her lips, as if she were praying. "Which means somebody else has the Files."

ABBEY SLIPPED OFF HER ROBE, HER BODY STILL DAMP FROM THE SHOWER. She slid into bed in the darkness beside Garrett. It was two in the morning, which was a time when she would usually be writing, but she found her nerves too frayed to think. She knew she wouldn't sleep, either. She couldn't keep her mind off the events of the previous night.

The close call she'd had with a killer.

The knowledge that someone wanted her husband dead.

And—she couldn't deny it—the return of Jason to her life.

She listened to Garrett's breathing next to her, and she turned her head on the pillow to watch him. He lay on his back atop the blanket, naked, barely visible with the lights off and the curtains closed.

"Are you awake?" she whispered.

He replied in a soft voice a moment later. "Yes."

"Can't sleep?"

"No."

"Me neither."

They were quiet for a while. Her fingers snaked over and held his hand. Then Garrett said, "Can I ask you something?"

"Sure."

"Are you still in love with him?"

Abbey knew he meant Jason. "No. I'm not."

"You don't have to lie, you know. If you are, you are. Don't tell me what you think I want to hear."

She propped herself on one elbow. "I *was* in love with him. Deeply. But that was the past. I couldn't live in his world, and he could never leave it behind. So we both moved on."

"Except now he's back."

"Yes, he's back, and he brought his world with him," Abbey said. "It reminds me how much I hate that world. It's dangerous. Violent. Dark. And Jason, he—he fits so well inside it. I can't be with someone who lives that way. Even if I once loved him."

"What about him? How does he feel?"

"He feels the same way. He told me he has someone new in his life. Someone who's more like him."

"If you say so."

But she could hear the doubt in his voice. She had to show him, not tell him. She came closer, molding her body against his. Her lips kissed his face. Her hand slipped between his legs and had no trouble arousing him. When she could tell that he was ready, she rose up and mounted him, feeling him slide easily inside her. They made love in the darkness, unable to see each other, but she could hear the catch of his breath and knew he was close. She pushed down hard, she squeezed, and she felt him give way in bursts of warmth. Her own body didn't respond, but this time was for him, not her. Slowly, she sank forward, embracing him and kissing him. Then eventually she slid herself free and stretched out beside him. She held him as he fell asleep, and then she turned over and closed her eyes.

Not long after, she finally drifted to sleep, too.

And then—how long was it?—she bolted awake.

Her body rippled with fear. She'd been dreaming. What was it? She had the sensation that Jason had been in her arms, but she was alone. She'd heard something. Was it part of the dream?

Abbey reached over in bed and realized that it was empty. Garrett was gone. She glanced at the alarm panel on the wall, which glowed green, and she swore at herself. In the passion of sex, she'd forgotten Jason's instructions and failed to switch on the alarm system.

Now she heard something outside. A shout. A struggle.

"Garrett!"

She got no answer.

Sleep fled. Abbey was wide-awake. In the darkness, she felt for her nightstand, and she yanked open the door and gathered her CZ P-01 9mm into her hand. With a smooth jolt, she racked the slide and scrambled out of bed.

Another shout. It came from the balcony. She heard the thud of something heavy hitting the wall. Cold air rippled across her naked skin, and she realized that the bedroom curtains were parted and the balcony door had been swept open. She ran out onto the sprawling, multilevel deck, and the wooden beams under her bare feet were slick with dew. Both arms outstretched, both hands on the pistol, she swung in each direction.

There they were. Two of them.

A body in black. Thin, tall, strong.

And Garrett, unconscious, being dragged down the stairs.

"Stop!" Abbey screamed.

She aimed the pistol high and shot off a round. The person in black—was it a woman?—seemed to see her for the first time. Something flashed in her hand, something glinted in the stars. It was a blade aimed at Garrett's throat. Abbey fired again, closer this time, and the woman dropped the body she had by the shoulders and ran, footfalls pounding down to the bottom of the deck. She disappeared into the trees toward Highway 1.

Abbey ran down the steps. She found Garrett on his back, his eyes closed. In the dim light, she could see him, could make out his face and beard, the bare skin of the man she'd made love to only minutes earlier.

Blood poured from her husband's head.

21

THE DEVELOPED LAND ON I-15 ENDED A FEW MILES SOUTH OF THE HEART
of Las Vegas. One last collection of cookie-cutter houses and clay roofs
baked in the sun, and beyond them, the scrub mountains took over
again like a moonscape. Johanna pulled off the highway on the motorcycle she'd rented at McCarran. She stripped off her helmet, letting her blond hair hang free, and drank from the bottle of water clipped
to her belt. A barren hill rose behind her, low brush clinging to dirt and
stone. To the north, she could see the towers of the Strip through smoggy
brown haze. Cars flashed by her on their way back to California.

Johanna hiked to a barbed-wire fence strung along the base of
the rocky slope. She was alone out here in the middle of nothingness, and the empty desert reflected the emptiness in her heart. It
bothered her. She'd spent her life shutting down anything that made
her vulnerable, and yet here she was, obsessing over Jason. Yesterday
she'd been caught up in the adrenaline of working with him again.
Sleeping with him again. God, they were good together.

But Jason was also the most dangerous man she'd ever met.

She couldn't lie to herself. She needed him. She *loved* him. She hated that he was on his way back to Los Angeles without her.

On his way back to Abbey Laurent.

Jason had sworn his relationship with Abbey was over. She wondered if that was really true. Months earlier, before he knew who Johanna was, before they'd become involved, he'd told her about Abbey. She knew he hadn't gotten over her. It was written all over his face. Now that they'd been thrown back together, it seemed impossible that they could stay apart. Johanna tried to keep the images out of her brain, but they assaulted her anyway. Jason in Abbey's arms. Jason in Abbey's bed. Her jealousy burned as hot as the desert sun. She wondered what she would do if she ever found herself face-to-face with Abbey Laurent. The two of them. Alone.

Could she stop herself from pulling the long dagger from her pocket and burying the blade in Abbey's chest?

Johanna shivered.

Behind her, she heard a car engine pulling off the highway. She took a breath, calming herself. Her skin was dry and red from the heat. She didn't need to look back to know who it was. The car engine cut off, but the door didn't open. Johanna turned around and studied the smoked windows of the silver Mercedes. Then she walked over to the passenger door and climbed inside.

Callie Faith sat behind the wheel, expensive pink sunglasses over her eyes. The stony line of her jaw revealed her impatience.

"Well?" Callie asked.

Johanna chose her words carefully. She assumed Callie was recording her. If push came to shove, and the congressional hearings began, Callie would throw her under the bus and see her rot for the rest of her life in a federal prison.

"The Files are a Chinese AI engine combined with an ongoing data hack driven by multiple apps," she said. "I know that much."

"I don't care where they came *from*," Callie snapped. "I want to know who *has* them."

"Bourne and I tracked down a programmer who was probably one of the lead coders in creating the Files. But the Chinese got to him first. He's dead. So are the other members of his team. I assumed that one of them would have been putting the Files on the market, but if it's not them, then I don't know who it is."

Callie clucked her tongue in disgust. "Do you think the Chinese know?"

"That's the good news. I doubt it. Or if they do, they don't know where the person is. If they did, they'd already have the Files."

"What about Bourne?"

"He's following up on Garrett Parker. Whoever has the Files wants him dead, and we want to know why. If we can figure that out, it should give us what we need to identify him. Then we move in."

"Or Bourne moves in on his own," Callie said. "He grabs the Files and gives them to Shadow, and you and I get fucked."

Johanna wanted to say: *I trust him.*

But she couldn't. Because she didn't. Just like he didn't trust her. Bourne had his own agenda in this hunt, and he was keeping the truth from her.

Why won't you tell me what's going on, Jason?

"You don't need to worry about Bourne," Johanna told Callie, despite her own misgivings. "I'll keep him close. When we know who we're going after, I'll get there first. Ahead of Treadstone, ahead of the Chinese, ahead of everybody. I told you I'd deliver, and I will."

Callie's fingers tightened around the steering wheel. "No."

Johanna's brow furrowed. "No? What does that mean?"

"No, that's not how we're going to play this. I let you run with Bourne because you said you could control him. I don't think you can. All we're doing is giving Shadow's agent a head start, and I won't take the risk of letting her win. Plus, we're running out of time. If the Files hit the open market, we have no idea in whose hands they'll end up. We need to act now before that happens."

"Then what do you suggest?"

"We do it my way," Callie snapped.

"Which is?"

"We make a deal. Whoever has the Files reached out to me. I say we give him what he wants."

Johanna heard the steel in Callie's voice. "I know you want action, and you're right, we need to move quickly. But this is a mistake."

"Why?"

"Because we don't know who we're dealing with. There's too much risk of it blowing up in our faces, even assuming the contact really did come from whoever has the Files. You have no idea who reached out to you. This whole thing could be a fake."

"It's not."

"How do you know that?"

"This person has information that couldn't come from anywhere else," Callie said.

"What kind of information?" Johanna studied the flush on the congresswoman's face. "Information about you?"

"That's not your concern."

"Is he threatening to expose you?"

Callie ignored her. "The bottom line is, I hired you to get the Files yourself, and you failed. You struck out. I can't give you any more time, not when there's an offer on the table right now. We do a deal."

Johanna raised her eyebrows. "The offer was for fifty million dollars. Do you have that kind of money lying around? Because if so, I'm raising my fee."

"Of course I don't."

"Then what's your plan? Can you redirect money from the intelligence budget?"

"In the past? Maybe. Not now. Shadow's watching the pipeline. If I go after the money, she'll know."

"So what do you want to do?" Johanna asked.

"We lie. We pretend we've got the money, and we set up the drop."

"The person behind this isn't a fool. Whoever it is will want to know how you did it. He'll want proof you can really make the transfer."

"Proof can be faked. *You* can fake it."

"Let's say you're right. We make them believe we can deliver the money. What then? What happens at the drop?"

Callie's head turned. Her brown eyes zeroed in on Johanna. She reached into her purse and took out her phone. With a cold smile, she switched off the voice recording she'd been making, and she deleted the file in a way that Johanna could see it.

"Then you grab the laptop and kill the bastard."

TATI AWOKE IN A HUGE WHITE FEATHERBED, SO PLUSH AND COMFORTABLE she felt as if she were floating inside a cloud. At first, she thought she was still dreaming. During the nights inside Cody's house, she'd escaped with Jason in her mind whenever she fell asleep. He'd come for her, and they'd run away together. She'd imagined the two of them speeding down a highway. Then she would wake up, and the gruesome reality of her situation would catch up with her. The rats. The guards. The fear of what lay ahead.

But not now.

Now she was free.

She got out of bed. Her room was located in the attic of a farmhouse, twenty miles from Cody and Narva. She wore cotton pajamas, soft and warm, which Frau Mikkel had given her. When she went to the attic window, she looked out on wide-open land, not a soul to be seen in any direction, just two horses exploring the snow-covered field inside the fence and a dozen pigs gathered for breakfast at the trough. As she watched, Herr Mikkel and his oldest son emerged from the horse barn. The two men crossed the field side by side, leaving their footprints behind them. The father's instincts must have told him she was there, because he glanced over his shoulder and waved at her in the high window, his plump face breaking into a kind smile. Next to him, Jan, twenty-three years old, did the same.

Tati waved back.

She couldn't believe how lucky she'd been. By all rights, she should be dead, frozen on the hard Estonian land somewhere. Or back in the hole of Cody's basement. When she'd panicked, seeing Kirill's body on the floor of the wine cellar, she'd fled the mansion with no clothes, no food, and no idea where to go. She'd run through the snow, her white skin growing even whiter as the frigid wind assaulted her. In minutes, her limbs stiffened, her feet growing numb from the snow, her fingers curling up like claws. But still she'd run and run, until Cody's estate disappeared behind her and she couldn't see it anymore. She'd run until her legs could take her no farther, and then she sank to the ground like a mannequin on the shoulder of a rural road that came from nowhere and went nowhere.

That was where the Mikkels had found her.

Friedrich Mikkel, heavy and happy, fifty years old. His wife, Berthe, forty-seven. Their four children, all boys. Jan was twenty-three, James twenty-one, Gerd twenty, and Franken just eighteen. The entire family had been stuffed into a tiny Škoda on their way back from a monthly journey for farm supplies, when they spotted the naked blond woman on the side of the road, frostbitten and unable to speak.

They rescued her. They took her home.

Fortunately, Tati had recovered enough in the warm car to beg them not to call a doctor and, most of all, *not* to call the police. If anyone knew where she was, she warned them, men would come to get her back. All she needed was a couple of days to rest and recover, followed by a quiet, anonymous drive in the trunk of their car to the Baltic coast. When she got there, she could finally escape the country—to Finland, or Denmark, or Sweden—and find a way to make contact with Jason. This chapter of her life would be over.

That had been two days ago. Two days of freedom, food, warmth, and laughter with a family that was generous and happy. Tati felt like herself again, her strength slowly coming back, her wounds healing. Today Herr Mikkel would take her to the ferry in Tallinn, and she would put away the nightmare of the past year. It didn't matter where she went, as long as it was far away.

Jason!

She had to find Jason.

Tati left the attic bedroom. She went down a narrow flight of stairs to a guest bathroom, where she stripped and showered. There was plenty of hot water. She stayed under the spray until her skin was pink, and she washed her hair twice. Ever since she'd come here, she'd washed her hair over and over, trying to lather away the smell of the wine cellar. But nothing got rid of it; nothing removed the terrible stench. She realized the smell was stuck in her brain, not her nose.

After drying herself with a thick towel, she wrapped it around her skinny body. As she returned to the attic, she found herself whistling, which she hadn't done in a long time. She was hungry, too. Downstairs, she smelled bacon. Her appetite had come back; she'd been starved in Cody's basement, and now she wanted to eat until she couldn't eat anything more. First, she'd have a big breakfast. Then she would say goodbye to Estonia.

Tati changed into fresh clothes. Berthe Mikkel was heavier than her, and shorter, so the clothes she'd given her didn't really fit. But Tati didn't care about that. She put on a loose sweatshirt that barely reached her waist, and she zipped up jeans and tied a belt as tight as it would go to keep them up. She looked around the cozy little room with the angled timbers, wanting to remember it forever. The red paint. The fresh flowers. The heavy duvet that had kept her warm.

She went back to the window to memorize the view.

It took her a moment, looking at the farm below her, to realize that something was different. Something was wrong.

Everyone—everything—had fallen down in the snow. To Tati, it looked as if some strange sleeping curse had rolled across the world.

The horses.

The pigs.

Herr Mikkel.

His son.

They all lay on the ground now. Then she looked closer. Where the bodies lay, the snow had turned red, like cherry slushies spilled around their heads. The color of blood. Tati's hand flew to her mouth. Her chest gagged with horror. They were all dead. The animals, the people. Shot. Killed.

She ran.

Below her, in the second-floor hallway, she came across Berthe's body first, three bullet holes in her back. Tati leaped over her and took the next set of stairs two at a time. In the ground-floor hallway, she found James, his throat cut like a grotesque smile, his blue eyes still open and wide with disbelief. A few feet behind him, there was Gerd, face down, not moving. Tati opened her mouth, but the scream that came out made no sound. She couldn't even drag the air out of her lungs.

Like a corpse, like a woman already dead, she shuffled toward the kitchen. They knew she was here; they were waiting for her. She came to the doorway, where the bacon was burning on the stove, smoke flowing from the pan.

"I'll have some of that bacon," Cody said when he saw her. "Get it for me, my love."

Tati complied without a word. She went and got a plate from the cupboard and tipped the blackened bacon onto it along with the grease, and put down the plate in front of Cody. He sat at the head of the table, where Herr Mikkel usually sat. His monster's body filled the chair. A heavy oilskin coat, drenched with blood, covered his huge torso. His dirty hair hung below his shoulders, thick and black. His pirate beard came to a point below his chin, and a devil's smile tipped up his mustache.

Half a dozen men stood around him, some with automatic rifles, some with pistols and suppressors, all of them pointed at her. But the worst of the scene was the kitchen table itself. Stretched across the large butcher block table was Franken Mikkel, the last of the family still alive. The teenager was tied spread-eagle to the four table legs, wearing nothing but old white underwear. His mouth was tightly gagged, muffled shrieks wailing from his throat. Franken squirmed and struggled, the smell of his body foul with fear. His eyes had the wild knowledge of everything that had already happened and everything that was about to happen.

Tears slipped quietly down Tati's face.

"Let him go, Cody," she murmured. "Show some mercy. He's a boy. Kill me instead."

"Kill you, Tati?" Cody retorted, chewing on the bacon, his voice booming. "No, no, no, I can't do that. You're my golden goose. Cain expects you to be alive. He needs an incentive to bring me what I want."

Tati stared at Franken. This poor, desperate boy. Every spark of life had drained out of her, leaving her voice sullen and lost. Her freedom had been snatched away, and her recklessness had killed the people who'd tried to save her.

"Then take me with you. I'll do whatever you want. Anything. Just let the boy live."

"You defied me, Tati," Cody replied calmly. "Defiance has a price."

Her eyes closed. She steeled herself for whatever he would inflict upon her now. For the pain that was coming. Nothing mattered anymore.

Oh God, Jason!

She would kill herself. That was her only way to escape now. When she was back at the mansion, locked in the wine cellar again, she would take one of the broken bottles and slit her wrists until she bled out. But it was as if Cody could read her mind and know what she was thinking.

"Kill yourself, and the boy dies," he went on in a silken voice. "Be a good girl, and he lives. You have my word."

Tati's eyes flew open again. "Oh my God! Thank you!"

"No more escape attempts?"

"No!"

"You'll be good? You'll do *everything* I say?"

"I will!"

"Excellent." The huge man's face hardened, becoming a mask of ice. "But I told you, Tati. Defiance has a price. It carries a debt that must be paid. If not by you, then by someone else."

Cody dug in one of his coat pockets. His hand emerged with a red-handled pair of farm shears, their silver blades long and sharp. Tati's relief vanished, and a wail of horrified anticipation burst from her throat. She couldn't take the agony. Not again. She wanted to run, scream, find a high building and throw herself to the ground.

But as bad as it already was, it got worse. So much worse.

Cody snapped his fingers. A guard came forward. He didn't go to Tati but to Franken. To the teenage boy tied to the table. The guard yanked the boy's underwear to his thighs, exposing him.

"You promised to do whatever I say," Cody reminded her. "It's time to prove you meant that."

He slapped the shears into Tati's hand, and he closed her fingers around the handles with his crushing grip. "You need to show Cain that my patience is running out. Show him what happens to those who get in my way."

22

"HOW IS GARRETT?" JASON ASKED.

Abbey sat on the brick hearth in front of the crackling flames of the fireplace. The Malibu house was cold, but the fire gave the room a semicircle of warmth. She took a sip of white wine, and her red hair fell across her face as she looked down. She didn't look at him. She'd barely looked at him at all since he arrived.

It was late. Dark. No light came through the windows. He'd waited for hours for her to get back from the hospital.

"So far, the doctors say there are no signs of a concussion," she told him, her voice flat. "No brain swelling. But they want to keep him for another night. I can pick him up tomorrow."

"I'm glad he's okay."

Abbey put down her wineglass. Her fists tightened, and her voice sounded choked. "You're glad he's *okay*? He's not okay. Neither am I. For God's sake, Jason, someone tried to kill my husband. *Again.* Can't you leave me alone? Can't you stop dragging me into your life? I can't take this anymore."

If she'd shot him, she couldn't have wounded him more deeply.

"Abbey," he murmured, trying to figure out what he could say. "The last thing I would ever want is to see you hurt. Or someone you love. You know that. If you want me to go, I'll go."

She got to her feet, and a long sigh breathed from her throat. "No. I don't want you to go. I sure as hell would never trust anyone else from fucking Treadstone. You didn't bring this with you, and whatever is going on, it would be happening whether you were here or not. But you have to understand how I feel, Jason. Nothing ever changes between you and me. Whenever I think I'm free, I'm not. Sooner or later, this latest thing is going to be over. And when it is—it kills me to say this, but I have to—I never want to see you again."

Bourne kept every emotion off his face.

"Don't think I blame you for that," he said. "Because I don't. You're smart. And you have my word. Next time I go, I'm gone for good."

She turned her back on him and stared at the fire. "So what do you want now?"

"Tell me about the person who assaulted Garrett."

Abbey shrugged. "I can't tell you much. It was dark. I think—I *think*—it was a woman. I'm not one hundred percent sure, but the physique didn't look right for a man. Regardless, man or woman, she was really fit. Strong. I mean, I know Garrett's not a big guy, but she had the drop on him. He said he heard something and went outside to check. Stupid."

"He was trying to protect you."

Abbey turned around again, her arms folded over her chest. "It wasn't this girl of yours, right? The one with no name? I mean, from what you say, she sure as hell could do it. And she doesn't like me."

"It's not her."

"You're sure?"

"I'm sure."

"Then who, Jason? Who's doing this?"

He shook his head. "I don't know yet. Right now, the first thing I'd like to know is *why* Garrett's a target. If the person who has the Files is behind this—if she's coming after him herself after Holtzman failed—then Garrett must know something that she's determined to hide. The most obvious thing is that he knows who she is, whether he realizes it or not."

"Garrett already told you everything he knows," Abbey said.

"Did he?"

"He told you about Jumpp and Mr. Yuan. It sounds like that's where all of this started."

"Except we think Mr. Yuan and his team are all dead. So there has to be someone else."

"If he knew, he'd tell you."

"Well, I need to talk to him again," Bourne said. "Tomorrow. When he's out of the hospital. I need to go through his life piece by piece, Abbey. Somewhere in there is a detail we've missed. He knows something. Or he knows *someone*. None of this is happening by accident."

Abbey finished her wine. She put the glass down on the hearth. "No."

"Excuse me?"

"No, you can't talk to him. I won't let you."

"Abbey, I'm trying to figure out who wants him dead."

"Then talk to someone else. Figure it out. You're good at that. But I don't want you anywhere near Garrett. He's jealous of you. He doesn't like you. He doesn't need you badgering him while he's trying to recover from getting smashed in the head. Don't you get it, Jason? Garrett's my husband. I may have rushed into it, and yeah, maybe part of me was on the rebound from you when I did it. But I'm married. I have to put him first. Are we clear about that? Stay away from him."

Jason stared at Abbey in the shadows. She'd always been strong, but she had a reservoir of determination now that made her even more attractive. His feelings for her hadn't died. They were embers that could be coaxed back to life with a breath of air. But he couldn't let that happen. The best thing he could do for Abbey was find the Files.

And then leave her alone.

"Fine," he said. "Whatever you want."

"Jason, look, I'm sorry—"

"No, you're right. Garrett's off-limits. But I still need information about him. Tell me who to talk to."

Abbey hesitated. "Well, you could always—"

She stopped as a bell rang, a muffled chime from Bourne's pocket.

He dug out his phone and saw that he had a text message from a number he didn't recognize. It was a video file, and below it was a brief note.

Tick tock, Cain.

With a frown of trepidation, Jason tapped the screen to play the video. As soon as he did, the screaming began, and he quickly muted the sound to keep Abbey from hearing the horrible soundtrack to what he was witnessing. He left the room and went out to the house's marble foyer and closed the door behind him. Then he turned the sound back on. As he watched, his anger rose in his chest like fire. His eyes blinked shut, then opened. For someone immune to the sadism of the world, Bourne had met few killers with the barbarity of the Russian strongman named Cody. This man was worse than Lennon. Worse than the Medusa operative Miss Shirley.

This man was pure evil.

He watched the video from beginning to end. Then he watched it again, his emotions now dead and chilled, watching for any details he may have missed. He focused on Tati's face. Tears pouring down her cheeks, mucus dripping from her nose, her mouth wide open as she pleaded with Cody not to make her do it. But the man had no mercy. He forced her, using his own bear paw over hers to squeeze the shears closed. When it was done, when the guttural moaning ended with the boy unconscious and Tati curled up on the floor, Cody spoke directly to Bourne on the camera.

"It gets worse from here, Cain. Get me the Files."

"Jason?" Abbey said.

She'd come into the foyer behind him. He turned around and shoved his phone back into his pocket.

"Jason, what is it? What's wrong?"

"Nothing."

A frozen silence hung between them. He knew she wanted to help, but he didn't need help. He needed to cool his thirst for revenge, uncoil the tension in his body that made him want to drive to the airport and fly to Estonia and take apart Cody limb by limb. He needed leverage. He needed the Files.

"Jason, tell me what's going on," she insisted.

His voice was harsher than he wanted it to be. "You can't have it both ways, Abbey. Either you're in or you're out. If you don't want to be part of my life, then don't ask me for details."

She bit her lip, accepting the rebuke. "Yes, okay."

"Garrett," he snapped. "Who do I talk to?"

"He has an assistant. Lana Moreno. She was in Seattle, but she followed him down here when he moved in with me. She's got an apartment in Santa Monica, and she works out of there. Lana knows everything about Garrett. She runs his whole schedule. She's been with him since Jumpp, and she stayed with him when he went out on his own."

"Lana Moreno."

"Yes."

"Okay, I'll talk to her in the morning."

He glanced at the front door. That was the way out. Open it, head out into the cool coastal night. Leave Abbey alone. Except he didn't want that, and neither did she. They stared at each other, only inches apart, desire rising between them. He could imagine his fingers running through her hair, feel their clothes falling to the floor, feel himself carrying her naked body to the bedroom. So much time had passed without her, and yet it seemed as if no time had passed at all. It would be so easy to pick up exactly where they'd left off.

"I need to go," he said, because in another moment, he would stay. All of the nerve endings on his fingertips wanted to touch her again, but the two of them were like magnets, pushing each other away when they got close.

"Yes. You better go."

She knew it, too. He saw the old flame in her dark eyes.

He turned for the door, dragging himself away from her. But her voice stopped him with his hand on the doorknob.

"Jason, tell me what's going on. Please. I can see it on your face. I know you too well. You need to talk to someone."

He waited, not looking back. She was right; she was always right.

"I'm running out of time," he said.

"Time for what?"

He opened the door, letting the ocean air blow between them, but he lingered on the threshold. "To find the Files. If I don't find them soon, a woman's going to die in a terrible way. And it will be my fault."

SHADOW WENT TO THE MINIBAR IN HER BEVERLY HILLS HOTEL. SHE FOUND a half bottle of champagne, unwrapped the foil, and smoothly popped the cork. She took one of the champagne flutes and poured a glass for herself, then went to the window and looked out on the intersection of Wilshire Boulevard and Rodeo Drive. Even after midnight, glamour couples walked the sidewalk, showing off skin and money.

She sipped her champagne, thinking about the transition in her life that the last few months had brought. For years, she'd been able to escape to her anonymous getaway on an island off the Northumberland coast. She could be a nobody there. She had no identity as Shadow. But all of that had blown up when Jason Bourne—when *David Webb*—returned to her life. She'd given up the cottage on the island; she could never go back there. Now she was head of Treadstone, and there was no escape from that responsibility. Rewards came with it—money, power, an elegant lifestyle—but some nights she missed who she'd been.

That was a weakness she couldn't indulge for long.

Choices had to be made. Hard choices.

She took her champagne back to the computer on the hotel desk. With a tap of the mouse, she rewound the video from the Treadstone camera and played it again, watching Jason in the foyer of the Malibu house and then seeing Abbey join him. She studied the chemistry between them, equal parts love and sex, with a clinical curiosity. The urge for them to come together battled with the need to stay apart.

Years ago, Bourne had looked at her that way. Same love, same passion. And she'd pretended to feel the way he did. Or at least, she'd allowed herself to believe she was only pretending. But her own emotions didn't matter. For now, she was only concerned with Bourne and what he would do next, and she'd known all along that if he would tell anyone the truth, it would be Abbey Laurent. That was why she'd bugged her house.

I'm running out of time.

Then a moment later: *If I don't find them soon, a woman's going to die in a terrible way.*

Of course. So that was the secret. That was what he was hiding from her.

Shadow reversed the video again and slowed down the playback. She analyzed Bourne's face, his eyes, his body, all the tells he hid from the rest of the world. But not from her. She still knew him inside and out, knew every strength, every weakness. She'd owned him, controlled him, danced him like a marionette for years without him even realizing she was there. She could predict how he would behave in every stressful situation.

By the time she shut down her computer a few minutes later, one thing was clear.

She had a problem.

23

THE TWENTYSOMETHING WOMAN RODE HER BIKE AT A FURIOUS PACE down the concrete path that stretched along Santa Monica beach, then braked sharply and stopped near the white high-rise apartment building. Behind her, a wide stretch of flat sand, riddled with footprints, ended at the blue waters of the Pacific. It was less than half an hour after sunrise, and the beach was still mostly empty at that hour, except for the beautiful people doing their early workouts. Lana Moreno was among them.

She was lithe and fit, wearing striped bicycle shorts over her long brown legs, plus a purple bikini top. Her skin shined with sweat. When she took off her alien-like bicycle helmet, she shook out her honey-colored hair, loosening the strands with her fingers. She checked her vitals on her smartwatch, then pulled her bike off the path and did a series of yoga stretching exercises on the sand.

Bourne waited for her, leaning against a stone wall in front of Lana's apartment building. After her post-workout was complete, Garrett Parker's assistant picked up her bike under one arm and trudged toward him. Her eyes zeroed in on him almost immediately, and she seemed to recognize that he was waiting for her.

"Are you Bourne?" she asked.

"I am."

Lana propped her bicycle against the wall and sat next to him, pulling her legs up underneath her. "Abbey Laurent told me about you."

"You're willing to talk to me?"

"Well, she says you're trying to help Garrett. If someone's really trying to kill him, then I guess he needs help from somebody. Since I can't see him myself right now, I guess I'll have to take her word for that."

Bourne noted an edge in her voice. "You don't like Abbey much, do you?"

"I barely know her," Lana said with a shrug.

"And yet your boss is married to her. Is that a problem for you?"

"Why would it be?"

"You followed him from Seattle. You must be pretty loyal."

"I am. So?"

"So I just wonder if there's anything personal between you."

"There isn't," Lana snapped. "Garrett's smart, and he's a good boss, and he pays me well. You can't fuck off good jobs these days. Plus, I didn't have any roots in Seattle. I went there for college, that's all, so nothing was keeping me there. If I can come down here and afford a place like this on the beach, why wouldn't I go?"

"True enough." Bourne glanced at the building behind him, which was prime real estate even by California standards. "Nice location. He must pay you well."

"He does. What of it? Tech bros make good money. His focus is his work, and he needs someone to run the rest of his life. That's how geniuses roll."

"Garrett's a genius?"

"Yeah, he is."

"How did you first hook up with him?"

"I applied to be his assistant when he was hired at Jumpp," Lana said.

"There must have been a lot of competition for that job."

"There was. But I made sure I knew his life story backward and forward before I met him. I read every article he ever wrote about AI and every article that had been written about him. I knew his dog's name when he was a kid. I knew how he ordered his coffee at Starbucks. I knew his favorite resort in the Bahamas, and I knew he'd had a thing for redheads ever since he fucked the girl next door."

Bourne's eyes narrowed. "The girl next door?"

"Yeah. Her name was Fawn. They were both in high school. He talked about it on a podcast one time, and I listened to it. Why?"

"There's an app called mygirlnextdoor. I was wondering if Garrett was involved with it."

"He consulted on the code on his old job when the site was in start-up. That was what the podcast was about, and that's why he told the story. So what? Some of the most advanced technology applications cut their teeth in porn. If you need day-to-day cash flow, there's always money in sex."

"Garrett told me he had nothing to do with the app," Bourne said.

"Was his wife there at the time?"

"Yes."

"Case closed," Lana said with a smirk.

"I get the feeling you don't approve of Garrett and Abbey," he told her.

"It's none of my business, but it all moved pretty fast, didn't it? They met in an airport, and next thing I know, she's got him uprooting his life for her. Do I not approve? Am I jealous? Not at all. I admire what a fast operator she is."

Bourne glanced at the apartment building again. He figured the units had to go for at least five thousand dollars a month. And that was probably for a studio that would make Superman squeeze to change clothes. He took another look at Lana and noticed how attractive she was, with a Camila Cabello face and a fit, petite body. He couldn't help but wonder if the relationship between Garrett and Lana went deeper than she was saying.

"Did Abbey tell you someone tried to kill him?" Bourne asked.

"Yes, that's what she said."

"You don't believe it?"

"I don't know what to believe. Technology is cutthroat, but murder is something else."

"Except, when China is involved, anything's possible," Bourne said. "You know about Mr. Yuan, right? Garrett's predecessor?"

"Yeah. I do. But that was in China."

"Have you checked out our southern border lately? Infiltrators from China are fanning out across the country."

Lana frowned. "You think the Chinese are going after Garrett? Why? He's not even at Jumpp anymore."

"That may not make him any less of a threat. Or the killer may be worried that Garrett will talk *to* the Chinese. The fact is, someone wants him dead. I need to know who, and I need to know fast. It seems like you're the only person other than Garrett who might know who it could be. You said yourself, you run everything in his life except the work itself."

"I do."

"Then who would want to kill him, Lana?" He added a moment later, "Abbey thinks it's a woman."

"A woman? Is she sure?"

"Yeah, she's pretty sure. Is it you?"

Lana's eyes flashed with anger. "Me? You're crazy. I . . ."

"You what?"

"Nothing. It's not me. That's ridiculous."

Bourne let it go, but he wondered if that sentence was going to end, *I love Garrett.*

"Then who?" he asked.

Lana kicked at the Santa Monica sand with one of her sneakers. She glanced around to make sure they were alone outside the apartment building. "Okay, look, I can think of one woman who might be wild enough to do it. It's been a while since we heard from her, but she was definitely a problem."

"Who?"

"Her name's Vix. That's what she calls herself. I don't know if that's a nickname or what. You mentioned the Chinese, right? Well, she's Chinese. She's a programmer from Shanghai."

"An AI coder?"

"Isn't everyone these days?"

"So what's her connection to Garrett?" Bourne asked.

Lana sighed. "Two years ago, when he was looking for a job, Garrett went to an AI conference in Washington. That's when he hooked up with the people from Jumpp. He also hooked up with Vix."

"As in?"

"They fucked. Sounds like it was hot and heavy. Garrett doesn't really talk about it a lot, but I got the impression they were really into each other."

"Who does Vix work for?"

"That's the thing," Lana said. "She worked for Jumpp."

"She was part of their AI team? I thought the whole AI team left after Mr. Yuan was killed."

"No, she didn't work in his section. Garrett thought there was some bad blood between them. I don't know, maybe she wanted in, and Mr. Yuan didn't think she was good enough to make the majors, you know?"

"So what happened after the conference?" Bourne asked.

"Garrett and Vix started a relationship. Rocky but intense. Except once Garrett got to Jumpp, she wanted into his section. She kept badgering him about it. In fact, he began to think that was the only reason she'd come after him in the first place. To fuck her way into the job she really wanted. But Garrett said he couldn't hire her, not with the two of them being involved. So she quit Jumpp."

"Where did she go?"

"That big dictionary word game based here in L.A. DicTrace."

Bourne remembered Garrett talking about the link between the Jumpp software and an app that fed a hack of his computer. *The only thing I could find that lined up was posting on Jumpp about my fucking word puzzle game.*

"Is Vix still there?"

"I have no idea."

"This must have been more than a year ago," Bourne said. "If Vix is going after Garrett now, why would she wait so long?"

Lana shook her head. "There's more. After Garrett broke it off,

Vix began stalking him. Sending him threats at all of his email accounts. Showing up at his door in Seattle. He blocked her online, but that didn't stop her. Except—except he didn't know about all of it."

"What do you mean?" Bourne asked.

"I didn't tell him that it kept going for a while. He thought it was done after he blocked her, and I didn't think he needed to know she was still trying to contact him. Vix was messing with his head. Getting in the way of his productivity. The police wouldn't do shit, so what difference would it make if he knew? I was the gatekeeper. I kept her away. But she kept at it for a while, and she—"

Lana stopped.

"What did she do?"

"It's not what she did. It's that she *knew* things."

"Like what?" Bourne asked.

"Personal things. Shit she shouldn't know or be able to find out. She was able to guess things about him that weren't online anywhere. Like somehow she'd hacked his whole life and could read his mind."

Like an AI engine assimilating data, Bourne thought.

"How do I find her?" he asked.

"I guess you could go to the puzzle people. Like I say, she worked there, but I don't know if she still does. It's been a while. She hasn't come after Garrett in months. I figured she got tired of the chase."

"What does she look like?" Bourne asked. "Do you have a picture?"

Lana rolled her eyes. "Oh yeah. More than I want to see, believe me. She used to send Garrett naked pics when they were together."

She reached over to her bicycle and unzipped a small pouch strapped to the frame. Her phone was inside. She opened it up and scrolled through her photos until she found what she was looking for, and then she handed the phone to Bourne. She was right. He found himself staring not just at parts of Vix, but at *all* of Vix. She had a taut body, skinny and all muscle—the kind of physique a woman would need to hit Garrett in the back of his head and drag him down the porch steps.

Jason felt the clues rearranging themselves in his mind like a word puzzle.

Vix.

An AI coder. A connection to Jumpp. A connection to one of the apps that went rogue on Jumpp's command. A connection to—maybe even an *obsession* with—Garrett Parker. Vix was exactly the kind of unstable mastermind who would know how to hack an AI engine and see an opportunity to use the Files for her own ends.

Bourne focused on her face. She had narrow, delicate features, deceptively hiding her strength. Her lips were ruby red against pale skin, her short black hair parted in the middle, her dark eyes huge between her almond-shaped lids and a little too close together. The effect he felt staring at her—particularly with her naked body on display in the rest of the photograph—was of someone who managed to be both submissive and scary at the same time.

"You see it, don't you?" Lana murmured. "She's crazy."

"I do."

But Bourne saw something else, too. Vix's face was familiar. He'd seen it before. Recently.

Where?

Who was she?

Then he remembered. He pulled out his own phone, and he found a photo he'd taken of the cover of *Wired* magazine that he and

Johanna had found in Chinatown. He studied the faces of Mr. Yuan's team and didn't see Vix among them, but when he looked more closely at the picture, he knew why.

Mr. Yuan hadn't refused to hire Vix for his AI team because he doubted her skills. No, he didn't want anyone to know who she really was.

Because Vix *was* on the magazine cover. She was there in miniature, in the large family photograph posed on the man's desk. The face was younger, from several years earlier, but it was definitely the same girl.

Vix was Mr. Yuan's daughter.

24

THE MARKETERS BEHIND THE WORD GAME DICTRACE HAD LICENSED A
cartoon image of Dick Tracy to go along with the app, but most of
the players used a different name when talking about it online. The
object of the game was to form the longest word possible out of a
large scramble of letters, and so most people called it Dick Race. In
one of the strange viral lightning bolts of the online world, it had
grown from obscurity to become the number one game app two
years earlier, with millions of people posting their longest words on
their social media accounts.

Like Jumpp.

In the process, Bourne realized, they'd unknowingly opened up
their computers and their lives to the Files.

He looked across the rooftop bar and restaurant called West at
the top of the Hotel Angeleno. It was near sunset. On the far side of the
cylindrical tower, at a window table overlooking the traffic of the
405, he spotted the man he was looking for, the man he'd been inves-
tigating all day. Martin Lee was the founder and CEO of DicTrace

and still its principal owner. The man sat by himself, scrolling through his phone and nibbling on an order of togarashi spiced tuna. He had a pink cocktail with a sugared rim in front of him.

Bourne made his way around the border of the restaurant beside the tall windows. When he passed the CEO's table, he stopped as if in surprise and whipped off his sunglasses. "Martin? Martin Lee? It's Charlie Briggs, Colby Lake Capital, Manhattan. Good to see you again. We met in the Nassau yacht harbor last winter."

Martin glanced up at him with no expression on his face. He was a slim Chinese man of about forty, with thinning hair and gold earrings in both ears. He wore a flowered silk Hawaiian shirt and ripped blue jeans, plus crocodile cowboy boots. No one would have guessed that he was worth a billion dollars. He took another sip of his drink and a bite of his tuna appetizer before replying. When he did, his voice was soft but direct.

"First of all, we've never met, Mr. Briggs. I remember everyone I meet. Second, I'm in no need of investment capital for my business, and I'm not interested in pitches for investing in other enterprises. Third, I don't appreciate my happy hour being interrupted. This is the only break I allow myself in my fourteen-hour days. So please excuse me."

"Oh, you'll want to hear what I have to say," Bourne told him with a wide smile. He sat down uninvited in the chair opposite the CEO.

"That's doubtful," Martin replied. "Do I need to ask the manager to have you removed?"

Bourne speared a piece of togarashi tuna with a fork. "This tuna is good. Excellent. I see why you come here every day. In fact, you spend exactly sixty minutes here while your driver waits for you in the Tesla Model Y downstairs. He carries a Ruger LC9, and he reads graphic novels while you're at your happy hour. That fruity pink drink isn't on the menu, but it's your favorite cocktail from your college days in Beijing. The bartender makes it special and has it waiting for you as soon as you arrive. You're a man of predictable habits, Martin. For someone with your resources, that's unwise."

Martin tapped a finger slowly on the table as he sized up Bourne with newfound curiosity. "Well. How interesting. You know a lot about me, Mr. Briggs. Congratulations on your research. Then again, most investment bankers are good at that. Know your enemy, I believe they say. Are you my enemy, Mr. Briggs?"

"That depends."

"On what?"

"On how the next five minutes of our conversation go."

Martin took another sip of his drink, then calmly licked his lips. "This isn't about money, is it?"

"No."

"And your name isn't Briggs."

"No, it's not."

"So what do you want, Mr. Briggs?" Martin asked, returning to his phone as if Bourne were nothing but a distraction.

"I need information about one of your employees."

"Talk to my HR department," the man replied. "I don't know the ins and outs of our personnel files."

"You know this person," Bourne said.

A hint of nervousness broke across Martin's face, but he covered it by dabbing at his mouth with a napkin.

"I'd like you to leave, Mr. Briggs. We're done here. If you want information about someone on my team, I'm sure you can do research on them the way you did your research on me. Now, as I told you, I'm a very busy man. I have work to do."

Bourne leaned forward, giving the man another hard smile. "Didn't anyone tell you that working too hard will kill you, Martin? Then again, so will the Glock I have pointed between your legs. Well, the first shot may not actually kill you. But trust me, you won't be winning any Dick Races after that."

Martin glanced at Jason's right arm, which had disappeared under the table. Bourne tapped the man's knee with the barrel of his gun, and the CEO's eye twitched with concern. "Who are you?"

"Who I am doesn't matter. The point is what I want."

"And what's that?"

"Vix."

Martin's face showed no surprise. "Vix. Of course. Well, join the club, Mr. Briggs. Everyone wants her. But I have no idea where she is."

"I find that hard to believe."

"What you choose to believe isn't my concern. Vix disappeared almost a year ago. I haven't seen her since then."

Bourne assessed the man and concluded he was telling the truth. At least about Vix. "Who else has been looking for her? Did the Chinese come calling?"

"I have nothing to say about that."

"Well, you better start talking. Now." He racked the slide on the Glock with a loud click that the CEO could hear.

"If I tell you anything, they will kill me."

"And if you don't, I will. I'm here, Martin. They're not. So let's try this again. Are the Chinese looking for Vix?"

Martin glanced around the restaurant, as if hoping for rescue or escape, but no one was coming to help him. "All right. Yes. I told you, she stopped showing up for work. A few days later, two men came to see me. Men like you. I told them what I'm telling you. I have no idea where Vix went or where she is."

"But you do know why they're looking for her," Bourne said.

The man's voice was clipped. "Vix is a thief."

"In other words, she has something the Chinese desperately want to get back. She's the one who stole the Files."

Martin said nothing, but his silence told Bourne everything.

"Did you know who Vix was when you hired her?" Bourne asked. "Did you know she was Mr. Yuan's daughter?"

Again, no surprise.

"I didn't. Not at first. Not when I brought her into the company. It was only after she disappeared that they told me. They didn't know at first, either. She fooled all of us. Mr. Yuan set her up with a false identity when he brought her to the U.S., and none of us had any idea. He wanted her close to him. Someone he could trust. I think he knew we would turn on him eventually."

"How did it all work? The Files. How did the plan get put into place?" When Martin hesitated, Bourne used his fork to take another bite of tuna, then placed the fork sharply against the vein on the back of the CEO's hand.

"You're about to lose the use of two of your fingers for the rest of your life."

Martin kept his face like stone, but he hissed in agony. "All right! Stop!"

Bourne removed the fork, and the man massaged the feeling back into his hand.

"The CCP were planning it for years," he said. "It started out as simply a data-hacking operation. After they breached the OPM in 2015, they were looking for ways to expand their reach. People outside government. Business, media, science. That was how Jumpp came into play. Just like TikTok, it was supposed to be a harmless social media operation that would plant spyware and manipulate American users. But Mr. Yuan saw potential beyond gathering the data itself. He was one of the original brains behind AI. As the technology grew more sophisticated, he realized the data could be mined by AI to reveal other, much more explosive secrets. That was the vision behind the Files. But they didn't want to rely exclusively on the coding for Jumpp to put it in motion. It would be too easy to discover, expose, thwart. So they created synergies between Jumpp and other apps."

"Like yours," Bourne said.

Martin nodded. "Yes. Like mine. Five years ago, I had the work done on the game, but I had no start-up capital to expand. A Chinese businessman came to me and said he wanted to help me with funding. I knew who he represented. I wasn't stupid, I recognized the hand of the government. But there was no way I could say no. So they became my silent partners. That meant giving them access to my code. Behind the scenes, Mr. Yuan and his team built a separate infrastructure, hidden away, under their exclusive control. They maintained it. I never even saw it. I had no idea what it was doing."

"So you knew Mr. Yuan?"

"Of course."

"Why was he killed? Why did they eliminate him and his team?"

"He began to raise doubts about the project and what it was doing. He saw how they planned to manipulate people. He opened his mouth. He protested. The fool! How could he think they would sit there and do nothing? So they took him out. They killed him and his wife when he went home for vacation. After that, the members of his team ran, but the Chinese tracked them down one by one."

"And Vix?"

Martin shook his head. "I told you, I had no idea who she was. She left Jumpp. I don't know why. Maybe she thought people there were getting suspicious of her. But she came here, and I assumed she was CCP. A plant to spy on me and my operations. I installed her in a separate division, but I got reports that she was hacking our code. Pawing around in the hidden systems. I didn't raise any red flags because I assumed she was working for *them*."

"She wasn't," Bourne said.

"No. She was trying to figure out how the whole system worked. How the data was hacked and stored. And most of all, how the AI engine integrated everything. It turned out that her goal was—"

"To steal it."

Martin finished the rest of his pink drink in a single swallow. "Yes. A year ago, she disappeared. So did her younger sister over in Shanghai. They must have coordinated it together. Vix obviously knew the CCP would use her sister as leverage as soon as they discovered what she'd done. She put her plan in motion over a weekend. I don't know what her motive was. Money. Revenge for her parents. Power. Maybe all three. But she relocated the cloud data to another server farm. We have no idea where. She downloaded the AI engine onto a laptop, and then she fed a virus into our systems to destroy it all behind her. After that, she vanished."

"With the Files."

Martin nodded. "With the Files. Wherever she is, Vix has them. And from what I hear on the street, she's using them."

———

VIX'S LAST-KNOWN ADDRESS WAS IN JAPANTOWN, NOT CHINATOWN. IT was a place where Chinese agents were unlikely to find anyone to act as spies.

Bourne made his way after nightfall to an apartment building on San Pedro Street in the heart of L.A.'s Little Tokyo. The street was quiet, the shops and restaurants all closed, but he eyed the windows around him to see if there was any obvious surveillance. Then he picked the lock on the building door and took the elevator to the top floor, where he let himself inside Vix's one-bedroom condo.

He didn't really expect to find anything, and he didn't. Whatever Vix had left behind when she ran was already gone. The apartment was empty. The furniture had been taken away, the closets and cabinets stripped. He didn't find so much as a scrap of paper or a package of frozen peas in the refrigerator that the Chinese had missed. The place had been thoroughly searched and sanitized. Even the walls had been opened up and checked, and then the drywall replaced and the entire condo repainted.

They'd left nothing for anyone else to find.

Except one thing.

When Bourne went into the bedroom, he knew he'd made a mistake. A green light immediately blinked on from a device mounted near the ceiling. A camera. The Chinese may have taken everything out, but they hadn't left. They were still watching the condo to see if Vix came back.

He spun around and charged for the apartment door, but before he made it halfway across the empty carpet, a man appeared in the doorway. He was Chinese, and he couldn't have been more than twenty-five. He wore red glasses and had spiky black hair, and he had a gold iPhone jutting out of the front pocket of his jeans.

Bourne had already seen him twice before.

Once at a café across from Rod Holtzman's building.

Once on the steps coming down from Feng's hideaway in San Francisco.

The killer pointed a Chinese-made QSZ-92 pistol at Bourne's chest. He kicked the condo door shut behind him with his heel, and he stepped closer, keeping a secure distance that was too far for Bourne to leap at him without taking a bullet.

"It's Cain, isn't it?" the man said.

Bourne shrugged and said nothing.

"I heard Treadstone was on the hunt for the Files," the assassin went on. "I figured it wouldn't be long until you made the connection to Vix and came looking for her. But I'm afraid for you, the hunt ends here."

"Killing me won't stop Treadstone," Bourne said.

"It'll slow them down. That's all we need. A few more days, and we'll have the Files back in our hands."

"How? Where's Vix?"

The kid smiled and didn't answer. "Get on your knees, Cain."

"I don't think so."

Never let your enemy know you want the same thing.

Treadstone.

"Get on your knees, or you won't have any knees. I have no instructions about whether to make it hard or soft for you, Cain. It's my choice. If you resist, that makes the decision easier."

"We're both professionals," Bourne said. "It's kill or be killed."

"That's right."

"Or we could help each other."

"We don't need your help. We simply need you out of the way."

"Vix is clever," Bourne told him. "She's Mr. Yuan's daughter. Don't be so sure she won't outsmart you."

"Enough stalling, Cain. Get on your knees."

Bourne stayed where he was. "Do you know why Vix is trying to kill Garrett Parker?"

Momentary suspicion flashed across the kid's face.

"You don't, do you?" Jason went on, because he knew the killer was wondering the same thing. "Don't you think you should figure that out before you try to take her down? Why is she so intent on getting rid of him when she's in the midst of selling the Files? Fifty million dollars, right? That's the price. For that kind of money, she could hire another hit man to replace Rod Holtzman and keep her hands clean."

"What do you know about Garrett Parker?" the kid asked.

"Put down the gun. Let's talk. I help you, you help me."

"Or you tell me what you know and I make it quick. Otherwise, you beg me to end it while you're screaming to Jesus." The killer lowered the gun to point the barrel at Bourne's left knee. "Last warning."

Bourne spread his arms out, his fingers wide. Slowly, he lowered himself to the carpet, one knee down, then the other. Without being asked, he laced his fingers behind his head, hoping the kid wouldn't notice, that he would think it was automatic. That's what you do when you've lost the game and you're out of options. You go to your knees, and you put your hands behind your head.

Right above the neck sheath that held his dagger.

He needed a distraction. Just one tiny break in the killer's

concentration. The kid slipped a finger over the trigger of the gun—
but Bourne didn't look at him and didn't look at the pistol. Instead,
his eyes drifted to the door, and a tiny smile crept along the corner
of his lips. That was all it took. The kid hesitated; he lost focus for a
fraction of a second. By the time he began firing, Bourne was already
moving as a bullet burned past his head. His right hand grabbed for
the knife handle in the sheath, and as he threw himself sideways, he
whipped his forearm forward, hurling the knife at the killer. He
aimed for his throat, but his aim was off, and the blade came in low
and hard, landing up to the hilt below the kid's collarbone.

The killer jerked but absorbed the impact. He tracked Bourne,
who rolled away, and the kid fired twice more as Jason yanked his
Glock from the rear of his back. A bullet blew into the wall near his
shoulder and threw up dust; another scored his neck, drawing blood.
Jason flinched, ducked, and fired back, but the killer was already
gone, tumbling to a new position near the apartment door. He came
up firing, but the blade had severed his shoulder muscles, leaving his
aim wild. Bourne fired on the run, but he missed, too.

For an instant between shots, their eyes met, their guns both
ready.

The killer made a calculation that killers make. He wasn't going
to win. Instead, he spun through the condo door. Bourne heard the
crash bar of the stairwell door on the other side of the hallway, and
he took off after him. The stairwell door hadn't closed as he slammed
through it. He spotted the kid halfway down the first set of stairs,
and he threw himself forward, his body landing on the killer's back
and crashing them both to the concrete landing at the base of the
steps. They hit hard; both of their guns went flying.

Bourne wound up on top.

He yanked out the blade of his knife and shoved it back in, up to the hilt again. This time the kid screamed.

"*Where's Vix?*"

"Fuck you," he hissed.

Blade out, blade in. Another squirt of blood and a howl of agony. Bourne leaned in, their faces inches apart.

"*Where is she?*"

The kid's breathing came fast. He clenched his teeth against the pain. "Kill me. I'm not telling you a fucking thing."

"Tell me, and I let you live."

"*Liar!*"

The killer slammed his skull forward, bone against bone. The impact dizzied Bourne for an instant, and the kid shoved against his body hard. Jason's hand was still clenched around the knife handle, and the blade came free as the killer squirmed away. As his brain righted itself, he saw his Glock, and he scooped it into his hand and spun, ready to fire.

But he had no shot. The assassin was gone. Far below him, footsteps pounded down the stairs for the street.

25

"VIX."

Garrett got up from the sofa in the Malibu house and wandered to the wet bar. He poured vodka into a shot glass. He downed it before Abbey could object, and then he returned to the sofa and sat next to her. Other than the bandage that covered part of his skull, he looked healthy. The color had returned to his skin, and he showed no signs of dizziness or distress when he walked. He put a hand on Abbey's thigh, and somehow Bourne thought the gesture was deliberate.

She's mine now. Not yours.

"Are you sure?" Garrett went on. "I haven't seen or heard from Vix in months. Yeah, she was unstable, but our relationship was a long time ago. I don't understand why she'd be coming after me now."

"Martin Lee from DicTrace confirmed it," Bourne said. "Vix stole the Files. She hijacked the AI engine behind the hack."

"And you think *she's* the one who's been trying to kill me?"

"It looks that way."

"Jesus." Garrett shook his head. He looked genuinely stunned, in a way that Bourne didn't think could be faked. "That makes no sense. You have to be wrong. I mean, okay, if Vix has the Files, fine. I can believe that. But why come after me?"

"Lana Moreno says Vix was making threats after you broke up. Did you know that?"

"Sure. Lana tried to protect me, but I knew. Vix was crazy. Brilliant, but off the deep end. But like I told you, that was months ago. We've had no contact since then. I don't think she'd be coming after me now."

"Well, she is. You need to wrap your head around that. For some reason, *you* are as important to her as selling the Files. I'd like to know why."

"Even if it's true, I don't see how it helps you find her."

"It helps me get inside her head," Bourne replied. "I can figure out her strengths and weaknesses, and I can try to guess what she'll do next. Plus, it's a piece of the puzzle that doesn't make sense, and I don't like that. Crazy or not, everything Vix has done up to now reflects a smart, calculated plan. Coming after you is part of that plan, and I don't think it's just obsession from a jilted lover."

"I don't know what to tell you. I still think you're wrong."

Bourne shifted his attention to Abbey, who was holding Garrett's hand as they sat next to each other. She looked at Jason, then looked away, with a flush that reflected the awkwardness between them. He wanted to be out of her life, and he kept coming back. He wanted to let her go, and circumstances kept reeling him in. Their relationship was over. But before he could walk away, he had to do something he was reluctant to do. He had to show her that her husband was lying.

Because Garrett was definitely lying.

"What are you hiding, Garrett?" Bourne asked sharply. "What are you not telling me? What are you not telling your *wife*? Because I think you know what's going on. You know exactly why Vix is coming after you."

The younger man's lip curled with anger. "Is this really about me, Bourne? Or are you just trying to turn Abbey against me?"

Jason tried to hide the contempt he felt for this man, but he failed. "Honestly? I don't care about you at all, Garrett. I do care about Abbey. As long as you're in the crosshairs, *so is she*. I only want two things out of this mission. I want to find the Files. And I want to keep Abbey safe. I really don't give a shit what Vix does to *you*."

"Jason," Abbey murmured, her voice chiding him. But he could see in her eyes that he was getting through to her. She turned to Garrett and said, "Is he right? Is there something more that you're not telling us?"

Garrett got up and stormed to the patio door and stared out at the California hills. "You too? Goddamn it, Abbey!"

"I *know* you're hiding things," Bourne went on. "I know you're lying. I'm not just guessing. Lana told me about mygirlnextdoor. You consulted on the code, but you told me you had nothing to do with the site. Why?"

"You think I wanted Abbey to know I was involved with a high-end escort site? I had a limited freelance role, and it was years ago. It had nothing to do with the Files."

"Mygirlnextdoor has everything to do with the Files. It's part of the whole scheme."

"Well, I didn't know anything about that."

"Of course you knew," Bourne insisted. "You're an AI genius.

There's no way you didn't spot problems with the code immediately. Even if you didn't know the endgame, you knew there was spyware at the heart of it. Is that why you went to Jumpp? Is that why you showed up at that conference and talked your way into a job? You wanted to figure out how the scheme worked."

Garrett's fists clenched. "You need to go. I want you out of here."

"Not until I get answers."

Garrett turned to Abbey, his voice harsh. "Get rid of him!"

She stared back, not with a wife's face, but with a reporter's face. "First I think you should answer his questions, Garrett."

"There's nothing to say. This is all bullshit!"

Bourne played his last card, and he hoped it was an ace. "Did you know that Vix was Mr. Yuan's daughter?"

Garrett didn't react. He didn't move; he didn't say anything; his face showed nothing. Abbey hissed with shock, but Garrett stood by the door like a block of ice. The lack of reaction told Bourne everything.

"So you did know," he said.

After a long silence, Garrett finally replied. "Yes."

"She told you?"

"Yes."

"When?"

"During our relationship."

"Strange that you didn't mention that," Bourne said.

Garrett went back and sat down next to Abbey, but as soon as he did, Abbey got up and walked away from him.

"Who did you tell?" Bourne asked.

"No one. I told no one. Even after we broke up, I kept her secret."

"Then why is she trying to kill you?" Bourne asked.

Garrett said nothing, and Abbey broke in from across the room. "I don't know what the fuck you're hiding, Garrett, but you need to *tell him.* You need to tell *me.* What have I gotten myself into by being with you?"

Her husband sighed. "It's possible Vix may blame me for the death of her parents."

"That was the Chinese," Bourne said.

"Yes, the CCP killed them, but it's more complicated than that."

"Then you better explain."

"If I do that, then *your* people will kill me," Garrett said.

"My people?"

"Treadstone."

By the glass doors, Abbey let an expletive burst from her throat. "*Fuck!*"

"How do you know about Treadstone?" Bourne demanded, emphasizing each word.

Garrett took a deep breath. "It all started with mygirlnextdoor. Just like you said. This was during my old job. Before Jumpp. I didn't write the code for the app. I just consulted on AI integration and where I thought the technology was going. Even back then, it was pretty obvious to me that soon you'd have completely artificial girls on these sites, interacting with clients using chatbots. So I was advising on ways they could be ready for the transition."

"And?"

"And I noticed some weird shit. Routines that didn't make any sense, sections of code that went nowhere. They seemed to have external references, like they'd be controlled from outside the app. I talked to the developers, and they got really squirrelly about it.

Turns out the whole app was being run from overseas. They wouldn't tell me where or how the code was supposed to work."

"What did you do?" Bourne asked.

"I posted about it on an AI forum. I wanted to see if anyone else had noticed shit like this on other sites. Next thing I know, my post gets deleted. Scrubbed. A week after that, a car pulls up next to me near Pike Place Market. This guy—a guy like you—says there's somebody who wants to meet me. A woman. She's part of a government agency, and she wants to talk about my post."

A woman.

Bourne knew what was coming. He could see it from a mile away.

"I figured we'd go to the downtown federal building, but we didn't," Garrett continued. "We went to the airport. An unmarked jet was waiting, and they flew me all the way to DC. But I didn't even get off the plane. Instead, this woman came on board to meet me. Blond, attractive, but not the kind you mess with, you know? She didn't even give me her name. She just said she was called—"

"Shadow," Bourne said.

Garrett stared at him. "Yeah. That's right. Shadow. She tells me she's part of an agency called Treadstone. Intelligence. National security. And she wants to know more about what I spotted inside this app. So I told her. I said it looked to me like the app was vulnerable. Deliberately vulnerable. With the right triggers, it could be used to hack into the personal data of the players."

"Then what?"

"She told me her team had the same concerns. They were worried about Chinese spyware and the kind of information hacking that could be done via apps and big social media platforms. One of them was Jumpp. I was from Seattle, and Jumpp was based in Seattle, so she asked if I'd be willing to work my way into the organization and find out what I could about their coding. They knew my reputation in the AI community. They figured I'd be taken seriously."

"This was while Mr. Yuan and his team were still there?" Bourne asked.

"Yeah. I knew *of* him. Everybody did. This woman—Shadow—said they didn't have any specific evidence that Jumpp was using spyware. But given that it was a Chinese operation, they wanted intel from the inside."

"So you did it."

"I did. I went to talk to Mr. Yuan. I tried to get him to hire me. I said he seemed to be doing cutting-edge AI applications, and that's what I wanted, too. We met two or three times. We spoke the same language, you know? We talked about trends. He didn't say anything about what was going on at Jumpp, nothing about spyware or hacking, nothing about AI engines to parse user data. That's what I reported to Shadow. I figured that was the end of it."

"So what happened?" Bourne asked.

"Two weeks later, Mr. Yuan quit. A month after that, he and his wife were killed. After that happened, Shadow came after me again. She encouraged me to go to the conference in Washington and try to get the people at Jumpp to hire me. They did."

"Not long after that, you testified before Congress that you saw no evidence of spyware in Jumpp's code," Bourne said.

"That was the truth. I *didn't* see anything. I had no idea what was really going on until I saw how DicTrace and Jumpp seemed to interact. Except—I wasn't the one who spotted it. Vix did. When she started working there, she saw what was going on, and she told me about it. We were still involved at that point."

"Did you tell Shadow?"

Garrett hesitated. "Yes."

Bourne shook his head. More lies from Treadstone.

Shadow had known about Jumpp from the beginning. She'd sent him on a hunt where she already knew where the evidence would take him.

"Why would Vix blame you for the death of her parents?" Bourne asked. "Martin Lee told me that Mr. Yuan had begun to question the uses for his code. He was having a crisis of conscience. That's when the Chinese pulled him out."

"Yes, but there was more to it than that," Garrett said. "He was also set up."

"Set up how?"

But Bourne saw the same invisible hand he always saw.

"Shadow," Garrett replied. "She leaked rumors to the Chinese that Mr. Yuan had been meeting with an American intelligence agent. Namely me, although I wasn't identified. The Chinese thought he'd been handing over secrets to the U.S. government about their hacking operation, and that's why they had him killed. Treadstone thought Mr. Yuan was a security threat, and they wanted him removed with no fingerprints coming back to them. They got what they wanted."

"They always do," Bourne said. "But if your identity was never revealed, how did Vix know *you* were a spy?"

Garrett shrugged. "How do you think? She ran me through the Files."

THE WOMAN DID TAI CHI ON THE PACIFIC SAND.

Every motion brought her body and mind together. It was so simple and yet so profoundly complicated. The exercises forced her to purge her brain of unwanted thoughts, to remove all distractions, to focus on the *now*. Her muscles worked as one, patient and fluid, like a slow-moving river through the forest. Her breath went in and out, and her heart slowed until she could hear its individual beats.

She didn't hear the ocean, but the waves rolled inside her like steady thunder.

She didn't feel the sun, but its rays warmed her from within.

She didn't hear the children on the beach, but their laughter connected her with her own inner child.

She went back to the past. To her earliest days of peace and joy. Inside her mind, this was more than just a memory. She literally traveled back to the gardens of Zhongshan Park in Shanghai and took strength from the presence of her family. They steeled her for the work that lay ahead. They instilled courage in her soul.

When her daily ritual was done, she turned her focus back to the house on the hill above her. The house where Garrett Parker lived.

All virtue was rewarded, all vice was punished.

Soon he would pay for his crimes.

26

TWO HOURS HAD PASSED. CALLIE FAITH STILL HAD GOTTEN NO RESPONSE from whoever was selling the Files.

"What's up with this asshole?" she asked Johanna. "Why the delay?"

"He's probably vetting the information we sent. That takes time."

"Or he's already spotted the fake, and he's talking to somebody else about buying the Files."

Johanna shook her head. "He hasn't spotted anything. You wanted a sophisticated story, and that's what I gave you. Even Warren Buffett would be convinced he was about to walk away from this deal with fifty million dollars."

"Take me through it again," Callie insisted.

Johanna sighed. She got up and went to the back of the Gulfstream G700, which was parked in a charter area of McCarran Airport in Las Vegas. They didn't know when or where the drop would be scheduled, but they were ready to fly anywhere in the world. She prepared herself a plate of mango, prosciutto, and chicken satay, and she poured orange juice in a champagne glass. Then she returned to the white leather seats in the middle of the jet and sat down across from the congresswoman. Callie already had an open bottle of Rombauer cabernet in front of her, with a glass of wine poured almost to the rim.

"We can't play with government money, right?" Johanna began. "We touch any of the defense or intel budgets, and Shadow is all over us. So the whole thing has to be privately funded. The only plausible private source for a payout like this is a billionaire who sees the Files as an investment. That's why I created a joint venture for you. You're in bed with an oligarch from Belarus. Literally. I planted AI-generated hidden-cam photos of the two of you fucking, in a place where someone who knows how to find such things would find it. Your oligarch is kind of a pig."

"Why is that necessary?" Callie asked. "Shit, what if someone else finds it?"

"It's the little details that sell the big lie. If anyone else finds it—well, they won't, because only someone who goes looking for it would find it. And no one will be looking for you fucking a man who doesn't exist, except for our friend with the Files. Anyway, your oligarch sugar daddy is named Maksim Zhuk. I created a legend for him. Look him up, and you'll find thousands of hits."

Callie stared at Johanna from over her glass of cabernet. "How did you do it so quickly? That's too much detail. There have to be holes in the story. You're too smart for your own good."

"Building legends that survive scrutiny is what Treadstone does," Johanna replied. "And it's not me doing the work. It's an AI interface. I create the parameters, and the software does in a few hours what would take me weeks to do manually. It builds an entire life. Dozens of newspaper articles—mostly in Russian and Belarusian, because that's where Maksim would get the most press. A few photographs, especially background shots, because he's a private guy. The most important piece of evidence for us is a Czech political podcast, with two guys talking on video—Czech with subtitles—about American sanctions that have hit Zhuk in his wallet and how much he wants the intelligence community to back off. They mention rumors that Zhuk has been cultivating a relationship with someone in the U.S. Congress who thinks American sanctions have gone too far."

"They have," Callie snapped.

Johanna shrugged. "Whatever. Do a little digging, and there you are. You met Zhuk on a congressional visit to Belarus four years ago."

"I've never been to Belarus."

"You have now," Johanna said. "You see? Anywhere you look, the story fits together. You're involved with an oligarch with vast financial resources who shares your interest in clipping the wings of the U.S. deep state. That's where the fifty million dollars is coming from. Oh, and Zhuk owns this jet, too, just in case our guy starts looking into how we get to the drop site. The ownership records lead back to him."

"Except Zhuk doesn't exist."

"Yes, he does," Johanna insisted. "He exists online. That's what counts for reality today."

Callie sighed. "Let's assume this bullshit story flies. What about the money? That's what he really cares about."

"I sent our friend a grid detailing routing and account numbers for six hundred and twelve separate accounts at banks around the world—all legit, all with computer-generated names—of random amounts that add up to fifty million dollars. With a push of a button on your phone, we can begin populating the accounts from Zhuk's various banks in Eastern Europe. I provided a list of those banks, along with multimillion-dollar balances. As a show of good faith, I transferred one hundred thousand dollars into the first of the accounts. Real money."

"Where the fuck did you get that?" Callie asked.

"Your IRA."

"Jesus, did you think to tell me about that?"

"If the deal goes as planned, we'll get it back," Johanna said.

Callie checked her phone again and scowled. "Except as of right now, we don't have a deal at all. I think he saw through your games."

"He didn't."

"You're goddamn arrogant."

"I'm goddamn good."

Callie harrumphed. She yanked a copy of the *Wall Street Journal* from her briefcase and snapped it open.

Johanna kept her seat belt fastened, despite the fact that they weren't in the air. The seat belt kept her from pacing, and she really wanted to pace. These were the moments in a mission that made her nervous, when all you could do was wait and see if the pieces fell into place. She wouldn't have admitted it to Callie Faith, but she *was* nervous about whether her AI creation, Maksim Zhuk, would stand up to the scrutiny of someone who knew what they were doing. But she'd done the best she could with the time she had.

Another hour passed.

Finally, a text tone sounded on Callie's phone, and she scooped it up. She read the message out loud.

You found a way to get the money. I knew you would.

"I'll be damned," Callie said, and Johanna exhaled with relief. Another text came in.

Does your husband know about you and Zhuk?

"Told you he'd find the pics," Johanna said.

"Yeah, great, now what? What do I say?"

Johanna grabbed the phone and typed a reply: *Fuck you. I have your money. Do you want to do the deal or not?*

"Too harsh," Callie said. "What if he walks away?"

"He won't. You need to be pissed off that he mentioned your affair. That way, he thinks he has you where he wants you."

I'm just saying, you're vulnerable in lots of ways, Callie. Don't cross me if you don't want your marriage falling apart like your congressional career.

"See?" Johanna said.

She typed: *You have the laptop?*

Of course.

We'll need to test it before we fund the accounts.

Fine.

When and where?

The Hollywood Bowl. Midnight tonight.

"Los Angeles," Callie said. "Jesus, I thought we'd have to fly halfway around the world."

Johanna frowned. "Yeah. I don't like that."

"Why?"

"He sounds rushed. Like he's moving up his own timeline. Something's going on. He wants to get the laptop out of his hands fast."

"That's good, isn't it?"

"Maybe."

I'll leave the laptop in the first row of seats. You won't see me, but I'll be watching you. I'll send you a code to unlock it. You'll have ten minutes to vet the Files before the code expires. Then you start the transfers. Once the money is in the accounts, I'll send a second code that opens it up permanently.

"I don't trust him," Callie said. "What if we transfer the money and don't get the code?"

"We don't have the money," Johanna reminded her.

"Shit."

Another text came in.

Fuck with me, and I destroy you.

Callie's mouth pinched into a tight line. "He can, you know. If he releases what he knows about me, I'm ruined. But it's too late to back out. If we don't show up, he'll take me down anyway."

"Then we'll have to figure something out," Johanna said. She typed: *I'll be there.*

Several minutes passed. There were no more messages.

"I fucking well hope you have a plan," Callie said.

Johanna nodded. "I do, but you won't like it. We need backup."

27

BOURNE SAW SHADOW EMERGE FROM HER BEVERLY HILLS HOTEL AT nightfall.

She'd been closeted in her suite all day, not taking his calls, not answering his texts, protected behind security in the lobby and an agent outside her door. Now he watched her pass under the hotel's stone archway onto Wilshire Boulevard, but she wasn't alone. Two Treadstone agents came with her, a man and a woman.

She waited on the street, as if posing for a picture. She wore turquoise jeans with white sneakers, plus a tweed jacket over a black shell. Her Coach purse was slung over her shoulder, which made an elegant holster for the Ruger LCP he knew she kept inside. Her blond hair was loose, her lips deep red as always. She eyed the street and then murmured something to the two agents with her.

Bourne stayed out of sight, but he wondered if Shadow sensed his presence. She knew he was coming after her.

He waited while she crossed the street to the Two Rodeo pedestrian mall. She climbed the steps beside a gurgling fountain, and the agents gave her space, taking up positions twenty feet behind her, one on the left, one on the right. Bourne followed. He didn't bother with a disguise. If Shadow saw him, a disguise wouldn't matter; she'd see through it. He let the crowd give him cover, but Shadow never looked back as she window-shopped along the cobblestoned walkway. The two agents in her wake watched for threats, and they were good, conscious of every face without drawing attention to themselves, hands ready if anyone made a move.

When Shadow went inside the Versace store, the woman agent accompanied her, and the man stayed outside, casually checking his phone while he kept an eye on people coming and going. His back was to the windows of Stefano Ricci, his stare fixed on the Versace doorway. Bourne approached him like a normal pedestrian, staying close to the store window, then passing in front of him. In the next instant, he spun back in a single smooth motion and cracked the man's skull against one of the building's stone columns. No one saw; no one heard. The man's eyes closed, and he slumped, and Bourne guided his body down to the sidewalk.

He slipped across the walkway to the Versace door. The woman agent came out first, her attention immediately focused on the disturbance at the opposite store, where pedestrians had begun to gather around the agent on the sidewalk. She didn't notice the man three feet to her right. Her mouth moved; she murmured the other agent's name into her radio and got no response. By instinct, she turned, ready to force Shadow back into the store. As she did, she spotted Bourne, and her eyes widened. Her lips formed the word *Cain* as she reached for her Glock, and Bourne's forearm had already launched a chop to her neck when Shadow stepped between them and deflected the blow.

"Enough!"

Bourne held up his hands. The woman agent stepped back. Shadow dismissed her with a flick of her fingers and continued at a casual pace down the middle of the stone walkway. Bourne fell into position next to her.

"How's Wolf?" Shadow asked, nodding toward the male agent on the ground.

"Hibernating."

"Was that really necessary, Jason?"

"You weren't taking my calls."

"I've had a busy day," she replied.

"Busy doing what?"

Shadow didn't reply. She stopped outside the window of David Orgell and nodded at one of the displays. "Do you like that Ritmo Mundo watch?"

"It's beautiful."

"Want me to get it for you? It's almost Christmas. It would look good on you."

"No thanks," Jason said.

"You don't want me buying you gifts?"

"What would the other agents think?" Bourne asked.

Shadow smiled at the joke. She reached into her purse—he could see the Ruger—and removed a pack of cigarettes. She lit one and inhaled. "That's better."

"I didn't know you smoked."

"Every now and then."

She used two fingers to draw the cigarette from between her red lips. It was always the same with her. The languid movements. The flirting. Sex was a more lethal weapon with her than the gun in her bag. "Since you're here, I assume that means you know about Garrett Parker."

"Why didn't you tell me about him?" Bourne asked.

"I knew you'd get to the truth eventually. Garrett was never an agent for us. Just a resource who provided me with information from time to time. I saw no reason to think *he* knew who had the Files. In the interim, I didn't want to prejudice your search. I couldn't be sure that the Files originated with Jumpp. It might have been TikTok or ChatGPT or something entirely different where the Chinese didn't have their fingers in the pie."

"Except I came to you about mygirlnextdoor from the beginning," Bourne said. "You never told me about the connection to Jumpp. And Garrett."

"Do you want me to apologize for being three steps ahead of you, Jason? The fact is, I always am. But like I told you before, it's irrelevant to me where the Files originated. The only thing that matters right now is who stole them."

"I think it's a woman named Vix," Bourne told her. "Do you know who she is?"

"A former coder with Jumpp, as I recall."

"She was also Garrett's lover. And Mr. Yuan's daughter."

Shadow's perfect dark eyebrows arched. "His *daughter?* Now, that is interesting. I thought Mr. Yuan's daughters were both in hiding in China. Or imprisoned in a labor camp somewhere."

"Mr. Yuan smuggled Vix out."

"And Garrett knew who she was?"

"He did."

"But he didn't tell me. What a naughty boy. That information could have changed everything. So Vix stole the Files to get back at the Chinese for what they did to her father. The pieces begin to fit."

"She also wants revenge against Garrett because she thinks he's a Treadstone spy who set up Mr. Yuan."

"Why would she think that?" Shadow asked.

"Don't act innocent. You leaked it. You wanted the Chinese to think Mr. Yuan was handing us secrets. That's what got him killed."

"I did no such thing."

"Garrett thinks you did. So does Vix. It came out of the Files."

"Then the Files are wrong," Shadow said. "I didn't know about Vix, and I didn't sell out Mr. Yuan."

Bourne studied Shadow's face, from her eyes to her mouth, looking for the tells that would prove she was lying. Because she always lied. She lied as easily as she could tell you the day of the week. But he saw no signs of deception now. Either she was very good—and she was—or she was telling the truth.

"I really have to go, Jason," she went on. "This was a short break, but I still have work to do. Is there anything else?"

"That depends. Is there anything you're not telling me?"

"I've told you everything you need to know."

Bourne shook his head. This time Shadow hardly even tried to hide the fact that she was lying. Something else was going on, but she was cutting him out of the loop. He'd been played by her once again, outsmarted and outmaneuvered. He'd given her Vix, and she'd given him nothing at all.

"Good night, Jason."

Shadow walked away with a toss of her hair and disappeared down Rodeo Drive. A few seconds later, the woman agent followed, trailing behind her, shooting Bourne an ugly look as she rounded the corner.

Jason turned around.

Johanna was right behind him.

She grinned at his surprise and then rolled her eyes. "A Ritmo Mundo watch? Seriously? What a bitch."

"What are you doing here?" Bourne asked, making sure no other Treadstone agents were staking out the mall. "If Shadow made you, she would have had you killed. You can't get that close to her."

"I love it when you get all protective." Johanna grabbed his face in her hands and kissed him. When she pulled away, she took his hand. "Come on. Let's get out of here. The exchange is going down, and I need your help."

ABBEY FOLDED HER ARMS OVER HER CHEST AS SHE STARED OUT THE WINDOW. The moon shined on the ocean in the distance, and a few headlights sped along Highway 1 behind the shroud of trees. The house was silent. Dead silent. She'd left the lights off because she thought better in the dark. And God, she needed to think.

Garrett was in his office working. They hadn't spoken at all.

Treadstone.

Fucking Treadstone.

She couldn't believe it. She'd given up the man she loved—she'd walked away from Jason even when it killed her to do so—because she couldn't live in the world of Treadstone. She couldn't exist among people whose only code was death and betrayal. She'd decided it was better to be alone than to love a killer.

But then she'd met someone else. She'd fallen in love again. She'd gotten *married*.

Only to have Treadstone come back into her life like a bad dream. Garrett was part of them, too. A spy. A liar.

"I'm sorry."

Abbey turned around. Her husband was in the doorway, and he didn't need to be a psychic to read her mind.

"I know I kept things from you," Garrett said. "I didn't have a choice. But that doesn't change how I feel about you. I love you."

She said nothing. She couldn't say it back. She didn't love him. Not anymore. She wondered if she ever really had. He came forward into the room, a shadow moving closer. When he took her hands, she pulled away.

"Abbey, let's go away tomorrow. First thing in the morning. You and me. We can forget about Jason Bourne and Treadstone and Vix and all of this bullshit. It doesn't matter anymore. Forget about Los Angeles. Forget about your book. Write something else. Let's just get away from this whole thing once and for all and start over. Okay? Can we do that? We could go to Seattle. I know people there. We can get a place on one of the islands. Or we can go somewhere completely different. I don't care. I just want to take you away from here."

She was silent for a long time.

It was tempting. She couldn't deny it was tempting. But she'd already learned with Jason that she couldn't run away. That world, that violent world, always caught up to her.

Treadstone.

"Abbey?" Garrett said. "Please. Tomorrow morning. We'll pack, we'll go."

She shook her head. "You pack. You go."

"Abbey."

"We're done, Garrett. You need to get out of here. Annulment, divorce, whatever it is, we're through. I'm sorry, but that's it. I don't want any déjà vu. I don't want to live with someone who can't be honest with me. I don't want to be married to a man who's been touched by a world I despise." She went on even when she knew she shouldn't. "If I could live with all of that, I'd be with Jason."

His voice was bitter. "You love him more than me."

"I loved him. I think I loved you, too. But not anymore."

"Give yourself some time. Give *us* some time."

"Time won't change this, Garrett."

"What are you going to do?"

She shrugged. "I have a book to write. People died in that fire. People lost everything. I'm going to figure out why, and I'm going to tell their story. That's what I do."

"You'd put that over us? A book? Jesus, you're making a mistake, Abbey. Don't walk away from me."

"I already have," Abbey said.

Garrett opened his mouth as if to say something more, and then he closed it. He stalked away, leaving her alone. Alone with the quiet and the darkness. She went back to the window and stared outside. She pushed everything else in her mind away, because that was the only thing she could do. She couldn't think about Jason, or Garrett, or Treadstone. All she could do was take her laptop and work all night.

Write the book. Tell the story.

That was who she was. Abbey Laurent, the successor to Peter Chancellor. Abbey Laurent, novelist.

She slid open the patio door, letting in the cool ocean breeze, but then she heard a muffled shout from deep in the house.

"Abbey!"

It was Garrett. She spun around, then hesitated. Her gun was in the bedroom; she didn't have it with her. Did she need it? But she'd heard nothing. No one was in the house. Just her and her husband.

Soon to be ex-husband.

"Garrett?" she called.

There was no answer.

She tried again, louder. "Garrett!"

Nothing.

She left the living room and found herself in the dark hallway. Ahead of her, on the right, the room that Garrett used as his office had its door ajar. The light was off. She walked closer, step by step, feeling a strange anxiety. With each step, she listened, but she heard no sound at all.

"Garrett?"

Abbey crept through the doorway. Her eyes adjusted slowly to the shapes inside. She saw Garrett's desk and the tall windows that looked toward the hills, mostly invisible. The glass door that led outside was open, bobbing in the wind. The alarm had been deactivated.

Garrett—where was Garrett?

She hurried forward, but she'd only taken a couple of steps when she felt a presence looming behind her, someone closing on her and wrapping an arm around her throat. Something wet and foul covered her face as the person hoisted her off the floor. She flailed, legs kicking, her body trying to twist away. Her foot hit something heavy, and she heard glass breaking against the wall. But the person held her tight as she struggled. She tried to scream, but the noise died in the rag. She tried to hold her breath, but all she could do was inhale the fumes. The silence turned into drums pounding inside her head, and the darkness became a merry-go-round, spinning wildly.

Then she was gone.

28

JOHANNA STOOD ON THE HIGH PROMENADE THAT WOUND AROUND THE
perimeter of the Hollywood Bowl. She clutched her Ruger tightly in
her right hand. Below her, dozens of curving rows of seats descended
to the bone-white amphitheater, which nestled in the middle of the
valley with the Hollywood hills rising behind it. Clouds came and
went across the moon, switching the darkness on and off. The area
felt remote, surrounded by woodland, but she could hear the traffic
and sirens of Los Angeles not far away. Row by row, she examined
the empty arena, looking for the person they were waiting for. For
the moment, she saw no one, but this was an area where they could
never really be alone. Even in the late hours, there were always
strangers sneaking into the Bowl, hiding in the trees, making love
and doing drugs. They were red herrings. Distractions designed to
slow them down. You could never be sure who your real target was
until you were right on top of them.

"Where is he?" Callie Faith asked impatiently. Her voice
sounded loud in the acoustic echoes of the arena. "Why haven't we

heard from the bastard? This was his time, his place. Is he going to show up?"

Johanna put a finger to her lips. She spoke quietly. "Odds are, he's watching. Just like we're watching."

"Watching for what?"

"Company."

She noted the time. It was a couple of minutes past midnight. The rendezvous hour had come and gone. Yes, he might be watching the arena, expecting a trap. Or he might be setting a trap himself.

She grabbed Callie's phone and tapped out a message. *I'm here.*

Two more minutes passed. There was no reply.

"Let him see you," she told Callie.

The congresswoman frowned. She took a few steps along the perimeter road and located a break in the green hedgerow at the top of the arena. She stood above the rows of seats, her hands on her hips. In the moonlight, her skin was white, and she had a baseball cap pulled low on her face. She wore a black turtleneck. Black jeans. Black leather jacket.

Johanna was dressed the same way. In the darkness, they could pass for twins. She sent another text. *Are we going to do this or not?*

Still no reply came on the phone.

Johanna studied the nighttime hills looming over the stage, sharp tree-covered slopes that surrounded the entire amphitheater. She couldn't see Jason, but he was there somewhere. Watching, like she was. Waiting to close in on the man with the laptop as soon as they knew where he was.

"Anything?" she murmured into the radio.

"*Nothing,*" Bourne replied immediately.

"Where are you?"

"West side. Halfway down the slope."

"Can you see Callie?"

"Yes."

"But no sign of our friend?"

"Not yet."

Callie returned from the arena steps. "I don't like this."

"Neither do I," Johanna admitted. It was now ten after twelve.

"If it's a setup, we need to get out of here."

"That's your call. If you want to go, we go. But we're not likely to get a second shot at the Files."

Before Callie could reply, a low chime finally sounded on her phone. Johanna checked the text message. *Section E, first row, west side. You'll find what you want. I'll call with instructions when you're there. Be ready to transfer the money.*

Another text arrived seconds later.

Remember, no games.

Johanna grabbed the baseball cap off Callie's head and shoved it on her own. Unless anyone looked too closely, she could play the role of Callie Faith long enough to get what they wanted before someone noticed the switch. And hopefully, Bourne would have the person disabled on the ground in less than five minutes. Threat over.

"I'm going in," she told Bourne.

Then to Callie: "Stay right here. *Do. Not. Move.*"

"Just get me the laptop," Callie snapped. "And don't try to double-cross me."

Johanna said nothing. She found the break in the hedgerow and hesitated at the top of the arena. She didn't wait long; she didn't want to risk giving the person with the Files a good look if he had a night vision scope. Slowly, she made her way down the steps. Her sneakers were silent. She still had her Ruger in her hand, but she kept it hidden inside the pocket of her leather jacket. Her eyes surveyed the area, checking each empty row, trying to spot anyone waiting for her near the arena stage.

Section E, first row, west side.

"Jason, he must be nearby. There's access to the walkway where the ground levels out. He could get in and out fast."

"I'm heading that way."

"I don't see any movement, but it's too dark to be sure."

"He won't go far from the laptop. He'll want to keep you in sight."

Johanna continued her slow trek downward through the arena. She reached the next section and turned left along the walkway until she reached another set of steps. Then she stopped. Her senses were hyperalert, and she heard muffled voices in one of the rows near her. Heavy breathing. The smell of weed drifted toward her in the breeze. She drew her Ruger out of her pocket. Quietly, she crouched low, then took four steps down and swung the gun toward the long wooden bench.

There were two teenagers lying there, naked and busy. They didn't even notice her, not until Johanna shoved the gun into the girl's head and clapped a hand over her mouth at the same time. The boy reared back, too shocked to say a word.

"Out!" she hissed at them. "Grab your clothes, and get out of here."

The kids didn't need to be told twice. Not bothering to get dressed or cover themselves, they shoved past Johanna in panic and disappeared. Johanna shook her head.

Distractions.

She continued toward the stage. It loomed larger as she got closer. At the next promenade, she saw a sign for section E, and she headed for the west side of the arena. She kept her gun aimed forward, her right arm outstretched, her left hand propping her wrist. Every few seconds, she spun to look behind her. The clouds overhead got thicker, and the moon stayed hidden, leaving the valley pitch-black. She could see a break in the wall ahead of her that led backstage. Behind it, a sharp hillside climbed from the sidewalk.

She felt watched. Was he there?

Did he know it wasn't Callie?

She waited to see if another text came into the phone, but nothing did.

Eight steps led up to the first row of seats, where a wooden bench ran along the concrete platform. She couldn't see anything, so she switched on the flashlight on the phone and let it guide her way forward. Ten yards away, something small and rectangular sat on the bench, with nothing else around it.

As Johanna got closer, the light told her what it was.

"The laptop," she said. "Jesus, it's here. I've got it."

BOURNE MADE HIS WAY DOWN THE HILLSIDE. IT HAD RAINED OVERNIGHT; the dirt was soft and loose, and he had to grab the branches of the trees to stay upright. A damp, wormy smell filled the air. He was nearly blind in the darkness, but he had a PVS-14 monocular that he used to check his surroundings. In the arena, he saw the green glow of Johanna's body through the scope, but he saw no one else. She was alone.

The same was true of the woods around him. He listened, hearing no sounds, no movement. Everything felt clear.

So why did he sense the jaws of a trap ready to spring shut?

Your instincts are smarter than your brain.

Treadstone.

If any of the other players in the race for the Files had caught wind of the drop, they'd be here. He thought about the young Chinese assassin with the red glasses, who'd arrogantly predicted that they'd have the Files back in their hands soon. Did the Chinese know? Were they waiting for Johanna to unlock the laptop before they moved in?

Where the slope ended, Bourne pushed out of the trees. He dropped silently from the retaining wall and found himself on the road that bordered the arena. He checked both directions—seeing no one— then stayed close to the wall as he headed downhill. He kept his Glock level, his index finger stretched along the barrel, ready to curl around the trigger. The only sound was the noise of his breathing, until—

What was that?

A branch snapped in the hills above him, as sharp as the crack of a bullet. He swung his monocular into the woods and, for an instant, he saw the glow of a man moving on a high trail before the trees sheltered him again.

A homeless addict haunting the Bowl?

Or a killer?

"We've got company," he murmured to Johanna.

"*Our guy?*" she radioed back.

"Can't be sure if it's friend or foe."

Bourne accelerated his pace as he jogged down the road. The goal now was speed. Get the laptop. Get Vix. Get away. He reached the base of the arena road, where the ground flattened. On his right, a walkway led into the rows of seats, and he could make out Johanna standing not far away. He used his monocular to assess the road that wound behind the stage, and then he surveyed the hill above him.

Vix would be close. Keeping an eye on her prize.

There!

Someone was crouched in the tall brush halfway up the hill. Not even thirty feet away! Was it her? The angle was right; from where she was, she had a clear sight line on the row of seats where Johanna had found the laptop. She could have made the drop in the arena in seconds and taken cover. Or she could retrieve it and be gone over the hill in less than a minute if anything happened.

Get her!

But as he prepared to move, Jason focused the monocular higher on the hill, and his breath left his chest.

Jesus!

Among the trees clustered at the summit, he spotted the ghostly glow of someone else hunkered down in the woods, stretched out on the ground, only the man's head and shoulders visible.

Plus the red beam of his laser scope. *A sniper!*

Bourne knew from the angle of the hill that he wasn't the target, but he knew who was. Swinging his Glock, he squeezed off several shots toward the top of the hill. He had no hope of hitting the man, but all he wanted was time, a few seconds, any kind of delay. Through the monocular, he saw the sniper pull back by instinct at the noise of the gunfire, but that wouldn't last long. Bourne ran, closing the short distance between himself and Johanna. His brain measured out the time it would take for the sniper to establish his position again, aim the rifle, and squeeze off the shot. It wouldn't be long.

A green hedge separated the walkway from the first row of seats where Johanna stood, the laptop in her hands. Jason dived.

The sniper fired a moment later.

Bourne landed hard against Johanna, her body spilling backward. In the same instant, the bullet left the rifle chamber; the crack of the shot chased it down the hillside. The sniper missed by inches, but as they fell, Johanna also hit the ground under him; he heard the crack of her skull on concrete. The laptop flew out of her hands.

He caught his breath and rolled off her. When he took hold of her shoulders, he saw that her eyes were closed.

"Johanna!" he hissed. He tapped his hand gently against her face. "*Johanna!*"

Her eyes blinked; she opened them slowly. He grabbed her body in his arms, one hand supporting her head, and he could feel the stickiness of her blood through her blond hair. But she was alive.

"Fuck," she moaned. "Goddamn, that hurt!"

Another bullet. Another crack through the brittle air. This one pinged off the concrete with a burst of dust inches away.

"We need to go," he told her.

"The *laptop*. Get it!"

He took a look around in the nearby rows, but saw nothing in the darkness. "I don't see it. We're in the open. We need to go *now*."

"No—"

Jason ignored her. He took his Glock and fired more shots at the hillside, buying them another few seconds to escape. Then he let Johanna sling an arm around his waist for balance as they limped down to the promenade, crossing in and out of view of the hillside just ahead of the next bullet that ricocheted on stone. When they reached the shelter of a concrete pillar, she managed to stand on her own, but she looked unsteady, dizziness in her eyes.

"No way he's alone. We need to get out of here."

"Jason, the Files—"

"Fuck the Files."

Bourne dragged her toward the arena stage. When Johanna lagged, he let her cling to his arm. At the stage itself, he lifted her onto the platform, then followed, barely escaping two more rounds that burned within inches of his back. But then the walls of the stage protected them from the marksman on the hillside. He helped her to her feet and propped her up as she stumbled beside him. They hurried for the far side of the arena.

The trap sprang shut around them.

The hot lights of the stage burned to life. Light towers around the circumference lit up the entire arena. They froze where they were. Bourne had his Glock in his hand, but his Glock was useless. A dozen men with tactical rifles approached from different directions, ahead of them, behind them, from the top of the arena, from the doors on the stage. They had no escape, nowhere to go.

"I'm so fucking sorry, Jason," Johanna murmured.

"It's not you. They knew we were coming."

The men with rifles tightened the circle. He bent and placed his Glock on the ground and kicked it away, and he took Johanna's Ruger and did the same. He lifted his hands, surrendering. The men drew closer, some on the stage, some below it. Then the armed agents directly in front of them parted to give access to a woman dressed in black.

It was Shadow.

Bourne realized that the assault team wasn't the Chinese. It was Treadstone.

Shadow snapped her fingers at two of the agents. "Get the laptop. It's on the other side of the arena. Hurry. *Now!*"

Two men broke off, jogging back to the area where Johanna had found the Files.

Section E, first row.

Shadow's eyes zeroed in on Johanna, who clung to Jason, her head bleeding profusely, ribbons of blood curling around her ears and down to her neck. "Hello, Storm," she said. "You and I have unfinished business. It's time to finish it once and for all."

"Fuck you," Johanna retorted. "Kill me if you want. I don't care."

Shadow gestured at Johanna. Four men came forward and ripped her out of Bourne's arms. She screamed; she put up a fight, her arms and legs flailing, but she didn't have much fight left. When she tried to break free, one of the men hit her hard across the face with the barrel of his rifle, and she slumped back into their grasp, unconscious.

Jason shouted and struggled to escape, but found himself staring down the barrels of four rifles pointed at his chest.

"Please don't, Jason," Shadow said. "Don't be foolish."

"You tried to kill her," he snapped, shaking his head. "And me."

"I warned you there would be consequences." Shadow nodded at the men. "Get her out of here. I'll deal with her later."

Bourne watched in helpless frustration as the men dragged Johanna out of the arena, her feet bumping along the stone walkway. When Johanna was gone, Shadow gave a signal with her hand, and the rest of the men let their rifles go limp in their arms. Shadow picked up Bourne's Glock and handed it to him, her fingers clutched around the long barrel.

"This is yours," she said.

"You trust me to take it? You don't think I'll kill you, too?"

"I know you won't. You're not a fool. You need to let go of Johanna,

Jason. She's done. She's out of your life now. But you and I still have work to do."

Bourne looked over her shoulder and understood. The two men she'd sent to the far side of the arena had returned empty-handed. In the tumult, Vix had slipped in and out of the arena.

The laptop was gone.

29

BOURNE AND SHADOW HIKED UP THE ARENA PROMENADE TO WHERE Callie Faith waited for them, surrounded by armed men, her wrists locked in handcuffs. She'd tried to run as the Treadstone assault began, but she hadn't gotten far.

"Callie," Shadow said to her, deliberately avoiding the title *Congresswoman*, as if she were sure that position wouldn't apply for much longer. "I don't need to tell you this, but you're in a lot of trouble. You've been a bad girl ever since the start of your political career, but now it's all about to come crashing down."

Callie's eyes went from Shadow to Bourne and then to the Treadstone agents guarding her. She tried to stay cool, but fear oozed from her body like perfume. "I haven't done anything wrong. Certainly nothing illegal."

"You're here in the middle of the night trying to purchase a hacked database for purposes of extortion," Shadow told her. "With money you don't have, using an armed ex–intelligence agent as your intermediary."

"Fooling a thief with fake money and a fake cover story isn't a crime," Callie replied. "I was simply planning to retrieve the database in order to hand it over to the appropriate authorities."

Shadow smiled. "Of course you were. You're such a selfless patriot. But I wonder what story Johanna will tell when I offer to spare her life in exchange for ratting you out. Will she back you up? Or will she admit what we both know? You were going to walk away with the laptop, and the person who stole it would wind up dead."

Callie frowned. She knew she was done. The game was over; she'd lost.

Bourne noticed that Callie didn't ask about Johanna. Her agent and ally had been taken away to rot in a hole somewhere, and this woman didn't care. That was what spies were to the powerful, just tools to be used and discarded. He hated this woman, and right now, he hated Shadow, too. Thanks to her intervention, his own plan to rescue Tati had blown up around him. He felt caught in a hallway with multiple doors, and no matter which door he chose to open, someone he cared about died.

"Johanna is hardly credible," Callie said, grasping for any kind of leverage. "You can't believe anything she says. You know that better than anyone."

"True, but I don't need her to take you down. I already have all the dirt I need on you. How long do you think it took me to figure out the significance of *ninety-six thousand dollars?* Not long at all, Callie. You launched your first campaign on the back of an illegal bribe from casino bosses. It's been downhill from there."

"You hacked my phone," Callie said, shaking her head.

Shadow shrugged. "Naturally I hacked your phone. I bugged your office. Your car. Your home. I've been watching your whole life in high definition for months. You're a fool to underestimate me, Callie."

"So what now? You arrest me? Let's see how that goes. You just admitted to illegal searches against a U.S. congresswoman. The Justice Department will never let that fly. You're the one who will wind up in jail, not me."

"Jail? Don't you understand what's happening here, Callie? We're way beyond the courts. Hell, if I wanted, I could make sure you're never seen again. Unless you tell me everything, you'll just *disappear.* A few days of headlines about the strange case of the missing congresswoman, and then everyone will simply forget about you."

Bourne caught Shadow's eye as she made that threat. Her stare was cool, and he knew this wasn't a bluff. Callie knew it, too.

"Fucking deep state," she muttered. "This—this right here—is why I've been trying so hard to take you all down. You think you're above everyone else. You report to no one. There's no accountability. Sooner or later, it's going to turn against you. Count on it."

"Maybe so," Shadow agreed. "We're all expendable in the long run. But I won't be taken down today, Callie. And not by you."

"You won't take me out," she snapped back. "You won't take that risk."

"I'll do what I have to do. But even if I choose not to eliminate you, all I have to do is let the rumors fly around Washington. The knives will be out in no time, Callie. That's how it works. You know that. Do you think Wilson Scott wouldn't love to know whose fingerprints were on the gun that shot him in the back? Do you think you'll keep your seat on the committee when everybody knows what you've done? Even if they don't pull a George Santos on you and kick your ass back to Las Vegas, you'll find yourself sitting all alone in the back of the chamber with zero power. I don't think you'll like that very much."

Callie did a slow burn, like a caged tiger pacing with nowhere to go. "What do you want, Shadow?"

"Isn't that obvious? I want the Files."

"Well, I almost had them tonight, and you fucked up the operation. Now they're going out to the highest bidder. It won't be me, and it won't be you. God knows who's going to end up with them."

"Then you better help us get there first," Shadow said.

"How do you expect me to do that? This was my one shot, and it blew up in my face because of you. Don't you get it? The Files are in the wind. I don't have a fucking clue who has them."

Bourne stepped closer to Callie, almost in her face. "Stop with the bullshit, *Congresswoman*. You manipulated Johanna and lied to her, and now you're lying again. You've been in the middle of this from the beginning. The Files were being used to help *you* gain power. That wasn't the Chinese. That was Vix. She took the Files, and then she reached out to you. Tell us why. Tell us what happened between the two of you. Because somewhere in there is a clue I can use to find her."

He expected the name *Vix* to land on Callie Faith like a sucker punch, pushing the air out of her lungs. Instead, confusion filled her blue eyes like a haze, and her forehead wrinkled as her mind worked furiously. When the fog finally cleared, her mouth bent into a cruel smile. She was arrogant again. Confident.

Her losing hand had somehow turned around, and he didn't know why.

"I want a lawyer," she said. "Now."

Shadow shook her head. "You still don't get it, Callie. There are no lawyers or judges in any of this. This is between you and me."

"Wrong. I want an immunity deal, and you're going to get it for me. All of it off the books, sealed, confidential. Nothing comes out about what I've done, *and* I keep my seat. My lawyer will negotiate with the Justice Department overnight. When it's signed and delivered, I'll talk. Until then, I'm not saying a word."

"How do I know that anything you say is worth that?" Shadow asked.

"Because you people obviously don't have a fucking clue what's really going on," Callie replied. "Without me, you're lost."

Bourne's eyes narrowed. "What do you mean?"

"You think Vix has the files? You're wrong."

"We're not wrong," Bourne insisted. "I got that info out of a Chinese contact who's running one of the compromised apps. He told me all about Vix. She's the one who hijacked the Files."

Callie smiled. "Yes, she did. I know that. Vix *had* the Files. But she doesn't have them anymore."

"Who does?"

"I have no idea. But if I tell you everything about our relationship, then maybe you can figure it out for yourself. Get me a deal. I'll talk. Without that, you'll be spinning your wheels until the Files are long gone."

Bourne shook his head. "How can you be so sure Vix doesn't have the Files?"

"It's simple," Callie replied. "Vix is dead."

PART THREE

30

BY MORNING, CALLIE HAD HER DEAL.

Bourne expected Shadow to resist, but instead she shrugged off the need to let Callie go, telling him that was how the Washington world worked. You made compromises. You gave your enemies what they wanted in order to get what *you* wanted. In this case, what Shadow wanted more than anything else was the Files.

Callie and Shadow sat across from each other at a table in Shadow's Beverly Hills hotel suite. The two women shared breakfast and mimosas as if they were friends now—friends who would put a knife in the other's back if given half a chance. Bourne stood by the window, eyeing the Wilshire Boulevard traffic below him. He wanted to rip the champagne glass out of Callie Faith's hand and get her to talk. *Now.* Every day, every hour, put Tati at greater risk. The clock was ticking, and he knew Cody wouldn't hesitate to send another graphic example of what he would do to her if much more time passed.

"How did it all start?" Shadow asked finally, sitting back in her chair. "Give us the details."

Callie used a fork and knife to cut a miniature raspberry tart in half. She looked on top of the world again, now that she had immunity and her seat in Congress was safe. "Vix came to me. Not in person, of course. I didn't know who she was at that point. She made contact with me anonymously."

"Why you?" Bourne asked from the window.

"I was only one member of the intelligence committee, but I'd gotten a lot of attention online and in the press."

"Yes, you're very good at that," Shadow commented.

Callie shrugged, ignoring the jab. "I'd made it very clear ever since I was elected how I felt about corruption in the U.S. intelligence services. I wanted to give them a buzz cut. Start over from the ground up. I'd also gone public with my belief that Chinese social media platforms were nothing but fucking spyware designed to brainwash our kids and gather personal data that could be used against us. My hearings focused on TikTok and Jumpp, among other apps that had foreign ownership. Of course, at that point, I had no proof of what was in the code, and they all denied it."

"So what happened?" Shadow asked. "How did Vix make contact?"

"I found a message one morning on the front seat of my car. Someone wanted to meet me at a DC parking garage. It was very clandestine, very *All the President's Men.* I suppose it was stupid to go alone, but I went anyway. I parked where the note told me to park, and a woman met me. I never saw her; she never got in the car. But I had the window down, and we had a conversation. She told me I was right."

"Right about what?"

"Right about everything. The spyware. The hacking. When I asked how she knew about this, she said that she'd worked inside two of the companies that were involved. One was Jumpp. The other was this word puzzle game, DicTrace. She said she'd spotted anomalies in the code that opened up huge vulnerabilities for users. But it wasn't just about stealing data. She said the scheme was much worse than I thought. That was when she told me about the AI engine the Chinese had built, how it could take reams of unrelated raw information and extrapolate personal secrets. It was scary as hell. She'd actually used it. She'd seen what it could do."

"Why did she go to you and not the FBI?" Shadow asked.

"Blame yourself for that," Callie replied. "She hated the intelligence agencies. FBI, CIA, all of you. That was another reason she turned to me—because I felt the same way about you corrupt assholes. She said she'd run her boyfriend through the Files and found out that he was working on behalf of a spy organization called Treadstone. She said people close to her had died as a result."

"Did you know she was talking about Garrett Parker?" Bourne asked.

"No. She didn't give me any names. That would have exposed her identity. But she said she wanted my help—not just to take down the Chinese operation but to take down Treadstone, too."

"And you were happy to oblige."

"I was."

"What did you do then?"

"I asked her for proof," Callie said. "It was a good story, and it confirmed most of what I already suspected. But I told her if she wanted my help, she needed to show me what the Files could do. She was already prepared for that question. She had information that she thought would interest me."

"Wilson Scott," Bourne concluded.

"Exactly. She had incriminating information about him—that he'd hired a hit man to kill his terminally ill wife. That he'd found this contact via a porn website involving Russian escorts. This was explosive. I asked how the hell she knew any of this, and she said— that's the Files. That's what the AI engine can do. If something's hidden, the software can find it. If you're hiding a secret, that sneaky little robot can parse a trillion bits of data and figure out what it is. Needless to say, I was impressed."

"And you used the information against Scott," Shadow said.

"Sure. You would have done the same. Don't pretend you wouldn't. If Wilson Scott resigned, I could make the dominoes fall in a way that put me in control of the intelligence committee. From there, it would give me the chance to take on my enemies. The *country's* enemies. So yeah, I destroyed him. I don't apologize for that. If you've got a weakness, someone will find it and exploit it. That's how the game is played. Scott should have known better."

"And Vix kept feeding you more dirt?" Bourne asked. "Al-Najjar? The general on the Joint Chiefs? A Space Coast CEO in Florida? And about a dozen others? Was that all you and her working together?"

Callie shrugged. "Al-Najjar, yes. I wanted to be sure Vix hadn't found out about Scott some other way. That the Files were really as powerful as she said. So she gave me al-Najjar, and I was satisfied. But I had nothing to do with the rest. They all came after."

"After what?"

She hesitated. "After Vix was killed."

"Who killed her?"

"I have no idea. Someone killed her and took the Files. That's when the rest of the extortion started, not just in Washington, but around the country. Except now the heat is on, and whoever has them is trying to sell."

Bourne approached the table and stood over Callie. "What happened to Vix?"

"She approached me a little over six months ago. She finally introduced herself and told me who she was—that her father was Mr. Yuan, that he'd built the AI engine and masterminded the entire hacking operation. After the Chinese betrayed him, she'd spent the past year undermining their plan from behind the scenes. Except now she was sure the Chinese were closing in on her. She'd already sent her sister in Shanghai into hiding. She wanted my help in getting free. Money. New identity. In return, she'd give me a laptop that included the AI engine. I'd have the Files for myself."

"You took the deal," Shadow said.

"Of course."

"But you didn't have the money."

"No. I didn't. Twenty million dollars? I couldn't bury something like that without someone like you sniffing it out. But I figured she was desperate. The Chinese were hot on her trail. I cobbled together a couple hundred thousand dollars. Cash. Plus, I used a contact in the FBI—one of my whistleblowers—to arrange for a passport and other documents. Once I met with her, I was going to tell her it was the best I could do. If I could get more later, I would. But I was sure she'd take the money and run."

"Because she didn't really have a choice," Shadow concluded.

"That's right."

"How did it go down?" Bourne asked.

Callie drummed her sharp fingernails on the table. She glanced at Shadow. "The deal covers everything I say? Right? Plus any actions or omissions related to other crimes? I don't want you coming back at me with obstruction of justice charges."

"What did you do, Callie?" Shadow asked coldly.

The congresswoman poured herself another mimosa from the pitcher. She sipped it, put it down, and picked it up again. "Vix was planning to leave the country. She'd booked herself passage on a freighter through the Port of Long Beach. She didn't tell me where she was going, and I didn't ask. Probably somewhere in South America. We were going to meet, exchange money and documents, and I'd walk away with the laptop."

Bourne waited. He felt a strange sense of horror growing in his chest. "And?" he asked.

"I rented her an Airbnb in the hills where she could hide for a few days," Callie said. "Fake name, fake everything. I set her up there under the name Debbie Robertson. Pretty generic ID, thousands of people with the same name. It was a wild-goose chase if anyone went looking for who'd really been staying there. Nobody could ever trace the reservation back to her or me."

The horror in Jason's gut spread. Why? Why did he know that name?

Debbie Robertson.

Shadow got to the truth first. She remembered the name, and her voice sank low. "The La Sienta fire."

Callie's face darkened. "Yeah. The house I rented for her was in the La Sienta Ranch development outside Malibu. I flew into town to meet Vix, and I was on my way to the rendezvous when I saw the smoke. I turned on the radio, and it was all over the news. A massive fire. It kept spreading, and they couldn't stop it. It engulfed the whole town. My God, more than a hundred people died! I knew it wasn't an accident. Someone got to Vix first. They killed her, they took the laptop, and they started the fire to cover it all up."

"But you said nothing," Shadow murmured.

"What was I going to say?" Callie retorted. "You think I was going to admit any of this? I was paying off a source and helping her leave the country, all to grab a laptop that I was planning to use against my enemies. Instead, a town was destroyed, and dozens of people died. It would have been the end of my career."

"But now you've cut a deal and saved your neck," Bourne hissed.

"That's how the world works."

"Are you sure Vix died?" he asked. "Maybe she started the fire herself to fake her death. Maybe she knew you were going to double-cross her about the money, and she walked away with the laptop."

Callie shook her head. "There was a body found in the house where the fire started. They weren't able to identify it, but the corpse was female. It had to be her."

Jason backed away.

The hazy wave of horror he'd been feeling came into focus and became a monster. A fire demon. He went to the window and tried to find breath in his chest, but he could barely inhale. It was as if the smoke of the fire were choking him, poisoning his lungs.

He knew.

He knew what it meant. Vix. The Files. The La Sienta Ranch fire.

There were no coincidences. There was only a cold-blooded scheme to make sure the truth never came out. The trouble was, one woman had stumbled into the middle of it by writing a book that was going to get her killed.

Abbey.

31

BOURNE PARKED OFF THE SHOULDER OF HIGHWAY 1 AND CAME UP THE winter-green hillside toward Abbey's Malibu rental house on foot. He had his Glock ready. He moved slowly and soundlessly through the tall weeds, climbing higher. Above him, he could see the sprawling mansion terraced into the slope, leaning on high stilts. The signal from Abbey's phone told him that she was still inside the house, exactly where she should be, but he didn't trust what the signal told him.

He'd tried calling her phone over and over. There was no answer. *Where are you?*

His fears for Abbey threatened to crowd out his concentration, and he couldn't afford to be distracted. He needed to focus. But he kept seeing her face, and he kept beating himself up for missing the secret that had been in front of him the whole time. Abbey wasn't in the middle of this by accident. She'd been set up. Fooled. Seduced. As soon as news hit the media that novelist Abbey Laurent was writing a book about the La Sienta Ranch fire, she'd become a threat. If she dug into the conspiracies behind the fire, then she might find her way to the truth about Vix. And the Files.

That was something Garrett Parker couldn't allow.

Garrett Parker. AI engineer. Treadstone source. Murderer.

Focus! Channel your anger!

Bourne forced his rage into a box and locked it away. Through the trees, he saw the driveway that curved up the slope toward the house. When he listened, he heard the distant thunder of the ocean and the buzz of bees in the California poppies. And something else.

Somewhere near the house, a sharp metallic click cut through the morning silence.

A car door.

He broke from the trees onto the strip of blacktop pavement. The garage and the front door—the area where he'd fought Rod Holtzman—were barely fifty yards away around the next curve in the road. He ran until he could see the driveway widen outside the house. A red Tesla Model 3 was parked there, its driver's door and trunk both open, next to Garrett's Lexus convertible.

But he didn't see Abbey's Audi.

Behind the Tesla, the front door of the house stood ajar.

Bourne ran to the far side of the driveway, where the wall of the garage gave him cover. He waited. Not even five minutes later, a woman emerged from the house, her face obscured by the two banker's boxes she carried. She brought the boxes to the trunk of the Tesla and squeezed them into the interior. From behind, Bourne recognized the woman's lush honey-colored hair and her shapely curves.

Lana Moreno.

Garrett's assistant.

Silently, he came up behind her. She didn't hear him; she was too busy arranging boxes in the trunk. When she finally shut the trunk and turned around, she screamed as she found herself staring into the barrel of his Glock six inches from her face. Her eyes widened as she recognized Bourne behind the gun.

"You!"

"Hello, Lana. Going somewhere?"

"Oh my God! Get that out of my face!"

"Then tell me where Garrett is. And Abbey."

Her eyes darted evasively. She tried to sound casual, but the arrogant confidence she'd shown during their first meeting had evaporated. Lana was scared. Someone or something had pushed her over the edge.

"Abbey's in the house."

Bourne glanced at the house, then waited a beat before saying anything more. "Then why isn't she answering her phone?"

"I don't know. Maybe she's got it muted or something."

"Where's her car?"

"Garrett took her car."

"Took it where?"

"He had a meeting in the city."

"Why not take his?"

"The brakes are rattling. It's not safe."

Bourne gestured at the Tesla. "What's with the boxes?"

"Garrett asked me to put some things in storage."

He pushed the Glock against Lana's forehead until it was denting her skin. "You know what I thought when I first met you, Lana? I thought you were nobody's fool. But it looks like I was wrong. Garrett's got you in deep. You better start looking out for yourself if you don't want to go down with him."

"I have no idea what you're talking about," she snapped.

"Then take me to Abbey. Because she's inside, right?"

Lana hesitated. "Right."

He jabbed the barrel of the Glock in the direction of the front door. Lana walked a couple of steps in front of him, and he waited for her to make her move. Because he knew she would. Her head kept bobbing toward the open fields, gauging when to run. Near the front door, she suddenly broke free, but he leaped like a cat, grabbed her by the belt, and threw her down to the blacktop of the driveway. His knee leaned into her chest, making her choke, and as she gasped for air, he shoved the Glock into her open mouth.

"Where. Is. Abbey?"

He yanked away the gun.

"Garrett took her," Lana gasped, spitting blood onto her lip.

"Where?"

"I don't know."

Bourne moved the gun back between her teeth, and Lana rushed on.

"I don't know! I swear I don't know where he is. I'm supposed to pick him up later, but that's all I know."

"Pick him up where?"

"He didn't tell me."

He shook his head in exasperation. "You know everything he's done. Right? You've obviously been his accessory from the beginning. Do you think he's going to let you walk away? This is not just fraud and extortion, Lana. Don't you get that? It's murder. One hundred and three counts of murder. Everyone who died in that fire."

"No! That was an accident! He swore to me!"

"He lied. He killed Vix to get the Files, and then he set the fire to

cover it up. What did he tell you, that the two of you will run away together? He'll sell the Files, and the two of you will live on an island somewhere? You really think that's the plan? Lana, as soon as you pick him up, he's going to kill you, too."

"Garrett would never do that! He loves me!"

"He *uses* you. That's what he does with women. Like he used Vix. Like he used Abbey. You do what he wants, and then he eliminates you." Bourne pinched her face hard between his fingers. "What happened overnight? Tell me."

Lana closed her eyes. When she opened them again, her stare had grown hard. "He called and said everyone was getting too close. The intelligence agencies. The Chinese. The Russians. He was sure the Russians were the ones who'd hired Rod Holtzman. He said if he didn't move fast, it was all about to come crashing down on our heads. So he set up a meeting with Callie Faith. The idea was to get the money for the laptop, and then we'd disappear."

"And Abbey?"

"He knew she'd never give up the book. Sooner or later, she'd figure out what he did. Plus, he—he needed her as leverage."

"What does that mean? Leverage against who?"

Lana swallowed hard. "*You.* He thought you'd get in the way of the deal. If he had Abbey, then he had something to trade. You walk away or Abbey dies."

Bourne's eyes burned. "I'm going to ask you again. *Where. Is. Abbey?*"

"And I'm telling you the truth, I don't know. Garrett drugged her. He tied her up and put her in the trunk of her car. He said he was going to drop her somewhere. He didn't want her with him when he was doing the deal."

"The deal fell apart," Bourne said.

"I know. He called me. He was out of his head. He still had the laptop—he said he barely got it back—but the whole thing was a disaster. We needed to run. Now. Today. He told me to gather up all of his documents so we could burn them. Then we'd get out of the country. He'd sell the laptop somewhere else. He figured there would be buyers in the Mideast who would pay ten times the price."

"What about Abbey?"

Lana blanched. "He had to deal with her first."

Bourne took the Glock and put it under her chin, tilting it so her eyes stared upward at the blue sky. He leaned down and whispered in her ear. "Listen to me, Lana. I need to find them. I need to know where Garrett took her. Either you help me or I pull the trigger. Right now, I'm at the end of my rope. I don't care what I do to you or anyone else. Do you understand me? Look in my eyes and tell me you understand."

"I do! I do!"

"Then how do I find Garrett?"

"There may be a way!" she told him, words spilling out one after another. "I don't know, but if Garrett forgot, there may be a way. He was so rattled he may not have remembered to get rid of it."

"Get rid of what?"

"A tracker. He hid a GPS tracker in Abbey's car a while back. He always wanted to know where she was. In case she—in case she turned on him."

"How do we find it?"

"I can probably call it up on his computer."

Bourne got to his feet and yanked Lana up with him. He pushed her ahead of him, and she led them inside the hillside mansion. It was quiet, and it smelled of Abbey's perfume in the hallway. But she wasn't here. He didn't even know if she was still alive. He felt urgency building in his chest, and he gave Lana another hard shove.

"Move. *Fast.*"

She practically ran into the room that Garrett used as his office, facing east toward the Malibu hills. Bourne followed, and he spotted the glinting shards of a heavy vase sprinkled across the plush carpet. He could guess what that meant. Abbey had struggled. She'd fought back. But she'd lost.

Lana sat in front of Garrett's computer, and Bourne put the gun barrel against the back of her head. "You have one minute. Then I shoot."

He heard her crying. Her arms shook as she tried to type. The computer was slow to awaken, and she banged her fists on the desk in frustration.

"Thirty seconds."

"I'm trying! I'm fucking trying!"

"Ten seconds."

"Here!" she screamed at him. "Here's the program! It's still active! It's still in her car!"

"Where is she?"

"La Sienta Ranch," she gasped. "Garrett took her to the fire."

32

ABBEY AWOKE, HER BRAIN LOST IN A FOG. HER EYES BLINKED OPEN, BUT nothing came into focus, and the images around her rippled like ocean waves in her head. A powerful smell filled her nose. Smoke. Chemicals. Burnt things. She felt dirty, as if a film of dust had caked onto her skin. Her burgundy hair fell in limp strands across her face. When she went to brush it away, she found that she couldn't move her arms. They were tied uncomfortably behind her in the small of her back, her wrists taped together. In panic, she tried to stand up, but she realized that her ankles had been bound together, too. She was seated, her back against some kind of stone wall, but she couldn't move.

When she tried to cry out—*Help me!*—she found a gag filling her mouth, a strip of cloth tied around her head to hold it in place. She couldn't say a word. All she could do was grunt and moan from the depths of her throat. She was a prisoner.

The world finally came into focus. What she saw was a holocaust. She'd been placed among the black-scorched walls of a destroyed house. One brick wall leaned inward, ready to fall. There was no roof over her head, just clouds and sky and the skeleton of a tree looming above the house like a bare cross. Charred debris littered the floor, which was a bed of wet gray ash. Roof shingles. Sheetrock. Broken pipes. Glass that had become lava. Melted silverware, melted plastic. Through the rectangular gap that had once been a doorway, she could see outside to the ruins of a street, where the hulking shells of cars still lingered where their owners had abandoned them as they ran.

The fire.

She was in the heart of the fire. She'd been here many times before, wandering through the moonscape of destruction.

But *why?*

Then she understood. A shadow filled the doorway, and in the dim light, she recognized her husband. Her momentary relief evaporated when she saw his face, which had a flat cruelty she'd never seen in him before. It was so obvious to her now, how she'd been fooled, how she'd walked into his trap months ago.

"You're up," Garrett said, watching her from the doorway. "I was thinking it would be easier if you were still unconscious."

Abbey squirmed, wanting to get up and go after him, wanting to rip off his limbs, wanting to pick up one of the chunks of metal or stone from the floor and beat his head with it. But she couldn't move.

He came forward, and she noticed a gun shoved into his belt. Her gun. He reached to a back pocket and pulled out a knife, which made her flinch. She tried to squirm away, but he caught her and sliced through the tape that held her wrists together. There was some kind of cloth below it, like a shirt. At first, she wondered why he'd taken care not to abrade her skin, but then she realized the truth, and the truth was worse. He didn't want any evidence that she'd been bound. When the gun—her gun—blew out the back of her skull, he wanted the death to look like a suicide.

She stretched her fingers; she coaxed life back into her arms. A part of her wanted to grab for the gun, but she didn't have the strength. Carefully, Garrett cut the knot that held the cloth around her face, and then he eased the gag from her mouth. She had to work the kinks out of her jaw.

Then she screamed.

Garrett just shrugged. "Scream all you want. There's no one around, Abs."

She shut her mouth again, saving her breath. Garrett put the knife back in his pocket. He took the gun from his belt and racked the slide, but he didn't point it at her. Not yet. Instead, he sat down in the ash a few feet away, his legs pulled up, his arms around his knees. His lips puckered with a kind of hollow regret.

"I'm sorry, you know. That doesn't mean anything, but I'm sorry it's come to this. I never thought it would, but I guess I was naive."

"Fuck you."

"Yeah. I deserve that."

Abbey shook her head. Every twist of her muscles brought pain. Her brain still felt as if she were crawling through gelatin. It was the aftermath of whatever drug he'd given her. She tried to put together the puzzle, but she didn't have all of the pieces. Even so, she guessed the biggest one. The one that started everything.

"*You* have the Files," Abbey said.

"Sure. The laptop is in the car. I've had it in a storage locker for months. I tried to sell it overnight, but your boyfriend fucked it up. That's okay. Once I get overseas, I'll find lots of buyers."

Her boyfriend. Abbey knew he meant Jason. The thought of him, the realization that he was still out there, gave her a glimmer of hope, like the sun creeping over the morning horizon. But they were in the middle of nowhere, and in minutes, she'd be dead. That was the reality. As fast as the sun rose in her mind, it disappeared into black clouds.

"What about Vix?" Abbey asked. "How did she fit into this?"

"She was a useful source of information," Garrett said. "I seduced her at the AI conference. Not the other way around. She was alone, and she needed someone to trust, and there I was."

"Like me," Abbey said bitterly.

"Yeah. Like you. I was gathering information for Treadstone, and Vix looked like someone who could help me crack the code of what was really going on at Jumpp. I wanted her brain, and her body was a bonus. She went to DicTrace because we both figured there had to be third-party apps involved. I'd already guessed that when I saw the anomalies at mygirlnextdoor. But after she went there, Vix was the one who figured out how it all worked, that it was way more than data hacking. Her father had built an AI engine to extract secrets out of the data—shit that no human being would ever have found. Shit that was *valuable*. That was when I began to think about my options."

"You mean you thought about getting the Files for yourself," Abbey said.

"Exactly. That's why I never told Treadstone who Vix was or what this was all about. This was my golden ticket, you know? Better than an IPO."

"Except Vix figured it out."

"She did. She was smart. She was able to guess her father's back door to gain access to the hidden code at Jumpp, and she was able to get hold of the AI software. After that, the first thing she did was run me through the Files. That was when she realized I was the one who'd set up her father."

"You. Not Treadstone."

"Yeah, me. I wanted Mr. Yuan out of the way. I wanted his job. So I leaked it. I knew what the Chinese would do. But Vix figured it out. She kept sending me threats after that. But all the time she was watching me—"

"You were watching her."

"Right. I needed to get the AI engine away from her. So I made her believe the Chinese were closing in, that they knew who she was. With that kind of pressure, I figured she would try to run, and she did. She approached Callie Faith about helping her, and I was watching. Callie set her up here. Right here. In this house."

Abbey closed her eyes. "You killed her. You started the fire."

"Yeah."

"Jesus Christ, Garrett. Did you know it would spread? Tell me it was an accident."

"I'll tell you whatever you want to hear, Abbey."

"You knew it was a windy day. You knew the hills were tinder-dry."

"Sure, I knew."

"You're a fucking monster."

Garrett rubbed his beard. Then he played with the gun in his hands. "Well, you wanted a conspiracy for your book, Abbey. You got it. One house burns down with somebody in it, the police are going to know something's wrong. A whole town burns down, and everybody thinks it's an accident. Downed power lines. A careless camper who didn't put out his fire. The only people who don't believe it are conspiracy nuts like your buddy Jerry. Nobody listens to people like that."

"Except me," Abbey said.

Garrett sighed. "Except you. Days after the fire, it looked like everything was fine. Vix was one of a hundred people who were unlucky enough to get caught by the blaze. The media was blaming the usual suspects. But no one was talking about murder. No one was talking about this house or a body that couldn't be identified. And then I read that you'd decided to write a book about the fire. Abbey Laurent. The queen of conspiracy novelists. You worried me, Abbey. You worried me because you're good at what you do, and people listen to you."

"O'Hare," Abbey murmured. "That wasn't an *accidental* meeting between us at the bar. You didn't just happen to be there."

"No. Lana found out where you were going to be. She adjusted my travel schedule to route me through Chicago. I found you at the bar. And I'd already done my research. I knew everything about you. So I knew what buttons to push."

Abbey swore under her breath. She hated that she'd made it so easy for him. Without any doubt or hesitation, she'd let him into her bed and let him into her life. She hadn't admitted to herself that she was on the rebound from Jason, that she needed to be in love again with someone else, anyone else. And here was this smart young nerd, sweet and innocent, who laughed at her jokes and loved Quebec and had been reading Peter Chancellor books since he was a kid.

All lies.

"You may not believe this," Garrett went on, "but I really did fall in love with you. At least a little bit. I never intended to take things as far as I did. Getting married, well, I guess I got caught up in it like you did. That wasn't part of the plan. It just happened."

"Do you think I believe that?" Abbey asked.

"I'm sure you don't. And to be honest, I was fucking Lana the whole time, too. She was my partner."

"Vix. Me. Lana. You're a real treat, Garrett. Are you going to kill her, too?"

"A loose end is a loose end," he said with a shrug.

He got to his feet. Abbey shrank into herself, knowing what was coming. They'd reached the end of the line. Her gun. A millisecond of light and pain, followed by nothingness. She'd be the last victim of the fire. She didn't cry or beg; she wasn't about to give him the satisfaction of watching her crumble. With a sharp intake of breath, she turned her fear into anger as he squatted in front of her.

"No one will believe I killed myself," she said. "Everyone will know it was you."

"Maybe so. I'm a good liar, but it doesn't matter. I have enough money to get away, and once I sell the Files, I'll be able to build a whole new identity in some corner of the world where no one will expect me to be."

He was inches away from her. That face—it was still a handsome face. The devil was never ugly; he always had charm. She'd stared into that face dozens of times when she made love to him. She wished she could burn those memories out of her head, but she knew that, in a moment, he would do it for her.

"Why don't you close your eyes?" he said.

"Why don't you go to hell?" Abbey replied.

Garrett lifted his arm. She watched the barrel of the CZ P-01 take shape like a black hole in front of her eyes. She tried to grab the gun; she tried to deflect it, push him away. But she still had almost no strength in her arms after being bound for hours. His strength forced her hands back, and the gun pushed into the smooth skin of her temple.

More than anything, Abbey wanted to close her eyes, but she didn't. Not for this man. She would force him to see the light go out of her eyes. His index finger slid down the barrel for the trigger, and all it would take was the tiniest pressure. Squeeze the trigger back, and end her life.

"You won't feel a thing," he said.

Abbey finally began to cry. She couldn't help herself.

But not because she was about to die. In the shadows of the ruined house, she saw a blur of motion, swift and sure, and she knew who it was. The next instant, the gun disappeared from her head, and Garrett's whole body flew into the air, as if a bolt of lightning had blasted him from the ground.

33

BOURNE COULDN'T FIRE.

He didn't have a clear shot, not without the risk of the bullet going wrong and hitting Abbey. So he dropped his Glock, closed the distance across the bed of ash with a few silent steps, and lifted Garrett into the air. He hurled him into the remains of the opposite wall, where the impact dislodged his gun and punched the air out of his lungs. The crumbling wall shuddered, dislodging a cascade of dust and stone.

Garrett landed on his feet. He staggered, his steps dizzy, and he searched the ash for the half-buried pistol. It hadn't gone far, but when he bent to retrieve it, Bourne kicked him hard in the chin and sent him flying backward, arms and legs spread wide. The butt of the CZ 9mm lay at Jason's feet, but he left it where it was. He didn't want to shoot this man. He wanted to kill him with his bare hands. He wanted to clamp his fingers around Garrett's throat and watch his skin turn purple and his eyes bulge out of their sockets.

Bourne closed on Garrett, who had struggled back to his feet.

The man swung a fist at Jason, but Bourne dodged it. Then he snapped Garrett's head back in a cloud of blood as he drove his knuckles into the middle of the man's face and broke his nose. Garrett screamed. He bent down and grabbed a charred length of pipe and swung it into Bourne's shoulder, but Jason shrugged off the blow. Behind Garrett, a brick tumbled off the damaged wall and landed with a puff of ash. Then a second brick did the same, popping from the middle of the wall like a missing tooth.

The wall was going.

A foul poison of blood, smoke, and sweat filled the air. Dust made a dense haze in the shadows. Garrett kept a wary distance from Jason. He sidestepped, his back to the wall, his eyes going from Bourne to Abbey to the two guns on the ground. There was no way to the door, no way out, and Jason didn't bother hiding the ice-cold intent in his eyes. Garrett wiped blood from his face. His chest heaved with each breath. Jason let him tire himself out like a fish wriggling on the hook.

The Glock was closest. When Garrett made a move, he'd jump for the Glock.

Bourne watched the man's eyes and waited. Like a base runner, Garrett dived with a grunt of energy, body crashing down into ash, fingers outstretched. Bourne spun toward him, but his shoes slipped on the damp ground. He lost a step, and in the instant it took him to recover, Garrett had his hand clenched around the butt of the Glock. As the man swung onto his back, Bourne landed heavily on his chest, but Garrett's finger made it to the trigger and squeezed off a shot.

On the opposite wall, Abbey screamed.

Jason wrenched the gun from Garrett's hand, then rolled away and saw Abbey, hand clutching her shoulder, blood leaking through her fingers. He ran to her. Her face was screwed up in pain, and a desperate whimper escaped from her throat. This was Abbey. Abbey— *shot!* Because of him. The sight of her drove everything else from his mind, and in that lost instant, Garrett struck again.

Abbey screamed a second time. A warning. "*Jason!*"

The knife drove two inches deep into his back, then made a bloody gash as Bourne twisted away by instinct. A stinging burn erupted behind his eyes. He spun, unleashing his fist, but Garrett slashed with the knife again, cutting across Bourne's torso and jabbing it into his forearm. The Glock dropped at his feet. He twisted Garrett's wrist sharply, dislodging the knife, and pushed into Garrett's chest with both hands. Reaching out, Garrett clung to his jacket and pulled him backward.

Both men stumbled, wrapped up in each other's arms. They jerked and spun in a crazy dance and then crashed into the wall, which groaned under the impact of their combined weight. Garrett let go, limping free, but as Bourne followed, he heard a roar. Like an avalanche breaking from the mountain, the wall collapsed, mortar and brick pummeling him and cracking against his skull. The impact drove him to his knees.

Garrett's eyes shot to the CZ, which still lay in the ash. Bourne saw it, too, but his dizzied brain reacted too slowly. He leaped, trying to separate himself from the rubble, but Garrett got there first, scooping up the gun and then jumping out of reach. A step at a time, Garrett backed away, half choking, half laughing. His face was a mess of dirt and blood, his whole body shaking. He stretched out his right arm, aiming the barrel at Bourne's chest. When his hand trembled, he supported his wrist with his other hand. The gun continued to wobble, but he was too close to miss.

"Didn't expect me to win, did you?" Garrett mumbled. "You can go to hell, Bourne."

Jason saw the man's finger begin to tighten on the trigger.

Then an explosion filled the ruined house. A gun went off, one shot tunneling into Garrett's head above his ear. The right side of his skull erupted in bone and brain, and he slumped sideways, dead, the CZ still clutched in his hand.

In the shadows, Bourne saw Abbey. She stood like a statue six feet away, blood soaking her shoulder, her other arm stiff, with Jason's Glock in her hand. She couldn't seem to move. Jason pushed himself slowly to his feet and took halting steps toward her, then carefully loosened her fingers from around the gun and restored it to his holster. He brought her arm down like the plastic limb of a doll. He ripped a sleeve off his shirt and tied it tightly on her shoulder to limit the bleeding, and she didn't even flinch at the pain.

"Come on," he murmured. "Let's get you to a hospital."

Abbey said nothing. She looked numb.

Bourne crossed the room to Garrett's body and found the key fob to Abbey's car in his pocket. He took the CZ—Abbey's gun—and secured it in his belt. He went back to her, but she still hadn't moved, her muscles frozen in place. Her eyes stared with horror and disbelief at her dead husband on the ground.

"I killed him."

"Abbey, you had no choice."

"I shot him. Me. I pointed a gun at his head, and I pulled the trigger."

"I know."

He felt a wave of blackness cross his soul. When they were together, he'd trained Abbey for a moment like this, because he'd known it would come eventually. A moment when someone came for her and she had to fight back. But training wasn't the same as reality. Shooting a target and shooting a man—her husband—were two different things. You never knew what you could do until you had to do it, and after that, you could never go back.

When they split up, he'd hoped that she was free. She could go on with her life and forget the things he'd taught her. Instead, here they were. Abbey now knew what Bourne had known for years.

What it felt like to be a killer.

Abbey's head finally turned. Her wide eyes stared at him. He watched her soul get ready to break, the numbness draining away. It only took a single touch of his hand on her face and she crumpled against him, sobbing with pain and anguish. He held her up because he felt her legs collapsing. Seconds turned into minutes as she cried, and then he gently separated her from him and wiped the tears from her eyes.

"We have to go."

Biting her lip, she nodded.

They turned to the light of the empty doorway. Abbey leaned against him as they walked outside. Her Audi was parked among the hulks of burned vehicles on a road that didn't exist anymore. He knew the laptop was inside. The Files. This was the end of the road; he had what he was looking for. But the women in his life had paid a terrible price. Tati. Abbey. Johanna. None of them would be the same.

His Highlander was parked behind the Audi. He guided Abbey that way, then stopped as he heard a voice.

"Don't move."

He didn't have time to draw his Glock from the holster at his back, not with Abbey in his arms. When he glanced to his left, he saw an Asian woman emerge from behind the ruins of the house. She held a Daniel Defense DDM4 V7 rifle nestled in her arms, ready to cut both of them down.

It was Vix.

"I WANTED TO BE THE ONE TO KILL THAT PIECE OF SHIT MYSELF," SHE SAID, "but at least he's finally dead. Thank you."

Bourne's mind raced, looking for options to strike back, but with Abbey wounded in his arms, there was nothing he could do. Even if he were alone, his Glock was no match for the firepower of a DD rifle. He could also tell, based on the way Vix was holding it, that she knew what she was doing.

"Aren't *you* supposed to be dead, too?" he asked.

"Garrett thought I was," Vix agreed.

Abbey pushed herself off Bourne's shoulder. Her voice was weak. "The body in the house. Who was it?"

Vix's eyes shifted to the burned-out house. A tight, stricken expression crossed her face. "Garrett showed up that day. I thought it was Callie Faith, but it was him. He hit me and took the laptop. He left me there, unconscious. Then he went to start the fire. If I'd been alone in the house, I never would have lived through it. But I wasn't. He didn't know that."

Bourne thought about the photo from the cover of *Wired* magazine. Mr. Yuan, his wife, and his *two* daughters. The one daughter was standing in the ash in front of him. The other had disappeared from Shanghai at the same time Vix went underground. But she wasn't in hiding on the other side of the world.

"Your sister," he concluded. "You got her out of China. You brought her to the U.S."

Vix nodded. "Once I sold the Files, she and I were going to make new lives together. She was upstairs when Garrett surprised me. When my sister realized the house was on fire, she came downstairs and revived me. By the time she did that, we only had seconds to get out. I made it. She was only steps behind me. But then the roof collapsed on top of her. There was nothing I could do."

"I'm sorry," Abbey murmured.

"Well, Callie thought it was me. So did Garrett. No one knew about my sister. I soon discovered that being dead has its advantages. I could make my plans and carry them out without the pressure of being on the run. Garrett destroyed my entire family, so I've made it my passion since then to destroy him. And get the laptop back. My father's legacy. With that, I'll be able to build a new life anywhere in the world."

"You hired Holtzman," Bourne said.

"Yes. I knew about him because of Wilson Scott. I wanted him to *take* Garrett. Torture him. Find out where he was hiding the laptop. Then kill him slowly. But you got in the way and stopped Holtzman. I took his failure as an omen that I should do it myself. I planned to do that today. But dead is dead."

"What about us?" Abbey asked. "Are you going to kill us, too?"

"You haven't wronged me. In fact, you were Garrett's victim, too. But the laptop belongs to me." She took a hand off the rifle long enough to gesture at Bourne with her fingers. "The keys to both vehicles. Toss them to me. Your guns, too. Slowly and cautiously. I'd rather not kill you, but I've traveled a long road, and I'm finally near the end. If you get in my way, I won't hesitate to use the rifle."

Carefully, Bourne withdrew the key fobs for the Highlander and the Audi from his pocket. He threw them across the short distance, where they landed at Vix's feet. She waited as he did the same with the Glock and CZ 9mm. He didn't bother with his knife, but that wasn't going help him now.

Vix took the guns and threw them over the ruins of the house. She sidestepped toward the Audi, the DDM4 still level and pointed at their chests. When she reached the car, she glanced inside through the window and smiled. Bourne didn't have any trouble reading the meaning behind her expression.

The laptop was there. She'd won the race.

"Leave me the keys for the Highlander," Bourne called. "I have to get Abbey to the hospital. Garrett shot her. She's still losing blood."

Vix shook her head. "You'll follow me."

"I won't. I only care about Abbey."

She opened the door of the Audi and glanced at the empty black landscape around them. "I'll drop the keys out the window a quarter mile down the road. You can retrieve them there. That should give me a sufficient head start."

When she climbed behind the wheel, she had to put the rifle down. Jason thought about charging at the vehicle. He had a one-in-a-thousand chance of getting there before she retrieved the gun and fired back. But he stayed where he was, holding Abbey. Something told him that Vix was a woman of her word.

Bourne stood there as Vix fired the engine of the Audi.

He watched her drive away with the Files.

34

JOHANNA HADN'T SLEPT. THE BRIGHT FLUORESCENT LIGHTS OVER HER head never went off, leaving her in constant daylight. She sat in the corner of a windowless room, her wrists and ankles in shackles. The room was empty except for a stainless steel toilet—no lid, no seat—and a camera watching her twenty-four hours a day from a mount on the high ceiling. She'd tried to keep track of the time since the Treadstone agents had hijacked her at the Hollywood Bowl, but eventually the endless light had played tricks on her mind. It had been at least twenty-four hours. She was sure of that. But it could have been much more, and she wouldn't have known the difference.

They'd left food for her, although she'd eaten nothing so far. Power bars. Plastic bottles of Gatorade. Smart. If they brought trays of food on a regular basis, they'd be giving her a chance to over-power whoever came inside. She appreciated that Shadow had respect for her skills.

But what came next?

Why was she here?

She was surprised that she was still alive. That probably meant Shadow hadn't been able to retrieve the Files that night. Something had gone wrong. But Johanna wasn't fooling herself about the future. As long as the Files were out there, then her skills might be needed, but as soon as Shadow had the laptop in her hands, then she would do what she'd wanted to do all along.

Kill Johanna.

She shook her head in frustration. God, she hated to lose. And especially to *her*.

Johanna pushed herself to her feet. The metal of the cuffs bit into her skin, and the chains rattled. She paced around the walls, counting off exactly one hundred transits. As she did, she played math games and word puzzles in her head. That was her way to stay limber and loose and keep her mind agile. If an opportunity came to escape, she wanted to be ready. To act immediately. And sooner or later, an opportunity would come. Someone would walk through that door.

When she was done with her workout, she decided not to resist her hunger anymore. Food was energy, and she needed to stay at peak energy. So she ate two power bars and drank an entire bottle of Gatorade. When she had to pee, she dropped her pants before sitting on the toilet and extended a middle finger at the camera.

Thoughts came to her. Questions and answers.

Where was she? Almost certainly still in the Los Angeles area. She'd regained consciousness in a Treadstone van, and they hadn't driven far. A couple of hours at most. They'd put a hood over her head, so she'd seen nothing when they unloaded her, and they'd only removed the hood when she was in this room. But if she was close to L.A., then Shadow was close, too.

So was Jason.

Jason.

Was he really still nearby? Was he even still alive? It seemed impossible that Shadow would kill him, but she'd learned long ago that Shadow was capable of anything. She didn't care about people. People were tools, nothing but means to her ends.

Johanna sat back down in the corner. She found herself getting tired. Crazy tired. The overhead lights made the room as bright as the sun, but her eyes drifted shut anyway. She wondered if they would wake her up by blasting Def Leppard into the room—keep her awake, keep her vulnerable—but she found her head sinking against the wall, and she slept without interruption. All she had were surreal dreams of sex and death. She had a vision of finding Jason in bed with Shadow, and she killed them both, stabbing their naked bodies over and over until their blood rose high enough to wash her away like a flood.

When she finally awoke, she had no idea how many hours had passed. But she realized immediately that this hadn't been sleep. She'd been unconscious. They'd drugged her. Fuck, fuck, fuck, it had been the power bars or the Gatorade! In the interim, they'd come into the windowless room and carried her away.

She sat in a new room now. It was larger, more like an office suite. There were windows, but the curtains were drawn, so she couldn't see where she was. She sat at a rectangular wooden table, and when she tried to move it, she found that the table was bolted to the floor. Her wrists were handcuffed to two metal rings, and her feet were shackled to similar rings on the floor.

Another camera watched her from the ceiling. She mouthed, *Fuck you.*

They were watching. They knew she was awake. Not even five minutes later, the heavy door to the room opened, and Shadow came inside. She closed the door behind her, and the lock clicked shut.

"Storm," Shadow said. "I thought we should have a chat."

Johanna said nothing. She hated being at a disadvantage to this woman. To her nemesis. It wasn't just that Shadow was free, whereas she was a prisoner chained to the table. It was also the fact that Shadow looked so annoyingly perfect, as she always did. Johanna wore the same clothes she'd been wearing at the Hollywood Bowl, and she was dirty, and she smelled, and her long blond hair clung to her skin in greasy strands. Shadow, by contrast, wore a smartly tailored burgundy business suit, every detail of her look perfect and attractive. Her hair swept over her head like an ocean wave, her blood-red lips had that kiss-me fullness, and her long, creamy white nails didn't show a single chip.

She carried no files, no pen, no phone. Instead, those elegant fingers bent around the butt of a Ruger LCP. As Shadow sat down across from Johanna, she put the gun on the table. The Ruger was part of the flag series, its rack decorated in red, white, and blue.

"Nice gun," Johanna said. "What do you want me to do? Sing the national anthem?"

A tight smile flickered across Shadow's mouth. "You may find this hard to believe, Storm, but I've always liked you."

"Well then, why don't you let me go?"

"Actually, I may do that," Shadow replied.

Johanna snorted. "Yeah, right. What do you want?"

"I want to end the vendetta between us."

"It ends when one of us is dead," Johanna replied.

"Yes, that's one option. But I'd like to propose an alternative."

"I'm not interested."

"Hear me out," Shadow said. "Don't you want to know what's going on? In case you were wondering, the Files are still out there. I don't have them yet."

"I figured."

"Callie Faith did a deal. She's free and clear."

"Of course she did. She's a survivor."

"So that leaves *you* in here, Storm. You're the only one paying the price for Callie's sins. Which is a waste of your considerable skills."

"Then why not test my skills?" Johanna replied. "Take off the cuffs. Leave the Ruger in the middle there, and let's see which one of us is fastest."

"Oh, I'm sure you'd win."

"You're right."

Shadow was quiet for a while, her stare looking inside Johanna's head like an X-ray. "You haven't asked about Jason."

"I figured you'd lie to me. Is he okay?"

"He's fine. He texted me a report this morning. He suffered a knife wound, but it's not serious. Garrett Parker is dead. Abbey was shot, and she's in the hospital. The bond between those two seems quite strong, doesn't it? I really thought he'd moved on from her. But apparently not."

Johanna's mouth tightened. She couldn't hide that Shadow had touched a nerve by throwing Jason and Abbey in her face. "Fuck you."

"Vix has the Files," Shadow went on, with an expression that said she'd gotten the reaction she wanted. "Callie thought she was dead, but she's alive and kicking. I imagine she's going to try to get out of the country with the laptop. Once she's overseas, she'll be able to find any number of rogue buyers. We need to stop her."

"Is that why you're here?" Johanna said. "Do you want me to get the Files for you? Because the answer is no. I'm not going to help you."

"No, I told Jason to go after Vix. I have faith in his skills. He'll find Vix before she gets away, and he'll get the laptop from her. He's very good. You both are, but in fairness, Jason understands people better than you do. He can read them. Anticipate them. Whereas with you, your amazing abilities are limited by what you are."

"Oh? And what's that?"

"You're a narcissist, Storm. The world is all about you. You can't sacrifice yourself for anyone else. You always come first."

Johanna shook her head. "Don't play your fucking Treadstone mind games with me and pretend you know who I am. We've been down that road before."

"Yes, we have. But that's why I know you better than you know yourself. I know Jason inside and out, too. In every situation, I know what the two of you will do before you have a chance to make up your minds and do it. That's *my* superpower. You can't play chess without knowing how to manipulate your pieces."

"You just want to fuck him again," Johanna snapped. "Now that he knows who you are, he's never going to let you do that."

Shadow leaned across the table, an arrogant sultriness in her blue eyes. "Please. If I want Jason in my bed, all I have to do is *snap— my—fingers*. Trust me, he'll come running, and he'll never go back to you."

Johanna jerked at the chains on her wrists, but they refused to yield.

Shadow sat back in the chair, a smile of smug satisfaction on her face. "Are you ready to hear my offer?"

"Take your offer and shove it up your ass."

"You haven't heard it yet."

"I don't need to."

"Give me five minutes, Storm. I have a mission, and you're the only one who can do it. I wouldn't trust this assignment to anyone else."

Johanna hesitated.

She was curious—and she was tempted—despite her hatred for the woman sitting in front of her. She wanted to spit, watching the expression on Shadow's face, but the bitch was right. She really did know how to get inside Johanna's head and push all of the right buttons.

"If I say yes?" Johanna asked cautiously.

"If you say yes, you'll be taken out of here. You'll be free. You'll have money, weapons, and access to the Treadstone jet to take you where you need to go. When the mission is done, you can trust me, come back to Treadstone, and I'll put you on the payroll as an agent again. Or you can take the cash I put in your account and go on your way. Either way, the vendetta will be done as far as I'm concerned. I won't be coming after you again." Shadow's face darkened. "Unless, of course, you make the mistake of coming after *me*."

Johanna's rage vied with her need to know more.

What mission was worth that?

"And what if I say no?" she asked.

Shadow picked up the Ruger and racked the slide. "If you say no, I'll put a bullet in your head right now. That will end the vendetta, too."

35

"YOU DON'T HAVE TO STAY HERE," ABBEY MURMURED FROM THE HOSPITAL bed. "I know you're looking for Vix. You have things you need to do."

Bourne stared out the second-floor window toward the Santa Monica hills. He turned back to Abbey, who was groggy from the surgery that had removed the bullet from her shoulder. Her face was pale, emphasizing her handful of freckles, and her dark red hair was pulled back and tied behind her head. His own wounds had been stitched and taped, and he felt nothing but a quick tug of pain when he moved.

"I'm waiting for someone. I can stay until then."

"Someone?"

He shrugged. "Treadstone."

Abbey closed her eyes with a sigh. He came and sat down in the chair next to the bed, and he took her hand in his. Her grip was limp.

"I'm sorry about Garrett," he went on.

"Thanks. The worst thing is, I feel like a fool. I always thought I was too smart to be manipulated by a man like that. I guess we all have our blind spots." Abbey's eyes blinked open. "Of course, most women don't have to shoot their husbands to make up for their mistakes. But you've saved my life so many times, I suppose I owed you one."

Jason smiled. "We're even."

"So what happens next?" she asked.

"Like you said, I have to find Vix. And fast."

"How?"

"We assume she's trying to leave the country with the laptop. There are lots of ways to do that. She could have a fake passport, but we've got facial ID surveillance on the airports and an alert out with TSA. She could head south to the Mexican border, but we've got her on the radar down there, too. Or she could head to another part of the country before trying to get out, but the longer she stays in the U.S., the greater the likelihood that she'll be spotted. So she'll want to move quickly."

"I'm guessing you have an idea how she plans to do that," Abbey said.

"Yeah. Her asset is the Files. Odds are, she's doing what she did with Rod Holtzman, finding somebody's weak spot and pressing on it. My guess is she's already got someone who knows how to smuggle people in and out of the country. Our advantage is, she's done it once before, so she'll probably go to the same person."

"Done it before?" Abbey asked. Then she made the connection. "Her sister."

"Right. She had to get her sister *into* the country. My bet is Vix will go to the same person to try to get herself *out* of the country. According to Callie Faith, she was trying to book passage for them via the port in Long Beach before the fire. I've got Treadstone doing research on likely suspects."

Abbey held his hand a little tighter. "After that, I guess you'll be gone."

"I already told you what I have to do once I get the Files."

"You did, but that's not what I mean."

"I know what you mean," Jason said.

She stared up at the ceiling. "I said when this was over, I wanted you to go far away from me. But now that it's really happening—"

"Abbey, don't do this now," he interrupted.

"If not now, then when? Isn't this the end?"

"We'll have time to talk."

She looked back at him with dark, troubled eyes. "Will we?"

"I'll make sure we do."

"You mean we'll have time for a proper goodbye?"

"I mean we'll have time for whatever feels right."

"Okay. I'll hold you to that."

Bourne felt the vibration of an incoming text on his phone. "I have to go."

He got up from the chair, but Abbey held on to his hand tightly. She didn't need to say anything, but there was a message for him in her face, and he watched her searching his own face for a reply. They were on dangerous ground. It would be easy, all too easy, to erase a year of goodbyes and go back to where they'd been before.

Her fingers loosened, and her hand fell back to the bed. She bit her lip and closed her eyes, rather than see him go. He turned away before he could lean down and kiss her, and he left her alone in the room.

Downstairs, Bourne exited the hospital into the warm California afternoon. He crossed to the far side of the parking lot, where he'd left his Highlander, and he found Shadow waiting for him, as cool and elegant as ever. He wondered what it would be like to be so untroubled by emotions, to be able to separate your feelings and duties into two separate boxes. She stood beside the SUV, her arms folded, her eyes focused on the rolling green hills. She heard him coming, but she didn't look his way.

"How's Ms. Laurent?" she asked.

"Abbey's not your concern."

"I'm just showing polite interest, Jason."

"She's fine. The surgery went well."

Shadow pursed her red lips, and as she always did, she seemed to read his mind. "Bad things happen to her whenever you come into her life. I'm sure you've thought about that. Remember the car bomb that nearly killed her?"

"I remember."

"It doesn't seem fair to do that to someone outside our world."

"That's why we broke up."

Shadow focused on him with the lasers of her blue eyes. "Did you?"

"You know we did."

"I know that's what you told me. I know that's what you've told yourself. But the past is the past, and that leaves the future."

"Move on, Shadow," Bourne snapped. "Abbey's role in this is done."

"All right. Whatever you say. Let's talk about Vix."

Bourne shook his head. "First tell me about Johanna."

"Johanna's not *your* concern."

"She sure as hell is. I want to know where you've got her. I want to see her."

"No."

"I wasn't asking," Bourne said.

"And I'm not negotiating. Forget Johanna."

"Is she alive?"

"She is. That's all I'm going to say. Let's get back to Vix and the Files."

"Maybe I'll just tell you to fuck the Files. Get them yourself."

"Is that what you want? If so, say the word. I'll throw you off the road like a flat tire and put on a new one."

Bourne tried to defuse his anger at this woman and her calm, infuriating superiority. The trouble was, she knew him too well. She knew when he was bluffing. He *needed* the Files. "If you're lying about Johanna—"

"I'm not."

Jason cut his losses and let it go. At least Johanna was alive.

"Did you have any luck with Vix?" Bourne asked.

"We did. Your instinct was a good one. We think Vix used a human-trafficking smuggler to get her sister out of Shanghai and into Los Angeles via a Chinese freighter. I'm assuming she paid to get her better accommodations than the poor bastards who wind up inside the cargo containers."

"Did you identify the smuggler?"

"With ninety percent certainty," Shadow replied. "The port's a big place. There are probably a hundred different smuggling opera- tions going on at any given time, from refugees to drugs to knockoff Birkin bags. Half of them have ties to China. Vix could have gone to a dozen different people for help. There's no way to know for sure how many of them would show up in the Files."

"But?"

"But in this case, we owe a debt to Garrett Parker. He was watching Vix. Even when they were involved, he had a PI put her under surveillance. I assume he already had his eyes on the prize. Remember we cloned Garrett's computer? Our techs figured out he kept data off-site using a third-party file manager. Video files, high-capacity stuff he couldn't keep on his local drive. I leaned on the CEO to give us access to Garrett's library. It turns out Garrett had files on Vix going back to when she was at Jumpp." Shadow hesitated. "Just so you know, he was doing the same thing to Abbey. He knew everything about her. That's how he was able to worm his way into her life so readily."

Bourne wasn't surprised. "What about Vix?"

"We're still going through the data, but I had the boys focus in on the time period within a month or so of the fire. I assume she wouldn't have tried to do a deal with Callie Faith until her sister was in the country, but she wouldn't have waited very long once she was actually here. So if she reached out to a smuggler, it was probably in that time frame."

"And you found something?"

"We did. Vix met twice with a man we were able to identify as Rufus Mack. He's in charge of nighttime security for one of the shipping operators at the Port of Long Beach. When we looked a little deeper, we found that Rufus has connections all over the Far East. China, Hong Kong, Vietnam, South Korea. He's a good choice if you want to move someone from Shanghai to L.A. under the radar. Rufus also wouldn't want his side business to come to the attention of his employer—or the FBI—so if Vix found him in the Files, she'd have been able to leverage him to do whatever the hell she wanted."

"And she still can," Bourne said.

"Right. If Vix is looking to get out of the country, Rufus Mack would be her first call."

VIX FELT THE THUNDER OF A FREIGHT TRAIN RATTLE THE WALLS OF THE motel.

She went to the window and peeked through the curtains, watching the graffiti-covered shipping containers rumble away from the port. It was dark outside, except for the city lights. Nearly nine o'clock. In another hour, her Uber would pull up outside the motel and drop her a few blocks away near the gangway of the *Xin Fang*. The ship would depart in the middle of the night after a wink and a nod from Rufus's man in U.S. Customs and Border Protection. She'd be hidden on board, silently holding her breath.

Next stop, Puerto Quetzal, Guatemala. She'd be free. Maybe not of the past, but free to build her future.

After that, who knew? She could go anywhere. Maybe Chile. Maybe through the canal and on to Turkey in the Mediterranean or somewhere in the Baltic. The cartels, the Eastern Europeans, the Iranians—they all would want a crack at the Files.

She went to the motel door and stepped outside into the cool evening air. She smelled the spice of the taco stand around the corner, where she'd had dinner. Electrical wires crisscrossed the sky. Among the parked cars in front of the motel doors, she heard the murmur of voices, and two men smoked cigarettes near the railroad tracks. But no one seemed to be watching her. She drew back inside, locking the door. Her nerves were rattled. She'd only relax when the *Xin Fang* was safely clear of the port and churning into international waters.

A few more hours.

Her duffel bag sat on the neatly made bed, filled with everything she owned in the world. Except for the laptop, which she hugged tightly in her arms. The laptop was back with her now, and she would never let go of it. It would never leave her sight, not until the final deal was done.

Vix checked her watch again. Almost no time had passed. These final minutes before she left for the ship felt glacial. The stress was unbearable, like a heavy weight pressing on her chest. Her stomach lurched, and she tasted acid in her throat. She ran for the tiny bathroom, and when she knelt in front of the toilet, her dinner came up in spasms, followed by dry heaves that left her aching and thirsty. She washed out her mouth, then went and stretched out on the bed. She didn't dare close her eyes and risk sleeping past the time she had to go. Not that she would have slept. Adrenaline poured through her veins.

Rufus had laid out the rules of the voyage. Arrive on time. Pay the captain in cash. Have plenty of money for bribes for the crew and for anyone else who asks questions. Keep to yourself until the ship arrives in Guatemala. Only get off when the captain tells you to get off, and don't draw attention to yourself in the port when you disembark. That was how it worked for different people on different ships a thousand times a day. Follow the rules, and you'll be fine.

But was Rufus lying?

He hated her because she knew all of his secrets and had threatened to expose him. When her sister had come over from Shanghai, she'd promised he would never hear from her again, but six months later, here she was, back with a new demand. For herself. Outbound, not inbound.

What if Rufus decided to do a deal of his own? Pay the captain or someone on the crew to get rid of her?

Wait until you're west of Mexico, then throw the bitch overboard for the sharks.

Or what if he'd realized she was more valuable to the Chinese? He could have named any price to hand her over to them. They'd be waiting for her when she got out of the cab, and they'd shove her inside one of their black SUVs.

Vix didn't trust Rufus. She didn't trust anyone.

She got out of bed again and paced. Only five more minutes had gone by. It occurred to her that if something had gone wrong, she wouldn't know. Her phone was powered down. Rufus had told her not to turn on her phone because phones could be tracked. But what if Rufus was trying to reach her, to tell her to stay away, to say that the plan was blown? She might be walking into a trap.

It would only be for a couple of minutes. Check her phone, then power it down and remove the battery.

Vix went to the window again. She checked outside for new cars in the parking lot, for new shadows on the street. But nothing had changed. She dug her phone from her pocket, inserted the battery with trembling hands, and waited impatiently for the power to go on and for the phone to search the sky for a 5G signal.

New messages.

None.

She went to the anonymous number—the number for Rufus's burner—and saw only the last message she'd sent him earlier in the day. *I'll be there.*

Everything was fine.

Vix went to power down her phone again, but before she did, a low musical ping announced that she had one new email waiting for her. The single digit on her home screen—*1*—taunted her. Who would be sending her mail? She thought about switching off the phone without checking it; she thought about going outside and putting the phone on the railroad tracks for the next outgoing train to demolish it.

Instead, she opened up the mail app and saw the empty screen of her inbox. Empty except for one message with nothing in the subject line. She didn't recognize the sender or the domain. The account writing to her was anonymous, just like her own mail account was intended to be anonymous.

How had anyone found her?

Vix opened the message. She began to read, but she hadn't even finished before she slapped a hand over her mouth and fell to her knees. Her eyes kept going back to the first lines of the email and reading them again and again.

I know who you are. If you want to survive the night, you'll
do exactly what I say.

36

BOURNE DROVE A STREET BIKE DEEP INTO THE PORT.

Railroad tracks lined one side of the shipping pier, and the deep waters of the oceanside channel bumped up against stone pilings on the other side. A cool breeze blew in from offshore, with a spitting rain in the air. Where the pier made a dogleg to his left, he drifted to a stop and hid the bike near the rocks. No one was likely to see it there. He checked both directions, but in this corner of the port, he had the road to himself.

It was midnight. Despite the late hour, industrial activity rumbled through the nearby inlets. He heard the thunder of engines and the bang of metal against metal. Light towers glowed against the night sky and threw ghostly shadows. Across the water, the high triangular silhouettes of cranes moved like giant spiders as they loaded and unloaded brightly colored cargo containers.

His Glock in his hand, Bourne slipped across the road. Flatbed railcars stretched out of sight in both directions in an unbroken line,

double-stacked with containers made of weathering steel. He
climbed atop the coupling that connected the two nearest cars, then
jumped down to the rocks on the other side. The next set of railway
cars made a wall, and he repeated the process, slowly cutting across
the parallel tracks toward the far side of the inlet.

Halfway through the maze, he heard a shot.

It was barely audible above the thumping noise of the port and
the plink of rain on the containers. The muffled report came from in
front of him; it came from where he was heading. Jason ran faster, up
and over the train cars. When he finally cleared the tracks, he
stopped, surveying a small parking lot next to the middle harbor.
The lot butted up to a barbed-wire fence, and he saw a two-story
building beyond the fence. It was built on a concrete platform to give
a vantage over the activity of the port. Stairs led up to a door labeled
SECURITY on the second floor, next to a few brightly lit windows.

That was Rufus Mack's office.

The door leading inside was wide open.

Bourne ran to the revolving security gate and jabbed the call
button. No one answered. He noticed a camera mounted on the
nearest light tower, but the camera had been shot out, and glass littered the pavement on the other side of the fence. Quickly, he
climbed the wet, slippery gate to the narrow steel platform, then
took wire cutters from the inside pocket of his jacket and snipped
the four rows of barbed wire and peeled them away. He lowered his
body from the platform, then let go and landed on the ground inside
the fence.

As he came off his knees, he swung the Glock in a semicircle.
Not even five minutes had passed since he'd heard the gunshot. He

examined the shadows of the building around him, but he saw no movement and heard no footsteps. Whoever had taken the shot had already disappeared.

Bourne ran up the steps to the building's open door. Leading with his gun, he spun inside. A large empty office looked out on the pier in every direction. Multiple monitors reflected video camera feeds from around the area. On the west side, he saw a monitor reflecting static, probably from the shattered camera at the gate below him. Below the monitor, he saw the body of a Black man sprawled on the linoleum floor.

The face matched the photo Shadow had given him. It was Rufus Mack, dressed in the brown uniform of port security. Vix's contact. Blood was spreading in a pool under his head from the bullet hole in the middle of his forehead.

Mack was dead.

Bourne swore. Someone had gotten here first; someone was ahead of him, but only by a few minutes. *Who?*

It didn't matter. Whoever it was had gotten what he needed out of Mack—the name of the ship that would smuggle Vix out of the country—and then killed the man to make sure he didn't sound the alarm.

Bourne went to the nearest windows. From where he was, he could see three huge container ships staggered around multiple docks, all of them weighted down with cargo and seemingly ready for departure.

Which one?

He returned to the body of Rufus Mack and searched the man's pockets. They were empty. He sifted through the mass of papers on Mack's desk, looking for any kind of clue that might point him to the ship where Vix would be hiding, but he found nothing. Then he noted a separate monitor that showed security camera footage on each of the three ships readying for departure.

The *Algeriana.*

The *Mirandelle.*

The *Xin Fang.*

He rewound the video feeds for each of the ships by two hours, then fast-forwarded, watching people come and go on the gangways that led inside the freighters. Whenever he saw anything that raised a red flag, he froze the video and checked it again. His review of the footage for the *Algeriana* showed nothing. Same with the *Mirandelle.* By the time he'd gone through most of the video for the *Xin Fang*, he was beginning to think Shadow was wrong. Vix's escape wasn't planned for tonight in Long Beach. Or it wasn't on a freighter located in Rufus Mack's area of the port.

Then he paused the video as someone approached the gangway of the *Xin Fang.* He backed up and watched the same fragment again. When he checked the time stamp, he saw that it had been recorded barely half an hour earlier. When Bourne zoomed in, the clarity of the feed was enough for him to recognize Rufus Mack. The security man chatted with a guard monitoring the gangway, and then he gestured the man away from the area with a handshake—probably a handshake that included a sizable bribe.

When the other guard was gone, Mack waved toward the shadows.

A woman in a hooded sweatshirt, with a duffel slung over one shoulder, walked into the light. Bourne couldn't see her face, but he knew it was her. Vix. She hurried up the gangway past Mack and disappeared into the interior of the freighter.

Bourne snatched Rufus Mack's port ID from the body and put the lanyard around his neck, with the badge flipped around on the outside of his jacket. He ran back to the steps and descended to the ground near the security fence. Quickly, he made his way to the water, where the long line of the pier stretched in front of him. He saw the *Xin Fang* at a dock two hundred yards away. He headed for the ship slowly, his hands in his pockets, one hand still curled around the Glock.

The closer he got to the ship, the more people he saw. Workers came and went, but no one paid attention to him. Overhead, giant cranes manipulated painted steel containers into cubes six and seven high, like enormous sets of children's blocks. He neared the gangway, which was guarded by a man in uniform waiting at the base of the ramp. The man had a radio and a gun, but this was not the same man who'd been monitoring access to the ship in the video he'd seen. Jason didn't alter his pace, but he shot a glance at the narrow corridors between the mountains of containers. He saw a body in the shadows; it had been dragged to a place where it was nearly out of sight.

The guard was a fake. This was the first watchman to protect whatever was going on inside the ship.

He was also Chinese.

The CCP was here for the Files.

As Bourne approached, the man tensed, his hand drawing near his gun. Jason let his own hands slip from his pockets, as if he were no threat. He didn't look like a guard, and he wasn't dressed like a guard, but all he needed was a cover that held for a few seconds. With a scowl on his face, he gestured at the hull of the ship towering over their heads, and he barked at the man in a voice that didn't tolerate disobedience.

"Hey, what the fuck? Didn't Rufus give you my message? I said I wanted *two* men on patrol tonight. The feds are all up my ass about counterfeits out of Dong Nai, and I don't want to give them anything that might slow us up." Bourne pointed over the man's shoulder. "Did that asshole with the clipboard ask you any questions? What did you tell him?"

Momentarily confused, the man twisted around to look behind him. In that instant, with a lightning blow, Bourne hit him in the throat. As the guard doubled over and choked, Jason threw him to the ground and slammed his head hard against the pavement until he was out cold. He looked both ways for anyone running toward him, but amid the rain and shadows, no one had noticed the fight. He rolled the body to the darkness at the edge of the pier, then ran up the rusting gangway to the stern of the ship.

For now, he was alone. The ship was designed to run with a skeleton crew, and whoever was here was likely above him on the navigation bridge. Looking forward, he saw a covered walkway, with containers rising above it to make a high wall. The superstructure of the ship rose over his head. He drew his Glock, then climbed to the next level and made his way through an open watertight door into the alleyway. The hum of the ship filled his ears. He checked the crew and officers' mess—both empty—then noted the cook and a couple of messmen at work with food in the galley. None looked back to see him.

He climbed to the next level. And then the next. He searched quickly, making his way from port to starboard and back.

Where was Vix?

Bourne checked all of the accommodation rooms on the upper decks and found no one in the cabins or recreation rooms. He climbed to the top of the ship, avoiding the bridge crew, then made his way back down to the alleyway on the main deck. He was ready to head forward past the stacks of containers when a scream rose from the bowels of the ship.

He slid down the railing to the upper platform of the engine decks. He found himself in a hot, supersized world of pipes, tanks, and boilers, thumping with the deafening noise of machinery and the hiss of hydraulics. He didn't need to hide his movements; no one could hear him. The equipment rooms were an erector set of fuel pumps and compressors, all whirring and banging, glistening in yellow and silver paint. His Glock outstretched, he made his way through the maze.

First the upper platform. It was empty. Then he descended to the middle platform just above the hull, where the pounding noise of the motors got louder, and he wanted to cover his ears. His head throbbed.

But he'd heard *something.* Was it a shot? A ricochet of bullet on metal?

Vix was here; she was close.

So were the Chinese.

The stifling heat intensified. Sweat poured in beads down his skin, soaking his clothes. The butt of his gun slipped in his hand. He squatted to survey the room below the machinery, but if anyone was hiding here, they were hidden behind a tangle of steel. His back against hot metal, he edged sideways past diesel generators twice his height.

There she was.

Huddled on the floor beyond the generators, her knees drawn up, her arms clutching a laptop to her chest, was Vix. She saw him, and her eyes widened. As Bourne ran forward, she opened her mouth to shout, but he recognized the warning too late.

Where the equipment ended, he charged into the open, and a vicious kick from his right sent him flying, his Glock skidding away across the floor. As he tumbled and then tried to get up, another kick threw him backward, his head and shoulders crashing into rock-hard steel. His eyes refocused, and he saw the Chinese assassin with the red glasses and spiky hair, the killer who'd dodged him three times before. The kid had his QSZ-92 in his hand, and he grinned as he brought up his arm to aim the gun at Bourne.

Ten feet away. Easy shot.

Then a wail of desperation distracted both of them. Vix shot off the floor and threw herself at the assassin, knocking him sideways against one of the generators. She ran, the laptop still in her arms, and the maneuver gave Bourne time to slither across the floor to grab his Glock. He scooped it up and rolled again, barely missing a shot from the killer's QSZ, and he fired back three times, hearing wild pings of metal. The third shot hit the assassin just above the knee, and the kid howled, his leg giving way. As the killer fell, he fired over and over, a random barrage of bullets that sent Bourne half crawling, half running to get away. Ricochets bounced like popcorn. Bourne leaped, hitting the metal wall, then crashed down to his left behind a web of yellow pipes.

He waited, breathing hard. He wiped his face and tried to dry his gun on his shirt. He listened, but he couldn't hear footsteps above the thunder of equipment. He couldn't hear the assassin getting up, moving left, moving right.

Where was he?

Bourne aimed at the wall and squeezed off a shot, trying to draw fire that would give away the killer's location. The assassin didn't take the bait. Bourne glanced to the six-foot gap between his hiding place and the row of generators, and he wondered if he could make it before the killer targeted him. He took the chance. He pushed off his knees and leaped, and again he drew no fire.

Then he knew why.

Bourne stood up. He kept his gun level, but he didn't shoot. When he eased past the machinery, he saw the killer on his back on the floor, a bloody, gaping gunshot wound where his left eye should have been.

A ricochet. A ricochet from one of the man's own bullets had taken him down.

Jason turned and ran. He had no time. *Vix.*

He bolted up the steps to the ship's main deck, colliding with and taking down two men who'd come to investigate the noises from below. Another man in uniform jumped to intercept him, and Bourne dodged him and flung himself outside through the watertight door. The gangway was immediately in front of him. Halfway down, he saw Vix, slipping and sliding on the wet steps. She glanced back and spotted him, and he took off in pursuit. When she reached the pier, she sprinted straight ahead into the mountainous cubes of stacked containers, and she vanished into the darkness.

Bourne followed.

The rain made a singsong music on the steel. The containers loomed like skyscrapers over his head, framed against the night sky.

He crossed into a wide track between the rows of cargo, and a shot bounced off the pavement and clanged against the metal. Vix stood a few feet away, the laptop under one arm, her other arm shaking as she tried to steady herself and fire. She squeezed the trigger once more and missed over Bourne's head. Then the next shot made zig-zag ricochets down the row of containers.

When she pulled the trigger again, it clicked and came up empty.

Vix dropped the gun. She pulled a knife from her belt and waved it in front of her.

Bourne pointed his Glock at her chest as he walked forward. "It's over, Vix. Give me the laptop."

She jabbed the knife at him. "Stay away!"

"Don't make me shoot you. I don't want to do that. But I will. I'll kill you, and I'll take the laptop anyway. Make it easy on yourself."

"No!"

"You can still escape. You can find a way out of the country and go wherever you want."

Vix dropped the knife and dug in her pocket. He watched her hand emerge with a pink stun gun, but before she could point it at him, he stepped inside her arms and knocked it away, then peeled the laptop from her fingers. He kept the Glock level as he backed up, and with his other hand, he lifted the lid and booted up the machine. The home screen glowed a few seconds later, with nothing but twelve white boxes blinking at him on a blue background and waiting for a password.

The Files.

"What's the access code?" he asked.

"Fuck you."

"I told you, I *don't* want to kill you."

"If you kill me, you get shit," Vix snapped.

"You're right, but that doesn't sound like an even trade, does it? Would your father think this is worth you dying like he did? Like your mom? Like your sister? Come on, Vix. Give me the code, and forget about the Files."

Vix stared at him through the shadows.

Then she rattled off a combination of letters, numbers, and symbols. Bourne tapped the keys as she did, memorized the code, and then pressed the ENTER button. The laptop screen changed, the password prompt disappeared, and three parallel lines appeared. A menu. He navigated the mouse arrow to the menu and clicked to see a lineup of at least twenty top-level search options. A guide to every secret that could be unlocked. Financial. Political. Personal. Sexual. He could almost sense a rogue brain humming inside the machine, an all-knowing genie with no moral compass ready to grant your wishes.

He had the Files.

"Thank you, Vix."

She said nothing.

He powered down the laptop and holstered his Glock. Vix looked surprised, as if she'd expected him to kill her anyway once he had what he wanted. He backed away until she was out of range, and then he finally turned around as he reached the next corridor between the shipping containers. He looked back one last time as he went deeper into the maze. Vix hadn't moved. Her face was lost in the shadows.

Bourne took a circuitous route back to the other side of the pier.

As he reached his street bike, he heard a text arrive on his phone. He checked it and saw a message from Shadow.

Do you have it?

Jason stared at those four words long and hard. He was at the point of no return.

Then he climbed aboard the bike and fired the engine, and with a flick of his wrist, he tossed the phone into the water.

37

CODY CHOSE A MEETING GROUND TWENTY MILES OUTSIDE OF NARVA, supplying GPS coordinates for the exact location. He would bring Tati at ten in the morning. Bourne would bring the laptop with the Files. Then they would make the exchange.

Jason awoke early in his hotel in Tallinn on the morning of the meeting. It had taken him three days to travel from Los Angeles to Estonia via six countries, avoiding any chance that Shadow and Treadstone might be able to track him. The last leg took him by ferry from Copenhagen, and he'd arrived in the early evening. He rented an Audi, ate a dinner of pork sausages and rye bread, checked into a cheap hotel on the outskirts of the city, and finally made a phone call to an old friend. For most of the night, he then lay on the hard bed, eyes wide open as he stared at the ceiling.

His mind worked through strategy after strategy, option after option, trying to find a solution.

Was there a way to rescue Tati and avoid giving up the Files? He saw no way to do so.

But if he handed the laptop to Cody, would the Russian keep his part of the bargain and let Tati go? Or would he kill them both anyway?

His instincts told him they'd be dead. So he needed a way to balance the scales.

At one in the morning, his old friend knocked on the hotel room door to make a delivery. After a large exchange of cash, Bourne had an AK-12 automatic rifle in his hands and plenty of extra magazines. The AK-12 was the standard service rifle for the Russian military, and he assumed that Cody and his men would be similarly equipped. Even if Bourne was outnumbered, he wanted comparable firepower.

Four hours before the meeting time, long before dawn, he headed out on the lonely Estonian highways. The rendezvous was two and a half hours away in the middle of nowhere, and he got there as the morning sun cleared the trees. The coordinates took him to the intersection of two unpaved roads covered by several inches of virgin snow. Dense stands of winter-bare trees crowded the roads in all four directions, and high towers carried electrical wires over his head.

He parked the Audi on the snowy shoulder of one of the roads and got out. He still had an hour to go before the meeting. With the rifle cradled in his arms, he hiked a hundred yards in each direction from the intersection, seeing no one. His breath clouded in front of his face. It was freezing cold under weak sunshine, and the empty area was unnaturally quiet. No birds. No car engines. Even the wind had died and left it completely still.

But Bourne wasn't alone.

In the darkness as he drove from Tallinn, he'd spotted the occasional glow of a single headlight as a motorcycle trailed him. A couple of times, he'd slowed to try to draw the driver in, but whoever was on the bike was smart. The rider never got close enough for Bourne to make them. Now, when he returned to the center of the crossroads, he knew he was being watched again. He heard no sound in the silence, but somewhere in the trees, sunshine glinted off metal.

A gun.

Cody had sent an advance scout to keep an eye on the Files.

Bourne removed the laptop and held it high in his hands, so whoever was there could see it. Then he put it on the hood of his rented car in plain sight. If he was being surveilled, he wanted the spy to report to Cody that Bourne had the laptop. The deal was on. When he was done, he returned to the middle of the road and waited. The rifle was still in his arms, its barrel pointed at the ground.

Cody arrived exactly on time.

At ten o'clock, Bourne heard the growl of engines breaking the silence. Between the trees in all four directions, black SUVs closed on the intersection. Each vehicle came within twenty yards of the crossroads and then stopped at an angle. Two men got out of each SUV, one on the driver's side, one on the passenger side, each man carrying an AK-12 that matched Bourne's gun.

Eight to one in a battle of automatic weapons. He didn't like his odds.

The back door of the SUV on the north side of the intersection opened wide. The vehicle shifted with the weight, and Cody climbed out. He had no rifle; the leader didn't need one, not when his men already had Bourne surrounded. But he had his Grach in a holster and the same long sharp knife dangling from his belt. The man wore camouflage cargo pants, boots, and an oilskin coat over his muscled chest. He was even larger than Jason remembered, and his long hair and beard made him look like a mountain man who'd been living as a recluse in the woods.

Seeing him, Bourne had flashbacks of what Cody had done to Tati. And what he'd made Tati do to the boy on the table.

This was an evil, dangerous man.

Cody noted the rifle in Bourne's arms, but he showed no concern. He grinned, revealing snow-white teeth, and it was the grin of the alpha wolf surrounded by his hungry pack. "You won't need that."

"No?"

"Not assuming you keep your end of the bargain. I told you before, Cain, I'm a man of my word. You can't do deals in my world unless people trust you."

"I don't trust anyone," Jason replied.

"That's fair. And smart. But look around you. There's no room for escape. You don't get out of here alive unless I say so."

"Kill me if you want." Bourne slapped the metal of his rifle. "But if you do, you'll be dead before I hit the ground. I'm a man of my word, too."

Cody chuckled approvingly. "I like you, Cain. A professional always respects another professional. Honestly, why do you waste your time with the liars of Treadstone? You say you don't trust anyone, so you know that you can't trust them. Why not change allegiances? Come to work for me. Be my personal assassin, like Lennon was to Putin. A handful of jobs a year, and the rest of the time, you're free. You can go live on an island somewhere and fuck native girls all day."

"No thanks."

"I hope it's not because of some kind of naive American patriotism.

Patriotism is for fools who march their way into the wood chipper while their bosses do deals with the enemy. That's not you."

"I make my own choices," Bourne said. "They don't include working for you."

Cody shrugged. He nodded at the laptop on the rented car. "Is that it?"

"It is. But first you give me Tati."

"That's fair. Just remember, no tricks, Cain. Any tricks, and it will go badly for both of you."

"The laptop contains the Files," Bourne said. "No tricks. There's a password that opens up the engine. Once I'm sure Tati is alive and hasn't been harmed, I'll give you the password. At that point, the Files are all yours."

"Agreed."

"But I can shoot you down in less than two seconds if you betray me, Cody."

The big man held up his hands. "Mutually assured destruction. I get it."

Cody gestured at the SUV behind him. The rear passenger door opened, and someone got out, but it wasn't Tati. This was a boy, no more than eighteen. He wore jeans and a gray sweatshirt, and he limped when he tried to walk. His feet were bare in the snow. Jason didn't know him, but he recognized him. This was the boy in the video that Cody had sent him. The boy that Cody had made Tati violate to send Bourne a message.

Franken. That was the name Tati had used.

Oh God, Franken, I'm so sorry, Tati had moaned.

Franken wrapped his skinny arms around his chest. He was cold. He stared at the ground, his messy brown hair falling across his eyes.

His skin was deathly white except for the rainbow-colored bruises where he'd been beaten. He had the defeated look of an animal condemned to a lifetime in a cage.

"A little bonus for you, Cain," Cody told him. "You get to take the boy, too."

"What did you do to him?"

"Only what was necessary to keep Tati in line."

"Where is she?"

Cody raised his right hand and snapped his fingers. Moments later, another figure climbed from the back of the SUV.

Tati.

She moved stiffly, her matchstick legs struggling to support her. Her arms were tied behind her back. Her black glasses were broken and had been taped together, but they hung off balance on her face. She'd always been skinny, but now she looked gaunt, her T-shirt and jeans swimming on her body. Coming into the bitter cold, she shivered, her limbs trembling. Her eyes squinted at the brightness of the day, and she looked around with frightened curiosity, seeing men with guns everywhere, obviously wondering if she'd been taken out here to be killed.

Then, as her head swiveled, her gaze landed on Jason.

A strangled cry burst from her throat. Her eyes glazed over with tears. She began to run, but her feet got tangled up with each other, and she pitched forward into the snow. With her hands tied, she couldn't get up, and one of the men with the rifles yanked her up by her loose red T-shirt. Her face was wet, her whole body damp. When she was standing, she ran again, directly toward Jason, and she spilled off her feet into his arms. He had to hold her up, and as she planted kisses all over his face, he slipped his knife out of his belt and cut through the zip tie that bound her wrists. With her arms free, she threw them around his neck and clung to him so tightly he could barely breathe.

"Oh God, you came for me," she breathed into his ear. "You're here, you're really here, I knew you'd come. I knew it. I never lost faith. Take me away from here, Jason. Please. Take me away. I never want to see this place again."

Slowly, he detached himself from her. "Soon. Soon we'll go, and you'll be safe."

Tati held on to his waist, her head leaning into his shoulder. She closed her eyes rather than look at Cody.

"Are you okay?" Jason asked. "Did he do anything else to you?"

"I'm okay. With you here, I'll be okay."

Cody looked amused by their reunion. "Satisfied, Cain?"

Bourne nodded. "I am. The laptop's yours. Take it, and we all go our separate ways."

"Naturally I need to verify its authenticity first."

"Naturally."

Cody flicked a finger toward one of the other SUVs. A small man got out of the back seat. He was in his forties, bald, with tiny silver glasses on his face and a cherry-red birthmark near his grim mouth. He wore a down bubble coat over a tailored business suit, and he carried a laptop of his own, along with cables and a small satellite antenna. When he reached Bourne's car, he spent a few minutes setting up the antenna and squinting at the sky as he booted up his computer.

"Starlink," Cody explained. "I just love Elon Musk, don't you?"

The tech man finally appeared to be satisfied with the setup, and he connected his own laptop to the machine that Jason had brought.

He powered on the computer that drove the Files, and Bourne saw the same blue screen with twelve white boxes that had greeted him when he took the laptop from Vix.

"Password," the man called in a flat voice.

Bourne gave him the code digit by digit, and the man keyed it in. When he was done, the password prompt vanished, replaced by the three parallel lines of the main menu.

"Well?" Cody called.

"So far, so good."

The man's fingers flew on the keyboard. Opening up the Files. Running searches. Turning the AI engine loose on a racecourse to see how it would perform. Two more minutes passed, and finally the man looked up from the laptop and gave Cody a thumbs-up.

"It's real."

Cody beamed. "Excellent."

Bourne tensed. This was the point of no return. Either Cody would let them go, or he'd betray them and bodies would start to fall. His finger slipped around the trigger of the AK-12, and he braced the butt against his shoulder. Cody was close. Not even ten feet away. In an instant, he could swing the rifle up and deliver a burst of automatic fire that would blow the giant man off his feet.

Of course, in the next instant, Bourne would be dead, too. So would Tati and Franken.

"Well?" he asked Cody. "Are you a man of your word?"

"I am. All three of you are free to go. But I'll also leave you with a warning, Cain. A bonus for keeping the deal."

"What's that?"

"Putin has a bounty out on you. He wants revenge for what you did to Lennon. Five million if you're dead. Ten if you're alive, so he can deal with you himself. Today you have my protection. Tomorrow we are adversaries again, and it's open season. So I'd suggest you not be in Estonia after midnight."

"I won't be."

"Then our deal is concluded."

Cody raised his hand over his head and spun his finger in a circle as a signal to his men. In unison, the eight men standing near the SUVs lowered their rifles. Bourne let go of his own rifle, letting it dangle at the neck strap. Step by step, he backed away, guiding Tati and Franken toward his car. He felt the eyes of every man, waiting for him to make a mistake. When he got to the Audi, he opened the back door and nudged Franken and Tati inside. He slammed the door behind them. Keeping his hands off the AK-12, he moved around the back of the car and then opened the driver's door. The keys were in the ignition.

The little man still had the laptop on the hood of the Audi. He began to disconnect his satellite hookup.

Then he screamed: "*Wait!*"

Cody's head snapped around. "What is it?"

"A virus! It's a fucking virus! The whole thing is disintegrating! The machine is worthless!"

The giant Russian didn't hesitate. Instantly, he jabbed a finger at Bourne and bellowed to his men: "*KILL THEM ALL!*"

The air exploded with a ceaseless, deafening barrage of gunfire.

Bourne dived behind the wheel of the Audi and screamed at Tati and Franken. "*Get down! Stay down!*"

He turned the engine over as every window in the car shattered and the metal of the chassis thumped with the impact of dozens of bullets. His foot jerked to the accelerator and jammed it down, and the Audi leaped backward, jerking across forty feet of rock and snow and crashing into the bodies of two of the men with rifles. The car kept going, slamming into the chassis of the SUV and pinning both men between the vehicles, their hips crushed.

"Stay there! Don't move!"

Bourne rolled out of the Audi. He fired a burst from the AK-12 to buy himself a couple of seconds, then skittered backward for cover behind the other vehicle. In front of him, Cody stood like a huge statue in the middle of the intersection, directing the battle while six other men converged on Bourne's location, not running, just marching like soldiers and firing as they came. The hailstorm of bullets froze him behind the SUV, unable to mount a defense. He couldn't stay where he was, and as soon as he tried to get Tati and Franken out of the Audi, they'd all be dead on the ground.

But above the frenzy of the assault, he suddenly heard fire from a new direction.

One of the men on the road danced a jig as bullets riddled his back, and he fell. So did the man next to him, nearly decapitated by rounds through his neck.

From the far side of the intersection, someone ran from the trees, her AK-12 bombarding Cody's men.

It was Johanna.

38

THE ASSAULT BROUGHT BOURNE BACK INTO THE FIGHT.

He watched the two closest men on his left swivel as bullets thudded into the snow and trees around them. He rolled free of the SUV, training his AK-12 on both men, and watched twenty rounds eviscerate their twitching bodies. They fell hard. There were now only two men left, caught in a pincer from ahead and behind, and they split their fire. One aimed at Johanna, the other at Bourne.

He rolled back to cover and slapped in a new magazine. More glass flew like shrapnel. The front tires of the SUV exploded. Inside the Audi, he heard Tati screaming and Franken crying.

When the barrage paused as the men exhausted their magazines, Bourne struck back. Johanna did the same. They swung into the open and attacked with a deadly, pinpoint cross fire, turning the white snow blood-red at the men's feet as their pulped bodies collapsed. Bourne's finger finally released the trigger. He reloaded, but the battle was done. Around him, a fierce silence replaced the blast of the rifles. Burnt smoke rose in the still air. Cody's men were all down. The tech specialist had dropped the laptop and run away into the woods.

At the center of the intersection, Cody stood alone, as stiff as an oak tree, his eyes wild with fury and disbelief.

Bourne hiked toward him, boots crunching in the snow. So did Johanna from the opposite side of the road. Cody still had his Grach in his belt, which was like a spitball against a cannon. He grabbed for it anyway, and as he yanked the gun free, Bourne unleashed a short round of tight, accurate fire that nearly severed the man's hand from his wrist. The Russian howled, watching blood spurt from his dangling limb.

Cody didn't move again.

Johanna walked up next to Bourne, her rifle still aimed at Cody. She wore white jeans and a white Lycra coat that made her look like a snow angel. Her long blond hair was tucked under a white beret, making her nearly invisible while she was hiding in the woods. One of her blue eyes winked.

"Surprise."

"Hey, I knew you were there," Bourne said.

"Did not."

He allowed himself a tight smile. "Well, I knew someone was there."

"Glad to see me?" she asked.

"Very glad."

Johanna nodded at Cody. "What do we do with Bigfoot here?"

Cody growled at them, his face contorted with pain. "You're going to kill me, so just fucking do it."

"I could cauterize the wound," Bourne pointed out. "That would save him. Or at least it would buy us time to get him to a hospital."

"Are you going to do that?" Johanna asked.

"No." Then he said, "Watch him, okay? If he goes for his knife, disembowel him."

Bourne walked back to the shattered Audi. He pried open the rear door, hearing the metal grind in protest. Tati and Franken huddled on the floor of the car inside, with Tati protecting the boy with her body. He helped them both out of the vehicle and made sure they hadn't been injured by any of the flying bullets or the fragments of metal and glass. They were unharmed.

The three of them returned to the middle of the intersection. Bourne noticed that Franken wasn't staring at the ground anymore. His eyes burned into the huge Russian, his young, bruised face reddened with a lust for vengeance. Tati, by contrast, didn't look at Cody at all. She simply stared at Jason, as if still unsure whether she was dreaming.

"It's up to you two," Bourne said. "You're the judge and jury. What do we do with him? We can save his life or we can kill him."

Tati and Franken glanced at each other and said in unison, "Kill him."

Bourne's index finger slapped the switch on the AK-12 to semi-automatic mode—one shot at a time—then curled around the trigger of the rifle. Cody stared back at him, defiant, his dark face aflame. The big man didn't have long to live regardless. Blood continued to pulse like a fountain from his wrist with each heartbeat. In another few minutes, he'd be gone, even if Bourne did nothing more. Jason thought about making the end hard, not soft. That was what his gut told him. Pay this sadist back for the things he'd done. To Tati. To Franken. To the boy's family. To countless young women. Make his last few minutes agonizing and slow.

Squeeze the trigger. A shot in the knee.

Again. A shot in the other knee.

Again. A shot in the groin.

Take the man's knife and peel back his skin. Let him scream for mercy before the devil took him away.

Instead, Bourne hoisted the rifle in one smooth motion, squeezed the trigger, and fired a single shot between Cody's eyes before the man had time to say another word. The Russian pitched forward, dead.

"Come on," Bourne said. "Let's go."

THEY TOOK ONE OF CODY'S SUVS.

On the long drive back to Tallinn, Jason kept a close eye on the mirrors, but no one from Cody's operation—or from Treadstone—showed up to follow them. They dropped Franken Mikkel at an apartment outside the city in Maardu, where his aunt lived. From that moment, Bourne knew the clock was ticking. He'd told the boy not to lie or hold anything back. The aunt would take Franken to the hospital, and the hospital would ask questions about his wound, and the entire story would come out when the police arrived. Soon enough, the Internal Security Service would be locating multiple bodies around Narva, and they'd be looking for the three of them at every border crossing.

All hell was about to break loose in Estonia, and Bourne needed to get himself, Tati, and Johanna out of the country.

He ditched the SUV in the city center. They shopped for new clothes and left their old clothes in the changing rooms. Then they took a cab to the port to catch the ferry to Helsinki, which was the fastest departure point. As they boarded, he wondered if Tati would remember the significance of this location. She did. The CIA had staged the death of her father—a Russian defector—in a ferry explosion at this port years earlier. He could see the memories casting shadows across her face. Tati went off by herself as the ferry cruised to open water in the Gulf of Finland, which left Bourne alone with Johanna.

They stood next to each other by the railing, with the cold breeze whipping off the water. Tallinn disappeared on the horizon behind them, and Helsinki was still two hours away. Johanna laced her fingers through his hand. Her pretty face was serene, her blue eyes lost in the sea, but that was an act.

They both knew time was short between them.

"I did a deal with Shadow," Johanna said.

Bourne nodded. "I figured."

"The deal was to save you. Otherwise, I wouldn't have done it. Anything else, and I would have spit in her face."

"If you hadn't been there, I'd be dead. So would Tati and Franken."

"Shadow knew what you were going to do," Johanna told him, which he'd already guessed. "She knew your plan. She knew you were going to steal the Files. Did you tell anyone?"

"Only Abbey," he replied.

Johanna stiffened. A frown crossed her lips. The name *Abbey* seemed to grate on her nerves like fingernails on a chalkboard. He understood the irritation. He'd told Abbey his secret, but not her. He'd trusted his old lover, but not his current lover. But the jealousy went deeper than that.

Then Johanna shrugged and let it go. "Well, I don't suppose she told anyone. Shadow must have bugged her house."

"I'm sure she did. That was a mistake on my part. I should have seen that coming."

"You better tell Abbey."

"I will."

"Because I'm sure you'll see her again."

"Johanna—"

She shook her head, brushing away the long blond hair that blew across her face. The gesture covered her hurt. "Forget it. I'm not her. That's the way it's always been. I know who you love."

He didn't say anything, despite everything he wanted to say. The silence dragged out for a while, with nothing between them but the rumble of the engines and the slap of the water on the hull. She pulled her hand away from his and rubbed her fingers together in the brittle cold to warm them.

"Officially, my job was to get the Files back," Johanna went on eventually. "Rescuing your ass was secondary. But Shadow knew I wouldn't do one without the other. That's why she picked me. Any other agent, they'd grab the laptop and not care what happened to you. Or the Russian girl. But I figured I could do both."

"Thank you, Johanna. I mean that."

"I know you do."

"But the Files are gone," Jason added. "Either Garrett or Vix must have loaded a time bomb. The password worked the first time. I checked it. Everything was there. It was legit. But using it the second time must have set a virus in motion that erased all of the code. Maybe the hacked data, too."

Johanna stared out at the water. "I guess that's the best outcome to the race. A draw. I didn't want the fucking Russian mobster to get it. Honestly, Jason, I can't believe you were willing to give it to him, but I understand. Your weakness is always the woman, isn't it? Anyway, Cody doesn't have it, but neither does Shadow. I wasn't crazy about turning it over to her, either."

The ferry cruised into choppy water. As the boat swayed, Johanna lost her balance. She fell against Jason, and he caught her. Their arms slipped around each other's waists. Their faces were close, lips nearly touching. Then she disengaged and pushed him away. She wiped her eyes, and if he'd asked her about it, she would have said it was the salt air. But they both knew they were saying goodbye.

He realized that was something he didn't want to do.

"What was the rest of your deal?" he asked. "What did Shadow offer you?"

"A truce. I can come back if I want."

"To Treadstone?"

"That's right."

"Do you want to?"

"And work for *her*? No way."

"What if you were working with me?" Jason asked.

Johanna's head turned. Her blue eyes tried to read the expression on his face, as if he must be making a joke. "You told me you only work alone."

"I do, but for you, I'd make an exception."

"So what would we be? Partners?"

"Why not? Like you said, we're good together."

"Are you serious?"

"I am."

She swallowed hard. The wind blew her hair into her face again, but she left it where it was. "No. It's tempting, Jason, but no. I don't want to be Treadstone partners. If you and I are together, I want to be *partners*. But that's not what you want from me. I get it. We can have sex. We can save each other's lives. But at the end of the day, you are in love with Abbey Laurent. Nothing I do, nothing you do, is going to change that. So go on back to her, and I'll get on with my life. It's better for all of us that way."

Jason waited a long time before saying anything more. "What are you going to do?"

When Johanna didn't answer right away, he added, "Are you still trying to destroy Treadstone?"

She sighed with resignation. "No. I'm done with that. I don't want Shadow coming after me anymore. It's not worth it. She set me free when she didn't have to, and I'll honor that. But it's not just to save my neck. Somewhere in these past few weeks, I realized that the deep state always wins. Take out Shadow, and someone worse replaces her. Take out Treadstone, and something worse replaces them. You may as well dance with the devil you know. I mean, that's why you do it, right?"

That was a question Bourne couldn't answer, even though he'd asked himself that very question many times.

Why? Why did he stay?

"So what will you do?" he asked again.

"I've been thinking about that. When Shadow had me locked up, I figured I was done. I'd never get out. But now that I'm free, I need time. At least a year. Maybe more. I need to be by myself. I'm going to buy a boat, sail around the Mediterranean, drink wine, look at the stars. I don't know. Somewhere along the way, I might figure out who I am and what the hell life is really about."

"I like that," Jason said.

"Yeah. Me too." She opened her mouth as if to say something, as if to ask him something, but she didn't. Clouds crossed her face. "Anyway, we shouldn't leave the ferry together. Eventually, they'll review the cameras. I'll head out on my own. You go into the city with Tati."

"Okay."

"Is the Treadstone jet meeting you?"

"Yes. Tonight."

"Well, don't tell Shadow my plans. I don't think she'll kill me, but then again, you never know with her."

There was nothing else to say, but they lingered together anyway. He felt the desire between them like a living thing, breathing and wanting. It would be easy to take her in his arms. It would be easy to tell her not to go. If either one of them had said a word, or made a motion, everything would have changed.

Instead, the moment passed. Johanna turned around, shoved her hands into her pockets, and stalked away from him. She didn't say goodbye, and neither did he. He stood there on the deck, watching her go. She reached the door that led inside, and she disappeared, leaving nothing but the faintest essence of her perfume in the cold air.

"You like her," said a voice at his shoulder.

He turned and found Tati next to him. The boat ride, the escape from captivity, had begun to revive her. She looked alive again.

"I do," he agreed.

"Maybe you love her?" she went on with a little arch of her eyebrows.

Bourne didn't answer, because he didn't have an answer. He heard Johanna's voice in his head. *At the end of the day, you are in love with Abbey Laurent.*

"You came back for me, Jason," Tati said, kissing his cheek, then wiping away the pink lipstick she'd bought for herself in Tallinn. "I knew you would. I knew you would save me."

"I wasn't going to leave you to that monster."

"That's sweet, but can I ask you something?"

"Sure."

"Why? Why did you risk everything for me? It's not like you know me so well."

Bourne smiled. "Because you needed help."

"And that's all?"

"That's everything. That's the only thing I have to hold on to. You've seen me, Tati. You've seen who I am and what I do. I have to take lives. But if I can't save a life sometimes, then I don't know why I'm here."

"Sweet," she said again. "You're sweet."

"I'm not so sure about that."

"You will take me with you?" Tati went on. "We'll go to America?"

"Yes."

"I'll finally be free there?"

Bourne nodded. "You'll be free."

39

SHADOW POURED MACALLAN WHISKY INTO TWO SHOT GLASSES AND GAVE
one to Bourne. They clinked the glasses together. "I'm pleased to see
Johanna's mission was a success. You're alive and in one piece. That's
a relief."

Bourne drank the shot in a single swallow. He went to the office
window and looked down at the neighborhood Christmas lights on
the quiet Washington street, where a light snow was falling. "Only a
partial success. We lost the Files."

"Yes, that's unfortunate. You're sure the laptop couldn't be restored?"

"Very sure."

"What did you do with it?"

"It's at the bottom of a lake on the road between Narva and Tallinn. I put about fifty bullets in it before I sank it."

"Well then, one or way another, it's gone for good," Shadow said.
"I'm sorry about that. But in the end, it's better that no one has the
Files than they should end up with the Russians or the Chinese."

"Or Callie Faith," Bourne said.

Shadow smiled. "Yes. Or Callie Faith."

She poured them more Macallan, and they sat on the office sofa next to each other. It was early evening, dark outside. The Treadstone jet had landed at Reagan National an hour earlier, and a black town car had whisked him across the city to his meeting with Shadow. Her office was located in a brownstone in the Bloomingdale neighborhood in the northwest part of the city. The new location—Shadow's choice—was a nod to Treadstone's origins in a brownstone on New York's East 71st Street years earlier. From the outside, it looked like an ordinary residential address, but the power, bandwidth, and security hid one of DC's most secret operations.

Shadow's personal office on the top floor reflected her tastes, with angled rooflines, gold-and-black wallpaper, heavy walnut furniture, and quiet piano music playing in the background. Bourne also knew that every inch of the office was covered by cameras and wired for sound. The room was warm, and the light was low. Shadow preferred Tiffany lamps to fluorescents. She was dressed for a late Washington dinner in a black cocktail dress that barely reached her knees. It was low-cut in front, and her blond hair swirled across her shoulders. Her lips were blood-red, as always, and her hard eyes drilled into him with a sensual combination of teasing and discipline. He didn't think it was an accident that she always seemed to be dressed to seduce whenever he was with her, and he never knew with Shadow whether he was going to get the lady or the tiger.

"You're taking this all rather well," Bourne said.

"What do you mean?"

"Well, didn't you say you'd kill me if I betrayed you? And I did. I stole the laptop rather than give it to you."

Shadow eased back into a corner of the sofa, seemingly not caring that her dress slipped up her legs to dangerous heights. Her skin was flawless, except for a scar on her thigh that Bourne recognized. That was where Johanna had shot her on top of an English castle a few months earlier.

"True, but I already *knew* you were going to betray me," she replied calmly. "I was listening to you and Abbey the whole time, and I made my plans accordingly. I could have stopped you. I could have made it impossible for you to get what you wanted. And yes, I could have killed you if you really got in my way. But I'm not heartless, Jason. If you could save that woman and I could get the Files back, then I wanted you to do so. Besides, if I'd tried to keep you on the sideline, you would have found a way back in, and that would have complicated all of my plans."

"You'll see that Tati gets a new identity?" he asked. "She'll stay here in the U.S.?"

"It's being taken care of. I'll find her a government job where she can work discreetly under a new identity but still contribute in a significant way to our climate research."

"Good."

"I take it Storm isn't coming back to join us?" Shadow asked.

"No. She's not."

She pursed her lips. "Shame. Storm is very good. When she's not trying to murder me, that is. But if I let that get in the way of who I hired, I wouldn't have much of a team. Treadstone agents are volatile psychologically. I count on that. It's part of what makes them effective."

"Like me?" Bourne asked.

"Definitely like you. But I knew that from the very beginning."

She draped an arm around the back of the sofa, and her nails brushed Bourne's arm. "Do you think Storm will continue to be a problem for Treadstone?"

"No. She's out. You gave her an escape, and she took it."

"Or maybe she's lying to you because she thinks you'll tell me about her plans."

"You don't need to worry about Johanna. As long as you keep your end of the bargain, that is. If you go back on your deal and send someone after her, then all bets are off. So I'd suggest you not do that."

"My only interest was in seeing Storm neutralized. I have no need for revenge."

"Then you have what you wanted."

"Excellent. But I do need to ask you one more thing, Jason."

"What's that?"

"Is there an emotional relationship between you and Storm? I know you fucked her as part of the mission. It happens. We all need to blow off steam from time to time, and I don't care about that. But if you intend to become involved with her in any meaningful way, that could cause problems."

"What kind of problems?" Bourne asked.

"She may be functional, but she's damaged. So are you. That's a dangerous combination. I don't want to see your efficiency compromised."

"You make me sound like a machine."

"You're not. Not at all. But you're a high-functioning agent *who lost his entire memory*. Storm is a high-functioning sociopath. Do you see why that combination would concern me? Jason, you need to accept the fact that I know you intimately. I probably know your mind better than you know it yourself. I studied you for months before you joined Treadstone. I studied you again for months when you finally came back to us after losing your memory."

"From behind a mirror," he pointed out. "I didn't know you were there. I didn't know it was you. I didn't even know who you were."

"That was for your own good. My point is, even with everything I know about you, I still don't know the true long-term impact of your memory loss. There are risks you can't begin to comprehend. You could lose your memory again—all of it, even the last few years. Or your memories could be manipulated, making you do things you would otherwise never do. Being with someone like Storm is an unacceptable risk."

Bourne reached for the bottle of whisky. He poured another shot, then drank it. Then he stood up from the sofa.

"It's strange," he said.

"What is?"

"Hearing you call Johanna a sociopath."

"Why is that strange?"

"Because she's not the sociopath. You are."

Shadow stood up, too. They were eye to eye, and he felt the same way he always did around her. Off balance. Out of control. Under her spell.

"Think what you want about me," she told him, her voice crisp. "But let me be very clear, David. Stay the fuck away from Johanna. That's an order. If I find out you're with her, my deal with her is off. I will send a team to slaughter her. Whether she lives or dies is on *you*. Is that understood?"

"Perfectly."

"Good. Then you can go. Take the jet if you want."

"I will."

"Where are you going next?"

"Los Angeles," Bourne replied.

"To see Abbey Laurent?"

"That's right. I need to rip out your listening devices from her house."

Shadow shrugged. "Do whatever you want. I don't care about her anymore. I don't really like your involvement with Ms. Laurent, but she's no threat to me. Not like Storm. Plus, I told you before. You can't hide from me, Jason. I'm always watching."

Bourne went to the office door, then stopped. "What exactly do you want from me, Shadow?"

"Obedience," she snapped.

"That's never going to happen."

"Don't be so sure, David. In a battle of wills, I'll always be stronger. You don't even know who you are, whereas I know every one of your weaknesses, and I'll never hesitate to push on them until you bleed. So go find Abbey and tell her you love her. It makes no difference to me. But when I tell you I want you back here, I expect you to come running."

Bourne knew she wanted to get under his skin, and he wasn't about to give her the satisfaction. His voice stayed dead calm. "You know, one of these days, I may have to kill you. I'm just putting that out there."

"Oh, I know," Shadow replied. "I fully expect it."

WHEN BOURNE WAS GONE, SHADOW WENT TO THE OFFICE WINDOW. SHE watched him emerge through the door below her into the December snow and take the steps to W Street. He climbed into a waiting town car, which took him away toward the airport. She wanted to make absolutely sure he'd left the building before she made her next move. With Cain, you had to anticipate surprises, but she'd never doubted that she would win the chess game in the end. The key with Bourne was to make sure he didn't know the game was being played.

She drank another large shot of Macallan, then went to a Mexican painting hung on her wall. It showed a skeleton dancing with a small child in a field of corn. She'd bought it on a mission in Tampico a few years earlier. She pulled the painting back on hidden hinges, revealing the door of a safe built into the cubbyhole. She used her thumb against the biometric sensor, then added in a supplemental code that unlocked the door.

From inside the safe, she removed a laptop and put it on her desk. When she booted up the computer, she saw twelve white boxes blinking at her on a blue screen.

"Does he know I made the switch?" a voice asked.

Shadow glanced up.

Vix stood in her office doorway. She was dressed in formfitting black clothes, with a duffel bag slung around her shoulder. She set the bag on the floor, then sat down in the heavy wooden chair on the opposite side of Shadow's desk. When she crossed her legs, her foot bounced nervously.

"He's smart," Vix went on. "I thought he might suspect what I did."

"He doesn't," Shadow replied. "Jason is convinced he destroyed the real laptop. So thank you. The virus on the alternate machine worked perfectly. As far as the rest of the world is concerned, the Files don't exist anymore."

Vix frowned. "Maybe it would be better if they didn't."

"If they didn't, you'd be dead," Shadow reminded her. "You made the right choice by helping me. Remember, Garrett Parker betrayed us both. He's the reason your family was killed. Now, give me the code, please. The correct one. If I activate a virus, there will be severe consequences for you."

"You don't have to worry about that." Vix bit her lip, then rattled off twelve letters, digits, and symbols, which Shadow keyed into the laptop.

The Files opened to the three bars of a menu.

Shadow couldn't suppress a smile of triumph. Her fists squeezed together in tight balls. She had what she wanted. The secrets of the world lay at her fingertips. Anyone who challenged her power would be laid to waste.

"Thank you, Vix. Well done."

"And our deal stands?" the woman asked.

"Absolutely." Shadow opened the top drawer of her desk and removed a sealed manila envelope. She handed it to Vix. "In here you'll find a new passport and a new identity that will get you out of the country, plus a summary of various bank accounts totaling twenty million dollars. You can go anywhere in the world you want. It's up to you. I have a car waiting for you downstairs. Once you're away, you'll have the resources to build a new life."

Vix clutched the envelope tightly in her hand. "That's it?"

"That's it."

"I won't tell anyone about this," Vix said. "I promise."

"I know you won't."

Vix got out of the chair. She shoved the envelope into a zippered pocket on her duffel bag, then hoisted the bag back onto her shoulder. With a tentative smile, she left the office and closed the door behind her.

Shadow powered down the laptop and returned it to the safe.

Tomorrow it would all begin. The next phase of Treadstone.

She took her phone from her desk and punched in a speed-dial number. A few seconds later, the driver of the SUV at the curb downstairs answered. His agent's code name was Zero. He was ruthless and reliable.

Obedient.

"She's on her way," Shadow told him. "You know what to do."

40

BOURNE WAITED FOR ABBEY OUTSIDE THE MALIBU HOUSE. HE SAT IN ONE of the Adirondack chairs on the balcony that overlooked the woods and the ocean. After midnight, when he saw headlights approaching on Highway 1, he knew it was her. The car turned up the long driveway, and Abbey parked outside the garage. As she headed for the front door, he called to her. She didn't look surprised to hear his voice.

She joined him on the balcony and took a chair next to him. Her mahogany hair was lush and loose. She wore a zipped nylon jacket over tight blue jeans, and her white sneakers were black with dirt and ash. He could smell smoke emanating from her body, and he knew she'd been at the site of the fire again.

"Still working on the book?" he asked.

"Still working on the book." Then her head swiveled, and her lips pushed together in a pale pink line. "No, actually, that's a lie. I'm sorry. I'm switching topics. The fire hits too close to home for me now. But I needed to see it again. I needed to see the place where I killed my husband."

"You didn't have a choice. Garrett put you in that position. This is on him."

"This is on Treadstone," Abbey said.

He couldn't really argue with her. Everything bad between them began and ended with Treadstone.

"They've been listening to you," Bourne told her. "And watching you, too. I went through the whole house. I took out all of their devices."

"Unbelievable." Abbey shook her head. "No, totally believable."

"I saw moving boxes inside," Bourne said. "Are you leaving?"

She sighed. "Yeah. I'm done here. No book, no need to be in this place. Plus, it has too many memories. I may go back to Canada for a while. Quebec. That's still home to me, and I need to be home right now."

"I understand."

"Do you think I'm safe being there, Jason? Am I safe anywhere? Or will Treadstone be keeping an eye on me?"

"I'd have your place swept on a regular basis," he admitted. "They may leave you alone, but they may not."

"Even if we're not together?"

"Yeah."

"Once I'm part of that world, I guess I'm in it forever."

"Hopefully not forever. If I'm not with you, they'll stop eventually."

Abbey stared at the distant ocean, looming like a black-and-gold shroud under the moonlight. "Did you save that woman?"

"I did."

"Good for you. I'm glad." She looked at him again, her face darkening with concern. "But if they had my place bugged, they knew what you were going to do. You told me your plan. They knew you were going to trade the Files for her life."

"Yes, they knew. But it all worked out. Johanna was there."

"Johanna?"

"She's the one I told you about."

Abbey's eyes widened. He tried to read the emotions crossing her face, but he couldn't. "Oh. Johanna. Pretty name."

"It's not really her name."

"Of course it's not." She seemed eager to change the subject. "Who ended up with the Files?"

"No one did."

"No one? After all that?"

"They were destroyed."

Her brow furrowed. "Really? Are you sure?"

Bourne thought about Shadow and the webs she spun to trap everyone around her. He pictured the enigmatic look on her face and the secret satisfaction in her eyes. *You're taking this all rather well.* "No. I'm not sure at all. On some level, I can't help but wonder if I was played. But for now, there's nothing I can do about it."

Abbey got up and went to the redwood railing, her back to him. She put her hands on her hips as she studied the darkness.

"No sling," he called. "Your shoulder's okay?"

"Better. I'm doing all right. My leg got better, too. Did you notice? From the car bomb last year. They thought the limp might be permanent, but physical therapy helped. I'm like ninety-five percent now."

"I noticed."

"So I guess I came out of my time with you alive and relatively unscathed." She glanced over her shoulder. "That was a joke."

"I know."

He joined her at the railing. They stood side by side above the woods that led down the hillside to the Pacific.

"I guess this is the talk, huh?" Abbey said. "This is where we lay it all on the line."

"I guess so."

She inhaled a slow breath, as if summoning her courage. "In Quebec a year ago, I said I couldn't live with you. I mean, with your world. With what you do. I was in love with you, but that wasn't enough. Since then, I've been running away from you as fast as I can. But when you showed up here—"

"You almost got killed. Again."

Abbey bowed her head, laughing quietly. "At least you're consistent."

"A year ago, I said you were smart to leave me," Bourne reminded her. "Nothing's changed."

"No, one thing has."

"What?"

"I've lived a year without you. I don't like it. I miss you. When I see you, I want to be with you. And then as soon as I take a step toward you, I want to run like hell again. It's crazy. I don't know what to do."

Jason leaned in and kissed her forehead, which was warm and soft. "What you need to do is say goodbye."

"What if I don't want to?" She took his face between her hands, and her gaze was intense. He couldn't remember how many times he'd lost himself in that stare. "What if I tell you to kiss me for real right now, Jason? And spend the night with me? What if I told you I wanted to try again? Despite everything. Despite who you are."

He shook his head. "We can't do that."

"If you're trying to save me, I don't need to be saved."

"That's not it."

"Then what?"

Bourne took a long look at her face. In that look, he saw their entire past, from the moment he'd seen her in his binoculars on the boardwalk in Quebec City, to the wrenching of his heart when he thought she'd died in a car bomb at the hands of Lennon, to the rage of seeing Rod Holtzman put her in danger again. It was hard for him, not having a past, to turn the page on any part of the past that he still remembered.

But he had to be honest with himself. And with her.

"Abbey, when I saw you again, I wondered the same thing about us. I thought it was fate. I thought we were brought together to *be* together. But in a year apart, everything's changed for us. I saw it in your eyes that first night when you looked at me. You miss me, like I miss you. You miss the past, you miss what we had. So do I. But the past is over. If we tried again, all we'd do is fail again. Because you're not in love with me anymore, Abbey."

He saw a glistening in her eyes, but she didn't deny it. She stared at him through the shine of tears and said, "What about you?"

Jason couldn't run away from the truth anymore.

He had to say it out loud, as much for himself as for her.

"I'm in love with someone else."

THE MEDITERRANEAN SUN BURNED, EVEN IN FEBRUARY. JOHANNA FELT the heat on the back of her neck as she strolled along Via del Brigantino in Positano, Italy. The stone walls of hotels and villas climbed the terraced hillside over her head. She avoided the teeming crowds by walking barefoot in the sand near the sparkling bay. She had two canvas bags slung over one shoulder, filled with supplies from the local grocer to get her through the next week on the water. Loaves of bread. Prosciutto and Parma ham. Pecorino, parmigiana, and mozzarella. Orecchiette pasta. Bottles of wine.

Each week a different port, a different country, different meals. One day on land, six days at sea. She'd never been happier. She'd never felt so carefree in her life.

Until two weeks ago.

Two weeks ago, they'd started following her.

The first time she realized it was on the island of Santorini. She'd been on the hilltop high above the water, strolling among china-white buildings, when she spotted a young Greek man watching her from an outside table at a taverna. He was handsome, with a broad nose, blue eyes, and oily slicked-back dark hair. He looked at her, smiled hawkishly, then looked away. That wasn't unusual. Men looked at her wherever she went, and European men hadn't been cowed into impotence like the Americans. They were open about what they wanted, and they wanted her.

But the Greek man was handsome enough that she remembered his face. She'd seen him before. She'd seen him in Athens when she was having dinner in the Plaka. She'd seen him at the fish market in Enez in Turkey. And then Santorini.

Three times in three different places.

Who was he?

He was definitely not Treadstone. She knew the type. So far, Shadow seemed to be leaving her alone. But if it wasn't her, then she had no idea who would be on her trail. Or why. Or how anyone had found her.

Now, in Positano, the Greek stud was back. He smoked a cigarette and admired the beachside watercolor paintings for sale at an open-air kiosk. People came and went around him, but he stayed where he was, thirty feet behind her, moving when she moved, stopping when she stopped. The same man.

Johanna didn't let on that she'd seen him. She felt no threat. If she wanted to take him, she could. She wore an oversized orange button-down blouse over jean shorts, and the loose top hid the Ruger in her belt. She could have ambushed him in the crowd with her gun or her knife, but killing him wouldn't have given her any answers. If she could have gotten him alone, then she could have sweated him for the truth, but he'd been careful to stick to crowded places. As if he knew she wouldn't dare go for him there.

What did he want?

She was tired of not knowing. She reversed direction. Time for the hunted to be the hunter. She headed straight for him, no longer hiding that he was in her sights. Their eyes met. He gave her a wolfish grin, then turned around, retreating. She followed, pushing through the crowd, keeping him in view as he moved in and out of the chattering tourists. He climbed the steps to Via Regina Giovanna and followed the cobblestoned walkway beside the water. He knew she was behind him, but he acted as if she wasn't there. He didn't hurry. Instead, he flirted with the tanned girls in bikinis and greeted the fishermen like friends.

Johanna closed the gap. He let her come.

Ahead of her, he climbed more steps, up the stone walkway that straddled the cliffside, with the rocky wall above him and the water slapping at the coast below him. There were fewer people here. The higher they climbed above the sea, the lonelier it became, until it was just him and her and no one else.

Why would he let her trap him? It made no sense.

Except when the trap finally sprang, it was on her.

She focused her attention on the Greek man, who was almost within reach, and she missed the man crouching on the stone wall above her, hidden by trees. His body hit her like dead weight, taking her to the rocky path, crushing the air from her lungs. In an instant, he had her on her feet, back against the wall. There were two of them now—the Greek, who'd retraced his steps, and his partner, who also had olive-colored skin, but was older and fatter. The Greek took her gun. The fat man, with a big nose and a scar down his left cheek, took her knife and pushed it hard against her throat, until she felt blood dripping down her chest.

His reptilian eyes showed no emotion. His mouth breathed tobacco in her face.

He said three words. *"Where is Cain?"*

Jason!

Oh my God. This was about Jason. She should have known. She should have anticipated it all along. They weren't looking for her.

They were looking for him.

"I have no fucking clue," Johanna spat back at the fat man.

"Liar! Of course you know. Tell us where he is, or I'll cut open your throat right here."

"I. Don't. Know. I haven't seen him in weeks."

She didn't wait for the next threat against her. Lightning fast, she drove her knee like a hammer between the fat man's legs, making him stumble backward with a howl of pain. Before he could recover, she jabbed her fist into his throat, and in the same motion, swung her arm hard and smashed the handsome Greek's head into the cliffside rocks. He crumpled, and she grabbed her Ruger out of his hand as he fell. Then she thumped the metal frame of the gun into the fat man's face, and he slid sideways to the ground.

Johanna ran.

Where there were two, there might be more. She sprinted along the cliffside walkway, then slowed as she reached the crowds by the water. Her eyes were alert, her adrenaline pumping. She hiked off the street onto the sand, and she kicked down the beach past dozens of sunbathers to find the teenager waiting at her Zodiac. She'd paid him not to move until she got back.

With a snap of her fingers and a quick glance behind her, she handed him five hundred euro and hissed, *"Non mi hai mai visto! Andare!"*

The kid ran up the sand without a word. Johanna splashed through the surf and dragged the Zodiac into deeper water, then climbed inside. She putt-putted past the yachts and sailboats docked in the harbor, and when she reached open water, she gunned the motor, the prow rising high as her speed increased. As the Italian coast grew smaller behind her, she began to breathe again. A few minutes later, she saw the white skybridge of her Fairline Squadron 65 looming where she'd dropped anchor. Around her, she saw no other crafts that might be closing on them or watching them, just the blue wide sea.

Her boat was called *Stormy Weather.* It seemed to be untouched. As she pulled up behind it and cut the Zodiac motor, she leaped to the stern and dragged the small craft onto the transom. Not hesitating, she ran to the upper helm, turned over the engines until they growled to life, and weighed anchor with the push of a button. She eased down into the leather seat and steered the craft at full speed south into the Tyrrhenian Sea.

She didn't slow until all the land was gone and the radar was clear. The breeze swirled her long hair, and she closed her eyes. Her heart finally slowed.

"Trouble?" said a deep voice behind her.

Johanna got up from the wheel. She crossed the varnished deck and wrapped one arm around his waist and slid the other behind his neck. He leaned into her, and she kissed him with hungry lips and felt him kissing her back. It was a kiss that could have gone on forever, but when she was sated and breathless, she pushed him away. Her blue eyes darkened.

"Someone's looking for you," she told Jason. "I think they know you're with me."